TALES OF A TRAVELER

BOOK ONE

Hemlock

N·J·LAYOUNI

Tales of a Traveler Book One: Hemlock

First Paperback Edition: May 2014

Edits suggested by Red Adept
Cover and Formatting: Streetlight Graphics

Connect with the Author:
Facebook:
https://www.facebook.com/pages/NJ-Layouni/405255156236485

Goodreads:
https://www.goodreads.com/author/show/8107337.N_J_Layouni

Twitter:
https://twitter.com/NJLayouni

Website:
http://njlayouni.blogspot.co.uk/

For Sami, Khalil, and Amira: 'To the moon and stars, and all the way back again.'

chapter one

In hindsight, hiking in the Lake District on a bitter day in November was not, perhaps, the best way to fix a broken heart.

Martha Bigalow looked up at the leaden sky and winced as a fat raindrop smacked her on the eyeball. "Ow!" She pressed the heel of her hand to the afflicted eye. "Spend a nice day in the country," she muttered, mimicking the gentle Irish accent of her Aunt Clooney. "It'll do you good, so it will, pet. There's nothing like a bit of fresh air and exercise to sweep away man troubles. Hah!"

The plan formed that morning over breakfast, snug and safe in the warmth of her aunt's Lakeland kitchen, wasn't exactly living up to Martha's hopes.

In the secret places of her mind, she'd imagined herself floating over the moorland like some despairing Bronte-esque heroine crossed in love, her heart mortally wounded by the hero's cruelty—not that she'd ever admit that one out loud. But the reality was nowhere near as tragically beautiful. She was freezing cold and soaked through to her skin. There was nothing remotely poetic about trudging along in wet knickers. On the plus side, she hadn't cried about Tony for the past five minutes. The loathsome fecker!

With the wind buffeting her from every direction, she

pulled back the hood of her parka a little and peered around. Was there a quicker route back to Littlemere?

Sleet-edged rain drifted along the valley in fast-moving sheets that dwarfed the highest peaks. The familiar landmarks were already swallowed up by low cloud. No, it certainly wasn't the best weather for going *off piste*. Squinting into the wind, Martha looked ahead, following the narrow path she was on until it disappeared beneath a tangle of rusting bracken. It was little more than a rabbit-way, really, but at least it led downhill.

Replacing her hood, she set off again, head down, hands thrust deep into her pockets. Raindrops hammered her hood, battering on the fabric like stones until her head vibrated with the constant tattoo. Unpleasant though it was, Martha wasn't afraid. These hills were old, if slightly grouchy, friends. Another hour and she'd be home and dry, sitting down to eat a steaming bowl of Aunt Clooney's homemade soup.

Stumbling and sliding through the wet bracken, she finally made it to the river. Martha heaved a sigh. All she had to do was nip across to the other bank and pick up the regular walking trail on the other side.

The river had other ideas. Swollen by the downpour, the ordinarily benign strip of water had been transformed into a tiger, hissing and grumbling as it raced towards the valley. Martha picked her way uphill until she reached the line of ancient stepping stones. They usually stood proud of the river, but now they lay semi-submerged beneath the froth of angry water.

No problem. Her coat might be crappy, but her boots were good. Taking a deep breath, she jumped and landed solidly on the first stone. Martha grinned and swiped the cuff of her wet sleeve over her face. One down, five to go.

Stones two and three weren't quite so easy. They wobbled with the force of the water pushing against them, minuscule movements as the shingle bed shifted beneath their immense weight.

She dithered on stone number three for quite a while, steeling herself to make the next leap. For the first time that day, a frisson of fear rippled up her spine. As she looked down, the speed and motion of the river made her head spin. Forcing her eyes upward, she fixed them on the opposite bank. It was so near. Just a couple more hops and she'd be on her way home.

With a final glance at stone number four, Martha exhaled like a weight-lifter and jumped.

As her foot touched the stone, it hit something slimy, and the world went sky down. Suddenly she was thrashing in the icy water, heart hammering, lungs refusing to breathe. Although the river wasn't deep, it was powerful, tugging at her body with unimaginable force. Flailing and splashing, she flung out her arm and hooked it about one of the stepping stones before the water swept her downstream.

Inch by painful inch, she dragged herself to safety, choking as a torrent of foaming water rushed into her nose and mouth. By the time she reached the shallows, she was exhausted. Trembling with cold and fear, she lay face down, forehead resting on her arms, gasping and totally spent.

Sweet baby Jesus. What just happened? Teeth chattering, she crawled from the river then collapsed onto her back on the soggy shore. The rain kept coming, belting down from the darkening sky. Her head felt fuzzy and muddled. She had to get off the hill. It'd be night soon, and she was already well into hypothermia territory.

Come on, Bigalow. Move it! Despite her inner drill-sergeant's best efforts, her body wouldn't obey.

What about her phone? Maybe it had survived? She reached into her coat pocket, her fingers claw-like with cold, and managed to scoop up her phone. It sloshed when she shook it, but ever the optimist, she pressed the on button. Nothing.

Stupid, flimsy, state-of-the-art piece of junk. What am

I going to do now?

Violent shivers wracked her body. In desperation, she forced herself to crawl a couple more paces, but the incline of the muddy bank was too much. Wrapping her arms uselessly about herself, Martha slumped back and closed her eyes.

As the river sang on, a slow lethargy invaded her limbs and sapped her will to move. Perhaps if she rested for a moment? Her head ached; Lord, she was so tired. A little rest couldn't hurt. Just to prepare her for the long walk home.

She sat up gasping for air, wrenched from an unpleasant dream involving herself, a pool-noodle, and a raging sea. It was dark, and her bed felt strangely lumpy and uncomfortable. When she reached for her bedside light, her hand struck wet stone. "What the...?" Reality restored her memory, but it failed to quieten her heart. This wasn't her bedroom.

The river. She must have fallen asleep by the river. So where was she now?

Motionless shapes rose out of the gloom as her eyes adjusted to the darkness. "H-hello?" Her voice bounced around a cavernous space. Whatever this place was, it was big. Like the inside of a cathedral, but much colder. Quieter too.

She battled against the urge to shout as the silence crushed down on her. Her spine prickled, the weight of the dark summoning all her long-forgotten childish fears. Steady, rhythmic *plink-plonks* of dripping water kept time with her ragged breaths.

She forced herself to breathe slower and deeper. A full-bore panic attack wouldn't help. Gradually, the indistinct shapes morphed into rough walls and a sweeping roof of stone. At last, the penny dropped.

How the hell had she ended up in a cave?

Huddling into a shivering ball, Martha wrapped her arms about her legs. They were bare, and as devoid of clothing as the rest of her. *Oh my God!* The only thing between her and total nakedness was her ill-matched underwear. An unknown someone had, quite sensibly, removed all of her saturated garments. Even so, she cringed, and the heat of a blush prickled across her cheeks.

Thank God whoever undressed her had been repelled by the sight of her off-white knickers and saggy old bra. Victoria's Secret they weren't. How humiliating.

Always wear nice underwear, pet. You never know when you might wake up in the hospital.

Aunt Clooney's voice spoke in her head as clearly as if she were sitting beside her. The old lady was forever spouting odd sayings, but that particular old chestnut was right on the money.

Martha groped around on the floor, hunting for her clothes. Instead, she found a woolen blanket. It must've slipped down when she'd woken.

She dragged it about her shoulders and huddled beneath its itchy folds, wrinkling her nose as the scent of leather and sweat enveloped her. At least it was warm. Shuffling her butt, she attempted to find a comfier spot on the thin bedroll.

Perhaps Mountain Rescue volunteers had brought her here? She frowned in the dark. So why hadn't they taken her back to the village? It wasn't that far away. And why leave her alone in a cave without so much as a flashlight or a foil blanket? No. Whoever brought her here had nothing to do with Mountain Rescue.

When she shivered again, it had nothing to do with the cold. Something wasn't right.

The darkness to her right was slightly lighter than the rest of the cave. That must be the entrance. Martha leaned toward it, clutching the blanket a little tighter to her chest. She couldn't sit here all night, half-naked, hoping her rescuer might return. *Rescuer?* He could be a serial axe-murderer for all she knew. A vivid imagination could be a terrible affliction. She chewed on her lower lip. Maybe she should make a run for it?

Then she heard the crunch of slow footsteps approaching the mouth of the cave.

Oh hell!

She swept her hands over the dirt floor in semi-circular motions, blindly hunting for something she could use as a weapon. The movement caused her blanket to slip, exposing her chest to the bitter cold. Cursing beneath her breath, she secured her wayward covering and continued the search one-handed.

Her fingers folded around a fist-sized rock. It was rough, heavy, and comforting. Just the right size for braining someone. She found it not a second too soon, for a large shadow appeared at the entrance to the cave, bearing aloft a flaming torch. Heart pounding, Martha flung herself down on the bedroll and pretended to sleep.

Blood pounded in her ears, almost deafening her. Martha tried to hold her breath, but pent-up air escaped in shuddering gasps.

The figure advanced. *Crunch. Crunch.* Closer still. His heavy boot-steps sent tiny bits of stone skittering towards her when his feet scraped on the dirt floor.

It had to be a man. No female walked like that.The whispering flames of his torch were audible now. Their fiery glow penetrated her closed eyelids like the sun.

Just how big was this guy? And, more importantly, could she take him? Martha opened her eyes a fraction, studying him from beneath her eyelashes. Her life might depend on knowing her opponent's strength.

The figure reached up and slotted the torch into a hidden place on the cave wall, close to where Martha lay trembling. The dancing flames transformed the shadow into a man.

A tall man, and a strong one too, by the look of him.

He turned and moved towards her.

Was he dangerous, though? Every fiber of her soul screamed out a unanimous *yes*.

Eyes tightly shut, Martha gripped the stone until her fingers ached. She sensed the man leaning over her prostrate form. What was he doing? Blindness increased her sense of vulnerability. She cracked her eyelids a fraction, and her heart went from a gallop to a stop. In his hand, he held a knife. A large and very shiny knife.

You'll only get one shot at this, Bigalow.

The rock's rough surface bit into her fingers. With a cry of fear, she lashed out at her assailant.

Not quickly enough. With frightening speed, a large hand grabbed her wrist in mid-arc. She gasped, writhing with pain as cruel fingers exerted pressure on her feeble bones, threatening to crush them into toothpicks. The stone fell harmlessly from her hand and hit the ground with a thud.

The knife clattered to the cave floor as the man grabbed the tops of her arms and hauled her against him. "What darkness are you?" he hissed from behind a mask that shrouded the lower half of his face.

Martha found herself up close and personal with the most incredible pair of eyes. Mesmerising eyes, glittering like coal in the torchlight. The concealing mask heightened the impact of his gaze. She couldn't formulate a response—not when pain had her whimpering like a puppy.

"Speak!" he demanded, giving her a hard shake.

"Ow! Feck! Let g-go of—"

"Answer me, woman!" The pressure on her arms didn't lessen. She struggled uselessly against him, her naked skin pressed to his woolen cloak.

"I'm Martha!" she cried.

"Armarther?" His beautiful eyes frowned, and the pressure of his hands eased. "What do you mean, Armarther?"

"Me!" She tried to pull away, but he was too strong. "I'm a...I mean, Martha. Martha B-Bigalow. L-let me go. Please!"

The panic in her voice must have reached him. Whatever it was, the immovable cage about her arms loosened, and she was free. The moment release came, she scuttled backward to the safety of the cave wall, arms crossed over her chest, rubbing at her throbbing arms.

The man sat back on his haunches and watched, his eyes never leaving her face. Uncomfortable seconds ticked by, and still he didn't speak. Only her panting breaths broke the silence.

Was he waiting for her to make the first move?

He picked up his knife from where it had fallen and slid it into a sheath on his belt. That was one less thing to worry about.

The weapon's disappearance gave her courage to study him, not that she could see much for the heavy cloak he wore. Even so, she could tell he was big. But not, she suspected, in the bulging and muscle-bound way. He was much too rangy for that. Hugging herself, Martha pressed back harder against the damp cave wall.

Hardly daring to breathe, she continued her wary inspection, her eyes moving over the shapeless grey cloak until they arrived at the place where his face should have been. A deep hood covered his head, and a broad strip of fabric shrouded his face, highwayman style. Only his eyes were visible. And what eyes they were. Her stomach lurched several times in quick succession. Thick dark lashes, the kind to make a woman weep with envy, framed his almond-shaped eyes. Jet-colored eyes that shone with a light of their own.

She gave herself a mental shake. It must be an effect of the crappy torchlight. Either that or he was wearing contacts. Who wore a cloak nowadays, or a mask, for that matter? Was he living out a deranged Batman fantasy? Was this place his BatCave?

Careful, Bigalow. Don't anger the crazy person.

The man held her gaze, not once looking away.

Martha glanced down at the cave floor, relieved to break the connection. If he was trying to out-stare her, he'd won. She had the strangest notion he could see all the things she preferred to keep hidden—especially from a creep like him.

Still he didn't speak.

His cold, silent scrutiny was beginning to piss her off. "Who are you?" she demanded, at last. "Why did you bring me here?"

"Such gratitude." His slightly husky voice held an accent she couldn't place. "Perhaps I should have left you outside for the wolves to feast upon." He tossed the blanket to her. She hadn't even noticed it was gone.

"Wolves? Yeah, right." Blushing furiously, Martha grabbed the blanket and wrapped it around herself. A flash of anger melted away the remnants of her fear. "Don't be so ridiculous! This is the Lake District, not... not..." She floundered for a country where wolves still roamed wild.

His black eyes narrowed. "No wolves, hmm? Where are you from, I wonder?"

The man threw back his head and emitted a long wolf-like howl that went on and on, echoing eerily around the cave. The hairs on Martha's arms stood up in legion, and icy shivers raced down her spine. His animal impression was very convincing.

She stared, open-mouthed. *He's as crazy as a box of frogs.* "Feel better now?" she asked when the last hellish note died away.

In reply, the man raised one leather-gloved finger and tilted his head slightly toward the cave entrance. "Listen."

And then her whole body erupted into a mass of gooseflesh. From far away, other wolf voices answered, continuing the stranger's song.

It had to be a dream. Jaw flapping, Martha tried, and failed, to put into words all the terrible confusion racing through her mind.

Were dreams this painful, though? Her head ached, pulsing with a slow symphony of throbs. Summoning her courage, she glared at the man. "I don't know what your game is, pal, but I don't like it."

She scrambled to her feet, and a sharp pain flashed down her leg. Her right knee almost gave way. She must have twanged it when she fell in the river. The man extended his hand, but she swatted it away. The blanket snagged beneath her foot and almost came loose. With a muttered curse, Martha yanked at it, managing to preserve her modesty at the final moment.

In one graceful movement, the man rose from his crouching position. He accompanied her to the cave entrance, keeping abreast of her as she hobbled barefoot over the uneven floor, but he made no further attempt to offer his help.

She stepped beneath the rocky arch into the outside world. Her hand flew to her mouth. For a brief time, she forgot the man existed at all.

The rain had stopped, and a bitter wind blew, leeching the remaining heat from her skin. She barely noticed. The valley below secured all of her attention. It was utterly dark. From this height, she should have seen roads down there, villages. There was nothing. Not a solitary light shone out in the darkness. A mass power cut? No. If that was the cause, she would have seen the friendly glow of a thousand candles. Besides, power cuts didn't affect car headlights, did they?

Her headache picked up speed. This was all so wrong. Littlemere was a popular tourist trail, for God's sake. It wasn't as if she'd been out hiking in the middle of nowhere.

But no matter how long she looked, she didn't glimpse a single light anywhere. Even the moon and stars had hidden themselves behind the heavy clouds. The skeletal shapes of trees, rank upon rank of them, clung to the sides of the valley, almost to the entrance of the cave.

Littlemere's hills were devoid of trees.

The surrounding landscape looked wrong. Sharp, soaring peaks replaced the gentle curves of the countryside she knew. Nothing was right.

"Where the feck am I?"

chapter two

Breathing much too quickly, Martha leaned back against the stone wall, her legs as wobbly as a newborn lamb's. Where was the Littlemere? An entire village didn't simply get up and walk away.

Impossible. She turned and glared at the masked man. This was all his doing. For some perverted reason, he must have drugged her, and then driven her out here—wherever the hell *here* was.

"Where's Littlemere?"

"You talk in riddles. Come back inside," he said in a gentle voice. "You will catch a chill, standing there wearing so little."

Martha glanced back at the silhouetted landscape, her body shaking with a combination of cold and raw fear. The man didn't sound perverted. If anything, he sounded concerned.

Well, of course he does. He's messing with your head.

Great. She was holding conversations with herself again. It was a stress thing. She'd been doing it a lot since she'd caught Tony— oh, forget him. Right now, her unfaithful ex-fiancé was the least of her worries.

"Why are you doing this?" Wrapping her arms about her shivering body, Martha raised her chin, holding the masked man's gaze. "Is it a power thing? Is that it?"

He took a step closer, eyes frowning over his mask. "What is it you imagine I am guilty of, m'lady?" He didn't look angry, only puzzled.

"Drugging me, kidnapping me, taking my clothes." Martha arched her eyebrows. "Any of this sounding familiar? How about when you tried to stab me—"

"I certainly did no such thing."

Now he was angry.

His eyes flashed like fiery coals. "You are free to leave whenever you choose. Go now, if you will." He gestured outside. "Your sodden garments are by the hearth. I was about to make a fire to dry them when you attempted to cave in my skull with your rock."

If he wanted an apology for that, he'd be waiting a long time. "So what did you need a knife for?"

The man took a deep breath and exhaled slowly. "The wood is wet," he said, with exaggerated patience. "Unless I first split and feather it, it will not burn." Shaking his head, he stalked back inside the cave, muttering snarly things beneath his breath.

Martha chewed her lower lip, her eyes darting from the strange man to the unfamiliar land outside. Now that he'd given her permission to leave, she was suddenly reluctant to go. Okay, he was a total fruit loop, but it was dark out there. An unfamiliar, howling kind of dark. Added to that, she had no idea where she was, and her clothes and boots were still soaking wet. Perhaps she should postpone her departure until morning. Decision made, she sidled back inside.

He knelt beside a circle of stones that marked the boundary of the fireplace. Martha crept toward one of the two log seats beside the hearth and sat down. The man didn't look up, too intent on what he was doing.

With her free hand, the one not occupied with securing the wayward blanket, Martha massaged her temples. The white-hot headache knifing between her eyes was fast becoming an absolute blinder. Hardly surprising, really.

It wasn't every day the world she knew disappeared.

Aunt Lulu would be pacing the floor with worry by now. Had she already alerted Mountain Rescue? They must be out looking for her by now.

There had to be a rational explanation for all this, something her muddled brain had overlooked. Perhaps she was having a mental breakdown of some kind? She hadn't been sleeping much recently. Misery had that effect on her. Or maybe it was the result of some terrible hallucinogenic illness? She might even be dead. Now, there was a comforting thought.

Her idea of heaven, however, was a place sunshine and peace, not of hypothermia, migraines, and twisted knees. And it certainly didn't come with a complementary wanna-be medieval cave-dweller.

Unless, of course, this was the *other place*. The basement. Martha shivered again. No. Hell would be warmer. So, by that reckoning, she must still be alive.

Huddled in her blanket, she watched as the weird man arranged small pieces of twigs in the blackened hearth. His movements were smooth and deft, as if making fire was second nature. Maybe he lived here, all alone in his horrible cave. What was he, a medieval re-enactor gone feral?

After arranging the twigs, he placed a layer of fluffy kindling on top. How would he light it? She craned her neck to see.

He fumbled in a leather pouch at his waist and produced a metal stick and some kind of stone. As he struck the two together, a shower of brilliant sparks rained down on the bed of kindling. A thin ribbon of smoke swirled upward in a lazy spiral.

No matches or firelighters for this guy. He really was living the survivalist dream.

Flipping back the hood of his cloak, the man pulled off his mask and threw it to the ground. Then, cupping the smoking ball in his hands, he raised it close to his face, gently blowing on it, encouraging the embryo fire to life.

Having ascertained she wasn't dead after all, Martha shuffled to the end of her log in order to see him better. If the veil was his normal attire, this might be her only chance to study him properly. The police were big on physical descriptions, apparently.

Oh, hello. Unexpectedly, her stomach flipped, and she sat up a little straighter. He was younger than she'd imagined; the old-fashioned way he spoke had thrown her. She began compiling a police report in her head.

Age? Early-thirties, give or take a year.

As he blew on the kindling ball a second time, tiny flames appeared, their light illuminating his face. The fire danced and flickered, reflecting in the man's dark eyes, lending him a demonic air.

Eye color? *Demon?* Martha sucked on her lower lip. No. She'd pass on that one for now. How about hair color? Freed from the confines of his hood, it hung down his back in a smooth black sheet, ending in a ragged line just beneath his shoulders. Making a sound of irritation, he flicked back his head to remove the hair from his eyes and the peril of the flames.

The newborn fire shone kindly on its maker. The Hollywood-perfect cheek bones were the ideal accompaniment to his firm and stubbled jaw line. Lovely. Not a sag or a bag anywhere. A little unkindly, Martha overlaid his profile with that of her ex-fiancé, mentally evaluating the two men. Tony lost. He'd gotten rather doughy around the edges of late. In comparison, the stranger's face was granite and marble.

Crossing her legs, she released her pent-up breath in a slow exhale. There was something rather sensual about his mouth, particularly the fullness of his lower lip. Set in such an angular face, it saved his face from harshness.

The man set the flaming ball in the hearth, tending to his greedy progeny as patiently as any father, feeding it small morsels of twigs until the flames were able to gorge on thicker pieces of wood.

Martha knew she was staring. She just couldn't help herself.

Perhaps sensing the intensity of her gaze, the man glanced around. "Have you seen enough yet, m'lady?" He rose smoothly to his feet, all six-foot-something of him. "Or perhaps you might like to see me dance a jig next?"

"Don't flatter yourself." Martha blushed, annoyed he'd caught her dissecting him. She needed a change of subject—and fast. "What have you done with my clothes? I take it you were the one who undressed me." The thought of him seeing her squishy bits made her cheeks burn even hotter.

"You would prefer I left you to freeze to death in your sodden garments?" He crossed the cave in two strides and selected another piece of wood from a pile of logs in the shadows.

"Yes... No..." She raked her hands through the wild frizz of her hair. "I don't know." Another flash of pure white pain pulsed through her head.

"I derived no pleasure from the experience, if that comforts you," he said, throwing the wood on the fire.

Yeah. Right. Her heart set off galloping as all her former panic resurfaced in a sudden crashing wave. "Enough with the games. Who the hell are you?" she demanded. "Where the feck am I, and what did you do with Littlemere?"

The man slung one long leg over the log and sat astride it. "Littlemere?" He began removing his leather gloves, one finger at a time. "Is that a person or a place?"

"The village!" She all but screamed the words at him. "You know what a bloody village is, don't you? Where am I?"

"The Norlands, m'lady. Erde, lest you have forgotten that too. The nearest hamlet is more than five leagues from here." Examining the stitching of his gloves with apparent interest, he added in an undertone, "I fear the cold must have addled her mind."

"Martha!" Heart pounding with fury, she leapt to her feet, grabbing hold of the blanket as it made yet another bid for freedom. "My. Name. Is. Martha. Where the bloody hell are the Norlands? Talk sense, why don't you? I don't want a hamlet. I want a proper village, preferably a town. Somewhere big, with shops and hotels. You know, decent restaurants, ATMs...cars...telephones?" A bitter laugh escaped her. "Is anything I'm saying even the slightest bit familiar to you? Feel free to jump in at any point."

The man picked at a small hole in the seam of his glove. "The town of Edgeway holds a market once a month during—"

"That's hardly the same thing, is it?"

"I really cannot say."

"Ow, shit!" Something sharp jabbed into the sole of her foot.

"Calm yourself!" Throwing his gloves aside, the man shot to his feet. Although he didn't shout, his voice was loud enough to get her attention. "Losing control of your temper will not benefit you."

Subdued by his superior height and proximity, Martha limped back to her seat to examine her wound. Just a spot of blood, but it hurt like crazy.

The man glanced at her foot. "Would you permit me to—"

"No. It's fine!" He'd touched her more than enough already. She pressed her thumb down on the bloody mark and winced. "It's nothing, really," she added in a gentler tone, throwing him a fake smile for good measure. He'd been fairly harmless so far, but she didn't want to piss him off. Not when they were alone in the middle of nowhere.

"Your words are strange to my ears, but instinct tells me your heart is truthful. Shall we begin again?" He stood before her, hand held over his heart. "Some call me Hemlock, but you may call me Vadim." He bowed his handsome head. "If it is within my power to do so, I will help you find your way home."

"Ch-charmed, I'm sure." Her stomach fluttered. "And I'm Martha, Martha Bigalow." Without thinking, she thrust out her hand. What the heck had she done that for? His old-fashioned manners must have rubbed off on her. "How do you do?" she added for good measure, then cringed.

"I do very nicely, thank you." After a momentary pause, Vadim took her outstretched hand.

Although his skin was rough, his touch was gentle. Warm. A pulse of electricity bolted up her arm. To her amazement, he raised her hand to his lips and brushed it with a feather-light kiss. All the time, those dark, knowing eyes bored into hers.

"'Tis my greatest pleasure to know you, Lady Martha," he murmured against her skin.

For a moment, she forgot to breathe. "J-just Martha will do. Thanks." What was she thanking him for? Blushing and flustered, she slipped her hand from his.

He made no attempt to stop her, but a half-smile played upon his lips.

Weird hermit, or an escapee from a secure unit? Whatever he was, Vadim knew what he was doing to her. Damn him. Martha shook her head to clear it. What was she thinking? *Get a grip, woman.*

While she wriggled her icy toes by the heat of the now blazing fire, Vadim retrieved her clothes from where he'd stashed them, and wrung out each sopping garment in turn, twisting them with his hands. Droplets of water pattered to the dry, dirt floor, quickly transforming it to a muddy ooze. It was strangely intimate, watching a strange man handling the things she wore next to her skin.

"What are the chances of my clothes being dry by morning, do you think?" she asked.

"Chance is something I seldom trouble to estimate,

m'lady." The tiny smile tugging at the corners of his mouth. "We have never been the best of friends."

"Not a gambler, huh?"

"This is strange fabric," he said, neatly changing the subject. "I have never seen its like before. What is it?" He raised her coat close to his face to examine it.

"It's a nylon mix. Don't ask me to explain what that means, I have no idea myself." She blinked. Did he just sniff at her parka? Lord knew what that smelled like after a day spent sweating in the hills.

"It is not a particularly serviceable garment." Vadim gave it a shake. As he did so, her water-logged phone flew out of the pocket and landed with a thud at her feet. His smile vanished, suspicion glinting in his narrowed eyes. "What is that?"

"N-nothing." Martha snatched up her phone and nursed it between her hands. "Just my phone. Don't worry. It doesn't work anymore."

Vadim threw down her parka. In two long strides, he was beside her, hand extended. "Show me."

Reluctantly, Martha obeyed. Great. She'd really blown it now. He probably thought she was going to call the cops. What would he do to her?

Vadim turned the phone over and over in his hands, frowning as if he'd never seen one before. "What is it?" he asked, prodding at the power button.

If that was the way he wanted to play it, fine. She needed to keep him sweet. "It's a telephone. I use it when I want to talk to someone who lives far away." If her voice was slightly patronising, it wasn't intentional.

"So you *are* a witch!" Vadim held the phone by his thumb and index finger and held it away from him. "This...thing is part of your impedimenta?"

Oh, for God's sake. She rolled her eyes and exhaled hard. He was taking this whole thing way too far. "It's just a phone, not a Book of Shadows, you great eejit."

"Then do it now. Speak to someone." He tossed the

phone to her.

She caught it one-handed. Was he for real? "I can't." The phone sloshed when she shook it. "It's full of water, see? It's probably ruined."

Thank God it was still on contract. Getting a replacement shouldn't be too difficult, though it pained her when she thought of all the data and pictures she'd lost.

"I see." Vadim held out his hand again, his black brows knitted together. "So it no longer has any value or power?"

Martha chucked the phone back to him. "Not any more." Besides, most of the stored pictures were of her and Tony. Maybe it wasn't such a great loss after all. "What the—"

Vadim dropped the phone to the floor and crushed it beneath his boot.

"What the hell d'you think you're doing?" she cried, leaping to her feet.

He shrugged, then crouched to gather up the shattered pieces. "By your own admission, it was useless."

"I-I don't care! It was mine." Her hand balled into a fist at her side, tingling with the urge to punch him. What, kidnapping her wasn't enough for him? Well, that Riverdance number he'd done on her phone had added a charge of criminal damage to the mental rap sheet she was compiling.

Vadim tossed the broken bits of phone into the hearth. "And now it is fuel for the fire."

Martha stared open-mouthed as the flames lapped greedily about the remains of her phone, melting it into nothing. "You bastard!" She cupped her nose and mouth with her hand as an acrid stench of plastic filled the cave.

A muscle set off pulsing in Vadim's jaw. 'Tis for the best. It would cause too many questions if anyone found it on your person. You are other-worldly enough as it is."

He was calling *her* other-worldly? *Pot, kettle, black.* With effort, Martha bit back the barrage of vicious retorts forming on her lips and resumed her seat, glowering in silence at the fire. Not as satisfying as punching him would be, but the way this day was going, she'd probably break her hand on his flinty face.

He picked up her coat from where he'd dropped it. "You would do better to wear a cloak," he said, as if nothing had happened.

Martha forced herself to look at him, pretending she was over the phone incident. "And end up looking look like an over-stuffed sofa? No thanks. I'll hang on to my fashion sense for a while longer, if that's all right with you."

Vadim shook his head, giving her a superior 'man look'—the kind she'd received a thousand times before. However odd he was, he was all male.

"Fashion has no place beyond the borders of Court, and certainly not here in the foothills."

Before she could quiz him on this, a rogue gust of wind entered the cave. As it hit the fire, it sent a great plume of plastic-tinged smoke straight at her face.

Martha set off coughing like a hardened smoker. The cave amplified her hacking barks until it sounded like a seal colony. She dry-heaved, tears coursing down her cheeks.

"Here." He thrust a soft leather bladder into her hand. "Water." It was already uncorked.

Gasping for breath, she took a little sip, somehow managing to swallow the liquid and not cough-spurt it into Vadim's face.

He moved behind her and patted her back, saying nothing until the coughing fit subsided into fish-out-of-water gasps. "Better?" He handed her a piece of cloth.

Nodding, Martha swiped the material over her teary face. Her lungs and throat ached as if they'd been savaged by a grater.

Vadim took off his cloak and swung it over her shoulders. "This will preserve your modesty better than the blanket, I think."

It landed with a heaviness that made her shoulders sag. Suddenly, she was basking in a super-heated cloud of man-scent and leather. Bliss to her icy skin. Curiously disturbing to her senses.

What on earth was he looking at now? Following his gaze down, she discovered the wretched blanket had come loose, treating Vadim to another eyeful of her cleavage—and the dodgy bra that failed to properly contain it.

"Oh, for f—" With an irritated little huff, Martha dragged the edges of the cloak together, trying to ignore his laughing eyes.

Now that the show was over, Vadim turned away to drape her clothes over a couple of large rocks at the opposite side of the fire. While he was occupied, Martha checked out his rear view.

He wore a long leather tunic, and a light colored shirt beneath it. A thick belt encircled his waist. Amongst the various bits of hardware attached to it, her eye was drawn to a long leather sheath hanging by his left hip. She caught the glint of a metal handle. Was that a sword? She gulped. Just how unbalanced was this guy?

"Tell me about the land you come from." Vadim spun about, having finished his laundry duties. "If you are willing, I should like to hear of it."

Martha schooled her face into neutral. "My world? Okay." She'd play along until morning, then she was out of here. Back to the real world, far away from Vadim's pseudo-medieval crazy land. Until then, she'd just have to humor him.

His barrage of questions soon had her tied up in knots. The modern world, it turned out, wasn't an easy thing to explain.

"So cars are a kind of horseless carriage?"

"Basically, yes."

"Like carts?"

"No." Martha ran her hands through her tangled hair.

"Cars are...well, motorised carriages, I suppose. They move by themselves. No horses required."

"No horses?" Vadim frowned. "Then what propels them?" He leaned forward, handing her another piece of the dry bread that comprised their supper. "Something must power them."

"That'd be the engine."

"The engine? You mean like a...siege engine?"

Oh God, no!

He cupped his chin in his hands, fixing her with his glittering eyes. Interest radiated from his whole being, and it was a good look for him, stripping away his veneer of stone. Unfortunately, she was about to disappoint him. Again.

"I'm sorry, Vadim. I can't even begin to describe the workings of a combustion engine to you. I have no idea how they work. I turn a key and the car moves. That's about the limit of my knowledge."

"Very well. Then tell me something else."

She'd always imagined that people from the present day were somehow superior in intelligence from their Dark Age ancestors. But as she talked to Vadim, she saw things in a whole new light.

This whole charade might be just a silly game, but she suddenly realized that those long-dead people had been just as smart, and equally as stupid, as their modern-day counterparts. They simply had a different set of life-skills.

And right now, Martha was the one feeling stupid.

"Wait a moment." She smiled, holding up her hand to ward off Vadim's eager questions. "Can I ask you something this time?"

He inclined his head slightly. "Certainly."

Careful now. Don't sound too eager. "Where did you find me?"

"Down by the river where the rowan tree grows. Close to the passing place. Why?" He raked back his hair one-handed, studying her intently. "Do you have some memory of it?"

"Not exactly, no." Excitement thrummed in her veins. The passing place must be the stepping stones. It had to be. "Is it, er, very far from here?" she asked, being careful to ensure her interest sounded casual.

"Not at all, though the terrain can be arduous in certain weather." As he spoke, Vadim gestured with his hand, unintentionally giving her a rough idea of the direction in which she should walk.

"Oh." Martha let the subject drop in case he became suspicious. "Okay, how about I have another go at explaining electricity for you?" she asked brightly.

***

The hour grew late. The strange woman slumbered on the bedroll, sheltered beneath his cloak. From his place by the fire, Vadim watched the steady rise and fall of her chest. Her occasional snores reminded him of one of his father's prized sows and of the contented sounds the piglets made when their bellies were full.

The old man...

Vadim took a deep puff on his pipe and exhaled slowly. Smoke spiraled about his face in a fragrant cloud. Why was he thinking of Father again when his family had been dust for so many years? With effort, he turned his thoughts from their bleak wanderings. The past was dead. The future did not exist. This moment was the only reality.

The fire burned low. He stretched out and threw another log onto the embers. Gentle flames caressed it, licking at the wood, coaxing it to become part of the blaze. The wood popped and hissed in protest but ultimately surrendered to its fate.

What fate had led him to Martha?

The chances of anybody finding her out there in that

exposed place were slim. It was fortunate for her he had been out checking his snares today. When he saw her lying beside the old river, he had at first believed her dead. She was unconscious, her skin tinged blue. Perhaps it would have been wiser to leave her there. Death would have surely taken her during the night.

Never had he encountered anyone of adult age so ill-equipped for survival. Nor so strangely dressed. Was she as innocent as her eyes declared, or was she an agent of the enemy? Where was she from? Where were her family? How could she have wandered so far on her own without being pursued by her men-folk?

Was she a witch?

He glanced over to where she slept, lost in her dreams. His questions would have to keep for another day.

Bedraggled as she was, Martha was certainly no peasant. Her smooth, white hands bore no calluses. Even her chestnut curls, mussed as they were, showed signs of regular maintenance.

And then there was the scent of her skin. Whilst removing her wet things, he had detected the faint sweetness of rose petals. Who but nobility had the time, silver, or inclination for luxurious bathing these days?

The soft, rounded curves of her body were most telling of all. Vadim shifted uncomfortably on his seat and took another long suck on his pipe. When they had arrived back at the cave, Martha's lips had been blue with cold. Although he needed to go out and gather firewood, he feared she would die if he left her. So, against his better judgement, he had crawled beneath the blanket with her and held her in his arms, warming her with his own body.

Even now, his skin recalled the sensation of the soft curves pressed against it. She was certainly well nourished. Only the nobles of these lands ate so well these days. The low-born frequently starved. No matter how bountiful the harvest, there was always a rich thief waiting to snatch the food from their mouths.

Martha's speech was neither noble nor peasant. He could only guess at the meaning of some of her words. Well-traveled as he was, he could not guess at her accent. In fact, he had never encountered anyone like her.

The woman sleeping beneath his cloak was a mystery. He disliked the unknown; it troubled him. His life did not require any more uncertainty.

Where were the places she spoke of, foreign places with names that did not exist? And what of the thin black box he had destroyed, and the other things she had tried explaining to him? *Carts without horses, indeed!*

Yet there she lay, asleep on his bed, her strange clothes drying by the fire, and the peculiarity of her speech still echoing in his mind. In the absence of any logical explanation, Martha's version of truth was all that remained. Whether she came from this world or another one, his problem remained the same.

What should he do with her now?

chapter three

When Martha woke, Vadim was gone.

It must be morning, but the light filtering through the cave entrance was weak and sullen, as though it resented another day here as much as she did. Martha grimaced and sat up. A night on the bedroll had done nothing for her back. She might as well have slept directly on the stony floor. Her spine popped and creaked as she stretched. Better. She could move again.

Where had *he* taken himself off to?

Last night's fire was now nothing more than a pile of glowing embers. As she stared at the faint red light, a sudden rush of longing to be home overwhelmed her. The fire shimmered before her teary eyes. The nightmare was real. All of it. What wouldn't she give to hear Aunt Lulu's voice calling her down to breakfast? Anything to rouse her from this awful dream. Instead, she was lost—only God knew where—and alone. Even the hot caveman had abandoned her.

Maybe he'd gone to fetch coffee? Ridiculous thought. Even so, she smiled, dashing away her tears as she pictured Vadim ordering two skinny lattes to go, while dressed in that insane outfit of his. Ooh, a steaming hot coffee would be heaven right about now. Her dry mouth desperately craved its regular morning fix.

There was one upside to her current situation. This was the longest she'd gone in weeks without obsessing over Tony. Being stuck out here in the wilds was grim, but at least she wasn't mooching around at home, weeping along to all the dreadful love ballads stored on her MP3 player. She even kept the songs in a special folder tagged "Mood Enhancement", of all things. *Ugh.*

Tony certainly didn't deserve her tears. For the first time, she was open to the possibility that wounded pride might be responsible for much of her previous misery. If she'd really loved Tony, would she have spent so much of the previous night ogling another man?

Vadim! Her stomach flipped. Handsome though he was, she had no intention of getting dragged into whatever twisted fantasy he was living out here. She had enough problems of her own. Pity, though. With the right medication regime, he might have potential.

Kicking off his cloak, she scrambled from the lumpy bed. As she did so, her knee gave a brief twinge of protest. She stood up, gingerly stamping her foot to test it. Nothing too serious, thank God.

Her clothes and boots were dry and toasty warm. Keeping one eye on the cave entrance, she dropped her blanket and dressed, her hands trembling and clumsy in their haste. Once fully clothed, she felt almost human again. It was amazing the difference her own clothes made, filthy though they were.

Her teeth had an unpleasant furriness about them, but she had no time to go looking for water. Fearing Vadim would return and force her to permanently inhabit the medieval dream world he had going on, she hurried out of the cave.

Daylight revealed in detail everything the previous night had hinted at. The alien landscape brooded beneath a gray and miserable sky. Absently twirling a long strand of her hair about her finger, Martha looked around. She still didn't recognise anything. This must be another valley, close to the place where she'd been walking, somewhere she hadn't visited before.

That's not very likely, said the voice inside her head, *You've lived here your whole life, Bigalow. You're really going to go with the Lost Valley theory?*

"Shut. Up." She growled through gritted teeth. Now, which way to the river? Closing her eyes, she replayed last night's conversation in her head. The Vadim of her memory obligingly waved his arm in the river's approximate location. Martha smiled and opened her eyes. Grabbing a sturdy stick from where it stood propped up against the cave wall, she set off walking.

Bye, Vadim. She cast a final glance at the cave. *Thanks for last night. It was...interesting.*

A thin ray of sunlight poked out from between the clouds as she picked her way downhill through the treacherous tangle of crunchy bracken and camouflaged rocks. The sun's brief appearance highlighted a twinkling ribbon of water in the next valley. Pausing, Martha shielded her eyes to look at it. The river. The sight of it lightened her heart.

The sun vanished, and Martha hurried on, ignoring the throbbing in her knee. Even if she couldn't find the stepping stones, it hardly mattered. All she had to do was follow the river. It would lead her to civilisation eventually. She might even end up at one of the big tourist lakes if she was really lucky.

At this rate, she'd be home by lunchtime.

Some time later, Martha wasn't quite so confident. Despite her best efforts, the river remained frustratingly out of reach. The trip-wire bracken and the steep gradient of the slope severely hampered her progress. Not wanting to add a broken ankle to her current tally of injuries, she'd slowed her pace to a crawl. Added to that, she'd somehow managed to get herself lost in the mini forest that clung to the hillside.

If there was an easier way down, she'd missed it.

Her growling stomach eventually forced her to take a break. Sitting on a flat-topped rock beside a gurgling stream, she rummaged in the deep pockets of her coat, hoping to find a boiled sweet or two. She hit the jackpot in the form of an old Snickers bar. It was flat and completely melted out of shape, but might still be edible. She tore off the wrapper and took a bite. Immediately, an explosion of sweet chocolate oozed over her tongue. It was so good, her eyes rolled back in ecstasy as she savored every wicked calorific moment.

On second thoughts, perhaps she ought to ration her meager supplies. Getting home was taking longer than anticipated. Reluctantly, after eating half the bar, she refolded the wrapper and stuffed the remainder back in her pocket. Just in case.

After many more endlessly toiling footsteps, she finally reached the river; and it wasn't the triumphant moment she'd imagined. Her knee throbbed to its own rhythm, and her face stung with the scratches of a hundred groping tree branches. Pausing to catch her breath, she leaned on her stick and smoothed back her hair. It felt like she had a woolly, leaf-infested beehive sitting on top of her head. Thank God Vadim wasn't around to see her now. She must look utterly vile.

Frowning, she looked up and down the deserted river bank. Which way should she go? Left or right? The scientific approach usually worked best. *Eeney, meney, miney, moe.* That way.

As she rounded a curve in the river, she finally caught a break. A lone tree leaned out over the slow-moving river. Was that the rowan tree Vadim had mentioned? She hurried toward it.

Only a few orange leaves and withered red berries remained, but it was enough to help her to identify the tree.

Definitely a rowan. So where were the— "Oh!" Her heart skipped a beat.

A little farther on, the shapes of six flat stones protruded from the river's dark surface, rather like the heads of breeching whales. This couldn't be right. She frowned and glanced in every direction. Why didn't she recognise anything?

A small inner voice whispered the secret dread of her heart: What if Vadim was telling the truth? A small frisson of fear trickled along her spine.

Impossible.

Tripping and stumbling over clumps of tussocky grass, she hurried towards the stepping stones. The dirt path leading from the height of the bank to the water's edge proved treacherous, and she surfed the greater part of the descent on her butt. With a muttered curse, she scrambled to her feet and limped over the crunchy pebble shingle of the fore-shore and hopped up onto the first stepping stone.

This couldn't be! She covered her mouth with her hands, eyes wide with disbelief. But the stones were the same. Exactly the same, right down to the distinctive grooves on their surface, marks made over many years by countless passing feet. She'd known these stones her whole life, played on them as a child. How...how...

The now familiar—unfamiliar—hills looked back at her. Frustrated and afraid, she jumped up and down on the first stepping stone. "Take me back. For God's sake, take me home!" She hadn't really expected anything to happen, but she repeated the process on all six stones, just to make sure. Zilch. The river gurgled and lapped over the top of the stones as if mocking her foolishness.

Finally admitting defeat, she clambered her weary way back to the top of the river bank and cast herself down on the prickly grass. What the hell was she going to do now? The sun took pity on her, sliding out from a thick cloud and bathing her in its warming rays. Martha exhaled. It was so peaceful here. A gentle wind stirred the dry stalks of grass, rustling them as it passed. In the distance, a curlew's lonely song echoed her feelings of utter isolation.

She tilted her head back. Even the sky looked different here, strangely unblemished by humankind. No vapor trails scarred the shards of pale blue patchwork. Not a solitary machine disturbed the silence. She strained her ears, listening. Even in the most isolated spot, the omnipresent rumblings of traffic and aircraft were usually present. Not here though. It was almost as if the modern world had packed up and moved on without bothering to tell her.

A cold lump formed in her stomach. This couldn't really be another world. Could it? She slumped forward, holding her head in her hands. No way. Stuff like that only happened in films and books. Didn't it?

Maybe leaving the sanctuary of the cave hadn't been the wisest course of action. What would it be like out here at night, with no fire or shelter—and with no kindly madman to defend her? With a shudder, she recalled those awful howls. What about the wolves? If this really was a different world, maybe they existed after all.

Oh, bugger!

As the sweat cooled on her skin, the wind felt less gentle than before. Shivering, she huddled deeper in her coat and zipped it up to her neck. The half-digested Snickers bar churned uneasily in her stomach.

Such a forbidding landscape. There wasn't a sign of habitation anywhere. Well, apart from the occasional rabbit hole she'd blundered into. It was a stark, cold land, empty of human life, and dominated by the dark soaring peaks of distant mountains.

As she miserably contemplated her own insignificance, she noticed a bird, a hawk of some kind, hovering over a patch of red bracken. It glided this way and that, battling to remain stationary in the wind. At least someone around here would be eating today.

She sucked in her lower lip. Maybe she should turn back? Vadim was a little weird, but he hadn't harmed her. Now she thought about it, he'd probably saved her life yesterday. Would he come looking for her? He'd know she was gone by now. Then again, why would he bother? She hadn't so much as thanked him for rescuing her from the river. She sighed. No. Wherever she was, she was on her own.

While she was dithering, trying to decide what to do, a sharp whistle drew her attention—a very human whistle. She got up quickly, swearing as her knee gave way and forced her to cling to her walking stick like an old woman. Stomach fizzing, she looked around.

There, only a couple of hundred feet away, was a man. But it wasn't Vadim. This one was on horseback. "Oh, thank God!" Stick in hand, she set off across the moorland at a brisk limp, all thoughts of returning to the cave gone. "Wait!"

The hawk she'd been watching for the past few minutes landed elegantly on the glove of the man's outstretched hand, flapping until it settled itself.

Martha quickened her pace, afraid he would ride off before she reached him. "Please wait!" she cried again, waving madly as she ran.

Head turned in her direction, the man sat back in his saddle and watched her stumbling through the heather towards him.

"Hello!" She reached him at last, panting but smiling. "For a moment there, I thought you hadn't seen me."

But there was no answering smile. The rider looked down his long nose, regarding her with obvious disdain. "Madam, no one could be so blind and deaf," he said in a smooth and cultured voice. "You have quite scared away my prey!"

The hairs on the back of her neck rose up like hackles. This stranger was even weirder than the last one she'd encountered.

Like Vadim, he wore a cloak, but his was a rich purple in color. The fine gold thread of its stitching perfectly matched the color of his shoulder-length hair. The man flung back his cloak, and the action sent the beautiful bird on his arm into a flapping, jingling panic. He placed a small burgundy hood over the bird's head which immediately calmed it.

"Well?" The man fixed her with a cold, blue stare. "Speak."

She gulped and took a step backward. His long, plum-colored tunic and fine linen shirt definitely weren't modern day. Neither were the exquisitely crafted over-the-knee leather boots he wore. Another re-enactor? What were the chances?

"Did you actually want something, woman? Or was your sole purpose to disturb my hunt?"

As he reached for the oversized cow-horn hanging by his side, his fingers glanced over the ornate and bejewelled hilt of a sword. Her stomach lurched. Another sword?

"I sincerely hope, for your sake, that is not the case. I warn you now, my men are close by. I need only blow this to summon them." He raised the horn to his lips.

She believed him. This wasn't a game. It was real. "I...I'm sorry." She took another hesitant step backward, away from the impatient hooves of his snorting grey horse. "I'm lost. I j-just needed directions to t-town."

One thing was for sure, she wouldn't be asking this guy for a lift there. Something about him made her blood run cold. He had serial-killer eyes, glacial and devoid of emotion. She felt more threatened by him than she ever had by Vadim.

"Town?" The rider's expression relaxed, even his voice lightened. "Oh. I suppose you are looking to join the house of Mrs. Wilkes." He looked her over in such a lewd way she felt like punching him. "Not bad, I suppose," he said, tilting his golden head to one side. "You might be desirable enough if you ever troubled to wash the filth from your person, and bothered to wear a dress. Men's clothing hardly flatters your figure."

Her cheeks flushed with a combination of anger and humiliation. Who the hell was he?

"You have quite a way to go yet. Edgeway lies ten leagues over yonder," the rider continued, waving his hand in the general direction. "But you might make the hamlet of Darumvale before dark if you march quickly enough."

What the hell is a league? "Thank you." Martha said through a gritted smile, biting back some of her choicest words. "You've been most...helpful." Wolves or not, she wanted to be alone again. For all the man's veneer of refinement, every fiber of her being urged her to run in the opposite direction from him.

A soft whooshing sound overhead had Martha and the man looking up in unison, scanning the sky for its source. There was a gentle thud in the vicinity of the horseman's saddle. A quivering arrow was embedded in the high back of the elaborate leather seat. The grey horse reared, almost unbalancing its ridcr. The man cursed, and the hawk flapped and screeched on his arm, bells jangling.

"Accursed outlaw!" The man sawed on the reins, fighting to regain control of his frightened mount.

Martha stumbled backward, away from the horse's wildly flailing hooves. She looked around to see who the rider was shouting at. A gasp caught in her throat, and a surge of unexpected joy filled her heart.

He's come for me!

There, striding through the bracken toward them, longbow in hand—looking just like Robin Hood—was Vadim. Despite the hood and cloak, and the face mask covering the lower half of his face, she knew it was him.

The rider brought the huge horn to his lips.

Before he could blow on it, Vadim nocked and loosed another arrow. It whooshed through the air, splitting the rider's horn in two.

The huntsman threw down his ruined horn, almost hitting Martha. "I shall hunt you down for this outrage, you pustulent dog!" Spittle sprayed from his mouth with the force of his fury. Gathering his reins, he brutally jerked the horse's head around and kicked the unfortunate animal into a canter. Without a backward glance, he left Martha to face her fate.

"Thanks a lot," she called at his fast-departing back. "You're a real gent." The hawk's outraged shrieks were her only answer.

Vadim approached, his long legs cruising through the heather, but Martha made no move to meet him. Watching and waiting, she put away her smile and forced her expression into neutral, to disguise her relief. It wouldn't do for him to get the wrong idea.

"You little fool!" Apparently Vadim had no such reservations about sharing his feelings with her. Casting his bow carelessly onto a cloud of heather, he stalked towards her, black eyes glowering. "What did you think you were doing?" He seized her arms, his fingers digging painfully into her soft flesh. "Do you know who that was? Do you?" He actually shook her.

A pulse of white hot rage ripped through her, evaporating every happy feeling. "Get off me, you bastard!" Wriggling madly, she battled for freedom. "Let me go!" The vice on her arms loosened, enabling her to lash out at him with the walking stick she still held in her hand. It connected with his shin bone with a satisfying *clunk*.

He released her, cursing violently as he did so. Although she didn't understand the words he used, she knew he was swearing. The venom in his words was clear. But her victory was short-lived. Grabbing hold of her walking stick, Vadim yanked it from her hand and pitched it violently into the air.

Martha watched it spinning away into the distance. "You great gobshite! I was using that." She turned on him, her legendary Anglo-Irish temper finally unleashed. "Who the feck do you think you are?"

"What did you tell him?" Vadim's voice was as cold as the horseman's eyes. He would've grabbed her again if she hadn't dodged out of his reach. "What were you saying to him?"

"Nothing!" she yelled. "He was giving me directions, that's all."

He snorted. "And you expect me to believe that?" Breathing hard, he ripped off his mask, wringing it through his hands as though he wished it were her neck, his dark eyes glittering with almost murderous intent. "Do not take me for a fool, m'lady!"

"I don't give a shit what you think, you... you... medieval caveman!"

He frowned. "A what?"

But Martha was in no mood to explain. Her blood boiled too fiercely. "What the hell is wrong with you people?" she demanded, hands on hips. "This, my friend, is supposed to be the twenty-first century. What sick fantasy are you living out here? And what's with the swords and daggers and stuff? Don't you and your colorful friend know it's illegal to carry lethal weapons—especially when you're both certifiably *insane*?" She actually screeched the last word at him, sounding much like the recently departed hawk.

She took a shuddering breath to calm herself. "Either I've got a brain tumor, or I really have fallen into a world of crazy people. Every ounce of logic I possess tells me you aren't real. You can't be real." She limped over and prodded at his leather-clad chest with her finger. "But you are. And none of this..." She waved her other hand at the surrounding hills, "...should exist either. The problem is, it does." Her voice softened as her rage tank flashed on empty. "It feels so real." Stepping closer, she stared up into his eyes, her hand still resting on his chest. "Is it me? Am I the crazy one around here? I don't know what to think any more."

The crushing weight of fear became suddenly unbearable. Stifling a sob, she turned away. There was nothing familiar to cling to. She was adrift in an alien sea. No one was coming to save her. This was it. Home might be gone forever. At that moment, all her anger melted away, and a great, walloping sense of bereavement took its place.

***

His temper cooled the moment he saw the defeated slump of her shoulders. "Martha?" Circling around, he found himself looking down on her tousled head. Was she weeping? He could not see her face; a tangled curtain of chestnut waves hid it from him. "Martha, look at me." He spoke with the same gentle tone he used to calm frightened horses, hoping it would have a similar effect on her.

"Go...away!"

Not precisely the result he had hoped for, but there was no real poison in her words. Vadim experienced a slight twinge of remorse. Perhaps he had been too harsh. But if she only knew how close she had come to... He shuddered. The mere thought of what might have happened sent a chill rippling through his blood.

Her strange words still rang in his ears. For both their sakes, he wished he could provide her with the answers she sought. The longer he spent in her company, the more outlandish she seemed.

Vadim laid his hand on her shoulder in a gesture of comfort. At once, Martha circled her shoulder and shrugged it off. Undeterred, he tried again, this time running his hands lightly up her arms. She pulled away, muttering another of her strange profanities.

Through the parted veil of her hair, he managed to glimpse her face. Martha's lower lip trembled with the effort of keeping her tears in check. With a heavy sigh,

Vadim reached for her again, and this time she made no attempt to escape. In a gesture of surrender, she slumped forward, resting her forehead against his chest. while her body quaked with silent tears.

Throughout the storm, Vadim held her quaking body, crooning soft words of nonsense against her hair. She did not wail, but her soundless misery cut him to the quick, all the same. He had never been able to tolerate a woman's misery. It had always been so. His guilt burned even brighter.

At last, the torrent abated.

"Thank you." Martha raised her head to look at him, managing a shaky smile. White runnels scored through the grime on her face, marking the tracks of her tears. "Sorry about that. This hasn't been one of my better days." Her voice was husky, still raw with sorrow.

"So it would seem." Vadim sighed, and wiped away a stray tear with the pad of his thumb. "As much as I wish to, I cannot give you the answers you seek. Those I do have will give you little comfort." He rested his hands lightly on her shoulders and stared into her glistening eyes. "As I told you yester-eve, this land is part of the Norlands. But there are other places on Erde. Many strange lands that lie across the great seas, countries where people speak differently."

Her mouth formed a silent "Oh".

It was a vain hope, but he felt compelled to ask, "Could you have crossed the seas, Martha? Might that be why you...why this place is so strange to you?"

Martha shook her head. "I don't think so, no. I've never heard of Erde, not before you mentioned it." She slipped out from beneath his hands, and began rummaging the pocket of her peculiar jerkin. Her brief search yielded a square of white cloth, with which she dabbed at her eyes.

Guilt still needled Vadim's heart. "I did not intend to handle you so roughly, my lady. But when I saw you with him..." He shook his head, quite unable to continue. Instead, he went to retrieve his bow from where he had dropped it.

"Is that your version of an apology?"

He looked up from the task of unstringing his bow. Martha was smiling again. The clouds in her eyes had cleared.

"In that case," she said, "I'm sorry for whacking you so hard with my walking stick. I do wish you hadn't thrown it away, though."

If she was angling for an apology for that, she would be waiting a long time. His shin still throbbed from the blow she had struck. Meek and mild Martha most certainly was not. "Come," he said. "We must not linger here, lest your new friend returns with reinforcements. Take my arm."

To his surprise, Martha obeyed. Without hesitation, her little hand slipped through the crook of his arm. The lightness of her touch made him tense.

"He did say that his men were close by." As she looked up at him, a frown marred the smoothness of her brow. "Who is that awful man, Vadim?" she asked. "Why did you shoot at him?"

"There will be time for talk later," he said. "For now, I suggest you save your breath for walking."

With that, she would have to be content. Martha had already inconvenienced him enough this day, and the encounter with the Earl had, as always, soured his stomach. Relating the history of their long-standing feud would only increase his malady. Its roots were too deeply buried in the past, a place he no longer visited. Not if he could avoid it.

chapter four

On the way back to the cave, Martha cast many side-long glances at her silent companion. Not that Vadim noticed. He was too occupied with looking over his shoulder, and everywhere else, for that matter. Everywhere but at her.

It was fascinating really, seeing him in hyper-alert mode. He reminded her of a meerkat on sentry duty, his eyes constantly scanning the horizon—not that Vadim was in any way cute and cuddly. A tad paranoid, maybe, but this was his playground, not hers.

As the gradient steepened, Vadim took her hand, all but pulling her up the most difficult parts. She was glad of his help. The pounding in her knee was fast becoming unbearable. It felt like she had a football slowly inflating beneath the material of her trousers.

A bird hurtled from the undergrowth, twittering madly. Vadim froze and held up his hand.

Oh, not again. Martha stood still, stifling a sigh. He'd only give her "the glare" if she voiced her irritation. But this was the fifth time they'd stopped, for God's sake.

"What exactly are you look—"

"Shh!" Eyes narrowed, he studied the skyline and the surrounding hills, scenting the air like a dark wolf.

Was that what he was looking for? Wolves? Did they

hunt in the daytime?

Suddenly, on the path ahead, something heavy crashed out of the undergrowth, moving at tremendous speed. She gasped, her heart slamming hard against her ribcage. Vadim swiftly drew his sword and shoved her behind him at the same time. Martha clutched the back of his cloak, peering at the creature from the safety of his body.

What the hell was that thing? It looked like a huge hairy boulder with legs. Then she saw two evil-looking yellow tusks pointing out of the creature's mouth, and the glint of a mean piggy eye. A wild boar? *Now there's something you don't see...ever.*

"Be. Very. Still," Vadim murmured.

The warning was hardly necessary. She dared not even breathe.

For untold seconds, they all stared at one another, as unmoving as statues. The boar was so close that its panting snorts were as audible as the blood rushing through her ears. Vadim stood rigid, arm extended, sword poised, ready to defend them if the animal charged.

For a moment, she thought it would. The boar pawed at the ground, its hairy back bristling with aggression. And then, with surprising agility for such a large animal, it turned on its hooves and bolted into the bushes.

In unison, they exhaled their pent-up breaths. Without speaking, Vadim turned to look at her and nodded, indicating they could walk on.

Now she got it. Suddenly, his caution seemed completely rational. She kept a wary eye on the undergrowth after that, straining to hear anything out of the ordinary. Whenever Vadim stopped, Martha stopped a heartbeat later, her stomach lurching unpleasantly.

When they broke free of the trees and onto the open moorland, Vadim visibly relaxed, even humming to himself on occasion. It was very reassuring sound. Finally, she dared to speak.

"Vadim?"

"Hmm?"

"I noticed deep scratches on a couple of trees back there. What made them—deer?"

"No, m'lady." His eyes twinkled as he looked at her. "That would be Old Harry's handiwork."

"And he is?"

"A bear."

"Oh!" *A fecking bear?* Martha felt light-headed all of a sudden, remembering how she'd wandered alone through those trees only a couple of hours ago.

"But you need not concern yourself about him," Vadim continued. "He has already taken to his winter cave."

"Th-that's a great....comfort." Wolves, boars, and bears? What was this place?

Vadim chuckled and took her arm, helping her over a narrow brook. Their run-in with the local wildlife hadn't seemed to rattle him at all. He was a peculiar man.

Where was his wife, she wondered. Did he have a Mrs. Vadim, stashed away in a cave somewhere? What was she like?

Don't start hero-worshipping him, Bigalow.

It was hard not to when he'd rescued her twice already. Three times, if she counted earlier on. If he hadn't come after her today, she'd now be facing the scary prospect of a night in the open. It was a sobering thought.

And don't go snivelling on him again, either.

Okay, that last one was an important safety tip. When she'd been in crying in his arms, he'd as good as sprayed her with a liberal amount of Eau de Vadim. Now, as her body warmed with exercise, she detected faint wafts of man-scent coming from her hair and clothes. It was a good smell, albeit disturbing. Leather and smoke combined with his own unique fragrance.

Get a grip, woman.

Thinking of a way out of this place would be a more profitable occupation than pondering Vadim's marital status.

Had she, somehow, fallen back in time? Was it possible? It must be, because here she was. Although Vadim was a little weird, on an instinctive level, she trusted him. She believed what he'd told her about Erde, and all the rest of it. Why would he lie? If he *was* some kind of sexual predator, he could have easily had his way with her yesterday.

Easily. Several butterflies flapped inside her chest, but she ignored them. In her experience, butterflies were misleading. Butterflies lied.

Back to business. If this really was medieval England, and the wildlife certainly suggested it was, how was it she understood the language? Martha was far from an expert in historical studies, but even she knew that Old English bore little resemblance to modern day speech.

Time for a spot-test. "Who's king these days?"

Vadim glanced over, frowning. "I beg your pardon?"

"The king. What's his name?"

"Erik." Vadim's eyes hardened into black ice. "Erik the bastard." He looked away up the trail, a tic pulsing in his jaw.

Okay. So her spot-test turned out to be more of a sore spot. Vadim definitely didn't care for King Erik, whoever he was. The name wasn't jingling any bells.

Maybe this was another world? *Yeah? So, how did you get here? By rocket? Or did the friendly neighborhood aliens give you a lift?* Oh, this was just getting silly. She gave an irritated huff.

There was only one rational explanation left—for the wolves, the boar, all of it. This craziness was nothing more than a vivid dream. None of it was real. Anytime now, she'd wake up at home, safe and warm in her own little bed. Until then, she might as well go with the flow.

"Would you like to rest for a few minutes?"

Martha blinked and returned to the present—wherever it was. They'd stopped beside a small spring that bubbled from beneath the earth, forming a small puddle between the rocks.

"A rest?" Vadim led her to the water and finally let go of her hand. "Your breathing is labored, and your face is as red as a berry." His lips curved into a crooked smile.

Oh? No wonder he hadn't attempted to jump her yet. "Thanks a lot." Kneeling on a flat stone, Martha plunged her hands into the chilly water and splashed it over her sweaty face and neck until her head felt like she'd eaten too much ice-cream.

If this was a dream, why couldn't she be all clean and sweetly coiffed, preferably wearing a sexy little black number? So unfair.

Without speaking, Vadim handed her his linen face-mask to dry herself.

The sun put in another appearance, chancing a peek at the world from between the mass of thickening clouds. Dabbing at her face and neck, Martha leaned back and looked at the vista before her. Sunlight transformed the bleak landscape into something more beautiful. The colors of discarded autumn peppered the hills in patches of reds, gold and browns. Away in the distance, the peaks of white-tipped mountains glinted, forming a shark-like smile. Big, scary towers of rock that loomed over everything.

A couple of years back, Tony—her scumbag of an ex—went trekking in India. That was what those mountains reminded her of. The places in Tony's photos.

India. She'd so wanted to go on that trip, but he'd put her off, saying it was a boys-only thing. It wasn't until afterwards, when she'd seen the photos, and the faces of various wives and girlfriends smiling out at her, that she understood the truth. Tony hadn't wanted her with him. But terrified of losing him, she'd kept her mouth shut, never questioning him about the presence of his friends' partners.

Martha shuffled on her stone, scowling at the mountains. How many years had she wasted trying to convince herself that Tony loved her? What a pathetic, cowardly idiot. Her, not him.

Vadim settled on the rock beside her. "The snows are coming," he said, staring off into the lands of the rock giants.

"Really?" She handed him the damp mask. "How can you tell?"

"The signs are clear for those who know how to read them."

And back into cryptic mode. "How...interesting."

Vadim rummaged about in the small pack at his feet and offered her a piece of hard flatbread. "Eat."

She didn't need telling twice. Her stomach had been growling like a rabid lion for the past half hour. She attacked the dry bread with enthusiasm, spraying crumbs everywhere. Where did he spend the winter months? Surely he didn't hole up inside the cave. How would he survive in such an isolated spot?

"What do you do in winter, Vadim? Do you have somewhere else to go? Apart from the cave, I mean." She smiled. "I bet you have some cunning plan or other up your sleeve."

"Cunning? No." He continued to look straight ahead, a furrow forming on his brow. "Once the snows come, I shall winter in Darumvale as usual."

"Oh? What's that? A village?" Her stomach lurched unexpectedly. "What about me?" The thought of being without him in this hostile place was now unthinkable, especially after the events of earlier on.

"You?" He turned, a shadow smile dancing upon his lips. "I admit, your arrival complicates matters a good deal, m'lady—"

"Well, pardon me for being an inconvenience."

"But there is a way to keep you with me, a way that will not offend the sensibilities of the good folk of Darumvale."

"Ye-es?" She wasn't getting a good feeling about this.

Vadim took a deep breath and fixed her with his coal-black stare. "You must become my wife."

His wife? "What?" Martha leapt to her feet, her eyes almost popping from her head. "No way!" She stumbled and sprawled head first towards a moss-encrusted rock.

In one smooth movement, Vadim plucked her from mid-air, securing her to the lean, hard length of his body. "Foolish girl! I meant in name only, a ruse to protect you." He set her back on her feet and released her as soon as it was possible to do so. "You cannot arrive there in my company as a single woman."

"Why not?"

"It would not be...proper."

Martha faced him, hands on hips, chest heaving. So the charade was for her own protection, was it? The BS detector in her head was saying otherwise.

Vadim looked down at the ground. "Surely you did not imagine that I would...we would..." He scuffed at the earth with the toe of his boot.

It was satisfying to see him in uncomfortable territory for a change. A suspicious beetroot undertone crept beneath the golden tan of his face.

"Would what, Vadim?" Martha asked, all wide-eyed and innocent, unable to resist teasing him a little.

"That we..." He cleared his throat, suddenly finding the seam of his glove fascinating. "That is, you should..."

"Darn your socks?"

Vadim's head snapped up. The puzzlement on his face sent Martha into fits of helpless giggles. She couldn't help herself.

"Martha?" Vadim wasn't laughing, and his frown made her laugh even harder.

"P-please don't, Vadim!" She bent double, clutching her aching sides, battling the urge to pee.

"I have done nothing. Are you quite well, m'lady? I assure you, it was not my intention to shock you so violently."

She flapped her hand at him, signalling him to

shut up. Eventually her giggles subsided into just an occasional snort.

"I'm sorry," she said when she was finally able to speak again. "I just couldn't help myself." She mopped at her wet eyes with a scrap of tissue.

""You were...baiting me?"

By Jove, I think he's got it. She nodded, slapping her hand over her mouth to prevent another burst of giggles escaping.

Vadim looked so serious, so stern. "Then you did not believe that I would expect you to—"

"Darn your socks? No."

"Ah!" He smiled at her properly for the very first time, and the force of it drove the breath from her lungs. She reeled beneath its impact, her stomach dancing with a whole swarm of demented butterflies.

Unlike Tony, Vadim's smile didn't end at his mouth. It involved his whole face. His dark eyes crinkled and twinkled, reducing his usual stony veneer to rubble. It was the brightest, whitest smile she'd seen on a man in a very long time—and he had the cutest set of dimples to go with it too.

Unable to stop herself, Martha took a step toward him, unable to look away. His eyes weren't black, she realized. They were much softer than that, more of a milk chocolate.

Vadim raked back his hair with one hand. "Then you understand, my intentions towards you are entirely honorable?"

"Yes." And she did trust him. A man she'd called crazy. Someone she'd known for less than a day. "You should smile more often, you know. It suits you."

"Indeed." Vadim's smile faded. He stared at the horizon as some inner darkness veiled him from her. "And perhaps one day I shall." Suddenly he was himself again. "Come. Shall we continue on our way?"

chapter five

On reaching the sanctuary of the cave, Vadim sent Martha to rest, for the final uphill stretch had almost finished her. Without argument, she limped over to the bedroll, and fell into a deep slumber almost at once.

He built a fire then made a start on supper. The rabbit carcasses still needed butchering if they were to eat this night.

He glanced at where Martha lay snoring. *Stubborn girl.* He would have willingly carried her home, but he had learned enough of her character not to offer his aid. Thus far, her behavior had exhibited a peculiar kind of self-reliance.

When he had returned to the cave that morning and found her gone, he had imagined at first that she was outside performing her toilet. But as his sense of unease increased, he had checked the bedroll and found the mattress stone cold. Martha had been absent much longer than he supposed. Ignoring the warning in his head, he had immediately set out to find her.

Locating the path she had taken was easy. A child could have followed its trail. Her marks on the land were as easy to read as footprints in mud. With hindsight, her escape attempt should not have surprised him, not when she had been so afraid and confused on the previous night. What had surprised him, however, was his decision to follow her.

His life would now be much simpler if he had let her go.

After gutting and cleaning the rabbits, Vadim chopped the meat into chunks and threw them into the small cooking pot hanging over the fire. The meat sizzled on contact, immediately releasing a delicious gamey aroma into the air, reminding him just how hungry he was. Adding a handful of herbs from his pack, he gave the pot another stir.

Martha's arrival had already upset his mealtimes. But he knew that in the days to come, a late meal would be the very least of the problems she caused. What was wrong with him? He was no callow youth, inspired to calf love by the glimpse of a pretty face. She was attractive beneath her grime; he could not deny it, but certainly no more so than other ladies of his acquaintance.

So why, within a few brief hours of her company, had he abandoned all of his customary caution? Those who knew him best would gape if they ever learned of it. And rightly so.

By nature, he was a solitary man. Wary. Mistrustful. Although he would die willingly for any one of his band of brothers, strangers frequently described him as cold and unfeeling.

True enough. Had he been in his right mind, he would have left Martha to die by the river. She was a stranger, an outlander. A possible threat. But what he had done today was far worse. He had deliberately tracked her down with the sole intention of bringing her back again. As for the fake marriage offer... Vadim shook his head and stirred cooking pot more vigorously. That was an act of sheer lunacy.

Perhaps he should call on Lady Juliana? His visit was long overdue. Maybe a few hours in her bed would rid him of this uncharacteristic behavior? She was always the most obliging of women, welcoming and eager to please. But the thought was fleeting and soon dismissed.

He glanced over to where Martha slept, covered by his own cloak. Was her conversation with the Earl as innocent as she claimed, or was she, in fact, his agent? Either way, the truth would come out eventually. In the mean time, he intended to keep his new *wife* close.

Was she a danger? *Undoubtedly,* whispered his heart. *And in ways you have yet to imagine.*

She woke a short time later, sniffing the air like a hungry fox cub. On discovering he had prepared supper, she sent him a smile that stirred the dark cobwebs in his heart. Vadim rubbed at his chest as if it could alleviate the unsettling sensation.

His fair guest was not the fussy eater he had supposed. She devoured her share of the stewed rabbit with impressive speed and then wiped her bowl clean with a piece of flatbread. When she had finished eating, she picked up her ale and drained the tankard in a few swift gulps. Vadim could not help but be impressed by her thirst.

Heaving a sigh of contentment, Martha dabbed her mouth delicately on the sleeve of her shirt. "Thank you, Vadim. That was lovely." A sudden frown creased her brow. "Why aren't you eating?"

"I ate earlier, while you were sleeping." The clawing in his stomach had been too fierce to ignore. "Forgive me."

"That's okay." She looked around. "Can I boil up that pan of water to do the washing up?"

"There is no need." Leaning forward, Vadim picked up a handful of white ash from the fire and threw it into the cooking pot. "After all, you are my guest." He swirled the pot around, combining the ash and warm fat into a rudimentary soap.

"No, really. I insist." Martha got up to suspend the pan of water over the fire, muttering beneath her breath, "It's a wonder he hasn't gone down with food poisoning before now."

He made no further attempt to dissuade her from her self-appointed task. Instead, he took out his pipe and lit it with a glowing taper from the fire, then he settled back to watch in comfort.

Martha glanced at him. "That's a bit of a grim habit you have there, if you don't mind me saying."

"Hmm?" He waved his hand in order to see her through the cloud of sweet tobacco smoke.

"If we're going to be friends, it's only right I warn you about the perils of the demon weed."

Vadim studied the pipe in his hand. It looked innocent enough. "What is wrong with a little well-earned tobacco after the trials of the day?"

"Haven't you ever heard about lung cancer or the effects of passive smoking?"

"I cannot say I have, no."

She gave a little tut. "Trust me on this. Smoking isn't good for you. It might even kill you."

The same could be said of a great many things in his life. Death stalked him on an almost daily basis. What was one more risk? "Is that so?" He raised the pipe to his lips and took another puff, ignoring her look of disapproval.

Wisely, Martha said no more on the subject.

When the first wisps of steam appeared, she lifted the pan from the fire and plunged the dirty vessels and spoons into the hot water, scrubbing each item in turn with a piece of rag and a stick. The force of her exertions sent dark tendrils of hair cascading about her face. He liked how she tried to huff them away when their irritation became too great.

She glanced up, her sweat-slicked face shining in the firelight. "Is something amusing you?"

To his surprise, Vadim found he had been smiling. He rectified this immediately. "'Tis nothing of consequence."

Fortunately, Martha was too intent on her task to pursue the matter. "Do you have any soap?" she asked.

"I can't shift this rabbit grease."

He handed her the cooking pot with its mixture of ashes and fat. "Daub this over the bowls. Let it soak in a little before rinsing them."

She looked inside the pot and wrinkled her nose. "Really?"

"Trust me on this." He deliberately used the same words she had used so recently on him. "It will help cut through the fat." How could she not know something so basic?

The hours before bedtime proved to be the most entertaining Vadim had passed in a long while. He could not recall when he had last been so diverted. Not content with cleaning his cookware until it shone, Martha's next mission was her own body. Near the back of the cave, she found a large rock with a natural depression at its centre.

"It's the perfect miniature bath," she told him with obvious delight.

Unconvinced, Vadim made no further comment. From his place by the fire, he watched with quiet amusement as Martha limped back and forth, boiling up pots of water and ferrying them to the back of the cave. It looked like hard work. And dangerous too. She had almost scalded herself twice already, politely declining all his offers of help. What more was a man to do?

"I don't suppose you have soap and a towel, do you?" she asked once her bath was prepared.

"No." He chuckled. She might as well ask for a copper tub to bathe in, or fresh linen sheets.

"Fine." She swiped her wayward hair from her face. "I'll just have to do without. Oh, I'll need to use your blanket as a towel, if that's okay?"

He shrugged. "As you wish." Her habits were most peculiar. "Why are you doing this, Martha? You will catch a chill."

"Why?" She fixed him with a hard stare. "Are you blind? Do you have no sense of smell at all? Look at me!" She performed a slow twirl, pointing out what she considered to be the worst parts of her appearance. "See? Filthy."

He grunted. "You look well enough to me." Indeed, she looked prettily dishevelled with her hair curling about her flushed cheeks.

"As much as I appreciate your input, V, you'll forgive me if I completely ignore that last comment, won't you? Now, off you go."

"Where am I going now?" he asked in surprise, pipe resting against his lower lip.

"Remember that talk we had earlier about sock darning?" Her blue eyes sparkled with mischief. "I'm not about to take a bath with you—"

"Oh!" *By the Spirits!* Vadim rose so swiftly he stumbled. "I quite understand. Forgive me." Gladly abandoning his comfortable spot by the fire, he grabbed his cloak and strode from the cave, out into the safety of the night.

The fresh air did little to calm his fevered imaginings. Huddled within the warm folds of his cloak, Vadim leaned against the cave wall, watching the tiny flakes of snow drifting from the heavy sky. They would need to head for Darumvale soon, before the weather worsened.

What was she doing now? He sucked so hard on his pipe it made him splutter. Impatiently, he tapped the bowl against the wall to empty it and ground his boot on the glowing embers. Imagining Martha's current state of undress was doing little to restore his equilibrium. She was disturbing enough even fully clothed.

With effort, he forced his mind away from the cave and turned it to a less pleasant subject. What was the Earl doing so far south of Edgeway? With winter so near, he should have been holed up at the castle by now. Perhaps Reynard would know the reason? He decided to pay his old friend a visit in the morning. Maybe he could assist him with another pressing matter: women's clothing.

Martha could not arrive in Darumvale dressed in her own outlandish fashion. The villagers were suspicious enough of strangers as it was. She at least needed suitable attire. But clothes were only the first layer of her disguise. If they were to pass the winter there, Martha must learn to act more appropriately. The strangeness of her speech and manner would be much harder to conceal.

Why was he doing it, thinking about her again when he had vowed not to? To punish himself for his weakness, he recited the lines of a long and tedious saga in his head, concentrating on each dusty word until his eyelids grew heavy.

"Vadim? Are you out there?" Martha's voice whispered into the darkness.

Rousing himself from the semi-doze he had fallen into, Vadim pushed away from the wall and shook the snow from his cloak.

Martha gave a squeak of fright as he advanced towards her. "Sweet Baby Jesus! You might have answered when I called."

Baby who? He looked her up and down. "I trust you have finished your...ablutions?" She had wound the blanket about her body in a makeshift gown which ended just above her knees. Wherever she came from, maidenly modesty must be in short supply.

Vadim cleared his throat, his eyes transfixed by the curves of her pale calves. The oversized boots, with their dangerously dangling laces, looked slightly comical attached to legs of such shapeliness. Suddenly recalling his honor, he dragged his eyes up to meet hers. "Where are your clothes?"

"I washed them, too."

Had she taken all leave of her senses? "Go inside at once." He spun her about and pressing one hand against the base of her spine, he gave her a gentle push. "Your obsession with cleanliness borders on lunacy."

Martha didn't move. "It's better than smelling." As she glared back at him, her scowl faded. "Oh, look!" She moved to the cave entrance and held her hand outside to capture a few of the thickening flakes. "It's snowing."

"I am well aware of it, m'lady." Vadim shook his head at the childlike wonder her voice contained. "And its arrival is ill timed indeed." It had been many years since snow had given him the same thrill.

She turned to him with a smile. "Are you always this grumpy?"

He could not think of a reply. Instead, he guided her back inside towards the warmth of the fireside.

Taking off his cloak, Vadim draped it over his seat to dry. Martha shuffled along her log to make room for him. Although unspoken, the invitation in her eyes was clear. Reluctantly, he sat beside her, being careful their legs did not touch. Ill at ease, he fiddled with his empty pipe.

Firelight suited her well. Damp curls of hair framed her pink-scrubbed face in a most becoming manner. From the way she was staring at him, it was clear Martha required some sort of comment upon her appearance. Unable to formulate an appropriate response, Vadim looked away. Almost immediately, he regretted doing so. Her clothes were all strewn out to dry at the opposite side of the fire, including her flimsy undergarments.

For the love of Erde!

A discussion on bathing it was, then. He cleared his throat. "You look...clean." Hardly a flowery compliment, but it was the best he could manage. Having spent so long in the company of men, he was well out of practice with discourse of this nature. It made him most uncomfortable.

Martha smiled. "Do I?" She tilted her head to one side and fluffed her hair with her hands as she dried it by the fire. "Good enough to find a place in the house of Mrs. Wilkes, perhaps?"

His fingers tightened on the stem of his pipe. "How

are you acquainted with Mrs. Wilkes?" he demanded. "I thought you were a stranger here, certainly not the type of young woman who—"

"Relax," she said with a smile. "I don't know her personally. It was just something the horseman said, that's all."

A ball of cold rage formed in his stomach. "He called you a...whore?" The barrel of his pipe creaked ominously between his fingers.

"N-no." Her smile faded. "When I asked him for directions to town, he assumed I was heading for Mrs. Wilkes' place."

The easy mood between them vanished. Barely able to contain his anger, he grabbed a lump of wood from the pile and took out his knife to whittle it. With each violent stroke, he imagined he was cutting into the Earl's scrawny neck. "You should go to bed now," he said curtly.

"And so I shall," Martha's voice remained calm and steady. "Right after you tell me who that man is."

Fortunately, his hair hung down over his face and concealed his grim expression. The last thing he wanted was for Martha to fear him. "He is Godric, Earl of Edgeway," Vadim muttered, though it sickened him to speak the name out loud. "And you were lucky to escape with your life today." He looked up, willing her to understand. "If your paths should ever cross again, you must walk away in the opposite direction from him. Give me your oath on it."

Martha nodded.

Vadim returned his attention to his whittling, but he sensed her curiosity reaching out to him in the silence. "Not now," he said quietly. He didn't look up from the work in his hands. "You have a right to the truth, Martha, but, please, do not ask it of me tonight."

He heard her sigh. "Okay. Then I'll just say goodnight."

"Take my cloak to cover you," he muttered as she passed by. Martha did not speak, but he heard the rustle of the garment as she picked it up.

***

Martha snuggled deep beneath the cloak and rubbed her feet hard and fast on the cold bedroll to warm them. If Vadim heard her shuffling, he took no notice. He scraped at his block of wood with smooth regularity, his strokes never faltering.

She yawned and watched the shadows of firelight dancing across the cave's knobbly roof. Why had the Earl of Edgeway rattled him so? This was far beyond mild dislike. Vadim obviously loathed the guy.

Okay, she wasn't exactly keen on him herself. He was obnoxious and more than a little creepy. Was that a good reason enough to hate someone? Then again, people frequently disliked one another over much less.

No. These two definitely had a history. The Earl must have done something terrible. She refused to consider the possibility that Vadim might be the perpetrator. So why hadn't he put an arrow through the Earl when he'd had the chance? Not that she wanted to see anyone dead, however creepy they were.

She yawned and snuggled deeper beneath the folds of Vadim's cloak. Its smell wasn't so offensive now. It was a tad musty, a little sweaty too, but there was nothing truly rancid about it. He must bathe occasionally, no matter what he said. She inhaled. It was a comforting smell, really.

Poor Lulu would be so worried by now.

Closing her eyes, Martha pictured her aunt in the tiny cottage kitchen, preparing a meal for a niece who might never return. In her mind, she saw her own snug room in the attic, with its soft bed, thick duvet, and the wonky walls hung with that hideous triffid-esque rose wallpaper. The little window overlooking the lake. The simple wooden cross hanging on the wall—right next to that awful picture of the Yorkshire Terrier puppy.

She sniffed as another wave of homesickness crashed over her. How idyllic her life had been. *Will I ever see it again?* Even Tony would be a welcome sight right now, and that was really saying something.

"Martha?"

Vadim's voice interrupted her miserable thoughts and dragged her back to an equally miserable present. Slowly her eyes flickered open. He was crouching beside her, though she hadn't heard him approach. Only minutes ago, his eyes had been cold, but now they glowed with pity.

"Were you having a bad dream?"

"I wasn't asleep," she admitted. "Just thinking."

"About home?"

Unable to answer, she nodded repeatedly and sucked in her lower lip. His sympathy was unbearable. Hot tears pricked behind her eyes, but she managed to hold them back. *Why doesn't he go away and whittle his wood!*

"Do not give up all hope. You may yet find a way back."

She bit down on her lip. If she'd been able to talk, she would have mentioned the Earl Evil again. That would stop him from being so horribly nice to her.

He made as if to stroke her hair, then seemed to think better of it. His calloused fingers hovered over her brow for a few brief moments then slowly retreated. "Try and sleep," he murmured. "Things usually look better in the morning."

The lump in her throat eased. "That's what Lulu always says."

"Lulu?"

"My aunt. Her real name is Clooney. I could never pronounce it when I was little, so I called her Lulu. I still do."

"Ah." Vadim smiled. "Then your aunt must be a wise lady." He stood up. "Would you like me to light another torch to banish the shadows a little?"

"No thanks. I'm good." It was a kind thought though. "Vadim?" She called to him as he moved away. "Where will you sleep? I seem to have taken the only bed."

He looked over his shoulder, his lips curved in a tiny smile. "I require little sleep, m'lady. Take your rest while you may. You need not concern yourself about mine."

And with that she was dismissed. *Strange man.*

chapter six

JUST LIKE YESTERDAY, MARTHA WOKE up alone. She knew Vadim was gone without needing to open her eyes. The cave felt empty, somehow.

At least he'd fed the fire before going walkabout. It blazed merrily in the hearth, beckoning her to sit beside it. She kicked off the cloak, her swollen knee grumbling in complaint, and went to check on her clothes. They were dry, if not much cleaner than they'd been before. Fearing Vadim might return at any moment, she dressed quickly.

Once decent, she went outside to use the accommodation's spacious en-suite facilities. The unfamiliar landscape had changed yet again, this time transformed by a thin blanket of snow. A low winter sun burned bright in the pale cloudless sky. Martha shielded her eyes from its brilliance. *I wish I'd brought my shades.*

Ablutions completed, as she headed back to the cave, she noticed Vadim's boot-prints in the snow. Long, even strides that headed downhill without evidence of a single slip. It was all right for some. She'd fallen twice already on her way to the toilet—or privy, as Vadim called it.

It was too cold to linger, so she returned to the cave and went to sit by the fire. On her seat was a linen-wrapped bundle containing a piece of flatbread and a strip of dried meat. Breakfast, medieval style. Vadim must have left it for her. That was sweet of him. She picked up the meat between her thumb and index finger, and sniffed warily at it. No. She wasn't that hungry. Not yet, anyhow. The bread would do for now.

It wasn't long before she heard the muffled crunches of approaching footsteps. Stomach fluttering, Martha leapt to her feet, her eyes trained on the door. What if it wasn't him?

Vadim breezed inside, dispelling her fears into nothing. The sweet scent of fresh moorland trailed in his wake. When he saw her standing there, his long stride faltered. "You are awake. I cxpected to find you still a-bed."

Did he have to sound so surprised about it? "Or halfway to the nearest town?"

"Perhaps." He smiled, shrugging a bulging pack from his back. "Did you consider it—another escape, I mean?" He came nearer, swinging the pack like a pendulum by its leather strap.

"Once or twice." Martha's cheeks suddenly ignited. What was with all the blushing all of a sudden? Back in the real world, she never blushed. Well, hardly ever. Now, after only a couple of days in Vadim's company, she was turning into a human brake light. "You sh-should have taken your cloak. It's cold outside."

"And deprive you of your bed cover? I am not so ungallant as that."

He stood before her, positively glowing with good health. His sable hair hung in a glorious wind-mussed tangle about his handsome face, tumbling down to rest on the shoulders of his leather jerkin. It was hard not to stare when he looked so good.

"Besides," he continued, "I walked quickly and had no time to feel the chill." He gestured for her to sit down, then thrust the pack into her hands. "Here. For you."

She arched her eyebrows. "Been shopping, have you?"

"You might say that," he replied, sitting down beside her.

Acutely aware of his nearness, Martha reached inside the linen bag and fumbled around. She pulled out the first item. A blanket? It had a similar weave. But as she unrolled it, the truth hit her like a truck. "A dress?" She looked up in disbelief. "You got me a dress?"

"A gown," he corrected. "It is necessary."

Taking the garment from her hands, he held it up so she could see it properly. Martha wished he hadn't. *Holy Mother of God. He's bought me a sack!* The dress was a horrible mold-gray colour, ankle-length, and long-sleeved. A criss-cross of lacing ran from the scooped neckline to where the waistline should have been.

"Darumvale is a small place," Vadim said, perhaps reading the shock on her face. "Its inhabitants will gossip if you arrive there looking..." He glanced at her parka and trousers. "Well...as you do now. We must not attract gossip, Martha."

Despite her best efforts to conceal it, she knew he'd guessed what she thought of the gown.

A crooked smile curved his lips. "It looks better on, I promise."

"Th-thank you." Her smile felt more like a grimace, but she did her best. It wasn't as if he had to take care of her, was it? "It's very..."

Vadim dropped the gown over the log and pulled the pack from her lap. As he leaned in, she breathed in a scent as sweet as line-dried laundry.

"There is more." He delved into the pack himself, since Martha was obviously more reluctant to do so.

"More?" *Oh, dear God.* Her heart sank. "You shouldn't have troubled yourself, Vadim." *Really, he shouldn't have.* "Though, I am grateful."

One by one, like a magician's trick gone bad, he pulled other things from the pack and held them up for her inspection. Each new item was as hideous as the one before: a thin linen shift with stains under the arms; grey woollen stockings; a pair of battered, leather shoes;

a thin belt, and a large strip of linen to cover her hair. The grand finale came in the form of a blue woolen cloak. As Vadim unfurled it, she caught a waft of rising damp and old cabbage.

At last, the pack lay empty. Martha looked at the pile of clothing on her knees, wondering if she trusted herself to speak. As if landing in a medieval world wasn't bad enough, now she had to dress up as one of its peasants.

Immediately, she rebuked herself for her ingratitude. In the past, she'd been a member of a local medieval re-enactment group. From what she recalled, the clothing on her knees would have constituted someone's whole wardrobe in years gone by. In real terms, she held a fortune on her lap.

With as much grace as she could muster, she took a deep breath and turned to look at Vadim. He silently watched her, his dark expression unfathomable.

"Th-thank you so much for the clothes. Forgive me if I don't seem grateful—I am—it's just that the truth of my situation has finally hit me. It's all real, isn't it?" She attempted another smile. "I hope my new wardrobe didn't cost you a lot of money?"

"It is on loan," he said, "from a friend."

A woman friend? His real wife perhaps?

She blamed the sudden twisting sensation in her guts on last night's rabbit. All that grease couldn't be good for anyone. "Then, please, thank your friend for me. It's very good of her to...help me."

"I shall." The stern line of his mouth twitched as if he was holding back a smile. "You may stop now, Martha. You have been humble enough for one day, I think." As his smile appeared, crinkles formed at the outer edges of his twinkling almond-shaped eyes. His sudden cough sounded suspiciously like laughter.

Martha glared at him. "Are you laughing at me?"

"Certainly not."

But as he turned his head away, she distinctly heard

the sound of chuckling.

"You gobshite!" Without pausing to think it through, Martha dug him hard in the ribs with her elbow, making him gasp. "It isn't funny, Vadim."

"Oh, but it is." He secured her hands easily in one of his, preventing her from taking another dig at him. "Your show of gratitude almost choked you, my lady. Admit it."

"You're wrong," she said as she attempted to pull free of his grasp. He'd removed his gloves, and the touch of those warm, rough hands was affecting her heart rate big time. "I *am* grateful."

"Oh?" He drew her closer, his smile suddenly fading.

Martha found herself up close and personal with Vadim's incredible chocolate-colored eyes. Tiny flecks of gold glittered from their depths. She was close enough to count each one of his long, black eyelashes. The heat of his breath brushed softly over her lips.

She was drowning. On dry land.

The hungry look in his eyes drove the air from her lungs. Suddenly, stupidly, she forgot how to breathe. Her heartbeat became one long drum solo. Every bone in her skeleton turned to a jelly-like mush. Everything faded. All she saw was him and the miniature Martha trapped within each of his eyes.

With his free hand, he stroked a strand of hair back from her face, his eyes flitting repeatedly to her lips. "Just how grateful are you, m'lady?" He stroked the rough pad of his thumb over her lower lip, his words brushing her mouth as he leaned in even closer.

Suddenly, her mind rebooted. "Not that grateful!" Thank God. Her mouth was back online. Whatever spell he'd been weaving was broken. Freed her from paralysis, she resumed her struggle for freedom.

Vadim blinked several times as if waking from a deep sleep, and released her hands as though her touch suddenly burned him. He scooted back along the log, hastily putting some distance between them.

Martha leapt to her feet, breathing hard. "What the hell d'you think you were doing?"

It was difficult to say who was the most shocked.

"Forgive me, m'lady. I do not know what—"

"I don't think me pretending to be your wife is such a good idea, after all."

"You have nothing to fear from me, I swear."

"Oh, really?" she sneered. "Then what was...*that*?" She gestured her hand rapidly back and forth between them. "Perhaps I ought to pretend to be your sister instead— "

"No!" The force of his protest made her jump. He got up so quickly, Martha took an involuntary step backward. Taking a deep breath, Vadim spoke more gently. "I had a sister. She was known to the people of Darumvale. They know she was my only sibling. You understand?"

Martha nodded. *Was? Past tense. She's dead?*

"Another female relative, then," she persisted. His morning visit to her mystery clothing benefactress had obviously fired him up big style. Attractive though Vadim was, Martha had no intention of becoming his surrogate lover in her stead. "Tenth cousin twice removed, maybe?"

"Impossible. You come as my wife or not at all. Have no fear of me, Martha. I will not touch you again." And his eyes were so cold she almost believed him. It was as though the events of last few minutes had never happened.

She crushed the sudden flicker of disappointment. "Good. Make sure you don't. I'm grateful you rescued me, but I've no intention of offering myself up as payment for your services. Are we clear on that?" She sounded like a prudish school ma'am, but she couldn't help herself.

"Perfectly clear, m'lady." Vadim inclined his head towards her with mocking civility. "I will be sure not to touch you again. Not without your prior permission, of course."

Of all the arrogant...

Instead of hitting him, Martha smoothed her hands over her khaki trousers, feigning a calmness she certainly didn't feel.

"That's hardly likely to happen, Vadim," she said. "I happen to be engaged to a wonderful man who satisfies me in every way."

"Indeed?"

If she'd meant to shock him, she was unsuccessful. "Then, let us hope we can find a way to reunite you with this paragon as soon as possible. Excuse me." And pausing only to collect his bow and arrows, Vadim turned and strode from the cave, leaving her to fume on her own.

Martha eventually regained her composure. But it took an anger-fueled frenzy of cave tidying to achieve it. After that, she had nothing left to do but think. Their near-kiss had shaken her badly, especially coming so soon after Tony's betrayal.

But Vadim was her only hope of survival here. She'd do well to remember that. Okay, he wasn't perfect, but he had saved her life. Twice. And by offering her the role of his pseudo-wife, he was protecting her again. He didn't have to do it. It couldn't be much fun for him.

So why had she acted like such a shrew? A kiss was nothing, right?

Because I'm jealous, that's why. Jealous of the woman who loaned me those awful clothes.

This revelation surprised her.

She was behaving like a victim of Stockholm syndrome, becoming emotionally attached to her captor. Okay, so he wasn't holding her hostage, but she did depend on him for her well being. Wasn't that roughly the same thing?

Being angry because he had a lover wasn't rational, but it wasn't right that he'd...what? Almost kissed her?

Big deal. Grow up, Martha. You're twenty-nine years old, for heaven's sake. And you're certainly no timid little virgin.

***

Vadim approached the cave with reluctance, uncertain what his reception would be. Perhaps Martha had run off again? He would hardly blame her if she had. He would have kissed her this morning if she had not prevented him. His conscience pricked him again for the hundredth time that day.

Taking a deep breath, he stepped inside the cave. His eyes widened as he looked around. The cave was unnaturally tidy, and there was Martha, sitting by the fire and smiling at him. He glanced over his shoulder, unsure if someone else followed behind him.

"Hello." She stopped poking at the fire with her stick and gestured toward his empty hands. "No luck hunting, then? Never mind. I expect all the animals are hiding somewhere warm out of the snow? Come and sit down. You look frozen."

Vadim edged into the cave and dumped his weapons in a noisy heap by the wall.

"By the way," she continued in the same friendly tone. "I chopped some more wood while you were out. I used your axe; I hope you don't mind."

"Have you been eating mushrooms?" That would explain her sudden change of mood.

"No. But I did eat that strip of meat you left for me. It wasn't bad at all."

'Twas not mushroom season anyway. Then why was she being so pleasant?

He approached the log with caution and sat beside her. He looked around. She had not lied. The log pile had tripled in his absence. The fire was so well stoked that sweat was already beading on his brow. He removed his gloves and loosened the ties of his tunic.

"We will set out for Darumvale first thing in the morning. I had hoped to set out today but—"

"Great." Martha seemed determined to be pleased

about everything. "I'd best get an early night then."

Vadim shrugged out of his tunic and placed it on the log between them. "Perhaps we ought to discuss...what happened earlier."

"Oh, no, we shouldn't!" A look of horror flashed across her pink face. "It's fine. Really. In fact, I think we should put it right out of our minds. Don't you? It never happened. What a lot of fuss about nothing."

"As you wish." He could not deny he was relieved. "Then we shall attempt to be as we were."

If she was willing to forget, he would endeavor to do the same. Though it would be no easy task.

By first light the next day, they were on the move.

Although Martha wore her new clothes, she refused to give up her boots for the sake of authenticity. She declared the flimsy leather shoes were useless for snow, and that she would not risk frostbite for anyone. Vadim conceded, seeing the sense of it. Besides, her gown was long. No one would see her feet.

To his annoyance, she insisted on wearing her trousers beneath the gown.

"There's no one else out here, Vadim." She hitched up the long, full skirt and tucked it into her belt, freeing her from the encumbrance of its heavy folds. "At least I'll be able to keep up with you this way."

The morning was bright and fair. There had been no more snow during the night, and the going was relatively easy. From time to time, he glanced at Martha as she trotted alongside him. She sang to herself as she walked, stopping often to examine something that caught her eye: stones, plants, or a piece of wood. In fact, she lingered so long he frequently had to call her to catch up with him. She was as determinedly cheerful this morning as on the previous night.

Perhaps thoughts of her future husband were responsible?

***

The trail became too narrow for them to walk side by side. As it dipped between two large grassy banks, the way ahead was often submerged beneath the constant run of melt water.

Martha stopped to admire some strands of drowning grass, dancing beneath the water of a deep puddle like the hair of a mythical sea creature.

"Who is he?"

"Who?" She looked up. Vadim had stopped to wait for her again.

"The man you intend binding yourself to. Does he have a name?"

Perhaps it was because of the exercise, but her cheeks felt very hot again. "Tony." She straightened up, inwardly cringing at the deception she'd begun. Anyway, why was Vadim so interested all of a sudden?

"What does your Tony do for a living? What is his trade?"

Martha grinned as she walked towards him. "You sound like a Victorian father: 'And what are your intentions towards my daughter, hmm?'" she said, mimicking a deep male voice while twirling her imaginary moustache.

Vadim didn't smile. "A man must be able to support his mate. There is nothing amusing in it."

In this world, maybe. "Then it might surprise you to learn that where I come from, women are quite capable of supporting themselves without a man's help. Believe it or not, some of us actually prefer it that way. There's a lot to be said for the single life."

She walked around him and took over the lead, continuing down the narrow track way with Vadim splashing behind her.

"Women live alone?" He sounded incredulous. "By choice?"

"Uh-huh."

"Without the protection of their menfolk or families?"

"Yes, and usually with their blessing, too."

"I can scarcely believe it! How do you support yourselves?"

"We work, of course."

"What kind of work?" His voice deepened suspiciously.

"Not the kind of work you're thinking of." Martha laughed. "Mrs. Wilkes isn't the only kind of employer in my town, you know."

"Most amusing," he answered sourly, giving her a gentle shove in the back. "Walk faster and tell me more. Do you support yourself, Martha, or does your Tony help?"

Why had she ever mentioned Tony? Even the sound of his name set her teeth on edge. "I work in a shop that sells women's clothing."

"Then you are a seamstress?"

"No. The clothes I sell are ready to be worn."

"Incredible!"

Finally, blessedly, Vadim lapsed into silence. She glanced down at her gown. The material was straining over her bust, so she tugged at the leather lacing to loosen it, hoping Vadim wouldn't notice. "How would I go about getting a new dress?" she asked. "It can't be that different here, surely."

"You must visit the seamstress. A new gown is usually ready within a couple of weeks, or so I am told, excluding fittings, and depending on the availability of cloth, of course."

"But of course." A couple of weeks? So much for instant gratification. Suddenly, her foot skidded from beneath her as it hit a patch of half-melted snow.

Vadim caught her as she fell, steadying her with a hand beneath her elbow. "Go more carefully here." His breath brushed warm upon her ear. "The way ahead is most treacherous."

"Thanks. I *had* noticed." She blamed the sudden hammering of her heart on the shock of almost falling.

Pulling free, she continued walking, this time with her eyes firmly on the path. For a time they were both silent, concentrating on the trail. Finally, the path broke free from the cover of the grassy banks and turned sharply downhill, bypassing a little coppice.

As her feet found their rhythm, she relaxed, lulled by the crunching steps of her boots. Walking gave her peace. It always had. Suddenly too warm, she flung back her cloak, welcoming the gentle breeze as it cut though her clothes and cooled her skin. Heaven. A small brown bird darted from the undergrowth up ahead, twittering a defiant song as it flew away. She smiled to hear it.

"Does Tony work alongside you in your shop?"

Oh, for fecksake!

Her good mood vanished. Why wouldn't he leave this alone? He was like a demented dog with a bone. What madness had possessed her to mention Tony in the first place?

"No he doesn't," she answered, through her gritted teeth. "He works in accounting."

"Ah! A counter of gold," he said, as if that explained everything. "Little wonder you have been forced into a life of paid labor."

"Do you mind?" she snapped. Tony was the last person she wanted to defend. "I'd rather not discuss my personal life, if it's all the same to you."

"As you wish." The path broadened and Vadim fell in step beside her again. "I was merely making conversation. I meant no offense."

"Huh." The way he was smirking, she wasn't so sure about that. However, she was too eager to let the subject drop to say so. "Tell me about Darumvale instead."

***

The day was all but gone when the lights of Darumvale finally came into view,

Vadim offered up a silent prayer of thanks. For the last two miles, Martha had suffered a good deal. Her knee was plaguing her again, their journey too long for such a recent injury. Although she had neither complained nor asked for his aid, her discomfort was apparent. When he offered her his arm, she accepted it with a mumbled word of thanks and leaned heavily upon it as she limped along.

Their progress was much too slow. A bitter wind swept down from the colder lands to the north, bringing with it the first flurries of snow. A storm was coming. Worse still, although he did not mention it to her, he knew wolves had picked up their trail. From time to time, amber eyes glittered out from the shelter of the trees, silently stalking them. A distant howl told him the pack had been summoned. Once they were gathered, they would attack.

"We are almost there, Martha," he said at last. "Look."

"Thank God." Then she lapsed back into her weary stupor.

From the valley below, cheerful points of light shone out into the night, beckoning them on. Darumvale. A dog barked, perhaps picking up their scent or that of the wolves. Soon, the quiet dusk was shattered as other dogs joined the chorus.

Vadim was relieved. Their noisy welcome meant whatever hunted them would have heard it too. With luck, they might have already turned tail, heading for safety. Wolves had no love for dogs nor their human masters.

As Darumvale loomed nearer, Martha slipped her arm from his, apparently wishing to attempt the remaining distance unsupported. He would not allow it, and clasped her hand. *Erde!* He felt the chill of her fingers even through his glove.

"You are freezing! Why did you say nothing before?"

He stopped walking and rubbed her icy digits briskly between his hands.

"Ouch! Enough, Vadim." She tried to pull free, but he held her too securely. Only when she whimpered with pain did he heed her pleas to stop. It must hurt. Well did he recall the burning sensation of hot knives in the blood.

Ignoring her protests, he removed his gloves and pushed them on her hands. They were far too big, but they were warm.

"Thank you," she murmured as she looked up at him. "But you didn't have to give me your gloves. We're almost there now."

"So we are." He began tugging at her skirts, freeing them from her belt and then arranging them into decency.

"I c-can do that myself you know."

"I do not doubt it." Nevertheless, he did not stop until all of her other worldliness was hidden from view. When they set off again, he kept her hand firmly clasped in his.

To reach Darumvale, they were forced to make a steep descent. By now Martha was weary beyond words. She limped on, biting her lower lip, frequently gasping with pain. The moment they reached level ground, he swept her into his arms, carrying her swiftly towards the long, single-storied building at the centre of the village.

For once, Martha made no objection. As he strode for the Great Hall, he felt the tension easing from her body. She pressed her face against his neck and sighed. The feel of her warm breath on his skin made him shiver.

The village dogs raced to meet them, surrounding them in a snarling, yipping mob. "Be gone!" Vadim aimed a kick at the big grey brute who just tried to take a piece from his boot.

"Who approaches this hall?" A deep, booming voice cut through the night and silenced the excited dogs.

"Seth. 'Tis I, Vadim."

"Vadim?" The stranger's voice relaxed into friendliness. "You are early, m'lord." He hastened to meet them.

"We had not expected to see you for another month at least. Has there been trouble? The Earl?"

"Not that kind of trouble, no." With a brief nod, Vadim indicated the bundle in his arms.

Seth came closer, frowning and rubbing at his red beard. "What have you there?"

Martha's eyes were closed, her lips slightly parted.

"A woman?"

"Not just any woman, my friend. Seth, I would like you to meet my wife."

chapter seven

WHEN MARTHA OPENED HER EYES, it was morning. Shards of brilliant sunlight streamed down through the gaps in a thatched roof, and a million dust motes danced, trapped within its narrow rays. She yawned and rubbed at her bleary eyes.

Where was she? A barn? It certainly looked like one, with its rough stone walls and the great crucks of timber supporting the huge thatched roof. It smelt like a barn, too, a combination of sweet hay and animal poop. At least she was warm. The mattress rustled beneath her as she rolled onto her back to stare up at the blue sky through the neat hole in the roof. Why had someone bothered to put a hole up there?

As a cloud of smoke engulfed the bed, she got her answer. She sat up quickly, coughing and spluttering, dislodging the mound of animal furs that were piled up on top of her. The movement attracted the attention of the small group of people who were sitting by a long fire at the far end of the barn. Was Vadim amongst them? She hoped so.

A tall figure disentangled itself from the group and strode through the haze of smoke towards her. "Good morning, my love. I hope our conversation did not disturb you?"

Her stomach flipped. Yes. It was him, all right. *My love?* Oh, it was way too early to be dealing with this—especially without the prospect of a coffee anytime in the next few centuries.

"How did you sleep?" he continued, with charm and concern oozing from every pore.

Let the games begin. "Very well, thank you, my little lamb chop." Martha smiled up at him, matching his tone.

Vadim's dark eyes flashed a warning as he sat beside her on the bed. The wooden frame protested loudly at their combined weight. "I am afraid the shock of our sudden marriage has left Seth and Sylvie reeling." With a smile, he nodded towards the two figures sitting by the fire—clearly listening for all they were worth. "Neither of them can quite believe it."

Martha flashed another saccharine smile. "I feel much the same way, dumpling." That comment earned her another stern look. Tough. She might as well have a little fun with this *marriage* of theirs. Well, it was only a dream, after all.

Leaning forward, she fluttered her eyelashes in a mock-flirty manner. "From the very first moment I saw you, I knew you were destined to be mine." Which book had she commandeered that line from? She couldn't recall it now.

"Indeed?" Vadim's eyes twinkled. "I had no idea you felt this way." He took her hand and slowly raised it to his lips. "Then, why did you fight me so hard, hmm?" He was enjoying this as much as she was.

"Oh, a lady must never appear too keen." Her mouth suddenly did that pouty thing it did whenever she was flirting in earnest. "After all, being pursued is half of the fun. And I *so* like the way you chase me." Okay, time to stop quoting the cheesy romance. The way his lips were moving over the back of her hand was bringing her out in massive shivery goosebumps.

Vadim's smile faded, and his eyes suddenly darkened. “I will have to remember that, m’lady.” As his gaze locked with hers, he turned her hand and placed a soft kiss against her palm. “But, be assured.” Another kiss. “I am a most determined hunter. Run where you will, my love. I will find you.”

Her jaw dropped, and her cheeks blazed like a blast furnace. The intensity of his gaze stunned her into silence. God, he was good. For a moment there, she almost believed he meant it. When he released her hand, time started moving again.

“Will you come and meet our hosts?”

How could he sound so normal when she was trembling so badly?

Mercifully, apart from her boots, she was fully clothed. Vadim helped her out from beneath the mound of furs, and like an obedient child, she sat at the edge of the bed while he slipped her feet into the awful medieval shoes he’d got for her—Prince Charming style.

“How is your knee today?” he asked, still playing the concerned husband.

What knee? How could she think about anything as mundane as a dodgy knee?

“Sylvie applied a poultice to it last night. She assures me the swelling will soon recede.” He tilted his head and looked at her, obviously expecting some kind of response.

“It’s f-fine, thanks.” Mentally slapping herself, she stood up, Vadim supporting her with a hand beneath her elbow.

Mooooo!

“Sweet baby Jesus!” The deafening sound drove her into Vadim’s arms, clinging to him in fright. She glanced over her shoulder. There, not ten feet away from her bed, stood a large brown cow. “What the hell is that th-thing doing in here?”

Vadim chuckled, holding her steady. “’Tis only a cow, Martha. I understand she is very friendly.”

As her heart rate slowed, she disentangled her fingers from Vadim's tunic and glared at the bothersome bovine. The cow swished its tail, regarding her with its huge brown eyes while emitting a heavy, wet, pattering sound from its rear end.

"Ugh! That's just gross." She wrinkled her nose in disgust and allowed Vadim—who was still laughing—to lead her to the fire.

A heavy-set man with long red hair and a matching beard rose from his seat to greet them. "My lady." He bowed his head. "I am Seth, Chief of Darumvale, and this," he said, indicating the little woman standing beside him, "is my wife Sylvie. We are honored to have you as our guest."

Martha smiled and inclined her head towards the couple while racking her brains for a suitable reply. "Thank you both so much for your hospitality and kindness." Her eyes flicked to Sylvie. "My knee is much improved, thanks to you"

Although her words felt stilted and formal, they seemed to do the trick, dispelling the tensions of introduction. Sylvie hurried to her side and, taking her hand, led her to a bench beside the glowing fire.

"Do sit down, my dear."

Sylvie was a tiny bird of a woman, probably somewhere in her mid-forties. Her merry grey eyes seemed to smile as frequently as her mouth. "You cannot imagine what a treat it is to meet the woman who has managed to capture the heart of the most wanted male in the locality."

Wanted as in *outlaw?* Or as in *desirable*?

"Sylvie!" Vadim said in a warning tone.

Ignoring him, she sat beside Martha and took her hand, squishing it between hers. "Let me have a proper look at you, my dear. I barely saw you when you arrived last night, for Vadim was so eager to get you into bed."

Oh, God! She daren't look at him. She could feel him smirking from here.

Blushing furiously, she waited for the older woman to

finish her inspection. After the trials of the last few days, she was sure to be a disappointment. What she wouldn't give for a hot bath and a bit of makeup.

"Perfect." Sylvie announced at last. "I could not have chosen a better wife for him."

Huh? Martha frowned. Was there something wrong with Sylvie's eyesight?

"You will both be very happy, I think," Sylvie continued. "Have a care, though. Not all the single maidens will take kindly to your stealing Lord Hemlock from beneath their noses."

Was Lord Hemlock his nickname or something? Martha shot Vadim a teasing glance. "Should I be worried, *Lord Hemlock*?"

"Pay Sylvie no mind," Seth said, leaping to Vadim's defence. "My wife speaks nonsense, m'lady."

"Oh, please. Won't you both call me Martha?" Being addressed as *my lady* made her feel like a pensioner.

"Martha, then." Seth's face flushed beneath his beard. "Know only this: you have the good fortune to be joined with the most honorable of men." He patted Vadim playfully on his arm. "He will treat you well."

"That's good to know."

Vadim looked down at her, his expression inscrutable. With his boot resting on her bench, he suddenly reminded her of a pirate, all cheekbones and stubble, and dark, flashing eyes. No wonder he was such a hit with the ladies. She wasn't exactly immune to his appeal herself.

Clasping Martha's hands tightly, Sylvie lightly kissed her on both cheeks. "Welcome to Darumvale. I wish you both every joy, my dear."

***

Following a breakfast of fresh bread, cheese, and warm milk, Sylvie removed the fragrant poultice from Martha's knee. Vadim cast many a surreptitious glance at the two women from where he conversed with Seth, his eyes lingering on the shapely curve of Martha's leg. The swelling had almost gone and apparently did not merit another dressing. With effort, he averted his gaze and attempted to concentrate on Seth's words.

When she was ready, Vadim invited Martha to accompany him to inspect the work being done on his house.

"I didn't know you had a house," she said, pulling her cloak tightly around her as they crossed the village's main, and only, street.

That amused him. "You imagined I dwelt in a cave permanently?"

"Honestly? I don't know what I thought."

She was still limping, flinching when she thought he could not see her.

"Take my arm. The way ahead is full of potholes."

Martha did as he requested. Over the recent days, much to his surprise, he had begun to enjoy the feeling of her little hand resting on the crook of his arm. He frowned as he touched her fingers. She was cold again, and he had left his gloves back at the hall. He would need to see about getting her some gloves of her own, along with some decent boots. She would need both if the weather proved to be as severe as the signs indicated.

They walked in silence for a time, following the road as it sloped gently uphill. Martha rapidly turned her head this way and that, taking in the sights of Darumvale. Such as they were.

As always, the fires of the smithy sent a steady stream of smoke up into the sky, and judging by the rhythmic clangs and clanks, Jared was already hard at work at his forge. Vadim touched the handle of his sword. Despite his best efforts with the whetstone, the edge of his blade was not as keen as he liked. Recent use had earned it several small notches that demanded more expert attention.

"Would you mind if I called at the smithy, Martha? My business there will not take long."

"Sure. Knock yourself...I mean, take your time." She smiled. "I'd like to have a proper look around."

Though Vadim experienced a brief pang of loss as her hand slid from his arm, he at once dismissed it as nonsense. Despite her sultry words back at the Great Hall, she was not really his wife. He would do well to remember it. "Wait here." With that, he ducked into the open doorway of the smithy.

Obligingly, Will, the smith's eldest son, and apprentice, dealt with the sword, leaving the two older men to exchange news. While Jared hammered at the strip of glowing metal on his anvil, they spoke briefly of the new taxes, the harvest, and other everyday matters, but Vadim could not bring himself to mention Martha. He was in no mood to receive any more joy or good wishes on the subject of his marriage.

Gradually, over the various clanks and hissing of the forge, Vadim became conscious of the sound of excited barking coming from outside. Without pausing to excuse himself, he hurried out onto the street.

He was just in time to see a huge gray dog leap at Martha.

Teetering on its hind legs, the great beast planted its two front paws on her shoulders in a grim parody of a dance, obscuring her from view. His blood chilled when he heard her squeal.

Erde! He ran, instinctively reaching for his sword, then cursing its absence. Without pausing, he drew his dagger instead. If he was not much mistaken, this very same creature had tried to take a chunk out of him on the previous night.

But as the shaggy gray animal dropped back onto all fours, Vadim realized his mistake.

Martha was not only whole and unspoiled, she was smiling. He slowed from a run to a trot.

She looked up and saw him advancing on her with a glittering shard of steel gripped in his hand, and her upturned lips slid into a disapproving line. "What the hell do you think you're doing?" The dog stood beside her, regarding him with equal suspicion.

Vadim stopped a little distance away from the pair. "Move away from the dog." He spoke calmly, though it cost him a good deal. He had seen such animals in battle. Fearsome creatures capable of shattering a man's bones between their massive jaws.

"Oh, I don't think so." To his dismay, Martha stepped between him and the dog, her arms crossed in defiance. "What is wrong with you? I'm not going to stand by and let you kill an innocent animal for no good re—"

"The dog has an evil temperament." Even as he spoke, the words sounded foolish.

"Really?" Obviously unconvinced, she turned to look at the beast.

If such a thing were possible, the animal proceeded to make Vadim look like even more of a simpleton. Flopping down in the half-melted slush, the dog rolled onto its back, exposing its bedraggled belly toward Martha, whining pathetically for her attention.

When she glanced back at him, the look in her eyes made him cringe inwardly. She obviously thought him a complete imbecile.

"Evil, huh?" She sighed and shook her head. "Put your knife away, Vadim. I think I can handle this alone." Then she crouched beside the dog, smiling broadly as she rubbed at his belly. "Are you a wicked boy? Yes. You. Are."

Rear legs thrashing, the dog groaned in delight, his lethal jaws parted in ecstasy.

"You big bad doggy, scaring the silly man." Her headscarf slipped back with the force of her exertions, but she seemed not to notice. "Naughty puppy!"

Vadim was unsure which offended him most: her insult, or the sickly sing-song voice in which she delivered it. As he replaced his dagger, Jared stepped outside, dabbing at his brow with a square of dirty linen. He gaped when he saw Martha fussing over the dog.

"By the moldy bones of the ancestors! Well, I never. Hey, Will?" The smith bellowed over his shoulder. "Come and see this, boy."

At the summons of his father, young Will hurried outside.

The three of them stood in line, watching Martha and the beast. "Who does he belong to?" Vadim asked at length. "I cannot recall seeing him before."

Jared puffed out his cheeks. "Well, I suppose that would be me, m'lord."

"Dad found him out on the moor last spring," Will supplied helpfully. "Someone had left him for dead with an arrow stuck through him."

The son had always been more of a talker than his father. In the months since Vadim had last seen him, Young Will had grown in width as well as height. His stout stature now rivalled that of his father. They were alike in many ways, even down to the way they wore their straw-like hair, tied back from their ruddy faces with a narrow strip of leather.

"For all that I nursed him back to health, the hound never behaved that way with me." Jared nodded towards Martha. "Nor with anyone else, come to think of it."

Comfort indeed. At least he was not the only one behaving oddly in Martha's presence, even if her other victim was a hound. Perhaps if he had left her to speak with Lord Edgeway the other day, the Earl's character might have undergone a similar transformation? The thought brought a grim smile to his lips. Nothing short of beheading would improve that man.

"Who is she?" Jared asked at last. "The young lady, I mean."

"Ah." Vadim turned to smile at the Smith. "The lady's name is Martha. And I, gentlemen, have the additional honor of calling her *wife*."

***

Martha limped after Vadim, with Forge trotting beside her.

What was wrong with the man? After briefly introducing her to the nice blacksmith and his son, he'd hurried her away, cutting both men short as they'd tried to offer their congratulations. Granted, receiving good wishes on their fake marriage made her uncomfortable too, but was it necessary to have been quite so rude?

Glaring at the back of Vadim's swirling cloak, she followed as best she could, holding onto Forge's shaggy back for support.

There seemed to be no one else about apart from a few wandering hens and a gang of nasty-looking geese that hissed at them as they passed. But Forge's rumbling growl soon sent them waddling in another direction.

Martha looked back down the hill, inhaling the cold, smoky air. Darumvale. A proper medieval village. And here she was, living the history. For real. Well, if a vivid dream counted as real.

The Great Hall sat at the heart of the village, dwarfing the other houses beside with its imposing rectangular shape. Smoke drifted from other chimneys, or roof holes, of other homes. A dozen or so. All much smaller than their lordly neighbor, but equally unique in their own ways. Some houses were round with sweeping turf roofs that almost touched the ground, while others were square, stone-built, and topped with thatch. A couple of houses were even whitewashed, and were much more familiar looking. Beside every home was a garden of sorts—now an empty plot of earth, probably waiting for spring planting.

There were no lawns or garden gnomes in Darumvale. Well, that was one good thing about it, she supposed.

The most obvious difference between these houses and the ones back home—excluding the lack of satellite dishes—was the absence of glass windows. One or two homes had window-like holes cut into their thick walls, but none of them were glazed. Most were covered with a piece of bright fabric.

As she walked, she heard voices coming from every home: male and female, the old and the young. Voices singing unfamiliar songs. People talking. Phlegmy coughs. Frequent bursts of laughter. She sighed, and paused to adjust her wayward headscarf for the hundredth time that day, suddenly feeling very alone.

Vadim's house was just off the main street, set back against the hill in its own little plot. His closest neighbors were some distance away. No surprises there. She got the impression he was a man who valued his privacy. Anyone who lived alone in a cave for long periods of time couldn't be classed as sociable.

She limped up the slight incline, her fingers buried into the warmth of Forge's shaggy fur, and found Vadim talking to a man up on a step ladder, which was leaned against the roof. As she moved closer, the breeze brought her the old man's words.

"...just needs a bit of patching, m'lord, no more than that." He patted the thatch almost affectionately. "She will keep you dry enough until spring."

"Good news indeed." Vadim glanced over his shoulder at Martha. "My lady wife is most anxious to have her own roof."

"Wife?" The man visibly wobbled on his ladder.

"Hemble, meet Martha. My wife."

Here we go again. Taking a deep breath, Martha plastered a bright smile on her face.

"Hello." She waved at the old man and came to stand at Vadim's side. "Is this your house, then?"

"It is." He slipped his arm about her waist, making her jump, and pulled her close to his side. "Does it suit you, my love?"

"Well, it's certainly better than a cave," she answered with a grin, trying to pretend the feel of his warm, hard body didn't affect her at all. Unfortunately, her hot cheeks betrayed her. As usual.

Vadim's house was similar to others she'd seen in the village. Sturdy, stone-built, and single-storied. But his had something the other houses didn't. "You have glass!" What was the matter with her? Since when was glass a cause for excitement?

Arching their eyebrows at one another, Vadim and the elderly thatcher exchanged a brief look—silent man-code for *women!*

"'Tis cow horn," Vadim corrected her, "but it works well enough in its stead."

"Oh." Pulling free from the shelter of his arm, Martha went to take a closer look. The old man on the ladder openly stared at her, his bushy silver eyebrows knitted together in a frown.

Now what? Had she said something wrong? Hadn't glass been invented or something? Being a medieval wife was harder than she thought. Then, something else caught her attention. "It has a proper door too." Some of the village houses only had a blanket tacked over the doorway. She rapped her knuckles several times against the solid wood. "This is great." She grinned at Vadim over her shoulder. "I love it."

"You have not seen inside yet, my love," he replied.

Although his tender smile was solely for the old man's benefit, it set off the butterflies in her stomach. She ignored them. In fact, she was getting quite used to them living there by now.

"Well, I shall be getting along for my pie and ale." The ladder wobbled as Hemble slowly made his way back to the ground. "I will return in an hour." He glanced at Vadim, his smile emphasising the deep wrinkles around his eyes. "If that will be long enough, m'lord?"

"Quite long enough," Vadim assured him, slightly inclining his head. "Thank you, Hemble."

Long enough for what? Had that dirty old man just implied they'd soon be doing...the marital jig? Swallowing hard, her eyes flicked to Vadim. How could he be so composed? When Hemble paused in front of her to wish her joy, even her ears glowed hot with embarrassment.

Mumbling something appropriate, she turned away to stroke Forge, refusing to look up until the thatcher was gone.

"Very virginal," Vadim remarked, once they were alone. "Your blushes are quite appropriate for the occasion. Hemble will make it his business to advise the entire village of my wife's modesty."

His tall shadow loomed over her. Was he laughing at her again? Martha looked up. Yes, definitely. "Most amusing, I'm sure." She planted her hands on her hips and glared at him. "Here's an idea. Since the opinion of the village matters so much to you, maybe you could stop taking the piss long enough for us to discuss the details of our courtship and marriage? I still have no idea what I'm supposed to say to people."

"Perhaps it would be better if we discussed this matter in private." Vadim's crooked little smile made her toes tingle. "It is customary, I believe, for the bride to be carried into her new home. No doubt we are being watched as we speak."

Before Martha could object, he swept her up into his arms.

"You'll break your back if you keep doing this," she said, sliding her arm about his neck. It was difficult to sound nonchalant when her heart was thundering so. "Don't come moaning to me when your back goes into lockdown." His hair felt soft beneath her fingers. She inhaled, unable to resist the temptation of breathing in his warm scent.

Oh God. Warm leather, plus man-scent, equaled too hot.

"Nonsense." His eyes darkened. "You weigh nothing at all. Excuse us, Forge," he said to the dog, "but we have needs that cannot wait." With that, he kicked open the door of the house and carried her inside.

chapter eight

THE COTTAGE WAS SMALL. JUST a single room with a low roof and roughly plastered walls. Even so, it felt welcoming. The moment the door was closed, Vadim set her down so she could explore.

The house had obviously been uninhabited for quite some time. A thin layer of dust covered every surface, and dust bunnies roamed wild on the wooden floor. Beneath the eaves was a bed—a long, low cot piled high with furs and several brightly colored blankets. Three large chests stood pushed up against the back wall, the tops of the two flattest serving as further storage space. Amongst the small collection of knives and mismatched pieces of bridlery, she spotted a pair of substantial-looking books.

Books! Her slippers tapped over the floor, scattering dust bunnies in her haste to check out Vadim's reading material. She was a firm believer that the titles on a bookshelf were a good indication of someone's character.

The plain, leather-bound cover of the first book creaked as she opened it. "Oh, my God." Brilliantly colored lettering and details leapt out at her, shining and glittering in the sunlight. She gasped. "This is just...beautiful."

Even though she couldn't understand the lines of small, even calligraphy, this was clearly a book of great value. Impossibly complex borders of band-work ran the length of each page, linking several exquisite miniature works of art. Vivid representations of people and animals sat side by side with terrifying demons. The book reminded her of Lindisfarne's famous illuminated gospels, but this book was newer, its colours fresher. *Illuminated* was certainly a great word for it.

A quick peep at the other book revealed the same dazzling quality of expression, written in the same unfamiliar language. The people at the British Museum would go nuts for these things. And rightly so. It felt like an act of sacrilege to be touching such incredible objects without the barrier of white cotton gloves. As she looked up, she caught Vadim watching her with a guarded expression on his face. "Wherever did you get these?"

He shrugged and turned away. That answered that. *Outlaw.* He'd stolen them. Why else would he be looking so shifty? She reluctantly closed the precious books and went to look around the rest of the cottage.

To her delight, there was a proper stone fireplace, equipped with all the hooks and gadgets essential for the medieval domestic goddess. And if she wasn't mistaken, there was a functioning chimney too, which was a definite bonus. Apart from a small table and two chairs sitting beneath the window, there wasn't much else to see. A peculiar light shone through the cow-horn window, giving the bleached wood of the furniture a faintly orange glow.

"The privy is out back," Vadim said as he took off his cloak. "But there is a pot beneath the bed for night-time use. When you empty it, might I ask that you use the pit outside and not the stream? Unlike other settlements, in Darumvale we prefer not to pollute our drinking water with excrement." He turned to hang his cloak behind the door, missing the look Martha sent him.

"I couldn't agree more." Apparently, Darumvale wasn't as backward as she'd thought. Even so, the prospect of life without indoor plumbing didn't fill her with joy. What she wouldn't give for the luxury of a flushing loo and hot, running water.

Vadim took off his sword and dagger and laid them on top of one of the chests with a clatter. "We have an hour at our disposal," he said. "Let us put it to good use." He went over to the bed and sat down, the wood frame creaking as it settled beneath his weight.

"I beg your pardon?" Martha pulled her cloak tighter around her body as Vadim began unlacing the ties of his leather tunic. Surely he didn't mean—

"Our marriage and courtship." He arched one black eyebrow at her, regarding the glow of her cheeks with amusement. "Their details?"

"Oh. Yes." Of course that's what he meant. What was she thinking? Pointedly ignoring the space beside him on the bed, she hurried to the table by the window and dragged out a chair to sit on. "What did you tell Seth and Sylvie last night?"

He'd told their hosts Martha came from a noble family based in the far south west, and that she'd run away because of a long-running family dispute—namely an arranged marriage to a man she despised. *Cherchez l'homme?* That made sense. In her experience, men were usually at the root of any trouble. But if they stuck to this story, no one would dare mention Martha's family or background within her earshot for fear of offending her. And, no one would be surprised if she went into hiding if a nobleman happened to pass through the village.

"The nobles do love to gossip amongst themselves. Imagine if word of your unsuitable match ever reached the ears of your loving mother and father?" Vadim said with a smile.

"But why would I need to hide?" No one was looking for her. Not in this world, anyway.

"The Earl saw you in my company." Vadim's smile faded. "For that, you are forever cursed. He will not easily forget you, Martha."

She didn't get it. "So?"

Vadim exhaled a long breath. "If you fell into his hands, he would use you to try and get to me." A muscle pulsed in his jaw. "In the end, you would be begging him for the death's sweet release."

Torture? Martha shuddered. "But I don't know anything."

"That will not protect you." A bleak smile curved his lips. "Many an innocent man has died screaming those very words. Ignorance is an ineffectual shield against Lord Edgeway's brutality."

Okay. It was definitely time to lighten the mood. She could feel a thick cloud of depression descending on the cottage. "So, tell me, *husband*, how exactly did we meet?"

The details of their *courtship* weren't a million miles from the truth. To begin with, they stuck to the real story, of how he'd found her unconscious in the hills and had taken her back to the cave to nurse her injuries. At this point, they embellished the tale a little, adding the character of a Traveler—a kind of wise, spiritual man—who had happened across their cave after they'd been alone together for several weeks. As repayment for sharing their fire and shelter, the kindly soul had offered to join them in marriage.

Martha exhaled. "Well, it's simple enough. But won't people think it's strange I know so little about you?" She was sure to betray herself sooner or later.

Vadim shrugged and leaned back upon the bed, making it squeak. "Why should they? We have not known one another for very long."

"But I don't know anything about you, Vadim." She raised her hands to her mouth and blew on her icy fingers. Did he have to lie there like that, tunic off, shirt open almost to his navel? Dark hair covered his well-defined chest. Not too much. Just enough to make him look manly. Swallowing hard, she averted her eyes from his nipples. "Wh-what about your home and family? Shouldn't your wife know something about them?"

A glacial look entered into his eyes. "That past is dead to me. Do not speak of it again, Martha. Be assured, no one else will."

"Suit yourself." She shrugged and stood up, going to look through the other window. At least she couldn't see him from here. Not that it was easy to avoid him in a house of this size. "Oh look." She squinted through the cow-horn windowpane. The thatcher was hobbling up the hill. "The dirty old man is back."

"So soon?"

The bed creaked, and suddenly Vadim joined her at the window, peering over her shoulder, much too close for comfort. From the corner of her eye, Martha saw black tendrils of his hair resting on her shoulder as the heat of his silent breath brushed against her cheek.

"Then I suppose I had better get ready."

Martha shivered, resolutely keeping her eyes fixed on the old man, pretending Vadim's closeness didn't bother her one way or the other.

When he finally moved away she didn't know whether she was relieved or disappointed. At least she dared breathe again, but she didn't look away from the window. As the thatcher approached the house, Forge raced to meet him, barking and snarling at their visitor. She clearly heard the old man's curses as he swiped at the dog with his stick, attempting to get by without being bitten.

A sudden rustling sound made Martha turn. Her jaw actually dropped. Vadim had removed his shirt and was now naked from the waist up.

"What the hell are you doing?" she squeaked, her eyes wide as saucers. Her mouth went very dry, and her knees actually wobbled, forcing her to clutch at the back of her chair for support. His perfect musculature seemed somehow graphically obscene.

Don't look at him! Turn away now.

Too late. His body was lean, without a trace of excess fat. Each muscle looked as if it'd been lovingly crafted from stone, carved by the hands of a master mason. Real beauty. The result of the life he lived, not courtesy of a gym. Her fingers tingled, suddenly aching to touch where her eyes lingered, and her long-dead libido suddenly roared back to life.

Several interesting scars adorned his abdomen, faint accents of silver enhancing the gold. But it was the intricate runic band tattoo at the top of his left arm that finished her off completely.

Unable to help herself, she simply stared, allowing her eyes to openly and quite brazenly roam his body. Propriety be damned. Taking her time, she followed the light covering of dark hair over his well-defined pectorals and down over his washboard abdomen to where it tapered away into a 'vee' just above his belly button.

Oh, sweet baby Jesus!

She gulped and forced her eyes back up. Vadim smiled, apparently enjoying her discomposure. *Damn him!* The image of that dark hair peeping just above the waistband of his trousers was now burnt onto her retinas.

"We were meant to have passed this hour within my bed, Martha." A slow, and quite wicked, smile curved his lips. "Old Hemble must be convinced that our marriage is normal and healthy in every way." He swept his hair back from his face with one careless hand.

"That old pervert has ideas enough of his own," she muttered, desperately battling to maintain eye contact. "Why encourage him?"

Vadim chuckled and opened the door, making a show of pulling on his shirt as he went to rescue Hemble from the dog. Martha shamelessly checked him out as he left, unable to resist the urge of doing so, and discovered the back of him was almost as good as the front.

What was wrong with her? *Okay, so it's been a while, but must you drool over the first semi-naked man you see? It's not as if you were ever that into the whole sex thing anyway. No wonder Tony—*

"Just shut up," she muttered to herself, rubbing her burning face.

From outside came the low rumbling exchange of male voices. Rather than be idle and fall victim to her own wayward thoughts, she went to straighten the rumpled bed covers. Vadim's discarded tunic lay where he'd left it. She sat down. The mattress still held the warmth of his body. An urge too powerful to ignore possessed her. With trembling fingers, she picked up the leather garment and raised it to her face. Then she inhaled—hard—filling her lungs with his scent. As she exhaled, an animal-like growl escaped from her throat.

What the feck was that, woman? That's a noise you've never made before. Not even when—

The door clicked, alerting her of Vadim's return.

She threw the jerkin down and leapt to her feet. When he walked in, she was standing red-faced in the middle of the room.

"That is a very guilty face," he said, closing the door behind him. "What have you been doing?"

"N-nothing." Breathing fast, she forced a smile. "Can we go now? I'm sure Humble...Hemble needs to get on with his work." She made to walk by, but Vadim caught her wrist, gently restraining her with his strong, warm hand.

"There is no hurry. Hemble will return later. He has another errand, it seems." He drew her slowly to him.

Hot and flustered, she couldn't look away from the deep neckline of his shirt and the temptation of the firm tanned skin that lay beneath it. *It just isn't fair.* Even her own body was conspiring against her. Her eyes were determined to get her into serious trouble today. With effort, she managed to close them. "I d-do wish you'd put some c-clothes on. It's freezing in here, or hadn't you noticed?" Her eyes snapped open when she heard his throaty chuckle. "And stop laughing at me!"

He cupped her face between his hands. "Poor Martha. Are you so unaccustomed to men? Can you truly be so innocent as your blushes proclaim?"

"Actually," she said, pushing his hands away from her face, "I've known plenty of men in my time."

"Oh?" Vadim didn't seem at all shocked. He leaned back against the door with the sole of his boot resting against it, effectively blocking her escape. "Socially or carnally? I am not convinced it can be the latter."

Carnally? Where did he find such words? The mere sound of it conjured a dozen deliciously sinful scenes within her mind. All of them featured Vadim in the leading role.

With difficulty, she found the strength to retaliate, hanging on to her rising anger in the hope it would save her from herself. "Not that it's any of your business, but I happen to have known a couple of men very intimately indeed." Hah. That had wiped the smile from his arrogant face.

"And is Tony one of these men?" he asked, stepping away from the door.

"Yes, as a matter of fact he is." She edged toward the window, eager to put some distance between them. The look in his eyes, so cold and brooding, was making her distinctly uncomfortable. In hindsight, she should've kept her mouth shut and let him go on thinking she was a virgin.

"And does he know he is not the only man to have shared your bed?" Vadim crossed the room towards her in a couple of slow strides.

The table prevented her from moving any farther, pressing into the back of her thighs. "He knows."

"Of course he does." He shook his head, his mouth curled with disgust. "From a man such as him I should have expected nothing less. I pity you, Martha, I really do. You deserve better."

"Really?" Another flame of temper ignited within her. Who was he to make judgements and feel sorry for her? What did he know about anything? "And what should he have done, in your considered opinion, hmm?"

A muscle ticked rapidly in his tense jaw line. "As your intended he should have called out the man who so dishonored you. 'Twas his right."

What stupid old-fashioned rot. "And what about my rights?" She faced him, hands on hips. "I have the right to make my own choices, don't I? I am not, and will never be, any man's chattel."

"A chattel?" Vadim looked shocked, his eyes widening. "You think Sylvie, or any other woman in this village, would accept a mate who treated her as mere property?"

"Don't they?"

"You should ask them before making such wild accusations," he told her in a low voice. "I do not understand your world, Martha, nor the dishonorable conduct of the men you associate with, but your knowledge of my world is equally inadequate. Have a care before you judge us too harshly."

She took a deep breath. "Then don't judge Tony and me by your standards. Our worlds are very different places, Vadim. We might never understand one another, but we can at least be respectful, can't we?"

"As you say." He bowed his head slightly. "But remember, Martha," he added quietly. "You are in my world now."

chapter nine

FOLLOWING THEIR SPAT, VADIM TOOK her straight back to the Great Hall, maintaining a stony silence the whole way there. He barely even looked at her.

Was he sulking? Well, that suited her just fine. She didn't want to speak to him either.

The moment they arrived, he strode over to the fire where Seth and several other men sat talking—a lively debate on the delights of hunting, by the sound of it. Martha hovered in the shadows, smiling to herself as the men began comparing weapons. They were all the same, no matter where, or when, they came from.

"Oh, I fear you have lost him now," a cheerful voice said at her shoulder. It was Sylvie, carrying a large basket of firewood in her arms. "No woman can compete with the glory of the hunt, not even a pretty new wife."

Martha grinned. "Men will be men, I guess. Here, let me help with that." She grabbed one handle of Sylvie's basket and, together, they carried it over to the log pile.

As they unpacked the wood, Sylvie said, "Tell me. Do you have any arrangements for the rest of this day?"

Martha glanced at Vadim. He was examining another man's bow, and shaking his head, obviously not impressed with the thing. She sighed. "It doesn't look that way."

"Good." Sylvie's grey eyes shone. "Then I can introduce you to the women of Darumvale."

Before Vadim set out with the hunting party, he came over to where Martha sat with Sylvie. The older woman politely excused herself and went to say goodbye to Seth, probably thinking the newly weds would value a private moment together.

Nothing could be further from the truth. Martha was still bristling from the way he'd spoken to her back at the house. She stiffened when he took her hand, raising it to his lips. This affectionate display was all for the villagers' benefit. Already, the deception was making her feel slightly sick.

"Will you not bid me farewell, m'lady?"

Sure. Why not? Anything to get rid of him. "Bye, Vadim. Have fun." Her smile felt forced and unnatural. He must have thought so too, for he released her hand and walked away without giving her a backward glance. He seemed as keen to be rid of her as she was to see him gone.

With the departure of the hunters, Martha's day improved. Sylvie was a very cheerful companion. As she trailed the older woman about the village, she gradually became acquainted with the other residents of Darumvale.

Unlike Vadim, Sylvie was extremely communicative. She talked constantly as they walked, rarely coming up for air, pointing out every home, barn and outbuilding. Each one, apparently, had a story to tell.

There were more houses than Martha first realized. Eighteen, in total, including the Great Hall. Although many homes were only slightly larger than Vadim's, according to Sylvie, parents, children, and grandparents all lived and slept beneath the same tiny roof—with only the occasional falling-out. Or so she claimed.

The small plot of land attached to every house was where families grew the food for their own tables. But there were larger fields on the outskirts of town, which the villagers farmed as a community. The main crops were wheat, oats and barley, enough to support the whole village. Any surplus stock was taken to sell at Edgeway's fortnightly market.

"Edgeway?" That name was familiar.

"The next big town, my dear," Sylvie replied. "Of course, we only attend during the growing season."

The plots and fields were empty now, the well-tilled earth waiting quietly beneath the snow for the cycle to begin again.

"I admit, Darumvale looks rather bleak at the moment," Sylvie said, perhaps guessing Martha's thoughts. "But you wait until next summer, 'tis a different picture then. Why, the whole town looks like a giant orchard, bursting with life and color."

Next summer? Hopefully, she'd have woken up by then. She refused to believe that any part of this elaborate dream was real.

Initially, the villagers and their children were as shy of Martha as she was of them. But shyness was a flimsy obstacle, lasting for as long as it took Sylvie to make the introductions. After that, only friendliness remained.

Martha soon found herself sitting on a stool outside the baker's house, encircled by a crowd of chatting women and laughing children. She sipped contentedly at the mug of warm ale someone had given her, basking in the fickle warmth of the winter sun. It appeared she was the centre of an impromptu street party. Everyone wanted to meet Vadim's woman.

The husbands of the village women—those not out hunting—were polite but somewhat reserved. Most of them disappeared just as soon as it was possible to do so.

"Ach! Pay him no mind." Rhea, the baker's wife, said to Martha when her husband had vanished back indoors after only the briefest of bows. "Men are all the same. They have no real interest in anything unless it's metal or sharp or shiny."

"Rhea!"her mother scolded, whilst Martha grinned and the other women laughed. "What kind of way is that to speak about the father of your children?"

Rhea was undeterred. "I speak the truth, Ma, as well you know." She was distracted by her son who was attempting to push a piece of twig up his baby sister's nose as she lay sleeping in her basket. "Connel!" Rhea excused herself and rushed off to save her daughter.

More chairs found their way out onto the street. An old woman began singing and other voices soon joined her. The song was in the 'Old Tongue', Sylvie said. Although Martha didn't understand a word of the song, she enjoyed the soft and haunting tune.

Snot-nosed toddlers constantly battled one another for the coveted position of Martha's lap, tugging at her skirts until she lifted them up, or until their mothers called them to 'leave her be'. Finally, one little boy fell asleep in her arms. Although her previous experience with children was limited, an unexpected wave of pleasure engulfed her as she held the child, snug and safe within the folds of her cloak.

She regarded all the smiling faces with a sense of wonder. As Vadim's wife, and in such a short time, these people had accepted her into their lives. It was a good feeling. Simple acceptance. Tony's friends had never fully accepted her. Not really.

Just for a second, she wished the dream was real.

However, there was no time to analyse this thought further. A pretty, snub-nosed young woman came across, introducing herself as Orla. She had the most beautiful auburn hair that lay in a thick, shining plait down her back. Martha was puzzled. All the other women, herself included, wore headscarves.

"I know this is probably a really stupid question," she

said, once the introductions were complete, "but why is your hair uncovered?"

Orla giggled. "Why, to indicate my maidenhood, of course, m'lady. And," she added with a sparkle in her green eyes, "so that my future husband might recognise me."

"Oh. Right." Did men display their singledom in a similar way, like wearing their daggers on the right side of their belts, for instance? Not that she dared ask. She felt ignorant enough already.

As luck would have it, Orla was a seamstress, and Martha wasted no time in making enquiries about a new gown. Compared to the other women, she felt downright dowdy. Although their garments were undeniably well worn, their cloth was brightly colored, and the addition of small pieces of glittering gold jewelery made them much more stylish, in a very medieval way. They made arrangements for Orla to visit the Great Hall to take Martha's measurements on the following day. She just hoped Vadim wouldn't mind footing the bill when it came.

The mother of the sleeping boy arrived to claim him.

"He's so good," Martha said as she stood up, transferring the soft, warm bundle to the safety of his mother's arms.

"I shall remind you of that the next time he disturbs the whole village with his wailing." His mother smiled. "Why do children always seem to cut their teeth at night?"

Martha confessed she didn't know. Children had never featured in her plans for the future. Or perhaps, they'd never featured in Tony's plan, and, like the fool she was, she'd gone along with his wishes, at the same time sacrificing her own.

There was a sudden, pained *yelp*. Looking down, she realised she'd accidentally stepped on Forge. Unnoticed by anyone, the dog had managed to sneak between everyone's legs, finding a place to settle near her feet. Now she'd gone and trodden on him.

"Oh, baby." Crouching down, she cuddled the big

dog's head to her chest. "I'm so sorry."

Bren, the smith's wife, shook her head as Forge licked Martha's face. "May the Spirits forgive me for doubting my own man. So, Jared was right, after all."

"Sorry?" Martha frowned, certain that she'd missed something vital.

"That dog...fawning all over you like that. I never knew him take to someone so, not even his own master." Bren smiled, displaying a rather gap-toothed grin. "Like him, do you?"

"I love dogs. Have you had him very long?"

"Only since last spring. Jared found him out on the moor, half dead with an arrow sticking out of his leg. We all thought he would die, for he was ill with a fever for days."

"How awful." Martha kissed the dog's head and stood up.

"Doubtless he once belonged to some noble who wearied of such a useless hunting dog and wanted rid of him." But Bren ruffled Forge's shaggy head, displaying an affection absent in her words. "Not that he ever shows us any gratitude for the trouble we took with him back then. Nasty old beast that he is."

A change in weather finally broke up the party. Thick, dark clouds lumbered in from the mountains, blotting out the sun. A bone-chilling wind sent the villagers back indoors to the comfort of their hearths. After saying their goodbyes, Martha and Sylvie walked back up the gentle hill that led to the Great Hall.

"Forgive me for being so ignorant," Martha said as they walked, "but I heard the women refer to Seth as 'The Chief'. What does that mean?"

"Why, that he is the Chieftain of Darumvale, of course." Sylvie looked at her with a curious expression in her eyes. "He has held the position for five years now. I thought Vadim might have told you."

"He didn't." Martha flushed, feeling stupid again.

What must people think of her? "I'm so sorry. Perhaps I should have addressed him in a certain way?"

"The villagers call him 'Sir' or 'Chief', but there is no reason for you to do so, Martha. Not since you so kindly dispensed with the formality of address that is yours by right."

"Huh?" What right? She certainly couldn't ask Sylvie about it, not unless she wanted to blow her cover.

But Sylvie was no fool. Surely she must know that Vadim had told her nothing about his past, or about anything else of consequence for that matter. Her blush intensified. *She probably thinks we didn't have much time for talking!*

Sylvie smiled, linking her arm through Martha's as they walked. "Your handsome husband has much neglected your education, my dear. Ah! Seth and I were just the same in the early days of our own marriage. We had no need of words, either, not when we were so much in love."

The hot flush spread to the tips of Martha's ears.

"Enjoy it whilst you can," Sylvie continued, "for there will eventually come a time when the outside world and all of its concerns will intrude into the bliss of your marital bed. It will pull your lover right out of your arms if you allow it." A shadow crossed her face, extinguishing her smile. "These are the most precious of days, my dear," Sylvie said as she opened one of the heavy wooden doors at the entrance of the hall. "Keep them warm in your heart. Then no matter what the future brings, there will always remain a place where you can be happy."

"Wait." Martha gently caught Sylvie's arm as she made to go indoors, hardly sure of what she wanted to say. "Is anything wrong? Is Seth all right?"

A smile flickered on Sylvie's lips.

That was her armor, Martha realized. Smiling kept her troubles at bay.

"You have a good heart, m'lady," the older woman

said softly. "Please, do not vex yourself on my account. We are both quite well, I assure you."

Worms of guilt ate at Martha's insides. Sylvie was such a nice little woman. She didn't deserve lies, especially from someone she'd welcomed into her home. The urge to confess all almost defeated her. Only Vadim's disapproving face, scowling within her mind, stopped her from doing so.

"Not everything is as it seems. Not for any of us." It was a cryptic comment, but as honest as she dared.

"Oh?" Sylvie searched Martha's eyes. "Secrets are a heavy burden, arc they not? No matter how much we long to rest, we can never set them down."

Martha nodded, absently sucking her lower lip as she wondered about Sylvie's secrets. The older woman looked haunted, the fine lines on her face appeared deeper without the disguise of her smile Whatever burden she carried was obviously eating her up inside.

How long before I look like that?

"You can talk to me about anything," Martha said. "I promise not to tell a soul—not even Vadim."

Something flashed across Sylvie's gray eyes. For a moment Martha thought she might confide in her. But just as soon as the look came it was gone again.

Sylvie clasped Martha's hand. "You are a good girl," she said. "I hope Vadim appreciates you as he should. Now, come." Her smile returned with a vengeance. "Let us seek the fire before we freeze."

***

The hunters returned at dusk with much loud talk and laughter, bringing with them the first flurries of snow.

It had been a good day. Tethered by their feet to sturdy wooden poles, the carcasses of two young bucks rocked from side to side as they were carried triumphantly into Darumvale, borne on the shoulders of the hunters.

Alerted by the noise, women poked their heads from their homes and called greetings to the men, while the roaming village dogs barked and got underfoot. Children, who should have long since been in bed, took turns running beneath each swinging deer, their laughter and squeals adding to the general cacophony.

Vadim walked slightly behind the main group, snatching a few moments' peace away from the excitement.

He was responsible for the first kill of the day. It had been an easy shot. The buck had all but walked into him as he hid in the undergrowth. But the men cared little for such details. Instead, they kept proclaiming him their good-luck talisman until he grew weary of their teasing banter. But the other men were not to blame for his sour mood.

A yearning for silence and solitude had stalked him since he had taken Martha back to the Great Hall that morning. Her admission of having two lovers affected him more than it had any right to. The moment the words left her lips, it was as though she had stuck a cold, dull blade into his guts and then twisted it without mercy. The pain within him had subsided now, settling down like the red heat of a post-wound infection. It was bearable. Just.

He did not relish the prospect of facing her again. Whilst out with the hunting party he had managed to forget her. Now the images in his mind had returned, stronger and more vivid than before.

"Vadim." Seth's call shattered his reverie. The Chief waved, summoning him to the Great Hall. Vadim returned his wave and reluctantly followed.

Within those walls, Martha was waiting. Somehow he must behave as an affectionate husband and continue the deception they had begun. It would not be easy.

***

"Sylvie? Sylvie!"

The doors to the Great Hall flew open and Seth strode in, grinning broadly. "What luck we have had this day!" he cried, oblivious of the swirl of cold air and snow that followed him inside.

"Welcome home, my dear." Sylvie set down her darning and hastened to her husband, raising her face for his kiss. "Tell me all. Did you catch a deer?"

Wide-eyed, Martha looked up from the stocking she'd been attempting to mend under Sylvie's patient tutelage. Vadim would be here soon. Would he still be in a bad mood?

And suddenly, there he was, his tall shadow looming in the doorway. Skirting around Seth and Sylvie's happy reunion, he headed in her direction.

Stomach clenching, she slowly rose from her seat. How should she greet him? From the opposite side of the fire, Seth's elderly mother directed a broad, gummy smile Martha's way. Obviously some kind of wifely display was expected.

Oh Lord!

As though her legs were controlled by another force, she set off to meet him, her darning still clutched in her hand.

As Vadim approached, the flickering light of the rush lamps enhanced the angles of his face, the deep shadows painting him harsh and forbidding. When he finally looked at her, his eyes resembled glittering lumps of coal. The eyes of a demon, eyes no mortal man should possess.

"H...hello." Her voice cracked in her suddenly dry throat. "D-did you have a nice day?"

Without warning, he grabbed her, crushing her body to his. Not exactly the response she'd been expecting.

"Hello, wife," he growled, resting his forehead against hers. He smelled of snow and sweet, cold air. "Did you miss me?"

The handle of his sword pressed painfully against her ribs. Before her befuddled mind could formulate a suitable response, his mouth came down hard on hers.

It was a parody of a kiss, rough and grinding, with not even a pretense of tenderness. Shocked, Martha pressed her hands flat against the hardness of his chest and pushed, but it was useless. Her struggles were nothing when matched against such superior strength. She tried to turn her head, but only succeeded in grazing her lips painfully against his stubble.

As a last resort, she relaxed her mouth, feigning surrender. As Vadim made to press his advantage, she sank her teeth into his lower lip. And she wasn't gentle. With a gasp of pain, Vadim broke the kiss. But he didn't release her from his arms.

"Witch!" He ran his tongue over his wounded lip. "You have bloodied me." But he smiled down into her furious eyes and didn't seem particularly upset about it.

"Bloodied you!" she hissed, her arms still braced against his chest. "I'd do a lot more than that if we didn't have a fecking audience, you bastard!"

Judging by the amount of laughter, Seth, his wife and his mother were all enjoying the floorshow.

"Indeed?" Vadim rubbed his nose against hers, Eskimo style. "Then, I shall look forward to being alone with you, my love."

"If you don't let me go, I swear I'll..." She couldn't think of anything bad enough.

But there was no need to think up more threats. The cage about her suddenly relaxed, and she was free again. Breathing hard, her face scarlet with embarrassment, Martha darted him one last venom-laden glare and stormed outside, heading for the privy.

chapter ten

VADIM PICKED UP MARTHA'S DARNING from where it had fallen and, chuckling at the memory of her outraged expression, went to speak to his hosts.

Seth laughed and slapped him manfully on the back, obviously much impressed with the way he had handled his new wife. Sylvie and Ma, however, only shook their heads and returned to the fire, leaving the men to their bluster.

As Vadim's blood cooled, his conscience awoke, and Seth's voice gradually blurred into a meaningless noise.

Poor Martha. What must she think of him?

Although the impudent wretch deserved some form of punishment for the way she had spoken to him back at the cottage that morning, the vengeance he had exacted was unequal to her crime.

Her *crime?* 'Twas a curious choice of word. What law had she broken? What was Martha actually guilty of? Having lovers was not a crime, not even in this world.

Seth's mouth was still moving. He paused, apparently seeking some kind of response.

Tilting his head to one side, Vadim made a non-committal sound at the back of his throat. It must have been the correct answer, for Seth smiled and continued conversing with himself.

Vadim ran his tongue over his wounded lip. The sweet taste of her still clung to him. It had an unexpected potency, inflaming him, body and mind. Suddenly he knew the reason for his earlier brutality, and it had nothing to do with her faceless lovers. He was angry because she had promised to bind herself to another man.

Ridiculous. He gave himself a mental shake. He could not keep Martha like a stray dog, and neither did he want to. His life had no room in it for a woman, especially one such as her. No, Martha belonged somewhere else. His duty, albeit self-enforced, was to keep her safe until he could find a way to send her home, wherever that was. Nothing else mattered.

***

Eventually, Martha composed herself enough to return to the hall. Not that she wanted to go back in there, but she had nowhere else to go. Besides, the privy was freezing, and she hadn't got her cloak to protect her from the cold. Reluctantly, she pushed open the ornately carved door and stepped inside.

"Martha." Vadim stepped out of the shadows by the entrance, making her jump. "May I speak with you for a moment?"

She pressed a hand to her pounding chest. "You have nothing to say that I want to hear." The time she'd spent in the stinking privy had done nothing to cool her anger. She tried to march past him but he stepped into her path, blocking her escape. Luckily for him, he didn't attempt to touch her.

"Please." He held out her cloak. "Walk with me."

There was no reason she should obey him. She hated him. But...there was something in the way he looked at her, a look so appealing, she found herself nodding.

"Oh, very well." She snatched the cloak from his hand and flung it about her shoulders, ignoring the inner voice that accused her of not having a backbone.

"Thank you." Vadim's expression relaxed a little. "I will detain you for long. Though, I doubt we will be missed."

That was true. In her absence the hall had become full of people. They stood around the long hearth in the center of the room, laughing and talking, good-naturedly arguing the best method of roasting a deer.

"There is to be a feast in honor of our marriage," Vadim told her. "The whole village will come to celebrate it."

"I'd rather they didn't."

"You would prefer to offend everyone?"

"No." She glared up at him. "I'd prefer not to continue this charade a moment longer," she said. "My marriage to you isn't all I hoped it would be."

"Come outside." He held open the door. "We should not discuss it here."

"Fine." Martha stalked back out into the cold night. "But don't you try anything with me."

They pulled up their hoods and, by mutual accord, set off in the direction of Vadim's house. When he offered her his arm, she refused it. He wouldn't fool her again with his fake gentlemanly manner.

Fat white snowflakes fell in a thick blanket about them, the intermittent moans of the wind stirring them into ghostly whirlwinds. Small snowdrifts were already forming against the doorways of the houses.

Once they were clear of the houses, Martha turned on him. "How dare you treat me like that!" She stopped walking and punched him hard on the arm. "This marriage isn't real, remember? You saved my life, and I'm grateful, but don't think you can use my body as a means of payment for your services. I am not a whore!"

"I know." Vadim rubbed his arm where she'd hit him. "Believe me, Martha, I sincerely regret my actions. It will not happen again."

"Hah. You've said that before," she said, recalling the near-kiss incident, back at the cave. "'I will be sure not to touch you again. Not without your prior permission, of course.' That *is* what you said, isn't it?"

"I did. And how well you remember my words, my love," he said with a mocking smile.

"Why wouldn't I?" she demanded, hands on hips. "It was only a couple days ago, for God's sake. Or is there something wrong with your memory as well as your manners? Let me make this as clear as I can for you, Vadim. I am *not* your love, and I never will be. Have you got that?"

He was fool enough to laugh.

Of all the infuriating— Martha's temper flashed. Balling her hand into a fist, she lashed out, aiming for his arrogant face.

But, this time, Vadim saw it coming and seized her wrist before her fist had a chance to make contact. "Enough, Martha. You earned one swing at me, I admit, but not two."

"Get off me!" The force of her struggles made her scarf slip.

"Not until you calm yourself."

As she stared into the fathomless depths of his eyes, her anger vanished like smoke in the wind, and a sapping weariness took its place. "I don't want to do this anymore, Vadim," she said quietly. "I really hate lying to these people. Can't we just tell them the truth?"

"The truth?" He released her wrist. "That you come from another world, a world where women dress as men and live alone? A place where physical intimacy is as commonplace as embroidery, but with none of its value? I think not." He looked grim. "You would be pronounced a witch and hunted all the days of your life."

When he put it like that, honesty didn't seem the best policy, after all. She sighed and huddled deeper in the folds of her cloak. "So, can I ask you something else?"

"Of course."

"Will you promise to give me a straight answer?"

"If I can."

"Why did you kiss me like that?"

"I was angry with you."

"Why?" She frowned. "Because of this morning?"

"Yes. The way you spoke to me, how you judged us." Reaching out, he brushed the snowflakes from her hair. "I did not care for it."

"But you judged me too."

"You have your answer, Martha. I did not say it would be reasonable."

"So what now?" She stamped her feet in the snow in an attempt to warm them. "I want to go home, Vadim. To my real home, I mean. Is there really a way, do you think?"

"I do not know." When he took her icy hands, she didn't pull away. "But if a way exists, I vow to you, I will find it." His thumbs stroked lazy circles on her hands. "In the meantime, we will continue as we have begun. However, there will be occasions when I shall need to touch you, Martha. But only for the sake of appearances, you understand?"

She nodded. It would look odd if they never touched, she supposed. "But not in the way you kissed me earlier. Promise?"

"You have my word." He raised her hands to his lips. "May I show you?"

At that moment, she'd have agreed to pretty much anything he suggested. The way he was looking at her sent shivers rippling along her spine. Had Tony ever looked at her with such intensity? Definitely not. No one could forget a look like this.

"Martha?" Vadim was still waiting for the green light.

"Wh...okay."

With a tiny smile, he lowered his head, pressing his warm lips to each unresisting palm in turn.

Her shivers quadrupled.

Transferring her hands to rest upon his chest, he placed his finger beneath her chin and tilted it so she could see the passion flaring within his dark eyes. Was he still acting? Damn. He was good. Her knees were already wobbling, and he'd barely even touched her yet.

"Relax, Martha," he breathed against her lips. "This will not hurt at all."

He lowered his head, brushing his lips against hers. At first, his touch was so gentle she barely felt it. Even so, it was enough to send the blood galloping through her veins. More kisses, each one as light as down, designed to seduce. Then his tongue flicked over her lower lip. He sucked gently at it before kissing her with the same gentle deliberation as before. She closed her eyes and shivered as a million goose bumps rose up all over her body.

Of their own volition, her lips moved beneath his. Her tentative response must have pleased him for he growled from deep within his throat. Slipping his arm beneath her cloak, he hooked her waist and gathered her closer.

The snow and the cold ceased to exist. She was only aware of the heat and the taste of him. His scent intoxicated her: leather with just a hint of tobacco, blended with his own unique male scent. A lethal concoction on her senses. Her hands slid up over his chest, testing the hard strength beneath them. She linked her hands about his neck, feeling the warmth of his skin seeping through the cool dampness of his hair. And then she became fully aware of the intimacy of their bodies. Up close and very personal. She was dissolving, melting into him. She couldn't fight it. She didn't want to.

He was holding back. She sensed it. Beneath his slow, chaste kisses, a fiercer need battled for freedom. What if she encouraged him, just a little? Without pausing to consider the consequences, Martha slid her tongue over the fullness of his lower lip in a blatant invitation.

Vadim accepted. He hauled her to him, slipping his tongue between her parted lips in a deep and hungry kiss.

She was with him every step of the way. Tangling her hands in his hair, she wantonly molded her body to his until he groaned from deep within his throat. He cupped one of her buttocks and held her even closer.

That's not a sword handle!

Her eyes snapped open. The hardness pressed against her belly thrilled her and turned her into a quivering mass of need. *God, I want him.* More than she remembered ever wanting anything. And that same desire was apparent in his eyes. It was difficult to believe. This gorgeous, sexy man actually desired her too.

"Martha." Her name was a ragged sigh against her lips.

Dragging his mouth from hers, Vadim cupped her face in his hands, anointing her burning cheeks with tiny kisses. Then he moved lower, his breath hot against her neck as he nuzzled, kissed, and tasted his way to her earlobe. The way his rough stubble brushed over her sensitive skin was an exquisite form of torture.

Still clinging to him, she tilted her head, silently willing him to take whatever he wanted. She ached for him in places that had been in stasis until today.

What would it be like if he explored all of her in this way?

A dog's intermittent barking broke the spell.

Although he still held her, she sensed him withdrawing. When she opened her eyes, she found him looking at her again in that familiar brooding way of his. Her own passion evaporated, cooling her blood and restoring her common sense.

"I-is that what you had in m-mind?" Her voice trembled, but it was the best that she could do.

"Hmm?"

"I don't know about you," she continued, "but I don't think we should do that in front of Seth and Sylvie." She forced a smile, casually twirling a strand of his hair about her finger. "We don't want to give them a heart attack, do we?"

Humor was the only defense she had.

"Perhaps not," Vadim agreed with a wry smile. "Our

marriage need not be quite so convincing." He pressed a light kiss to her forehead then released her from the warm circle his arms.

Suddenly, she felt empty. Alone.

Vadim pulled the edges of her cloak together, covering her against the cold, then swept the snow from her hair. "Shall we return to our hosts?"

She nodded, although it was the actually the last thing she wanted to do. "Do I look decent?"

"Far from it," he answered with a sexy smile. "Here, allow me."

He helped to fix her hair, smoothing the wild curls back from her face and tucking it beneath her scarf. "This looks a little sore..."

As he spoke, he grazed the pad of his thumb over her swollen lower lip. A shudder of response rippled through her. Vadim's eyes darkened.

With difficulty, she forced herself to look away. "Come on. Let's go back inside before we freeze."

NO ONE HAD MISSED THEM.

The great fireside roasting debate raged on. Two long benches were set by the fire, seating for the hunters and their families. Sylvie and Seth's mother—Martha didn't know her real name; everyone called her 'Ma'—roamed amongst them, ladling out steaming bowls of vegetable pottage to their supper guests. Seth, meanwhile, had opened a barrel of ale, ensuring no one went thirsty.

"Sit down and eat," Sylvie called as they entered the hall. Hands full, she gestured with her head to the two empty stools by the fire. With his hand in the small of Martha's back, Vadim escorted her to their place, then immediately fell into conversation with the grizzled-looking man to his right.

Martha accepted her food with a word of thanks. It smelled delicious, but she wasn't hungry. How could she eat while her stomach churned so badly?

When Seth stood up, the room fell silent. Raising his tankard skyward, he gave thanks for the food at his table and for the friends seated about it. The villagers bowed their heads, muttering "We give our thanks". When the prayer was over, everyone began eating again, resuming their previous conversations.

Martha could only pick at her pottage, rinsing it down with sweet watery ale whenever her swallow reflex needed help. No one noticed her distraction. Her companions talked loudly as they ate, the glow of the successful hunt still bright in their hearts.

She glanced at Vadim from beneath her eyelashes. He appeared quite untroubled and cleared his own supper with an ease she envied. Obviously their kiss hadn't affected him at all. But what had she expected? A kiss, after all, was just a kiss.

Kissing her was all part of the deception. His body's response was that of any healthy male animal, nothing more. Just another act in the play they'd written between them. And as she knew to her cost, some men were much better actors than others.

As a host of Tony-flavored memories flooded her mind, her throat went into lock down, refusing to accept another morsel of food. Fortunately, Forge came to the rescue. Without anyone noticing him, the dog had entered the hall and secured a place at her feet. With speed and discretion, he disposed of the pottage she 'accidentally' dropped to him.

When the meal was over, the men took out their pipes and the conversation took a darker turn. The name of the Earl of Edgeway roused Martha from the deep reverie she'd drifted into, lulled by the heat of the fire and the amount of ale she'd consumed.

"Curse him and his taxes!" Vadim's grey-haired companion spat onto the fire, making it sizzle and pop. "We will be lucky to make it 'til spring after all he has taken this season."

Martha sat up a little straighter, absently stroking Forge's head where it lay on her lap.

"Aye. There is no reasoning with him." Seth puffed thoughtfully on his pipe. "Only the Spirits know how hard I tried to make him see sense, Jem."

"No one blames you, Chief," the man assured him. "I

meant no offense by my words."

"And I take none, my friend," Seth replied. A bitter smile twisted his lips. "I only wish I could negotiate with the man without wanting to tear his heart out. It does not benefit our cause, I am sure."

Sylvie laid her hand upon Seth's thigh. "And I am sure no one could do any better, husband. The Earl cannot be reasoned with," she said quietly. "He wants us to hate him."

"Aye, that and to starve us and our children to death!" Jem's wife looked tenderly at the baby suckling at her breast. "If this winter is as long as the last one—"

"Hush now." Her husband put a brawny arm about her shoulders. "It will not be as bad as that, lass. Thanks to Vadim and the others, we have food the Earl cannot know about. We will outlast him." He smiled, adding. "At least the snows are a good defense against his visits."

One or two people chuckled, their laughter easing the growing tension of the room. Martha looked at Vadim's impassive face with new eyes. *He helps these people. How?* And who were 'the others' Jem spoke of? Unfortunately, she couldn't ask without rousing suspicion.

"I saw him on the road only recently," Vadim said in a quiet voice. He glanced at Martha then looked away. "Barely five leagues from here. Darumvale may not rest easy quite yet. Even now, the roads are passable."

"What?" Seth's eyes widened and he stroked at his beard. "So close?"

One of the younger men snorted. "He will not risk being cut off from his castle for three months or more. Our little village cannot compete with the delights of Edgeway." He grinned at his sniggering friends.

Edgeway must be the local fleshpot in these parts.

"Mind your tongue, young Will." An old, bald-headed man cuffed the lad over the head and glared sternly at him. "There are decent women present, in case you have forgotten it."

It seemed she was right.

"My apologies, ladies." The lad's ruddy complexion darkened. He bowed his head to Sylvie and the other women, including Martha, and looked suitably chastened.

"When I last saw the Earl, he was south of Darumvale, not to the north." Vadim looked slowly from face to face. "I confess, his closeness to this place makes me uneasy."

There was a rumble of agreement followed by a flurry of questions.

"Then he may come here yet?"

"Did he have soldiers with him? How many?"

"Was he dressed in mail, m'lord? Did wagons follow him?"

Vadim held up his hand. "Peace, friends. He was alone when I saw him, save for his hawk. Too distant to be challenged..."

Martha blinked at such a blatant untruth, but Vadim avoided her eyes.

"...He seemed bent upon his own pleasure rather than on ruining what remains of ours. Even so," he darted a look at Martha, "I will head out on the morrow, weather permitting, to track his movements."

At this, there were smiles and words of relief. Everyone was pleased about Vadim's intention. Everyone except Martha.

"You are a good man, m'lord." Jem nodded at Vadim over the lip of his tankard. "And a great friend to this village. The pity is that you cannot take up your true—"

"Quite." Vadim cut Jem off, very rudely. "But let us deal with one thing at a time, my friend."

His true— What?

"And so, Seth." He smiled at the Chief. "I must beg a favor in return. Will you protect my wife in my absence—"

"Vadim!" Seth cried. "Need you even voice such a request? We will care for her as our own family. Is that not right, Sylvie?"

"Of course." Sylvie smiled across at Martha. "She is

one of us now, an inhabitant of Darumvale."

"Your lady will be fine, m'lord," Jem added, winking at Martha. "We will all look out for her."

"I am much obliged to you." Vadim resumed his pipe, billowing out plumes of sweet, fragrant smoke.

"Thank you," Martha added, thinking she'd better say something too. "You're all very kind." Inexplicably, the thought of Vadim leaving made her eyes prick with tears.

Sylvie waved aside their thanks. "Just as long as you are back for your wedding feast four nights hence," she told Vadim, her grey eyes twinkling with mischief. "It would not be much of a celebration without you, m'lord."

Martha blushed at the good-natured teasing that followed. So she was very glad when one of the younger men took up a long whistle and raised it to his lips. As the first clear note rang out, everyone fell silent and listened to the lad play.

It was a sweet and melancholy tune. Although Martha was no musician, even she appreciated how gifted the lad was. The music seemed to speak of lost love and sadness. She closed her eyes, fighting to hold back scalding tears. As kind as these people were, they weren't her own family. They never could be. But what remained of her family now? Aunt Lulu was all she had. The only living person who returned her love.

Seth's mother began to accompany the whistle's song, and her voice was surprisingly sweet. She sang in the Old Tongue. Although the lilting lyrics were incomprehensible to Martha's brain, her heart recognised them well enough. When Ma's voice trembled over the saddest parts of the song, Martha had to bite her lip. She wondered if the old woman's secret memories were as painful as her own.

At that moment, Vadim reached over and took her hand. Martha clasped his strong, rough fingers, and found comfort in his touch. It felt natural and right somehow. He seemed to have sensed her sadness when no one else could. Not only did she like him, but she trusted him too.

Be careful you don't give him your heart as well.

The song finally ended, the last note dissolving into the heavy silence of the room. Everyone seemed to exhale at the same moment, a long communal breath, releasing them from the paralysis they'd fallen into. Vadim released her hand, and everyone stood up en masse, chatting loudly to one another again as they gathered their belongings and prepared to return to their own homes and hearths. Only Martha lingered by the fire.

It must be getting late. She had no concept of time anymore. In Darumvale, her body was discovering its natural inner clock. Sleep when it was dark, wake when it was light.

The force of her yawn took her by surprise. Belatedly, she covered her mouth and looked around to see if anyone had noticed. Predictably, Vadim's were the only eyes she encountered. He smiled and offered her his hand. Martha was glad to take it.

"Bed for you, my lady." He pulled her to her feet.

"I need the loo...privy first."

He sighed. "Very well. Do you wish me to accompany you?"

She rolled her eyes at him. "No thanks."

Once the demands of her bladder were met, Martha returned to the hall, shivering and stamping her feet. Vadim was waiting.

"It's getting worse out there," she said, flinging off her cloak and sending a shower of snowflakes into his face. "Oops! Sorry."

He smiled and wiped the melting residue from his eyelashes. "Bed. Now."

They were staying in the Great Hall again, for Vadim said Hemble had yet to clean the chimney of their house. So, bidding goodnight to their hosts and the last departing guests, he led Martha to the bed by the cow byre.

Sylvie had thoughtfully provided a jug of water and a bowl for washing. There was also a chunk of nasty-smelling soap that didn't lather very well. Martha washed her hands and face then rinsed, gasping as the chilly water hit her face.

"Finished?" Vadim asked.

She hadn't realized he was still there. Didn't he have anything better to do than stand around watching her wash?

"Almost." She dabbed her face with a rough piece of cloth, then began cleaning her teeth with the piece of twig that Sylvie had recommended, sitting on the bed in order to concentrate on the task.

"Just how long does your toilet take?"

Martha's hand stilled. "You don't need to wait," she said. "I'd much rather do this without you hovering and twitching over me."

"As you wish." Vadim turned smartly on his heels and walked back towards the fire.

She shook her head. *Men!*

When he returned, she was in bed, wriggling around beneath the mound of furs. Her dress, cloak, and scarf hung from a nail protruding from the wall and her shoes lay neatly together beneath the bed.

"Are you comfortable?" The foot of the bed sank when Vadim sat on it, creaking horribly beneath his weight.

"Do I look comfortable?" She kicked him when one of her feet moved too vigorously upon the mattress. "Sorry."

"What did I do to earn that?"

"Nothing. I'm trying to get warm, that's all." She glared in the direction of their bovine neighbor. "Must you keep doing that?" Her nose wrinkled as she detected an unpleasant gas emission. "Ugh!"

Almost as if it understood her words, the cow stopped chewing. Its expression was almost wounded. Martha's Catholic conscience released a flood of guilt into her heart. "Oh, I know you can't help it, but would you at least move away before you let rip?"

Vadim laughed. "You are aware she is a cow, Martha? She does not understand you."

He bent over, fiddling with the straps on his boots. "Hemble says the house will be ready tomorrow, though I would be happier if you remained here until I return." As he kicked off his boots, Forge gave a sudden yelp from the shadows beside the bed. "My apologies… Wait. What are you doing in here?"

Martha giggled. "What's that you were saying about talking to animals, hmm?"

"Dogs are different," he said, tugging at the lacing of his tunic.

"Different how?" Then it dawned on her. "What are you doing?" He was undressing.

"I should have thought that was obvious," he said, throwing his tunic to the ground. "Move over." He pulled back the bedcovers.

Her heart lurched. The cot was narrow for one person, let alone for two. "Move where exactly? There's hardly enough room for—"

"Roll onto your side." Vadim slid into bed and pressed his hand against her hip, pushing at her.

Beneath the thin fabric of her shift, her skin burned where he touched her. Heart pounding, she had little choice but to obey. They were guests in Seth's house. She couldn't argue with him here.

"Fine. But I won't be able to sleep, laying on my side." Huffing in irritation, she rolled over. Vadim immediately spooned up behind her, his warm, hard body much too close for comfort.

A cold draught was coming from somewhere. She tugged at the cover trying to arrange them, one-handed about her neck.

"Allow me." Vadim carefully tucked the furs about her, ensuring she was cozy. Then he held her to him again, his arm resting over her breast. "Better?"

Martha shivered as his warm breath brushed soft against her ear. "Smashing, thanks." At least she was warmer now. It was quite impossible to put any distance between their bodies, so she didn't bother trying.

One by one, the rush lights around the hall went out until only the red glow of the fire remained. Gradually the hall grew quiet as Seth and his family retired for the night. Only the occasional animal noise, and the distant low murmurings of Seth and Sylvie talking in their own bed, disturbed the peace.

Vadim entwined his legs with hers. "Your feet are still cold," he said in a low voice. "I can feel their chill even through my clothes. Give them to me."

"They're fine!" she hissed, pulling her feet away from where he'd trapped them between his long, warm legs. At least he'd kept his trousers on.

"Relax, Martha." He stroked her hair with a gentle hand. "Warmth is all I offer you this night. Your virtue is quite safe. I am too weary to pose a threat."

That much seemed to be true. Although her backside was pressed firmly against his most intimate region, she detected no response. Exhaling, she forced her bunched-up muscles to relax. This time, when Vadim took her feet between his legs, she didn't fight him. His heat soon penetrated all of her body, banishing every shiver from their bed.

He didn't speak, only held her securely against him. She stared into the darkness, listening to him breathe. Would she ever see him again after tomorrow? What if the Earl caught up with him? The thought distressed her much more than it should. Why did he have to go looking for the Earl anyway? Why couldn't someone else do it?

"Vadim?"

"Hmm?" He snuggled closer against her, his chin resting on top of her head. Already she heard the shadows of sleep in his voice.

"Are you awake?" *Please wake up.*

"What...is it?" He sounded so tired that she felt a pang of guilt, but only the tiniest pang.

"Do you have to go away tomorrow...I mean, why do you have to go?"

***

The vulnerability of her questions roused him from the lure of sleep. "It is my duty to protect this village. I must do all I can to keep it safe."

"Why you, though? The other men have weapons. Can't they protect themselves?"

"They can, to an extent. But they are mainly farmers and tradesmen, Martha. They are not soldiers; not trained to fight and kill."

"Not like you, you mean?"

"No," he agreed softly. "Not like me." If she only knew what his life was like she would recoil from him. A woman such as she should not be subjected to the horrors he carried within him. He could not tell her. Not now.

***

Martha took a moment to absorb this information. It was hard to believe that the man holding her so gently was a trained killer. "If that's so, why didn't you kill the Earl when you had the chance? Why did you lie to Jem earlier?"

She felt him tense behind her. She knew he would have moved away from her if he could.

"Because I made a vow to...someone, long ago," he said at last. "A vow that forever binds my hands. I cannot kill Edgeway, no matter how much I wish to. If I could undo my foolish vow I would do it in a heartbeat, but I cannot." He sighed. "Only one person had the power to release me, but she has been in the ground for many years now. My fate is set in stone."

As his voice trailed away into the darkness, Martha caught a glimpse of the pain he carried inside him.

"Who was she, Vadim?" she asked softly. "You must have loved her very much to make such a promise." She would have turned over to face him, but he would not allow it. His arm over her breast tensed, keeping her where she lay.

"Of course I loved her," he replied huskily. "She was my only sister."

His sister?

"Go to sleep now, Martha. Ask me no more tonight."

"Just one more question," she whispered into the darkness, "and I promise I'll shut up. How long will you be gone? You won't stay away too long, will you?"

"That was two questions."

"Yes, but they're related. It's allowed."

He chuckled, banishing his ghosts for the present.

"Then here is a single answer for you. I will return by the eve of our wedding feast."

"Good enough." Martha closed her eyes and relaxed against him, ignoring the final morbid question flitting about her mind. But he must have heard it anyway.

"If I have not returned by then," he murmured against her ear, "you must go to Seth— and only Seth, mind— and tell him everything. Ask him to find Madoc the Seer. Do you understand?" She nodded. "Good girl."

He spoke no more. Not long afterwards, Martha detected a change in his breathing. It became slower and deeper. The arm resting across her chest suddenly felt very heavy. She knew he was asleep.

For her, sleep proved more elusive. How could she possibly sleep now?

Vadim's final words played in her mind on a constant loop. *If I have not returned by then...* The thought of 'then' made her feel sick.

What if he never came back?

Yes, Seth would look after her. Of that she had no doubt. But it was Vadim's fate that concerned her more than her own.

In such a short time she'd become very attached to him. And it wasn't all to do with the kissing either. Yes, he was easy on the eyes, but that wasn't it. Somehow, he'd managed to change from a stranger into a friend without her noticing. It was as if he'd always been in her life, that she'd always known him.

Closing her eyes, Martha smiled. Whatever tomorrow brought, for tonight at least, she was in the safest place imaginable.

chapter twelve

"Martha? Martha, open your eyes."

"Huh?" Her heavy eyelids refused to obey the gentle summons. She was just too comfortable. "Just five more minutes..."

Something tickled at her nose. She swatted it away.

"Wake up, little sluggard."

Another tickle. Martha scrubbed at her nose with her hand.

"Go away!" As her eyes flickered open, Vadim's face swam in and out of focus.

"At last." He smiled. "I had begun to think you would never wake." He brandished a piece of her own hair and moved it towards her nose again.

"Stop it!"

She tried to move her head away. Then, in a flood of wakefulness, she noticed their sleeping position was different from how they'd started off the previous night. Now they lay face to face. Very close together, in fact. Their noses were almost touching.

"May I get up now?"

He glanced down, and Martha followed the direction of his eyes. To her horror, she discovered her arm was hidden beneath his shirt, wrapped around his naked waist. And if that wasn't bad enough, her hand splayed across the firm warmth of his back, holding him.

Oh. My. Lord!

Vadim looked amused. His smile broadened even more when she blushed.

"I am *so* sorry." She hastily retracted her arm and attempted to dive out of bed. But Vadim slid his arm about her waist and prevented her escape.

"You need not apologise, Martha." He stroked the hair back from her burning face. "I liked it. And had I not plans for today, *wife*, I would be more than content to spend it within your arms." He glanced down at her lips. "Alas. Duty calls me away."

Excitement churned in her stomach as she watched his eyes darken. *He's going to kiss me!* The prospect didn't dismay her as it should have. She *so* wanted him to kiss her again. But to her disappointment, he didn't.

With a rueful smile, Vadim set her away from him, threw back the covers, and swung his long legs out of bed. "This shall be gone when I return." He rubbed his hand over the scratchy-sounding stubble on his face. "Little wonder your poor face is so raw." He touched her chin with his thumb.

Did that mean he planned on kissing her again, sometime in the future? She shivered. Vadim's kisses were a lot more exciting than Tony's infrequent, slightly soggy offerings. Maybe she shouldn't get her hopes up too high in case she was disappointed.

She sat up. "What time is it, anyway?" she asked on a yawn.

The hall was still thick with shadows. Only the glowing embers of the fire penetrated the darkness. Seth's deep resonant snores drifted from the other side of the hall. It looked like the middle of the night. Even the cow and the goats weren't awake yet.

"'Tis almost cock-crow." Vadim bent to strap on his boots. "I wanted to make an early start."

Hugging the bedcovers about her, Martha watched

him dress. She suddenly felt very cold.

Once his boots were in place, Vadim stood up and grabbed his sword belt from where it lay on a hay bale. It clanked noisily as he strapped it about his waist. The sight of the weapon gave Martha the shivers. Finally, he adjusted the position of his dagger and reached for his cloak. He was almost ready to go. She had to say something. Anything. But what?

"Aren't you going to have any breakfast? It *is* supposed to be the most important meal of the day, after all."

Really? That's the best you could come up with? Why couldn't she ever say what she wanted to say? She frowned. What did she want to say?

"Is it indeed?" Vadim smiled and stroked her cheek. "I must remember that."

He lifted his pack from the floor, making Forge grumble, for the dog had been using it as a pillow.

"Hush, beast," Vadim scolded, but his voice was kind. "Take care of your new mistress until I return, hmm?" He ruffled the dog's shaggy head, and the action elicited a slow tail-thumping response. Then he looked at Martha again. "Farewell for the present, m'lady. Keep out of trouble if you can."

"Wait." She scrambled out of bed and crammed her bare feet into her shoes. "I'll see you off."

"There is no need," he said. "Go back to sleep."

She took no notice. Vadim smiled as he watched her take her cloak from its peg. He looked almost pleased.

"I'm awake now anyway," she said, swinging the cloak over her shoulders. "Besides, I need the privy."

Tiptoeing over the floor rushes, Martha followed him outside. *Quick. Fling yourself around his legs and beg him to stay.* Perhaps not. Maybe she should have stayed in bed after all.

The village lay blanketed beneath a thick fall of snow and glowed unnaturally in the pre-dawn light. A bitter wind sliced through her clothing as she stood on the stone threshold of the Great Hall. Heavy snow clouds hung low in the sky, blotting out the mountain tops.

Martha frowned. “It’s not really the best weather to go traipsing about in the mountains, Vadim.”

“I am used to it,” he said, tapping a gloved finger against the tip of her nose. “These hills have been my friends in all weathers. I shall not come to harm in them now. Stop fretting and go back to bed.”

When he opened his arms, she gravitated helplessly to him, burying her face into leather tunic. “Be careful.” Her voice wobbled a little. “Hurry back.”

Vadim hugged her and planted a brief kiss on the top of her head. “I shall.” Without another word, he pulled free, striding through the virgin snow and out of the village. He didn’t look back.

Martha watched until he was out of sight. Even after he’d gone, she lingered. Leaning her head against the doorpost, she stared at his departing tracks in the snow, wishing him back. Suddenly, she felt more miserable than she had at any point since arriving in this strange new world.

“There you are.”

Martha turned. Sylvie stood in the doorway with a shawl draped about her thin shoulders, her hair hanging free in a long silver sheet.

“I was concerned, you have been out here so long.”

It was true. The numbness of her hands and feet was a testament to how long she’d been blindly staring at the mountains.

A cockerel crowed, shattering the peace of the village with his lusty call.

Sylvie slipped her arm about Martha’s shoulders and guided her back indoors. “I feared you might have gone with him.”

“He wouldn’t have taken me, even if I’d wanted to go.” Even as she spoke the words, she knew they were true.

Sylvie made her sit on a bench beside the long hearth

while she busied herself with coaxing life back into the fire.

In silence, Martha stared at the growing flames. She felt like a balloon with a slow leak, weak and floppy. The numbness of her extremities had spread to her heart, but she was grateful for it. Only cold rational thought could stop her from losing the plot now. Emotions would hinder her survival. Vadim's departure had unleashed all the concerns and fears she'd buried within herself; Aunt Lulu, Tony, home, her real life. Would she ever see them again?

If this world really was a dream, why wasn't she waking? It couldn't be real. It wasn't possible.

"Here you are, my dear." Sylvie pushed a steaming tankard into Martha's hand. "Drink up. 'Tis fresh from the cow, and old Mab was not happy about being woken so early, I must say."

She'd milked the cow? Martha hadn't even noticed she'd left.

Pull yourself together, Bigalow. Don't lose it now. Or do you want to end your days in whatever qualifies as a medieval mental asylum?

She sensed vultures of madness circling her mind. If she weakened, she would become their next meal. So she drank the milk, obediently swallowing the warm creaminess, though it made her want to gag. Then she made appropriate responses to Sylvie's chatter, and forced herself to smile.

Sylvie, however, wasn't fooled. "It is never easy being parted, especially when you are newly wed." She sat beside Martha and squeezed her hand. "Vadim will return, my dear. Never doubt it."

Taking a deep breath, Martha looked into Sylvie's compassionate eyes. "And until he does, I want to work, Sylvie. I *need* to work."

"Yes, I know you do," Sylvie replied. "And in Darumvale, there is always plenty of work to be had."

Over the following days, Martha embraced each new daily chore with the fervor of a convert. Nothing was beneath her. No job was too unpleasant to be tackled. Along with the other women, she helped butcher one of the deer, preparing joints of meat for drying in the conical-roofed smokehouse.

It was cold outside, but the task was too messy for indoors, so they worked quickly. The packed snow beneath their feet soon turned red with blossoming blood droplets. Their butchery attracted a devoted audience; the village dogs watched with hungry eyes, pacing and whining in the hope of snatching a stray piece of meat.

To begin with, she had little skill with her blade, but there was always someone on hand to help when she struggled.

During a break, Martha flexed her stiffening back and looked around. There was another small hut at the other side of the road. The wooden door lay open, and the carcass of the other deer hung suspended from the roof, already skinned and gutted. Hanging by its hind legs, it swung gently in the bitter breeze.

"Aren't we going to butcher that one as well?" she asked Bren, the blacksmith's wife, who happened to be taking a break at the same time.

Bren grinned. "No, lass." Still holding her blood-smeared knife, she wiped her brow with the back of her hand. "That one is for your wedding feast. It will need to hang for another two days yet."

Martha was appalled. "Won't it go bad?"

At this, Bren guffawed, her hazel eyes twinkling with amusement. "In this weather? How could it go bad?" She shook her head, causing a lock of wild red hair to pop from beneath her scarf. "Even my youngest grandson could tell you that fresh meat needs to hang a while before it's cooked. Your education lacks much, my lady."

Martha blushed. Everyone must think she was really stupid.

"I know," she said quietly. "But I'm willing to learn if you'll help me."

Bren's haggard features relaxed into another smile. "That I will," she replied. "We shall make a proper wife of you yet."

If the gaps in Martha's education surprised anyone else, unlike the blunt-speaking Bren, they were too polite to mention it. Under the patient tutelage of the village wives, she gradually became acquainted with the everyday tasks of their lives.

She learned how to transform wheat into flour using a small circular grinding stone. It was hard work. It took forever to make even a little bit of flour. Later, she helped to turn this flour into the unleavened bread that was so popular in Seth's house. Sylvie was such a good teacher that even Martha's efforts were edible.

In another lesson, Sylvie taught her how to milk the cows and the goats. Martha redeemed herself a little in this task at least.

"You are a natural, my dear," Sylvie declared. "So quick and gentle, and not one drop spilt."

At least I'm good at something. Martha was fast coming to the conclusion that she just wasn't cut out to be a medieval wife.

On the third afternoon after Vadim's departure, during a prolonged break in the snowfalls, she tried her hand at soap-making.

They built a fire outside the Great Hall and suspended a cauldron over it. Soap alchemy, she discovered, was a very smelly business indeed. While Sylvie and Ma threw handfuls of rendered animal fat into the cauldron, constantly bickering over the recipe, she stirred the disgusting, simmering soup with a long-handled wooden spoon. Once the soap mixture had cooled, it was poured into a large wooden mold which was then taken into one of the outhouses for curing.

By the end of the day, Martha felt filthy. The smell of fat clung to her clothes and hair, making her feel slightly sick. "I really need a bath," she said, wrinkling her nose as she discarded her grim apron. "I stink like a dog otter."

Sylvie laughed. "Well, you are welcome to bathe in front of our fire. Or you could do so in the privacy of your own home, now that Hemble has cleaned the chimney. I believe Vadim has a tub stored somewhere in his outbuilding."

"Does he?" She was thrilled to hear it. Maybe she could wash her clothes at the same time. One set of clothing was proving to be a bit of a challenge. She hoped Orla would finish making that new gown for her in record time.

"Take these for your fire." Sylvie reached into her apron pocket and handed Martha a flint and steel. "Keep them if you will, I have another set."

"Thanks, Sylvie." It was funny. Only a week ago, she wouldn't have known what these items were, let alone how to use them. Now she could light a fire almost as quickly as anyone in Darumvale. "Er...would you mind if I didn't come back to the Hall tonight? I have so much laundry to do."

The older woman frowned. "But we promised Vadim—"

"I'll be fine," Martha assured her. "After all, what can happen to me in the village?"

"Very well," Sylvie said at last. "But take the dog with you." She nodded, indicating Forge who was sniffing at an interesting stain on the hem of Martha's gown. "We will visit you later though, to make sure all is well."

chapter thirteen

MARTHA COULDN'T REMEMBER ENJOYING ANY bath as much as this one.

The wooden tub was small, barely wide enough to accommodate her hips, but the steaming hot water felt like heaven on her skin. With a sigh, she closed her eyes and rested her head against the tub's high wooden back, listening to the crackles and pops of the fire in the hearth.

She fumbled under the water for the chunk of the scented soap Sylvie had given her and lathered her hair until it was stiff with lavender-scented bubbles.

Forge lay in a prime spot by the fire. Raising his head, he grumbled in protest when she splashed him during her rinse cycle. With one last sour look, he put his head back between his paws and went to sleep.

When the water grew too cool to sit in, Martha stood up and gave herself a final rinse using another bucket of water that sat warming on the hearth. Then, wringing out her hair—now sweetly fragrant and squeaky clean—she stepped from the tub and wrapped herself in the linen sheet Sylvie had given her.

The older woman had packed many other things into the small wicker hand basket she'd thrust on her, back at the Great Hall. As well as the cleaning supplies, there was also bread, cheese, milk, and a bladder of ale.

Martha had laughed. "Anyone would think I was going away for a week." But she appreciated Sylvie's kindness. Without her, the last few days would have been very bleak indeed.

Vadim's absence gnawed at her insides, niggling away, no matter what she did or how tired she was. And the sorrow of losing her aunt along with the rest of the twenty-first century wasn't getting any easier to handle, either, no matter how hard she tried to block them from her mind. Not thinking too much was the only way she knew to hang onto her sanity. If she was actually sane to begin with.

One thing was for sure. As each day passed, it grew harder to cling to her dream theory. This world felt very real indeed.

She rummaged in one of the chests and found one of Vadim's old shirts. She dared not wear her modern clothes, just in case anyone decided to pay her a visit, so Vadim's stuff would have to do. The shirt was a little threadbare and much too big. The hem stopped just above her knees, and the neckline was positively indecent. But it was clean and bore only the faintest trace of man-scent. She resisted the urge to sniff it, determined to get her silly crush back under control.

Braving the cold and the snow, Martha hauled the tub outside, water sloshing everywhere. With difficulty, she managed to empty the water into the pit without seeing any of their neighbours. Then she dragged the tub back indoors and filled it with more hot water, this time for her stinking clothes.

She reached for another chunk of soap, this piece designed specifically for laundry purposes, and began scrubbing at her dress. Her mind began to drift as it usually did when occupied with simple tasks.

Of all the things she missed from her old world, excluding her aunt and indoor plumbing, it was communication she missed most. If Vadim lay dead or injured upon the mountain, how would she learn of it? In Darumvale, mobile phones weren't even a distant dream, especially since he'd thrown hers into the fire.

From what she could gather, the villagers relied on peddlers—travelling salesmen—for much of their news. The knowledge they brought with them was often far more valuable than their wares.

In summer, the villagers got their news fresh from the 'Big Smoke'—as she called Edgeway—at the weekly market. In winter, however, this was impossible. The High Born—the nobles—might communicate with one another by hawk or pigeon mail, but this method was beyond the means of most ordinary folk.

Who would they communicate with anyway? Most local girls seemed to marry a boy from the same village—or maybe from the next one if they were particularly daring. News was usually only walking distance away. And if the nobility had news for the villages under their control, they certainly had the money and the means to make it widely known.

She squeezed her dress, wringing the scummy soap water from it.

This world was certainly much smaller than the one she'd left behind. Most of the people she'd met hadn't ever travelled further than Edgeway; the world beyond its borders was as mysterious to them as it was to her. Darumvale was the centre of their universe. It was the place they were born and, most probably, where they'd die.

So where did Vadim fit in?

Darumvale might be his winter base, but she got the impression it wasn't his permanent home. He seemed too large for the village, somehow. Perhaps he really did belong in the mountains? Or maybe with the woman who had loaned her the dress. She should have asked him about her, but she wasn't brave enough.

It's none of your business anyway. She diverted her

attention back to her laundry. There was no point torturing herself about his mystery woman. Vadim and his personal life were none of her concern. The sooner she got that into her thick skull the better. All that mattered was getting home again.

She wrung out her clothes until her hands ached and then arranged the damp garments by the fire, draping them over the chair backs.

Laundry complete, Martha dragged the tub outside to empty it.

Enormous snowflakes tumbled from the sky, obscuring everything. She could barely make out the Great Hall anymore. Even the mountains had vanished into the whiteout. Shivering, she propped the tub against the wall of the house then hurried back indoors.

After the chill of outside, the heat of the cottage hit her like a physical blow. It was like walking into an overheated department store on a winter's day. She slid the doorbolt and went to check on her steaming laundry.

The embers in the hearth glowed hot and red, and flickering shadows danced about the whitewashed walls. Forge looked up, his tail thumping a welcome on the thick wooden floor.

"Do you want to go out? You must need to pee by now."

In reply, the dog gave a huge yawn and flopped onto his side. Apparently not.

Actually, taking a nap wasn't a bad idea. The bed looked so inviting, all heaped up with blankets and furs. So what that it was only late afternoon? She was tired and, until her clothes were dry, she couldn't go anywhere.

The lure of the bed was impossible to resist. Martha crawled deep beneath the covers like an animal about to hibernate. The furs felt like silk against her skin. Eyes closed, she listened to the wind as it blew itself into a gale, moaning like a soul in torment beneath the eaves of the house.

Snuggled up safe and warm in her cozy cocoon, she

felt sleep beckoning her. Was Vadim safe and warm, wherever he was? She hoped so. Although she was not a particularly godly person, she offered up a silent prayer for his safe return.

Bang. Bang. Bang!

Sweet Baby Jesus! Martha sat bolt upright in bed, heart pounding. *What the feck was that?*

Forge was going crazy, barking and scrabbling at the door.

"Be quiet, lad!" She swung her legs out of bed. "It's only Sylvie and Seth, you great eejit!" They'd promised to call on her before bedtime.

She pattered barefoot across the wooden floor, and shoved the dog to one side with her hip. "Wait a minute," she called. "I'm coming." They probably wouldn't hear her over Forge's thunderous barks of displeasure.

Grabbing the dog with one hand, she slid the door bolt. "It's open." She pulled Forge away from the door, clinging to his scruff so he couldn't attack her visitors. He was certainly riled enough.

The latch clicked up, and the door swung open, a blast of snowflakes gusting in on the howling wind.

Along with Vadim.

"Never open the door without first knowing who stands on the other side!" His brows merged into a mono-brow, he scowled at her so fiercely. "I might have been anyone." With that, he kicked the door closed behind him.

Martha's heart swelled. The joy of seeing him standing there, stamping snow from his boots and looking so thoroughly out of humor, welled up in her chest like a huge bubble of helium. "You're back!"

She released Forge and flung herself into Vadim's arms. If her greeting surprised him he didn't show it. With only the briefest hesitation, he hugged her until her ribs creaked.

"Foolish girl," he muttered against her hair. "When will you ever learn caution?"

Holding her shoulders, he set her away from him and looked her up and down. His eyes widened as they encountered the low neckline of her shirt. "Whatever are you wearing?"

"It's yours. I hope you don't mind. My things are still drying...oops!" As she followed the direction of his gaze, she saw just how much skin the garment revealed. Grabbing the edges of the neckline, she pulled them together before Vadim's eyes prolapsed completely.

He cleared his throat. "And you consider that a suitable garment for answering the door?" His mouth curved into a slow smile. "What if I had been old man Hemble?"

Martha grinned. "He'd have probably suffered a heart attack. Anyway, I thought you were Sylvie."

"An easy mistake, I am certain." Vadim released her and swung off his cloak, showering the room with thousands of tiny ice crystals that fell tinkling to the floor. "Though I doubt Sylvie would have the strength to batter at a door with a sword handle for so long. I had begun to think you were dead." He hung his cloak behind the door.

Martha giggled. "Stop exaggerating. You only knocked three times." Her head swam with the delight of seeing him again.

He took off his sword belt and lay it on of one of the chests. "I was not pleased to discover you had abandoned Seth's worthy hall."

"But I needed a bath. It's impossible to get any privacy there. You know that."

"Anything could have happened to you."

"In this village?" She arched her eyebrows at him and snorted. "I sincerely doubt it."

She stroked Forge's head as he leaned against her legs. The dog still eyed Vadim with silent suspicion.

"Besides," she continued, "I had Forge for protection,

just in case the Evil Earl decided to ski across country and find me. Not that he even knows who I am."

"Martha." Vadim frowned, not appreciating her levity.

"Did you find him, by the way?"

"No." He crouched down and unfastened his sodden boots. "I received word he is back in Edgeway castle. We were lucky he chose another route. He will not be travelling further abroad for some weeks. Nor will anyone else, for that matter. I barely made it back myself."

Martha nodded, very grateful that he had. "Who told you where he was? One of the 'others' Jem mentioned the other night?"

He stiffened and looked up at her. "Yes."

"Is he like you? Does he live in the mountains too?"

"He is an outlaw, just like me. Yes. Perhaps we might discuss this later?"

"Oh. Yes, of course." He looked so tired. The dark smudges beneath his eyes spoke of his fatigue. What was she thinking? "Come and sit down." She hurried over to the fire and tugged her drying shift from the chair so he had somewhere to sit.

***

Once he had removed his boots, Vadim glanced over to where Martha stood prodding at the glowing fire with a metal poker.

By all that is sacred!

He shook his head and looked away. "Perhaps you... might wear your cloak until your gown is dry."

"Why?" She turned her head to look at him, apparently oblivious of what he had seen. "I'm not cold."

Vadim could not meet her eyes, such was his discomfort. "Your shirt..." He cleared his throat again. "The fire has rendered it almost...transparent."

"Shit!" Martha threw down the poker and backed away, her arms folded over her breasts.

Vadim fixed his eyes on a swirling knot of wood, high up on one of the roof beams. At last, he heard the whisper of fabric upon fabric.

"Okay. You can look now."

Vadim exhaled and turned around. To his relief, Martha was safely shrouded from neck to ankle in thick, serviceable wool. She disturbed him enough when she was fully clothed. But, to his cost, he could not un-see what he had just witnessed. The vision of her body's gentle curves outlined beneath that thin shirt was now etched onto his memory, adding more fuel to the inner fires he battled to conceal.

Throughout his scouting trip, Martha's ghost had been his constant companion, tormenting him with the memory of her kiss and the feel of her soft body pressed to his. And now that he had tasted her, he wanted more. Much more.

But he was her protector. If he seduced her, she would have a claim on him. His life was dangerous enough without the added burden of a woman. He clenched his hands into fists at his sides, resisting the urge to wrench the cloak from her shoulders and press his lips to her smooth, pale skin.

"Are you hungry?" Martha asked, lighting a candle with a taper from the fire. "Sylvie sent lots of food if you want something." Without waiting for his reply, she hurried about preparing supper, chattering as she worked.

Vadim barely heard her words, too intent was he on mastering himself. As he sat beside the fire, the heat gradually penetrated his icy limbs and banished the primal lust from his blood. Martha was safe. For now.

With a bright smile, she handed him a wooden platter heaped with food. Then she shooed Forge away from the front of the hearth so that he could stretch out his legs.

"Thank you," he said when she sat down beside him. "You are most kind."

While he ate, Martha regaled him with tales of all she

had done during his absence, including the finer points of soap-making.

"How is it that something so wonderful starts out so vile? I had to swallow back a vomit burp more than once." She grinned. "I don't think Ma and Sylvie would have appreciated that in their cauldron, do you?"

Fortunately, he had finished eating.

"Probably not," he agreed with a chuckle. "Though by all accounts, you have been working very hard recently. The ladies of the big house had only the best things to say about you when I called on them earlier."

"Really? It's nice to know I've managed to impress someone here. But you might want to talk to Bren before you go believing the good stuff. She thinks I'm useless, and quite rightly too."

"Bren can be...plainly spoken, but she has a good heart."

"I know. She's one of the nicest people I've met so far."

He took another sip of his ale. It was weak and watery, unlikely to get him drunk no matter how much he imbibed. Which was just as well. For both their sakes.

Suddenly, Martha leaned forward, studying his face. "I thought you said you were going to get rid of your beard."

"You do not like it?" Vadim touched the black stubble upon his chin. "I thought I might keep it after all. It is certainly much warmer than going about bare-faced in this weather." And it might serve as a reminder not to kiss her again.

She shrugged one shoulder. "It's your face. Whatever floats your boat, mate."

"I beg your pardon?" Some of her expressions were difficult to fathom at times.

"I mean," she explained, "you should do as you wish. If you like your beard, keep it. Besides, I'm currently growing one on each of my legs, so I can't pass judgement." With a grin, she parted her cloak, giving him a brief flash of her shins. "See?"

His jaw dropped. “You remove the hair from your legs? Whatever for? Is it a custom where you come from?”

“I suppose it is. I hadn’t really thought about it.” She took the empty platter from his lap and stood up. “Do you want any more ale?”

Patting his tunic in search of his pipe, he watched as she moved about the cottage, illuminated by firelight. Were all the women of her world as singular as she, or as beautiful? He shook his head, upbraiding himself for thinking such a thing.

She is not yours, and she never will be. Remember that.

***

That night, Martha sensed a shift in their relationship.

Admittedly, she had her emotions on a tighter rein, refusing to listen to the insistent whisperings of her heart. But this was something else. Something from him.

Vadim was different. Withdrawn. Oh, he was still courteous and friendly, but that was it. His eyes no longer burned when he looked at her. And when they were forced into close proximity, the air did not fizz and crackle as it had before. Not on his side, anyway.

It was as if someone had reached inside his head and flicked an inner switch to the ‘off’ position. Had she only imagined those kisses in the snow?

Their wedding feast was a large and merry affair, and the entire village turned up to celebrate it. The Great Hall glowed as bright as day with dozens of torches and expensive beeswax candles, and at the center of the event was a delicious spit-roasted deer.

Fiddles and flutes played irresistible tunes, toe-tapping music that made it impossible not to want to dance. Everywhere she looked, Martha saw smiling faces. The sounds of conversation and laughter competed with the music. The Great Hall seemed to come alive. It really did feel like the heart of the village.

Seth rolled out more barrels of his beloved ale for the celebration, fueling another round of toasts to the 'happy couple'. Some of the bawdier wishes made Martha blush to her ear tips. Vadim only smiled and raised his tankard in reply. He wove his fingers with hers, giving her hand a gentle, reassuring squeeze.

Fortunately, the music resumed. A slower tune this time. "Shall we?" Vadim set down his beer—which he'd barely touched all night—and led her to the middle of the hall.

Folded in his arms, she swayed to the music with her head resting upon his chest. She closed her eyes for a few moments, savoring the feel of him. His warmth and man-scent caused the bunched up muscles in her shoulders to sag. She sighed, kneading the softness of his loose linen shirt with her fingers, pretending their closeness was real.

Vadim hummed softly to himself as he held her. The low sound rumbling through his chest and into her head. Where was he now, she wondered. Who was he with? Not her.

"Are you enjoying yourself?" he murmured at length, his lips moving upon her hair.

Reluctantly, Martha raised her head to look at him. "Yes. Are you?"

He smiled and touched her cheek. "I hardly know."

Oh, for goodness sake. "What's to know?" she asked, cross with him now. "It's a simple enough question."

He stroked her cheek with his thumb, its roughness grazing lightly over her skin. "For you, perhaps. Ah, Martha. Your view of life is so simple. I envy you that."

Great. Now he thinks I'm simple.

At that moment, the music stopped, saving her from saying something she'd probably later regret.

As much as she despised the deception of their 'marriage', it was nice to be the focus of so many good wishes. The villagers presented the 'happy couple' with small gifts: a carving in the shape of a horse, several pieces of pottery, and a matching pair of matching cloak pins, to name but a few.

The best present of all, however, came from Bren and her husband, Jared.

"Here." Bren shoved a beautifully worked leather collar into Martha's hand. "We may as well make it official since Forge practically lives with you now."

"You mean?" Her eyes shone as she looked into Bren's slightly horsey-looking face.

Bren nodded. "The dog is yours."

"Oh, Bren!" She hugged the older woman hard and planted a kiss on her ruddy cheek. "Thank you so much. Both of you." She directed a smile at Jared.

"Yes. Thank you," Vadim added. "We are overwhelmed by your generosity." He sounded more than a little sarcastic.

Jared guffawed with laughter and slapped Vadim energetically on the back several times, almost causing them both to spill their ale. "No, my friend. 'Tis I who should be thanking you for taking that ungrateful beast off my hands."

For the remainder of the party, although Vadim remained by her side, Martha became increasingly aware of the distance between them.

Had it always been there? Had she imagined it all? What she felt for him was real enough. She couldn't stop looking at him, willing him to look at her.

Vadim must have felt her staring, for he glanced at her, his lips curving into a brief smile before returning to his conversation with Seth.

At old man Hemble's insistence, and much to the delight of the other party guests, Vadim was eventually persuaded to kiss her.

"We might as well surrender, my love," he said with

a smile, taking her in his arms. "They will not leave us alone until we do."

Martha shrugged, feigning the same indifference. "Might as well." She tilted her face towards his, her heart leaping somersaults in her chest as she recalled the last time he'd kissed her.

Vadim drew her closer, but not close enough. He didn't crush her to him as he'd done before. Lowering his head, he gently brushed her lips with his. The crowd roared in approval, and the fiddlers set off playing another up-tempo tune.

That's it? Seriously? It was positively chaste. Like being kissed by an aged relative. Apart from the sensation of his well-groomed beard tickling her face, she'd felt nothing from him.

Whatever magic they'd had, it was well and truly gone. For him, at least.

More people arrived to shake Vadim's hand. All Martha could do was stare up at him from beneath the shelter of his arm. He hadn't been the same since the night they'd kissed out in the snowstorm.

Tony hadn't liked kissing her, either. He'd said kissing was for teenagers. Funny how he'd forgotten about that on the day she discovered him with his tongue stuck down the back of his boss's throat.

Were her kisses really that terrible? She looked at Vadim, who was smiling at something Orla had said. Yes. She supposed they must be.

The days slipped by, gradually turning into weeks. Despite Martha's hopes that Darumvale was nothing more than a vivid dream, she never woke up. At last, she was forced to admit that it was real. All of it.

Somehow, she'd fallen into a medieval world, and there seemed little hope of getting out again.

Vadim was seldom there. No matter how early she woke, when she opened her eyes, he would already be gone, his bedroll folded and neatly stashed away. It was as if he'd never been in the cottage at all. Although she'd offered to let him have the bed sometimes—without her in it, of course—he always politely refused.

At first, his morning vanishing act upset her. But now, as with so many other things, she'd grown accustomed to it, accepted it. It was just another cog in her routine. Like knowing she wouldn't see him again until nightfall.

She sought solace from her misery in her daily routine. Today, as every other day, once her solitary breakfast was over, she washed and dressed then set out for the Great Hall, Forge snuffling in the snow beside her. She smiled. The dog was the only joy she had.

Up at the big house, Sylvie and Ma were always pleased to see her, accepting her presence without question. They always had plenty of chores to keep her occupied. Of course, she could have cooked, baked, and darned at her own house, but Martha preferred the company of other women to the alternative of endless hours of solitude.

"You need a baby in your belly, lass," Ma commented when Martha asked Sylvie for cloths to deal with her period, which had finally decided to arrive.

"I don't think I'm very fertile," she replied with a shrug, ignoring the fleeting and delicious thought of carrying Vadim's child within her. "Thanks, Sylvie." Taking the bundle of rags, she headed for the privy. But in her haste to get outside, she dropped one of the cloths. As the door closed behind her, it snagged the rag beneath it. Cursing beneath her breath, Martha pushed the door a little, attempting to pull it free.

From where she crouched, she could clearly hear Sylvie and Ma's conversation. They had their backs to the door and were so engrossed with dipping candles into a pan of melted tallow they didn't notice she was still there.

Ma shook her silver head with concern. "There is something not right there, you heed my words, daughter."

"Yes," Sylvie agreed."She has certainly not been her merry self of late. And even Seth has commented on Vadim's long absences, and he seldom notices anything of a delicate nature, as you well know." Sylvie attached her candle to the drying rack. "Could they have quarreled, do you think? But, no. They always appear so united in public."

Martha finally yanked the rag free and stood up. *They're talking about me!* Her cheeks burned hot. Although eavesdroppers rarely heard anything good about themselves, she listened anyway.

"As do many a couple trapped in a bad marriage," Ma remarked grimly. "How long did they know one another before they were joined?"

"Only a few weeks, I think." Sylvie took the candle Ma handed her, being careful not to bend it as it was not properly set.

"Ah, the foolish lad. Whatever was he thinking? The life he leads is unsuitable for any woman, let alone one who is a danger to herself when left unsupervised. Do the Nobles teach their daughters anything of value, I wonder? I have—"

Unable to listen to anymore, Martha marched away to the privy, anger burning in her stomach. Even Ma and Sylvie thought she was useless. And they were right. In this world she was nothing but a burden. No wonder Vadim couldn't stand being around her.

When she returned to the Great Hall, she believed she had her anger back in check.

Sylvie looked up from her task. "Oh, there you are, my dear. We were beginning to wonder where you were. Come and sit down."

The compassionate look in Sylvie's eyes was more than she could bear. Even Ma's eyes were glistening. She knew what they were thinking. *Poor Martha. She can't even get pregnant, let alone keep her hot new husband interested.*

Martha forced a smile and approached the fire. No wonder they'd been talking about her. Her fake marriage didn't even convince *her* anymore. Everywhere she went these days, she was aware of the sympathetic glances and whispers that followed her. The women thought Vadim had married too soon and was now paying the price: trapped in a loveless marriage with a woman who couldn't even provide him with a son and heir. It was humiliating. Vadim didn't have to suffer the gossips as she did. She longed to shout the truth, to be free from this miserable deception. But she couldn't.

She was trapped. Caged in on every side. And no one could hear her screaming.

Enough was enough. A new feeling of strength washed over her. "Actually," she said with a brightness she certainly didn't feel, "I think I'll take Forge for a walk." She rubbed her stomach. "These cramps are absolute murder. A bit of exercise usually shifts them."

Her statement generated more sympathetic glances.

Martha clenched her fists, her cheeks prickling. If she didn't get out of this place in the next ten seconds, she really would scream.

"Of course, dear," Sylvie smiled. "Do not wander far, though. There will be more snow before the day is out."

Martha ground her teeth, *Really? More snow. What a bloody surprise.* She was sick to the gills of the wretched stuff. And of everything else here, too.

"I won't." She grabbed her shawl and headed for the door. "Come on, Forge." The dog hauled himself up from beside the fire and trotted outside after her.

chapter fourteen

SEVERAL OF HER NEIGHBORS CALLED out to her as she marched from the village. Martha smiled but kept on walking, not being in a suitable mood to exchange more pleasantries. With a sigh of relief, she stepped out of Darumvale and onto the North road. Despite its grand title, it was little more than a mud track, edged on either side by tall, naked hedgerows which protected it from the worst of the snow.

She found she could get up quite a pace in her new leather boots. Vadim had given them to her one night after returning from one of his mystery jaunts. She thanked him but didn't ask where he'd got them from.

More loans from his secret woman, no doubt. It was fortunate they shared the same shoe size.

Martha walked for miles, seeing nothing and hearing nothing. Rage fueled her pace. The flames of anger within her heart burned out of control, unchecked for once. It was good to be herself again. Angry. Miserable. But free. She was so sick and tired of pretending.

Martha cursed and swore as she marched—venting her spleen, as Aunt Lulu called it.

Stupid, gossiping people with their narrow views on life. What the feck did they know? Who were they to feel sorry for her?

Ever so slowly, her temper burned itself out. Only when her heart fell silent, finally rid of all its fury, did she stop walking. Panting and red-faced, she sat on a snow-covered rock at the side of the road. Her butt was soon wet and cold, but she didn't care. What did it matter? What did any of it matter when she was stuck in a place that shouldn't even exist?

She looked up at the perfect sky. "I just want to go home!" she yelled, startling several sparrows into flight. Forge ambled over and laid his head upon her lap, regarding her intently with his wise brown eyes.

"Don't you start." Martha laughed bitterly as she stroked his head. "I don't need anyone else feeling sorry for me today."

To her dismay, she couldn't stop laughing. She laughed until her ribs ached, and tears streamed down her cheeks. And just when she thought she would die from it, the insane laughter ended. Then the sobbing arrived. Quietly at first, it built in violence until her whole body quaked with the force of her misery. The sorrow she'd kept locked away for so long broke free, gushing from her eyes in a hot, bitter torrent that left her weak and trembling in its wake.

Wake? That was exactly it. She felt...bereaved. As if her home, life, family, and friends had died en masse on one extraordinary day. Even the woman she used to be was gone, leaving nothing but a pale ghost in her place.

If my world really has gone for good, what am I going to do?

Obviously, being Vadim's *wife* wasn't the answer. The role only added to her misery.

The weak winter sun broke through the clouds. Closing her eyes, Martha tilted her face to absorb its gentle rays, welcoming its pale warmth into her body. In her haste to escape the village, she hadn't bothered to fetch her cloak. At least she'd brought her shawl. But as she reached over her shoulder to find it, she discovered her shawl was gone. Dropped somewhere on the road between here and Darumvale, no doubt.

"Shit!" She shivered as the sweat cooled upon her skin. Crossing her arms, she gave herself a hug. God knew she needed one.

For the first time that day, she noticed the scenery. Huge mountains dominated the skyline in every direction. White summits brushing against the fat gray clouds, blocking their way and forcing them to travel in another direction. Martha felt as if she were looking out from the mouth of a gigantic imaginary crocodile.

And there, stretching out in the distance, lay a thin, dark ribbon of road weaving its way to... *Where?*

Shielding her eyes from the sun, she looked back along the road she'd traveled. Far, far away were the hills where Vadim had found her. Where was he now? Plotting and scheming with his fellow outlaws, no doubt. Poor Vadim. He might be an arse, but he was a well-meaning arse. He didn't need the added complication of a woman in his life. Especially one who meant nothing to him. But he was a man of honour. She knew that he wouldn't abandon her now.

Yeah. That'd probably violate some obscure law of his Outlaw code.

As a small symbol of rebellion, Martha took off her hated headscarf and let her hair flow free for once. The breeze took hold of the chestnut waves and tossed them playfully into the air, tangling them into a wild mess.

She didn't care.

No matter what it took, she wanted to be herself again. She looked down at the dress she was wearing. Yet another part of her disguise.

Perhaps out of pity for Martha's non-existent wardrobe, Orla had finished the burgundy gown in record time. It fit beautifully, flattering her curves. The front lacing was supportive and kept her boobs in such good check beneath the scooped neckline that she no longer needed her tatty old bra. Her figure had never looked so good. Everyone said how well the dress suited her.

Everyone except Vadim.

When she'd arrived home, wearing the gown for the first time, he just looked up from the arrow he was fletching and asked how much silver Orla required for her services. When Martha told him, he threw a couple of coins onto the table before returning his attention to his stupid arrows. That was it.

His lack of interest hurt. The Vadim she'd known was gone, along with everything else that mattered. Apart from Forge—she looked over to where the dog lay sleeping on a patch of dry earth he'd found beneath the hedgerow—she had no real friends. Sylvie and the other women were great, but the need for secrecy prevented her from the honesty true friendship required.

If they ever discovered how she'd deceived them, they'd hate her.

She yawned, suddenly weary to her bones. For the past week, she'd slept badly, haunted by dreams of her former life. As the sun vanished behind a dark cloud, she became aware of how bitterly cold it was. Perhaps it was time to head back to the village. She got up and rubbed her numb backside.

"Come on, Forge. Let's go home."

Home. If only it were that simple.

Dusk arrived, and the snow Sylvie had predicted came with it, drifting steadily from the leaden sky. Martha chewed her lip. She'd been walking for what seemed like hours, and still Darumvale was nowhere in sight. Fear twisted her stomach. A night out in the open was a death sentence. She stumbled, clutching at Forge's furry back to steady herself. To his credit, the dog made no protest and continued to pad quietly at her side.

"Wait a s-second, sweetheart." Shivering violently, she wrapped the headscarf about her face as a flimsy barrier against the biting cold. It wasn't much, but it helped a little.

They kept moving, plodding through the swirling snowflakes as day turned to night. By now, she was beyond cold. She couldn't feel her fingers and toes anymore. Why the hell had she walked so far? *Idiot.*

As darkness fell, Forge came to a sudden stop in the middle of the road, his muscles tensing beneath her fingers. Something was out there. He began barking, a deep booming sound that shattered the night.

"Shh. What is it?" Martha crouched beside his head. "What have you seen?" Had someone come looking for her? It wouldn't be Vadim. He seldom came home before bedtime. Squinting through the gloom and the snow, she saw the faint shape of a fast-moving horse. Maybe it was Seth?

No. It couldn't be. According to village gossip, Seth wasn't much of a rider anymore. A new and horrible thought occurred to her. What if the rider was, in fact, the Evil Earl? Unlikely as it seemed, she wasn't taking any chances.

"Come on, Forge," she hissed, trying to drag the dog to the side of the track in the hopes they'd find a hiding place beneath in the hedgerow. But the stubborn animal wouldn't move. Maintaining his position in the middle of the road, he barked louder than ever.

She darted a look at the rider. He was getting closer. What should she do now? Hide and abandon Forge to his fate? Never. Loyalty won. Using a combination of brute force and coaxing, she managed to edge the dog to the side of the road as the horse thundered towards them. Martha clutched Forge's hairy coat with her deadened fingers. With luck, the rider would simply pass them by.

But he didn't. The horse reined in, coming to a shuddering halt a little way from where they stood. Clouds like dragon's smoke puffed from the huge animal's twitching, snorting nostrils. Martha took a small step backward.

Shrouded by a cloak and hood, the rider dismounted.

He strode towards them, boots crunching through the snow. Forge stopped barking and began whining instead, his long tail wagging like a whip.

Martha's knees wobbled, but not through fear. She knew who the rider was.

"Where in the name of all the Spirits have you been?"

Vadim! But her relief was short-lived.

He threw back his hood and ripped off his mask. "Well?" His eyes flashed beneath his dark, scowling brows. "Have you nothing to say for yourself?" Before she could stop him, he ripped the scarf from her face. "Answer me!"

"I-I just went for a walk." She couldn't look away from him. Beneath his beard, a tic pulsed away in his firm jaw line. A sure sign of his anger.

"A walk?" Finally, the explosion came. "You are still a league from home, you foolish girl, and you have been gone all day!" He glanced down at what she was wearing. "And without taking so much as a cloak?" His lips curved into a sardonic smile which increased her shivers. "Most rational people would consider that rather more than a simple walk."

Her temper flashed back to the 'on' position.

"Don't you dare shout at me!" she cried, facing him with her hands planted on her hips. "Who the hell do you think you are? I'm not your *wife*. I'm a free woman, and I'll do whatever I choose, whether you approve or not, your lordship!"

Vadim's eyes widened. He looked as though she'd slapped him, surprised and a little hurt too. "I was merely concerned about you, Martha," he said in a softer voice. "We all were."

Were they indeed? *Good.* "Well you know what? You can take your concern and stick it up your—"

"Martha!" Vadim reached for her, pulling her rigid body toward him. "Have I wronged you somehow?" His eyes searched her face as if they might find the reason for her outburst there.

He really didn't get it, did he? At least he wasn't yelling at her anymore.

"What is it?" he asked kindly. "Will you not tell me, hmm?"

"No." She tried to pull free, but he held her too firmly. His kindness was the last thing she needed. "You wouldn't understand."

"I might."

"Please don't be nice to me. I don't want to hear it. It's all too little, too late, Vadim. Just... Oh, leave me alone." She wanted to scream at him. She really did. But after the trials of the day, her anger was all used up. She bowed her head, too exhausted for an argument. What was the point in fighting anyway? It wouldn't change anything.

***

Vadim lowered his head, attempting to look into her eyes. "Ma thinks you are disappointed because I failed to plant my son in your womb this cycle," he said with mock seriousness. "Could she be right, perhaps?"

Martha's giggle reassured him immensely.

"Oh, no!" As she looked up, her mouth curved into a smile. "She really said that?" Her swollen and blotchy eyes were irrefutable evidence of the many tears she must have shed this day.

"Indeed she did. And a good many other things besides." Vadim kept his voice light, though the scene back at the Great Hall had shaken him a good deal. "Seth's womenfolk attacked me the moment I arrived home. It appears I am lacking in the attributes every decent husband ought to possess."

He pinched her chin gently between a gloved thumb and forefinger and smiled. "They wondered how I ever persuaded you to accept me in the first place. At this moment, I believe they consider Forge a better man than I."

They looked over to where Forge lay curled up beneath the hedge. He wasn't stupid enough to stand out in a snowstorm, even if they were.

"What am I thinking? Come here." Vadim opened his cloak and enveloped Martha within its folds, sharing his heat with her. "You are frozen," he said, stroking the snow from her hair. "Are you ready to come home now?"

"No." Martha sighed. "Not yet. There's something I need to tell you first."

"Oh?" He held her hands beneath the shelter of his cloak, massaging her icy fingers. He looked into troubled eyes. "Then, speak. I am listening."

She took a deep breath. "You aren't my husband, Vadim, and Darumvale isn't my home. It's not fair that you should suffer for performing one good deed for the rest of your life. I won't let that happen—"

Whatever was coming, could not be good. "Martha— "

"Please, don't interrupt," she begged. "This is difficult enough as it is." Her eyes and expression were deadly serious. "I've been thinking about this all day, and I know it's the right decision for both of us. As soon as spring comes, I want you to take me to Edgeway and leave me there—"

"No!" The denial burst from him so fiercely, it made her jump. "I forbid it." He would never consent to such an ill-conceived plan.

"Don't you see? It's not your place to forbid me anything." Slipping her hands from his, Martha stepped out from the protection of his cloak. "You aren't my father, my guardian, or any other relative." She seemed oblivious of the swirling snow, so intent was she on leaving him.

"So, I am nothing to you?" he demanded. "Is that what you mean to say?"

"No. That's not what I mean at all." She drew closer

and pressed her palm against his chest. "You're a good man, Vadim. Probably the best man I've ever known." She smiled up at him. "You're my friend...sort of. And because I care, I won't let you suffer for your good deed a moment longer than necessary." She took a breath to steady herself.

His heart raced beneath her hand. Could she not feel it? Let her say her piece and be done. Whatever she said, she was going nowhere. Not without him.

"I shall go to Edgeway as a respectable widow," Martha continued. "I'll find a job and somewhere to live, and you'll go back to Darumvale and tell everyone I upped and left you." She smiled with a little of her former sauce. "You'll be free to live your life again, and everything will be as it should."

But Vadim did not smile. "Except for you."

"Yes," she agreed. "Except for me."

"So you have given up all hope of returning home." It was a statement, not a question.

"I have." She looked so beaten, it tore at his heart.

"Have faith, m'lady. When spring comes I shall continue my search for Madoc the Seer. He is wise in ancient lore. I am certain he will know what to do."

Martha gave a bitter laugh. "Even if this chap does know how I got here, do you really think he'll know how to send me back again? Wake up, Vadim. I thought I was the only one who still believes in fairytales. Just forget about it. I'm going nowhere."

When her lower lip trembled, Vadim took her in his arms again, enfolding her with his cloak. He closed his eyes, holding her close. It felt good, to hold her. He wanted to warm her, to banish every trace of cold from her flesh.

With a small sigh, Martha relaxed, and lay her cheek against his chest.

At length, Vadim roused himself. The snow was getting

thicker with each passing moment. “We should return to Darumvale before they send out a search party.” Reluctantly, he set her away from him. “We will continue our discussion later.”

“This discussion is over,” she said. “I won’t change my mind.”

chapter fifteen

When they reached Darumvale, people streamed from their homes and onto the street.

A voice cried out, "All is well. He has found her!"

A crowd of villagers swarmed the horse, all talking at once, voicing their concern.

Martha smiled until her face ached. "I'm fine," she repeated, over and over again to the kind enquiries. "I just walked further than I realized."

Seth hurried down the hill, with Ma and Sylvie clinging to each arm, slipping in the snow. "You scared the life from us," he said sternly as they reached the horse. "Never wander off like that again."

"I thought the wolves had eaten you for sure," Ma said, dabbing at her eyes with a corner of her food-smeared apron.

Martha's remorse was swift. "I'm sorry, Ma...everyone. I really am. I didn't mean to be gone so long."

"Take her, Seth." Vadim lowered Martha from the horse and into the Chief's capable arms. The moment her feet touched the ground, Sylvie flung Martha's forgotten cloak about her shoulders and hugged her hard.

"I have seen how unhappy you are, Martha," she whispered fiercely against her ear. "I should have spoken to you about it—been a proper friend."

"Shh." Martha kissed Sylvie's cheek. "I'm fine, really. You have nothing to blame yourself for."

After surrendering his horse to the care of one of the village boys, Vadim took Martha's hand. "We appreciate your concern, friends," he said in a loud voice, addressing everyone. "But the best thing for my wife at this moment is the comfort of her own hearth. We bid you all a good night." It was apparent he thought the reunion had gone on long enough.

"Not without some food inside her first" Sylvie glared at Vadim so fiercely even Martha flinched. "I have made up a small pan of pottage. It only requires a little heating."

Vadim bowed his head. "You are kindness itself, m'lady," he said with strained politeness.

It wasn't easy watching two people she cared about being so cool with one another. But what could she do about it? Nothing. Not until spring, anyway.

***

Whilst Martha visited the privy, Vadim stoked the fire and prepared supper. He donated a generous bowlful of the pottage to Forge. The dog disposed of his share in a few quick mouthfuls, then, with a contented little groan, he flopped down in his usual spot in front of the fire.

The latch clicked, and Martha entered the house. She looked pale and weary to his eyes.

"I really need a bath," she said, hanging her cloak on the hook behind the door.

"Eat first." Taking her arm, he guided her to a chair beside the fire, and placed a steaming bowl of food into her hands. "I have already put your water on to boil."

Her eyes widened as she saw the little wooden bathtub at the other side of the hearth, little wisps of heat curling up from its depths. She smiled. "I must really stink like a dog otter if *you're* encouraging me to bathe."

"Not at all." Vadim picked up his own bowl of food and sat in the chair beside hers. "I have merely become accustomed to your ways, that is all."

It was a pleasant meal, during which they avoided any topic of conversation likely to end in a quarrel. When supper was over, as Vadim prepared more hot water for her bath, he told Martha about his day in the mountains. Nothing of great consequence. Simple things, which he hoped might divert her from her melancholy, such as the plants and animals he had seen.

Although she appeared to listen, nodding her head occasionally, Vadim knew other matters consumed her mind. *Like moving to Edgeway.* A foolish notion if ever he heard one. No matter what she might think of his interference, he would not allow it. At length, she lapsed into silence, staring into the fire as though the flames held the answers she sought. Answers he could not give her.

For the sake of his honor, he had avoided her as much as possible during the past few weeks. By physically distancing himself, he had hoped to smother the increasing attraction he felt for her.

This method, cowardly as it was, had met with limited success. Although he could now share a room with her without needing to touch her, his hunger remained. It still lived and breathed within him, locked away in the darkest recesses of his soul, quietly resenting him for its imprisonment.

What else could he do? Her heart belonged to another man and another world. Had she not said so on numerous occasions? If his frequent absences wounded her at all, it was only because she missed the security he provided as her guardian. Nothing more. The people of Darumvale needed him in much the same way. No. Martha did not require anything else of him, and it was just as well. He certainly had nothing of any value to offer her. Not anymore.

Love was the most excruciating pain of all. The peril of

its lethal knives was too great a risk. His heart still bore the scars of wounds that had almost killed him. Love and loss were too closely intertwined. Only a fool would court its dubious pleasure for a second time.

My heart must remain empty. I have not the courage to face that kind of torture again.

He poured the final pan of steaming water into the tub. Even the splashing of the water did not rouse Martha from her reverie. Lifting his pipe and tobacco from the mantelpiece, he called to her.

“Hmm?” Blinking several times, she finally dragged her gaze from the fire.

“Your bath awaits. And I have business with Seth.” He smiled at her. “Have no fear, I shall not return too early, my lady.”

“But you are coming back?” she asked quickly. “We have things to discuss, remember?”

Vadim chuckled. She had no intention of letting him off the hook, it seemed.

“Tomorrow will be soon enough for talk. Have your bath, and go to sleep.”

“Uh-uh.” She shook her head, sending wild waves of chestnut hair about her pink face. “I’m not as green as I am cabbage-looking. You’ll be up and away to the mountains before cockcrow. By the time you get back, it’ll be too late to discuss anything at all. I’m wise to your avoidance tactics by now.”

“Why are you comparing yourself to a vegetable, Martha?” He chuckled and swung his cloak about his shoulders.

“It’s an expression,” she replied tartly. “And that’s another tactic of yours—changing the subject. Just when are we going to have our talk, hmm?”

When she pursed her lips like that, she looked most severe. “Incredible. You even sound like a real wife—”

“Vadim!” She stood up and grabbed his gloves from the trunk, pitching them at his head in quick succession.

One missed its target, but the other hit him squarely in his face.

"Very well, m'lady." Still laughing, he salvaged his gloves from the floor. "Tomorrow it is, then. I will stay home all day, and you may nag at me as much as you please."

"And you'll give me straight answers. Promise?"

"You have my oath as a gentleman." He swept her a mocking little bow.

"Huh. For what that's worth." She sat in her chair again, her movements stiff and weary. "Off you go, then. Play nicely with Seth." As he reached for the door latch, she called to him. "And, Vadim?"

He turned. "Yes?" The warmth of her smile made his guts clench.

"Thanks for the bath, and for coming to find me...again."

"You are most welcome," he replied with as much calmness as he could muster. "Good night." Then, before his resolve could weaken any further, he opened the door and stepped out into the bitter coldness of the night.

***

True to his word, when Martha opened her eyes the next morning, Vadim was there.

"Good morning, little sluggard." He looked up from where he was crouched by the fire, stirring at a pan of porridge.

She sat up, blinking in the bright sunlight that streamed through the window.

"'Tis is a lovely morning. Forge and I have been awake for hours," Vadim continued.

There was something different about him. Martha rubbed her bleary eyes. Then it hit her. "You shaved off your beard!"

"Indeed." He stroked a hand over his smooth cheek. "Does its absence improve me at all?"

Martha swallowed hard before trusting herself to speak. "You might say that."

The familiar black whiskers were gone, and the cheekbones were back. *Hooray!* She'd almost forgotten how attractive he was. Not that his stubble had rendered him ugly by any means. But it was criminal to hide a face like that beneath a beard. His smile looked even whiter today. Even his eyes looked different, more chocolate-brown than black.

"You look...younger." *And so hot, my eyes have blisters from looking at you.*

He chuckled, turning away to ladle out the porridge into two wooden bowls. "I am flattered."

"Not that you looked old before," she assured him quickly. "The beard made you look a bit grumpy, that's all."

"Have a care." He brought a bowl over and thrust it into her hands. "Your generous compliments might swell my head. Move over."

Martha obeyed, shuffling over to make space for him on the narrow bed. He sat beside her and proceeded to eat his own porridge. "I thought we might go for a walk today, if you are willing," he said, in between mouthfuls. "The day is too good to waste indoors."

"Okay." She toyed with her spoon, suddenly no longer hungry. *Oh-oh! It's back.* His nearness was affecting her stomach again. Why did he make her feel queasy when absolutely nothing about him revolted her? Quite the reverse in, fact.

Vadim didn't appear to share her symptoms. "Would you like more honey?" He had finished his porridge whilst hers still steamed, barely touched, in her hands. "No doubt you prefer it sweeter than I take mine."

"No. It's lovely, thanks. I'm just not that hungry today." She cupped her fingers about the wooden bowl to warm them.

He nodded his dark head in apparent sympathy. "Ah! Women's problems, I expect."

"You could be right." She was unwilling to entertain any other possibility, even to herself.

As soon as she was dressed—wrapped up as if she were about to embark on a polar expedition, thanks to Vadim—they left the house.

Forge bounded ahead of them, galloping through the snow like an overgrown puppy, his tongue dangling in a wild grin. Martha waved to Bren as they passed by the smithy, then hurried to catch up with Vadim and Forge.

Vadim turned onto a narrow trail she hadn't noticed before. As they followed it the path travelled up and over a little hill before snaking off into a forest. Hardly any snow lay on the ground here. The trees were tightly packed together, the dry, compacted ground giving a dull, echoing thud with each footfall.

She didn't like it. Somehow, the silence was too loud. Not even birdsong penetrated the oppressive stillness. As her eyes accustomed themselves to the gloom, she stumbled over several tree roots. Vadim offered her his arm.

Martha held up her hands. "I can manage, thanks." Touching him wasn't good idea. Not if she wanted to get her heart rate back under control.

Vadim raised one dark eyebrow but made no comment.

The path narrowed again, forcing them to walk in single file. She followed in Vadim's wake, constantly battling to wrench her cloak from the grasping evergreen bushes that attempted to pull it from her.

This wasn't her idea of a nice walk.

Her dislike of the forest increased with every step. It made her feel claustrophobic, even the air tasted old and stale. Just as she was about to ask how much farther they had to go, the path forked. Without hesitation, Vadim turned onto the trail leading uphill.

He glanced over his shoulder at her. "Do you wish to rest for a moment?"

"No, thanks. I'm good."

"The path becomes a little steep from here," he warned.

"But, I assure you, it is well worth the effort."

'A little steep' didn't quite cover it.

The path left the stifling confines of the forest and, with no preamble, shot straight up a large hill, using the most direct route possible. Martha envied the ease with which Forge tackled the incline, bounding up the shifting slope of snow-covered scree. He even had the energy to snuffle about for rabbits. The lucky thing.

Martha labored upwards using Vadim's footprints whenever possible. Her lungs burned, and sweat beaded on her brow. Because his stride was so long, she plunged knee-deep in snow at every other step. The bottom of her dress hung heavy and damp about her legs, clinging unpleasantly to her calves, further hampering her attempt to tackle the brute of a hill.

Her breathing resembled random notes from a wheezy old accordion. She pulled off her headscarf, dabbing it over her face and neck. Just then, a cold and gentle breeze danced over her hot skin, its icy caress making her sigh with bliss.

Vadim waited for her on a small rocky plateau. He frowned as she approached. "Is it too much for you, Martha? I know you are a little...unwell."

"I'm...fine." She bent over, attempting to slow her breathing.

"You do not look fine. Perhaps we should turn back?" He, to her disgust, didn't sound even slightly out of breath.

"I have a period," she snapped. "I'm not dying of the plague." She stood upright again. "See? I'm fine."

"Then stop being so stubborn and take my hand." He proffered his right hand. "If you do not, I will take you no further."

Forge barked at them from higher up the hill. Martha shielded her eyes to look at him. His pink tongue lolled from his mouth, and his tail thrashed with happiness. It would be unfair to deprive him of a day out just because she was afraid of 'The Vadim Effect'.

"Whatever." She shrugged and let him take her hand. "Though it's hardly necessary."

When his warm, rough fingers closed around her hand, the swarm of butterflies in her stomach went crazy. This was getting ridiculous. Tony had never affected her in this way. Not even at the start of their rocky relationship.

As they walked on, she was very glad of Vadim's hand. The steep ascent didn't let up for a moment. For the hundredth time that day, she wished she'd worn her trousers and sturdy walking boots, rather than a stupid, impractical dress.

Her thigh muscles burned. Uphill walking had never been her strong point. But the pain was the price she paid for reaching the high places she loved.

Finally, the agony ended.

Vadim guided her to a large boulder at the top of the hill and let go of her hand. They sat together in silence, looking at the view.

Before her lay the most amazing vista. The jagged peaks of a mountain range glittered white in the winter sunshine, set against a backdrop of the bluest sky she'd ever seen. The mountains dominated everything. She felt as if she could simply reach out and touch them.

She managed to speak, finally putting her appreciation into words. "Wow!"

Nothing interrupted the majestic panorama. Shielding her eyes, she looked up into the sky. No aeroplanes and not a trace of a vapor trail anywhere. *Did you really expect to see any?*

When she looked down into the valley, she couldn't see Darumvale, but the fields outside the village were clearly visible. They looked like patchy gray postage stamps from this vantage point of eagles. She made out the road she'd travelled on the previous day, following its course for as far as she could. If she'd walked long enough, she'd have eventually reached a lake. Its waters flashed from far away with a diamond-like brilliance.

"How far away is that lake?" she asked, suddenly aware of Vadim staring at her.

"Five leagues," he replied gruffly. "It is the main water supply of Edgeway."

Really? She screwed up her eyes and peered harder. *That's about...fifteen miles, I think.* There was no sign of the town.

"Put it out of your mind," Vadim said curtly. "You are not going to Edgeway."

She tutted, scowling into the sun as she looked at him. "There you go again. Will you *please* stop trying to command me?"

"I would if your decisions were rational, not foolish whims of fancy. You know little about our world, Martha—"

"Only because *you* won't tell me anything. I'm not allowed to discuss it with anyone else, am I?" She glared at him. "God! It's like living with a member of the Secret Service sometimes. What *is* your problem?"

"It is...complicated." He looked towards the horizon and treated Martha to the sight of his attractive profile. His dark hair billowed about his face. At that moment she was too cross to care how handsome he looked.

"I'm sure it's very complicated." With effort, she remained calm. "But unless you start dishing out some information, I'll be going to Edgeway whether you like it or not. So, what's it to be?"

Vadim was silent for so long, she began to think he'd forgotten she was there. *He can take all the time he wants.* Forge laid his head on her lap, wanting to be stroked. Martha ran his silken ears through her fingers. *I'll sit here all day if I have to.*

"This land once knew peace," Vadim said at last. His voice was so low, she strained to hear him. "Real peace. Her rulers were just, and the people were content. Life was a little ordinary, but it was safe. For the most part, we were happy with our lot. The fields and barns were always full of food, and our children never knew hunger."

A shadow of bitterness crossed his face. He stared at the glorious view, but Martha knew he wasn't seeing it. "Why do we never appreciate the value of anything until it is taken from us?"

"What happened?" she asked gently, when he lapsed into silence again.

"The king was murdered, and a usurper stepped up to claim the throne. The old king had no children, you see. His queen died young, and he had not the heart to take another one." Vadim sighed. "It was a time of great change and turmoil for us all.

"The new king was an upstart, but a powerful one. He had few friends amongst the existing nobles, so he set about 'cleaning house'. He deposed the rebel lords—a sentence of banishment was considered very good fortune back then—and promoted his allies to positions of power.

"A few of the old families managed to hang on to their lands by swearing fealty to the new monarch, but these instances were rare. The king did not feel safe, and he wanted his own people about him. In the beginning, it was only the noble houses that fought against the king. They wanted to preserve the lands that had always been theirs. Eventually, the fighting spread further. Ordinary men were forced to pick a side and fight, even spilling the blood of their own kin at need. Can you imagine such a thing, Martha?"

"A civil war." Feeling cold, she huddled deeper within her cloak and cuddled Forge against her. The dog licked her hand as though he sensed his mistress's disquiet.

"You have experienced this in your own world?"

When Vadim turned to look at her, she was shocked. Within the space of a few minutes he had changed, and not for the better. His eyes were black and empty-looking, almost as if he'd lost his soul. A death-like pallor robbed his face of color

"Not first hand, thank God," she muttered. School history lessons didn't count.

"You should be grateful. War is always a terrible thing but this was..." He shook his head and drew his hand over his eyes.

Martha's heart ached for him. No wonder he was so reluctant to discuss his past with her. She would have liked to hold his hand, but something in his manner prevented her from doing so.

"I was only a boy at the time," he continued speaking in a flat and empty voice, "but I remember everything so clearly." He looked away into the distance again. "There was a young man back then, a minor cousin of the new king. His engagements took him away from his estate, traveling his new lands and visiting the people under his rule. By some misfortune, he happened across my sister Lissa when she was visiting friends in the next village."

Vadim sighed and a tiny smile curved his lips as he spoke of her. "All the local boys wanted to marry Lissa, and with just cause. Her beauty glowed from the inside out. I loved her. She never seemed to mind having an irritating younger brother who trailed her everywhere. I was there, the day she met Godric."

Martha's eyes widened. "The Evil Earl?"

"The very same. But he wasn't an earl, not back then." Absently, Vadim patted at his pockets, seeking the comfort of his pipe.

"You left it on the mantelpiece," Martha said, wishing she'd brought it for him. This wasn't going to be a happy tale, she knew.

"So I did." He stopped frisking himself and continued with his story. "The moment they laid eyes on one another across the market place, it was as if something came to life within each them. Although I was young, even I could see it. An acquaintance introduced them, and from then on Godric was a frequent visitor in my father's house. Not that the old man liked him. There was something beneath his civil veneer that always troubled Father. But he could not afford to offend the king's cousin, you see?"

She did. What an awful situation to be in.

"As for myself, I hero worshipped Godric. I was at that impressionable age where a good horse, fine clothes, and a shiny sword were sufficient proof of someone's good character. How brutally my hero was to betray me."

Martha watched a tic pulsing in his jaw, unable to look away.

"I shall not go into the specifics of their affair; it grieves me too deeply to dwell upon it. All you need to know is Lissa became pregnant with Godric's child. In a rage, my father finally banned her from seeing her lover, but it was all much too late. Of course, he should have put a stop to their affair long before, but fear of the consequences always held him back. As it turned out, delaying his decision proved worse. To give him his due, Godric proposed marriage, but my father would not hear of it. He had heard enough accounts of his character by then to be violently opposed to the match. Godric's handsome face concealed wicked cruelty."

Vadim drew a shuddering breath. "Late one night, he returned with a troop of soldiers. He broke into the house and took my sister by force. Once she had ridden away under escort, he directed the remainder of his men to deal with the rest of the household."

Martha's stomach lurched.

"No one was spared. Godric cut my parents down in front of me, and I-I could only watch them die. I was too petrified to hide or to help—"

"Oh, Vadim!" Martha clasped his hand tight, her eyes full of tears. She didn't want to hear any more. But Vadim continued speaking as if she hadn't interrupted him, his bitter words spilling out like poison.

"I can still see their blood, pooling about my boots. But at least their end was swift when it came." Vadim paused to clear his throat. "Godric laughed when he saw me standing there, trembling in the shadows. He said, because he liked me, I had a choice. I could meet death in the same way as my parents, or I could attempt to outrun his arrow." His lips curved into a bleak smile. "You can guess what I chose, I think."

Some choice, Martha thought. The image of a pale-faced boy appeared in her mind, alone and petrified before such wickedness.

"When Godric picked up his bow, life returned to my frozen limbs. I ran, but I was barely halfway across the street before his arrow brought me down like a deer. I cannot recall much else after that."

Vadim raked back his hair with one-handed, impatiently pushing it away as the wind billowed it about his face. "I remember being rolled onto my side—the movement of the arrow in my back must have roused me—and I saw him looking down at me. He thought I was dead and left me where I fell. Strangely, I felt no pain. The last thing I remember were the screams of the women as his men went on the rampage." He scowled. "Then everything faded away into blackness. It was Seth who eventually found me, bleeding out onto the street."

"Seth?" Martha sat up a little straighter.

"He was my father's...friend."

His momentary slip did not escape her. What had he been about to say? She had no time to dwell on it as Vadim went on speaking, almost as if now that he had begun he couldn't stop.

"He and Sylvie saved my life. They hid me until I was well enough to travel, and took me away to Darumvale. It has been my home ever since. They raised me alongside their son, treating me as their own child. Now you cannot wonder why I regard them so highly. Seth and Sylvie are much more than friends. They are my family too."

Martha nodded. "I imagine they put themselves at

great risk when they took you in."

"Indeed they did." Suddenly, Vadim roused himself, looking about him as if he'd just woken from a long sleep. "Let us walk a little further," he said. "There is something I want to show you."

chapter sixteen

THEY WALKED ALONG A HIGH ridge that boasted even more spectacular views, but they were wasted on Martha. She hadn't the heart for them now. Trudging along in silence, her mind whirling with terrible images, she cast frequent glances at Vadim. His mouth was set in a thin line, and his features were twisted into a grim mask. She could only wonder how he'd managed to stay sane.

"Stop it, Martha." He looked over, probably feeling her eyes boring into him. "I do not need your pity."

"No. What you need is a bloody big gun to shoot that bastard with," she declared. "I wish you'd told me all this before I ran into him that day."

Vadim chuckled, the sound of it chasing the shadows from his face. He was himself again. "What would you have done? Shot him with your gun—whatever that might be?"

"Maybe," she replied hotly. Not that she really could kill someone, no matter how evil they were. But it felt good to say so.

Still laughing, Vadim took her arm, leading her off the main ridge and onto a narrow path that lead to another smaller crest. There wasn't much snow here. The large gray mountain in front of them seemed to have acted as a snow-break of sorts. Even so, there was still enough snow on its summit to make her twitchy.

"Won't we get avalanched?" She chewed the inside of her mouth.

"Not today," he replied. "Do you imagine I would have brought you here if it was unsafe?"

"That all depends on how much you want to be rid of me. Will you be quiet, Forge?" The dog was up ahead, as usual, barking loudly, apparently irritated by their slow progress. "We're coming. Leave the mountain in peace, why don't you?"

Vadim pulled her to a standstill, a frown creasing his brow. "Why would I want to be rid of you? The only reason I told you my story was to prevent you from leaving...Darumvale."

Darumvale? Her heart skipped a beat. For a second there, she'd thought he was going to say something else. *Get your eyes back on the ball, Bigalow.* Putting words into Vadim's mouth wasn't a good idea. So she said, "Okay, let's talk about that. I'm still not clear why you think me leaving is such a bad idea."

"I have not yet finished my tale, m'lady," he replied with a dark look. "You will understand when you have heard the whole of it."

She wasn't sure she wanted to hear any more about Vadim's past. But it was too late now.

Walking in single file, Martha followed Vadim along the ridge. As it headed closer to the mountain, it formed a natural bridge between the looming rock face and the sloping foothills they'd just left. Where was he taking her? She was hardly dressed for altitude.

Forge disappeared into a cave up ahead, and they followed him inside.

The passageway echoed with the sounds of their footfalls and the constant drip-dripping of water. After the brightness of outside, the innards of the mountain were very dim indeed. The air was so frigid it hurt to breathe.

Clutching the back of Vadim's cloak, she trailed her other hand against the wall of the passage. It felt like ice: cold and smooth, with a slightly slimy feel.

"Almost there." Vadim's voice bounced eerily off the walls of the passageway. "Be careful," he said, taking her hand. "The path becomes a little steeper here."

The going became much more challenging. Martha's feet constantly slid from beneath her. The soles of her leather boots were no match for such a slippery floor. On one occasion, she almost pulled Vadim down with her as she fell, but he managed to right them both at the last minute.

"I shall have to put some nails in your boots. I should have thought of it before."

"Crampons might be more appropriate. Shit!" She giggled as her feet slid from under her again, and clung to Vadim's arm. "What is this stuff—ice?"

"Yes."

Somewhere ahead in the darkness, she could hear Forge scrabbling frantically to find purchase on the treacherous floor. At least she wasn't the only one having trouble. Just then, a blast of arctic air struck her. She gasped, her lungs recoiled from inhaling too deeply. It was like walking into a freezer on a hot summer's day. The hairs on her arms stood up on end. Peering around the dark shape of Vadim's body, she saw that the darkness had lessened. Now she could see the walls of the passageway, glowing white in the distance.

When they stepped out of the tunnel, Martha gasped. They were inside a vast cavern.

"Oh. My. God!" The barrage of natural wonders bombarding her eyes flooded her mind with superlatives.

The roof soared above them—easily over two-hundred feet high—brilliant sunshine flooding in through a large hole at its centre, illuminating the heavenly space with its dazzling rays. The wet walls twinkled as if they were carved from diamonds, bathing everything in with an almost unearthly light. If Heaven had a cathedral, this would be it. Only the singing of an angelic host was missing.

But the centerpiece of this magical grotto was the colossal waterfall that spanned the cavern from roof to floor like a fantastic ice sculpture. Its turbulent waters lay silent, frozen in mid-flow, as if the rules of gravity didn't exist. A brief snapshot of a moment in time.

The ice creaked and groaned as if a living, breathing creature struggled for freedom from beneath its frozen shackles.

At length, Vadim broke the silence. "Do you like it?" He was still holding her hand, his breath forming clouds in the frigid air.

Like it? She shook her head, looking into the dark warmth of his eyes. 'Like' was much too minuscule to describe the sight before her. "I've never seen anything so...beautiful in all my life," she whispered, reluctant to taint this heavenly place with a voice that could never do it justice. "Thank you so much for bringing me here. It's the nicest thing anyone..." She couldn't go on. Eyes burning, she looked away. For some reason, she felt perilously close to tears.

Vadim put an arm about her and pulled her close, planting a kiss on top of her head. The sensation of his lips moving against her hair made her shiver, but she blamed it on the sub-zero temperature.

"We shall return in the summer," he said, "when the waters are free. 'Tis quite a different place then, but equally lovely."

They stood in silence for a few minutes more, Martha shuffling her feet. The cold penetrated the soles of her boots, numbing her toes. Shivering, she huddled deeper beneath Vadim's arm, seeking his warmth.

He must have sensed her discomfort. Calling to Forge, who was snuffling at the base of the waterfall like a pig hunting for truffles, by common consent, they departed.

It was a relief to be outside. Sitting on a flat rock, Martha closed her eyes and tilted her face towards the sun, enjoying the warmth of its gentle rays. Her mind reeled with all the things she'd seen and heard today. And it wasn't over yet.

"You must be hungry." Vadim sat beside her. She heard him foraging about inside his backpack. When she opened her eyes, she found he'd brought a picnic. Along with a small loaf of bread, he'd brought a slab of cheese, a bladder of ale, and a couple of withered-looking apples.

Right on cue, her stomach grumbled.

Vadim looked up and arched one dark eyebrow at her. "Little wonder your belly protests. A wise woman once told me that breakfast is the most important meal of the day, and you barely touched yours."

"Do as I say, not as I do," Martha replied with a grin. "I've always excelled at not taking my own advice."

When lunch was over, Vadim frisked his cloak with his hands again until she reminded him he'd left his pipe at home. "You're a complete addict. It's not good for you, you know. Smoking, I mean."

"Why not?" Vadim leaned back, his strong forearms braced against the rock, he closed his eyes, basking in the sun.

"It'll kill you."

He chuckled. "So may a good many other things in my life. I am a hunted man, after all."

She frowned. "You don't even care, do you?"

He shrugged, not bothering to open his eyes. "Why should I?" His long, sooty lashes flickered softly upon his cheek. "Death is a natural part of the cycle of life"

"There's nothing natural about having a sword run through your..." She cringed, mentally cursing herself for making such a thoughtless remark.

"You are doing it again." Vadim opened his eyes and

fixed her with his intense dark gaze. "Feeling sorry for me." He smiled. "There really is no need. The past is gone. It cannot harm me now."

"Oh?" She wasn't so sure.

"What happened earlier...up by the waterfall?" he asked, neatly changing the subject. "You said, 'it is the nicest thing anyone...' and then you became upset. Why?"

"No reason." Martha looked at her hands and began folding the material of her skirt into pleats. "It was a nice thing for you to do, that's all."

"Nice!" He snorted, as if the word was an insult. "What about Tony, your intended? Are you upset when *he* is nice to you?"

Tony. She ground her teeth. The last thing she needed was Vadim going on about him again. "Actually," she said, "I've been meaning to talk to you about that."

"Being nice?"

"No." She gave an irritated huff. "About Tony." Vadim's sudden scowl puzzled her. What was wrong with him? Perhaps the sun was in his eyes.

"I hope you will forgive my bluntness," he said with icy politeness, "but I have no wish to hear any more about your beloved."

"Me neither. But you mentioned him first."

Vadim tilted his head to one side. "I think I must have misheard you."

"There's nothing wrong with your hearing," she assured him. "You aren't the only one with secrets. And as it seems today is the day for trading them, here's mine." She took a deep breath before speaking. "Tony broke up with me a month before I came to this world."

Vadim sat up, his scowl slipping into a frown. "Broke up with you?"

"Ditched me. Gave me the old heave-ho—"

"I understood you perfectly." The crease between his eyes deepened. "What I want to know is, why he would do such a thing?"

Martha laughed. "Oh yes. Because I'm such a catch, aren't I?"

As usual, her sarcasm was wasted on him.

"You might be considered so—yes. Did he at least have the decency to offer a good reason for backing out of your agreement?"

Good enough.

How could she tell him that Tony had two-timed her for months with his boss? His very attractive and single *male* boss. The truth only came out because she'd caught the two of them snogging at a party. His betrayal had been a double whammy. Although having an affair with his pretty secretary was a cliché, somehow, that would've been easier to take.

Reluctant to meet his eyes, she stared at the ground and made patterns in the snow with her boots. But all the time, she was aware of Vadim staring at her, waiting for an answer. Truth time. Taking another deep breath, she said, "Let's just say that you're more Tony's type than I am." With that, she began refolding the linen cloths that had contained their lunch.

"Ah!" In that one syllable, she almost heard the penny drop. "He likes men." There followed a brief silence. "So why did he embark on a relationship with you in the first place?"

It was nice having someone so apparently annoyed on her behalf.

"In denial, I suppose." She shrugged. "And I could forgive him for that. But what I *can't* forgive him for..." She picked up Vadim's pack, stuffing the linen napkins into it with unnecessary force. "...is for having sex with someone else when he was supposed to be with me. He lied and cheated for weeks. And you know what the worst of it is?" A bitter laugh flew from her lips. "I never suspected a thing. How stupid am I?"

"Martha. Stop." Vadim stilled her violent hand, his fingers gently encircling her wrist. The kindness in his voice was almost too much to take. "Look at me."

She did. What she saw flipped her stomach. The tenderness in his eyes melted her.

"Be angry," he said. "You have every right to be. But do not think less of yourself. The fact that Tony prefers men does not mean you are less of a woman. The two things are quite separate. You do understand that?"

And there he had it. Right on the nose. At that moment, she suddenly understood the true nature of the injury Tony had dealt her. *He simply prefers men.* There it was, plain and simple. It wasn't her fault. There was no reason to feel ashamed. But she did, she realised. Losing your man to another woman was one thing. Losing him to a man was quite another.

Despite herself, she smiled. "You're the last person I expected to understand. How did you get to be so wise?"

"I was bred from good stock," Vadim answered with mock seriousness. As he let go of her wrist, she experienced a flash of regret. "So why did you lie about him? Why did you tell me you were betrothed?"

"Oh, come on," she said, her humor returning. "It's not exactly rocket science, is it?"

"Is it not? I have no idea. Rocket, what?"

She tutted. "You're incredible, Vadim. You manage to unpick the tangle of my hang ups in ten seconds flat, but you don't know the answer to this one? I needed Tony as protection, of course."

"From me?" He raked back his hair with one hand, frowning again.

"No. From the monster in the woods." She laughed. "Of course from you. Look at it from my point of view. I arrived in a strange world with only a grumpy caveman for company. Wasn't that reason enough to adopt a fake fiancé?"

A slow smile curved Vadim's lips. "I could have dishonored you anyway, with or without him."

"True." She nodded, half wishing he had. The way he

said 'dishonored' sent a delicious frisson tingling up her spine. "But I hoped you wouldn't. And it seems I was right to trust you."

"Thank you for your honesty." Vadim inclined his head. "It means more to me than you know."

The way he looked at her made hot blood prickle beneath her cheeks. "You're welcome. It's the least you deserve for taking care of me." She pulled her cloak about her as a fat white cloud drifted over the sun. "You can't keep me indefinitely, Vadim. You know that, right?" she asked, suddenly serious. "What about your own life? You must want a woman, and a family of your own. How can that happen with me hanging around like a bad smell?"

His expression became as impenetrable as stone, impossible to read, but she ploughed on regardless. "If I can't go home, then I must make another life here. Edgeway—"

"No! I will never consent to it. Do not waste your breath." He leaned forward, eyes flashing. "Whether you choose to leave me or not, everyone now acknowledges you as my wife. Lord Edgeway knows I survived my wounds to become a man. If he ever heard his enemy had taken a wife..." His voice trailed away leaving her to absorb the unspoken peril.

"Oh." Vadim's protection came with its own dangers, it seemed. "How does the Evil Earl know you're still alive?"

"Ah, that." He moved his neck from side to side as if trying to ease tension in it. Forge ambled over and lay down heavily on Vadim's feet with a loud grumble. "He knows I am alive because I challenged him just as soon as I reached manhood"

"You what?"

He shrugged. "I had some skill with the sword by then, for I had trained for years under Dareth, a master swordsman of his time. He was dour and strict but an excellent teacher. And I was his most eager pupil; a young lad with a heart set on revenge."

Her eyes widened. "You could've been killed." *Duh!*

What was she saying? *Talk about stating the obvious.*

Fortunately, Vadim was too polite to mention it. "True. But as it turned out, luck was with me that day. I escaped without a scratch. Edgeway, however," he gave a wry smile, "was not so fortunate. Fuelled by anger rather than much skill on my part, I managed to cut him badly before his guards interceded. The pity is I did not have time to finish him."

"But I thought you'd promised your sister—"

"This encounter was before I made my foolish vow." He scowled at the distant mountains. "Over the years, I had managed to meet with Lissy in secret. Edgeway had made her his wife, omitting to mention he had slaughtered our family before she bound herself to him. When she learned the truth, the shock of it made her lose the child within her womb." He shuddered. "She never bore him another. As you can imagine, theirs was not a happy marriage."

"Why didn't she leave him?" How could any woman remain with such a man?

Vadim sighed. "She had her reasons. I cannot pretend I understand them. In spite of everything, she loved her husband, just as much as she loathed him. Edgeway Castle was her home. She had no living family in the outside world, save a hot-headed brother with a price on his head." He turned, fixing her with a cold, black stare. "I do not know what it is like in your world, Martha, but here a woman needs her family, especially if she does not have the protection of a man. I was angry with Lissy for a long time, but I finally came to accept her choices, even though I did not agree with them.

"After I had wounded him, Lissy sent word she wanted to meet me. It was to be the last time I saw her." He swallowed hard. "She looked so ill. It shocked me to see the changes a few short months had wrought upon her. Lissy had always been of slight build, but when I saw her next she resembled a walking corpse. Her fine clothes hung from her body, and her bones jutted from beneath them.

Her cheeks were no longer pink but yellow, and her lovely eyes seemed too large for her face. Of course, she insisted she was well, that she had recently recovered from a fever. And because I could not face the reality, I accepted her words."

He shook his head. "How blind and foolish I was! I should have taken her away with me, but I did not. Even then, her thoughts were all for Edgeway—though he had several mistresses by this time and rarely sought her bed or company. She begged me never to harm him again on my oath as her brother. And because I loved her so well, I gave her my vow." His jaw tightened perceptibly. "She died three days later."

Martha's hand flew to her mouth. "Oh, Vadim!"

"I did not attend her interment." He picked up a small stone and threw it hard over the edge of the ridge. "She had been in the ground for two months before I learned of her passing. And with her death, all that remained of my blood family was gone."

"Have you visited her grave?" Martha asked in a gentle voice.

"Once. Though it took me some time to find it. Edgeway guarded Lissy as jealously in death as in life. The sad thing is, in his own twisted way, I believe he loved her."

She looked at him, as though seeing him for the first time. "Just who are you, Vadim? Are you from a noble family?"

He gave a heavy sigh. "Does it matter?" He stood up. "Yesterday is gone. Today, I am exactly what you see."

And back into cryptic mode again. But she didn't push it. He'd re-lived a lot of awful stuff today. Did it really matter? Neither of them were who they'd once been.

"Let us head back." He glanced at Martha, who sat shivering beside him. "We have lingered here too long."

chapter seventeen

THEY DIDN'T SPEAK MUCH ON the way back down the mountain. After a day of so many revelations, there wasn't much else to say.

For once, Martha wasn't troubled by Vadim's silence. His thoughts, she knew, were in the far away and long ago. Everyone had a past, or carried some form of emotional luggage, but Vadim was hauling an entire baggage train around with him. No wonder he was sometimes so...withdrawn.

She shivered, glad to be on the move again. It was turning colder. A bank of thick clouds had moved in and swallowed up the sun.

When they reached the village, the light was already fading from the sky. The days of winter were still all too brief.

Seth saw them returning, and he strolled over to speak to Vadim. As the men talked, Martha stared at the red-haired Chief, seeing him with new eyes. His bravery had saved Vadim's life. Her heart glowed with gratitude.

"You will be dining with us this evening, I hope?" Seth turned his head, addressing the question to her as well.

"We'd love to." Martha gave him a warm smile. "That is," she glanced at Vadim, "if you don't have other plans?"

"Nothing that will not keep." Her sudden consideration of his wishes seemed to amuse him.

"Then, thank you. We will." To the surprise of both men, she planted a kiss on Seth's hairy cheek.

The Chief flushed crimson and raised his hand, touching the place she'd kissed. "What did I do to earn that?"

"You're a lovely man, Seth," she said. "You've been very good to...me." She caught a glimpse of the frown forming in Vadim's eyes. "I think I'll go and see if I can help Sylvie and Ma with anything." With that, she hurried away to the Great Hall with Forge at her heels.

Supper was a cheerful occasion. Sylvie and Vadim had apparently buried their differences, and the two of them chatted easily together, with none of the hostility of the previous day.

"You seem happier tonight, lass," Ma commented later as the two of them washed the supper things. Her rheumy blue eyes twinkled. "I take it you and Vadim have found an accord between you?" A wet-sounding chuckle escaped her throat. "You have seldom looked away from him all evening."

Martha flushed. If that was the case, she'd better take care Vadim didn't notice it too. "We've had a talk—yes." She returned her attention to the cauldron she was scrubbing, avoiding Ma's shrewd gaze.

"He loves you a good deal, you know," Ma continued, oblivious of the impact of her words. "I never thought I'd live to see him settled and content."

"Settled?" Now she did look up, blaming the heat of the water for her burning cheeks. *If this is settled and content, what the hell was he like before?* "He's rarely here," she said. "Why? What makes you think so?"

Ma shrugged her thin shoulders. "'Tis in his eyes every time he looks at you, girl."

Martha opened her mouth to speak, then closed it again. What could she say without giving the game away? The old lady must be mistaken. But that didn't quieten her dancing heart.

"Surely you cannot doubt his feelings?" Ma asked. "I know the early days of a union can be difficult, but even so..."

Martha said nothing and scrubbed the cauldron with enthusiasm.

"Let me see your hand." Ma extended her thin, liver-spotted hand towards Martha.

"What for?"

Ma tutted. "So I may read what lies there, of course." She gave a gappy grin. "I have the gift of The Sight. It seldom leads me false."

"Oh, very well." Martha wiped her damp hands against her apron then proffered her right one to the old woman. "Not that I believe in this kind of thing. Do I have to cross your palm with silver first?"

"Do not be flippant, child," Ma scolded, gripping Martha's hand with a strength that belied her years. "The old wisdom should never be mocked. Not even in fun. Now..." She held Martha's hand close to her face, almost pulling her off the little stool she sat upon. "What have we here?" Squinting at her palm, she traced its lines with a hooked finger. "Oh!" She glanced up. "You have indeed traveled far." Then she returned her stare to Martha's hand. "I see a man, a pale man with golden hair..."

That must be Tony.

"And another man; a dark man. Wait, he is turning to me now. Ah, yes!" Ma smiled her approval. "'Tis your husband."

"Really?" Martha leaned forward, suddenly very interested indeed. "What's he doing?"

Ma's smile faded. "He is...bleeding." She peered closer.

"His sword lies...broken at his feet."

"What?" Martha's heart lurched. The thought of it made her feel sick to her stomach. "When? How?"

"I cannot know that, child." Ma lowered Martha's hand, her wrinkled face twisted in pain and sympathy. "Time cannot be seen."

"Look again!" She thrust her hand back in Ma's face. "Am I there? What am I doing?"

"No." Ma shook her head, refusing to look. "You are gone. I cannot see you."

"What does that mean?" Martha was aware of how shrill her voice had become, but she couldn't help herself. "Am I dead?" *Or transported home again?* "Who did this to him? You must know something." *Please, God, don't let him die.*

"Listen to me." Ma gripped Martha's hands, darting a quick glance towards Vadim, who was heading towards them on an intercept course. "Trust no one," she hissed. "You will be betrayed by someone close, someone you consider a friend. If you love your man as I know you do, you must protect him and all of his secrets. Just as he protects you and yours. Do you understand—do you?" Ma's grip increased when Martha didn't answer swiftly enough.

She nodded. "Yes." Hot tears blurred her vision and slid down her cheeks when she blinked. "I understand."

Their whispered conversation ended with Vadim's arrival.

"Have you been reading Martha's future, Ma?" he asked, looking from one woman to the other.

Martha hurriedly swiped a hand over her face in a useless attempt to disguise her tears. He knew. She saw it in his smile; it looked unnatural, forced.

"So? What awaits us down the road, my love?" The lightness of his voice was unconvincing. Extending his hand to Martha, Vadim pulled her to her feet. "Are our children going to be troublesome? It cannot be good news, for you look so unhappy."

"N-not at all." Martha switched on her own fake smile. "Ma was just...suggesting a treatment for my chapped hands." They were a little rougher these days, true enough.

"Indeed."

As feeble as her lie had been, Vadim didn't challenge it. There followed a brief, uncomfortable silence. He studied her face as if he'd find the truth there, if he looked hard enough. Afraid that he would, Martha looked away.

"I shall have something ready for you tomorrow," Ma muttered, rising stiffly from her seat. She picked up the cauldron full of clean utensils and hooked it over her arm. "Now, I must put these away."

As soon as Ma was gone, Vadim drew Martha toward him until she was within the warm circle of his arms. To the casual observer, it must've looked as though the newly weds were having a cuddle. The truth was much less pleasant.

"What did she see?" He murmured against her ear. She shivered as his warm breath brushed over her skin. "We have no secrets between us now, remember?"

How can I ever forget?

"It's nothing." Martha looked into his eyes and attempted another fake smile. "Just a bit of nonsense, that's all. I certainly don't believe in such rubbish."

Vadim stroked the back of his hand over her cheek. "Ma's ability is not nonsense. Her visions have saved me many times. What did she tell you?"

"I can't." She looked down at her hands, palms resting on his leather jerkin. "Please don't ask me."

"But I must." He raised her chin with his index finger, forcing her to look at him. "Tell me, m'lady."

Unable to resist his will, she caved and whispered the prophecy to him. As she spoke, Martha played with his hair where it rested on the breast of his jerkin. Vadim listened without interruption.

"Is that all?" he asked when she fell silent.

"That's not enough for you?" She accidentally tugged at his hair, making him flinch. "Sorry." Disentangling her fingers from his hair, she continued her whispered rant. "Oh, why did I ever let her read my hand in the first place? What am I talking about? It's a hand, not a book. No one can really predict the future."

"Ma can," Vadim replied. He took her hands, holding them within the warmth of his. "It is fortunate we have warning of what lies ahead."

She envied his calmness. "Forgive me if I don't see it in quite the same way." Did nothing ever ruffle his feathers?

"The future is not fixed, Martha. It shifts and changes like pebbles in a river."

"Really?" She didn't believe him, however nice he made it sound. "So, why couldn't Ma see me? Have I gone home or—"

"You will not die, my lady," he assured her, demonstrating some funky mind-reading skills of his own. He clasped her hands tighter. "That will never happen. Not while I am here to protect you." The way he looked at her made her heart flutter. "When spring comes, I will find Madoc, the seer, and attempt to find a way to send you home." He raised her hands to his lips, pressing a kiss upon each one in turn. "Believe in that."

Believe in me, his eyes seemed to say.

I already do. Was that why the prospect of returning home didn't thrill her anymore?

What am I thinking? She gave herself a mental slap. His tenderness was all for show. She'd do well to remember that. With a smile, she stepped away, reluctantly sliding her hands from his. Oh, he was fond of her. How could she doubt it? But his affection was that of a kindly brother, not of a lover.

"I know you'll do your best for me, Vadim," she said softly. "You always have."

"Then do not vex yourself any further on this subject."

He offered her his arm. “Shall we rejoin the others?”

The short winter days gradually lengthened, and the snow retreated for another year. As the temperature climbed, the tips of fresh green shoots poked up shyly from beneath the soil, and swollen tree buds began to unfurl. Bird song resonated across the clear blue sky. Spring had finally come.

As life returned to the land, Darumvale woke from its long winter slumber. Suddenly, there were dozens of jobs to be done. On this particular day, Martha had been commandeered for field duties, and it was backbreaking work. The villagers hoed the earth by hand, preparing it for planting.

During the phase of the full moon—Sylvie told Martha it was important every crop be sown and reaped at its proper time—every man, woman, and child capable of work set to, planting the fields with, what would be, the first harvest of the year.

Martha straightened up from her stooping position, groaning as the little kinks in her back popped and cracked, and drew her sleeve over her damp brow. She was glad she'd worn her second-best dress. Her sturdy boots and the hem of her grey gown were already heavy with thick, cloying mud.

Taking a deep breath, she looked around. She was in the middle of a long line of villagers, each person allocated with a furrow to sow. A bag containing the precious seeds hung from the waist of every worker.

It was slow work. The human chain inched forward, stooping, scattering, and re-covering, before moving on to the next patch of bare furrow.

The sun felt hot on her head. For once, she was glad of her scarf's protection. Shielding her eyes from the sun's glare, she squinted into the blue sky. Sparse clouds like wisps of gossamer drifted overhead. It was so peaceful. She closed her eyes and listened to the bleats and moos of the livestock as they grazed themselves sick on the plump green grass in the top meadow.

A breeze tickled her face, chilling the sweat on her skin and giving her goose bumps. She smiled. It was impossible not to when she felt so good.

"What are you thinking about, milady?"

A voice to her left roused Martha from her waking dream. She turned to see Bren, a couple of paces ahead, grinning at her from an almost upside-down position.

"Have you heard news from your man today?"

"Actually, I have," Martha replied with a smile. "Not that it's any of your business."

But her words were meant as a joke, and the smith's wife knew it. Over the course of the winter, the two women had become close, their initial liking growing into friendship. While Martha loved Bren's bluntness, Bren seemed to appreciate having someone around who never took offense at her words—and who frequently gave as good as she got.

"A tinker called at the hall this morning, asking for me." Martha bent over and continued planting, hurrying until she drew level with Bren.

"And do you intend telling me what this tinker had to say?" Bren pushed a piece of grizzled hair back under her scarf with a filthy hand. "Or perhaps it is too depraved to be repeated in polite company?"

Martha snorted. "Polite company—you? Hah!" She reached into the bag at her waist and withdrew a fistful of seeds. "If you must know, Vadim sent word that I should expect him by the end of the week. Satisfied?"

Even repeating the words was enough to set her blood racing. The killer butterflies in her stomach went wild. Vadim had been gone for three weeks this time, his longest absence yet. At first, it was difficult without him, especially at night, but she'd adapted. Eventually. But it disturbed her to learn just how much she'd come to depend on him.

Living with Vadim was easier than she'd ever imagined it would be. They'd whiled away the long winter nights in conversation, frequently shunning the bright lights of the Great Hall in favor of their own fireside. While Vadim educated her about Erde, Martha, in turn, described life back in her world. The hours were too brief for all they had to say.

In all that time, Vadim behaved like a true gentleman, not once stepping over the invisible line of friendship—much to Martha's disappointment. It was like living with her best friend.

This time, he'd been gone too long. She missed his companionship, his voice, his smile, and even his snoring. In short, she missed...him. Standing there, in the middle of the field, sweating and ankle deep in mud, Martha finally accepted what her heart had known for some time. There was no point denying it to herself anymore.

I just love him.

She smiled. The words made her fizz with happiness from head to toe.

It wasn't a sudden revelation, borne on the wings of thunderclaps and accompanied by the trumpets of an angelic host. For her, love had come slowly, dripping into her heart, bit by bit, day after day. Now, it was full of Vadim. How had he managed to become so very dear without her knowing it?

"I am heartily glad to hear it," Bren said, dragging Martha back to the present. "You have been as dour as Old Mother Galrey since he went away."

"I have not." Mother Galrey was renowned for her gloomy disposition. "I've just been a bit tired, that's all. Some of us aren't accustomed to rooting about in mud all day long." That was true enough. On some nights, she was asleep before the birds had sought their beds. This new life made her body ache, unaccustomed as it was to the demands of such regular physical toil.

"Is that so?" Bren straightened up and stretched her back. "Then, perhaps you ought to return to your former life, *milady*," she sneered. "Let us hope your noble family do not object *too* strongly to having an outlaw for a son-in-law, hmm?"

"God, you're an evil woman, Bren." But Martha laughed. She felt so happy she would have laughed at anything. "I don't know how poor Jared puts up with you."

"He has no choice." Bren gave a horsy-looking grin. "We are bound until death. He cannot escape me now."

As Bren stared off into the distant mountain range and took a well-earned breather, Martha returned to her planting, nursing her new-found love within her heart.

One of the women began to sing. Other voices, male and female, joined in. Soon the field was awash with song. Although some of the singers weren't particularly tuneful, taken as a whole, it was a fairly harmonious sound. Martha found her rhythm again, humming along as she worked.

Life as a glorified farm laborer was hard, but it was strangely satisfying. There was something about physical labor, the kind that left a person bone-weary and sore at the end of the day. She'd never slept better nor felt so at peace. Even thinking about Tony didn't bother her anymore. His betrayal no longer caused her pain. Aunt Lulu was her only regret. A fleeting thought crossed her mind.

What if I stay? With the exception of Lulu, what did home have that was worth going back to? Not the material stuff, but the things that really mattered.

She instantly pushed the thought aside, dismissing it as rubbish. She didn't belong in this primitive place. It wasn't her home. Was it?

Could you leave him now, even if there was a way?

Before she could give the matter any more thought, Bren called to her again. "It seems he could not wait until the end of the week, after all."

"Huh?" Martha straightened up and looked in the direction Bren was pointing.

"Is that your lord and master?"

A fast-moving horse and rider hurtled down the road towards them, kicking up dust behind it. Martha shielded her eyes and squinted—long-distance vision wasn't her thing. Her heart skipped. It looked like Vadim. The man's face was covered, his cloak billowing behind him in a dancing grey banner. But as he drew nearer, she realized her mistake. It wasn't him. The rider was too short, his build was too broad, and his hair wasn't black but a golden-brown.

From its glorious expectant heights, her heart crashed back down to earth. "It isn't him."

Bren put a clumsy arm about Martha's shoulders. "I am sorry, lass. Curse my weak eyesight."

The sound of approaching hooves had roused the other villagers. Rising as one, they stood up from their sowing and watched the rider's progress.

When he reached the boundary of the field, the man reined his horse to a swift halt. Swinging one leg over the horse's neck, he leapt to the ground, and marched across the field to where Sylvie stood waiting, hoe in hand.

The rider stopped before her, briefly bowing his head. "I must speak with the Chief on a matter of urgency," he said.

"Seth is out with a hunting party." Sylvie wiped her dirty hands on her work apron. "Perhaps I might serve in his stead?"

The rider seemed to consider her offer.

Why hadn't he removed his mask? Except for a pair of intense blue eyes, the man's face remained hidden. Was he another outlaw? One of Vadim's merry men?

He watched warily as the villagers gravitated to Sylvie's side. They were protecting Sylvie. The village had closed ranks against an outsider. Flock mentality or not, Martha drew closer to Sylvie too. Although the rider was the only one wearing a sword, he was vastly outnumbered. Simple farmers though most of the villagers were, Martha wouldn't fancy getting a clout from one of their hoes.

"Very well," he said at last. "Then perhaps we might speak in private?"

Sylvie nodded. Dispersing her human shield with a glance, she accompanied the stranger from the field.

They spoke together for several minutes.

During that time, no one returned to work. Instead, the villagers leaned motionless on their tools, fixing the rider with the considerable weight of their combined stare.

"Who do you think he is?" Martha whispered to Bren, unwilling to disturb the silence which had fallen on the field.

Bren shrugged. "Looks like one of Vadim's outlaw friends to me. They do visit us occasionally, although we never see their faces. This fellow must be new, though. I do not recognize him or his horse."

When Sylvie came back, she looked pale. For once, her ready smile was absent. "Grim tidings, my friends. The Earl and his company are on the road as we speak. They will be with us within a few hours. It is likely they will spend the night here in Darumvale."

At this, there were many groans of dismay.

Sylvie scanned the assembled faces until her eyes rested on Martha. "Martha, my dear," she said gently. "You cannot remain here, not whilst the Earl and his men are in residence. You understand why."

Oh, shit. Her stomach plummeted. Not only was she supposed to be Vadim's wife, but a runaway noblewoman too.

"Go home and prepare. You may be gone for several days, but pack lightly..."

Several days?

"...you are ready, come to the Hall." Sylvie picked her way through the furrows towards her. She took Martha's hand, her grey eyes glistening. "I must ask you to go away with this man—"

"Him? No way!" The protest flew from her lips before she could stop it. "I don't know him from Adam. For all we know, he could work for the Evil Earl. Does anyone here recognize him?" She glanced at the other villagers for support. There were several murmurs in her favor. "See?"

"Please, m'lady." Sylvie grasped her shoulders. "We are wasting time. Harken to me, Martha. Do you believe I would send you away with someone I did not trust? This is one of Vadim's men. We have passwords for such occasions as these, and since the gentleman has provided me with the correct answers to my questions, I am assured he is who he claims to be."

Martha chewed her lower lip. She didn't want to leave the village in the company of a complete stranger. Like it or not, Darumvale was her home now, albeit temporarily. It was familiar...safe. Her blood ran cold at the prospect of leaving, but it seemed she had little choice in the matter. If the Earl recognised her as Vadim's companion, the villagers would pay the price for sheltering them. "Okay," she said. "I'll go and grab my things."

Bren accompanied her back to the house, helping her cram her few belongings into one of Vadim's spare back packs. Martha attached a small knife to her belt then pulled on her cloak, Ma's warning still ringing in her head: *'Trust no one.'* She had no intention of doing otherwise.

As they approached the Great Hall, Forge lolloped up, barking and whining, sensing an adventure in the offing. The rider stood waiting, surrounded by a crowd of villagers, holding the reins of his huge black horse. The large animal pawed at the ground, obviously eager to be gone. A bundle of food hung from its saddle, courtesy of Sylvie and Ma, no doubt.

When Martha arrived, the rider bowed his head. "We will have to share the horse," he said. "I hope you have no objection."

"None at all," she replied. "Just as long as I get to ride at the back." The last thing she wanted was him breathing down her neck. No, she wanted him right where she could see him.

The stranger seemed as impatient as his horse, stamping his feet and fiddling with his gloves while the women hugged and said their goodbyes. Eventually, he swung up into the saddle of his restless steed, and extended his hand down to Martha. "Come," he said.

With great reluctance, she gave him her hand, and with the help of two old men, boosting her up from behind, Martha was finally seated behind the rider.

"Return to your work," he told the assembled crowd as his horse skittered beneath him. "The Earl must suspect nothing."

"Take care of her," Bren growled, "or I will be after you, young man."

"I consider myself amply warned, lady."

Martha barely had the chance to shout goodbye before the man gathered his reins and cantered swiftly from the village.

chapter eighteen

THEY TOOK TO THE ROAD, heading north. The hedgerows burst with green life, no longer the stark skeletons Martha recalled from the previous winter. Forge kept pace with the black horse, his pink tongue lolling from his mouth as he ran.

"Send him home," the rider growled over his shoulder.

"No." Martha stuffed her pack firmly between their bodies. "If he can keep up, I'll be glad to have him with me." She clutched at the high back of the saddle, watching the scenery as it whipped by. "Where are you taking me? Are we going to Edgeway?"

The man grunted.

She tried again. "How do you know Vadim?"

"We are brothers," he answered curtly.

Martha tensed. "He doesn't have any brothers."

"I was speaking figuratively, of course."

"Oh. Did Vadim send you to fetch me?"

"No. I have been watching the village in his absence."

"Did he ask you to do so?"

"Why else would I be here, lady?" He was beginning to sound slightly irritated by her barrage of questions, but Martha didn't care.

"He asked you to take me away if the Evil Earl reared his butt-ugly head?"

The man snorted. She couldn't tell whether he was amused or disgusted. "Of course. You do ask a lot of questions, m'lady."

"What did you expect, that I'd follow you like a little lamb?" She settled back against the high back of the saddle. "If Vadim told you I would, then I'm afraid you've been sorely misled, my friend."

"So it would seem." But the man didn't seem upset about it. "I am beginning to feel much sympathy for my Lord Vadim."

"Watch it." Martha prodded his back. "I am still here, you know."

He sighed. "I am only too aware of the fact, lady."

When he lapsed into silence again, she didn't mind. Their brief conversation had settled much of the panic within her heart. He was definitely Vadim's man. If he'd been sweeter and more polite, she wouldn't have trusted him at all.

They traveled along the North Road for another mile or so, then turned left up a narrow track heading for the remains of an abandoned homestead. The stranger dismounted and walked the horse around the back of the tumbledown buildings. When they reached a rickety wooden gate that led to an area of open pasture, the man looked up at her. "We can take the horse no further," he said. "From here, we travel on foot."

Martha dismounted with difficulty, hampered by her long skirt. The man stood by and made no attempt to help. As soon as her feet touched the ground, Forge trotted to her side, panting and wagging his tail, covering her hand in hot doggy drool. She was relieved he'd managed to keep up.

While she fussed over Forge, the man untacked his horse, and, after giving the animal a brief pat, he turned it loose in the meadow. Then he stashed the saddle and bridle inside the open doorway of the ruined house and set off walking. He didn't look back to see if Martha was following.

She sighed. What choice did she have?

Unlike Vadim, this man didn't wait for her. He strode up the steep, grassy gradient as easily as if it were level ground. For all she struggled to keep up, the man drew farther and farther ahead. From experience, she knew it was better to find her own pace than attempt to match someone else's. So she stopped trying to compete. Gradually, her breathing slowed, and her heart rate settled into a less frightening rhythm.

It was hot though. She plodded uphill, occasionally swiping her cloak over her sweaty face—the horrid, itchy thing. But wearing the garment was easier than having to carry it.

The man walked on, soon becoming a small dot on the horizon.

Martha was glad of Forge's company, particularly when they reached the treacherous scree slopes. As the rocks shifted beneath her feet, she clung to his collar, her knuckles white with fear. It was a long way down to the bottom of the hill.

Keeping to her slow and steady pace, Martha gradually began to enjoy the walk. The gentle sounds of the wind rushing through the grass, and the songs of hidden curlews accompanied her panting breaths. When she dared to look up from the narrow path, she saw swallows soaring and diving in the sky overhead.

The man was nowhere in sight.

She didn't see him again until she crested the top of the hill. He was sitting on a large rock, his face uncovered, drinking from the bladder he carried on his belt. As Martha approached, he hurriedly rearranged the fabric mask around the lower half of his face.

"Don't mind me." Martha flopped down on the rock beside him. "There's no need to cover up on my account. My hubby is an outlaw too, remember?" Forge jumped up and settled himself on the rock behind them, basking in the sunshine.

"I do not doubt your loyalty, m'lady, but a good torturer can extract the truth from even the most trustworthy," he replied. "It is better this way. After all, you cannot tell what you do not know."

Martha shuddered. How easily he spoke of such terrible things. "In that case, I guess there's no point in asking for your name."

The man shrugged and offered the bladder to her. She sniffed suspiciously at the contents before raising it to her lips. Ale. Warm, sweet ale. The perfect lubricant for a parched throat. After taking a few hefty gulps, she handed it back. "Thanks. Have another drink if you like. I promise not to look at you."

She stared straight ahead, her mind spinning with the events of the day. And it wasn't over yet. Why had she ever considered staying on in this mad world? As much as she loved Vadim, the stranger's arrival was a timely reminder of just how stupid an idea it really was. If the opportunity to leave ever presented itself, she was gone.

"You would have done better to marry a farmer," the man commented, unconsciously reading her mind. "Not that anyone here is truly safe anymore."

Martha had no intention of discussing her 'marriage' with him and quickly changed the subject. "Where are you taking me?"

"'Tis not far now." He stood up. "Shall we proceed? I am keen to return to my duties."

"And what might they be? If it's not a state secret, of course."

"I will continue to observe Darumvale. We follow the Earl's movements closely, m'lady. Like a poisonous snake, it is always better to know exactly where he is at all times." They set off walking. This time, the man shortened his stride to match Martha's.

"So why hasn't someone chopped off this snake's head before now?" she asked, glancing at Forge who'd found a little stream to drink from.

The man made a sound of grim amusement from behind his mask. "You make it sound so simple. Unfortunately, the Earl is seldom without his guards. Even when he is, he is far too slippery to hold. Whatever spirit watches over him guards him well. Many men have died attempting to end Lord Edgeway's life."

At length, they reached a series of caves burrowed into the mountainside. The man took Martha inside the largest of them. "What is this fixation they have with caves?" she muttered as she explored her new surroundings. But he heard her.

"They are a haven for us. Even the Earl's men dare not stray too far into the mountains. These are our lands." His blue eyes glittered above his mask. "Not even the King can claim them."

She dropped her pack to the compacted, hard floor then took off her cloak. "Is that what happened to you? Did someone take your lands? Vadim told me what happened to the old noble families. Is that why you're doing this?"

The man regarded her curiously, staring as if she'd suddenly grown another head.

"You must ask your husband," he said at last. "It is not my place to tell you anything."

Great. Yet another mystery.

"The woodpile is over yonder." He gestured toward the back of the cave. "There is a spring outside that is safe to drink from. Your friends gave me plenty of food." He indicated the pack he'd brought with him from the village. "Is there anything else you require of me before I leave?"

He was going already?

"No—I'm good, thanks," she heard herself reply. Crouching down, Martha unrolled her bedding by the doorway. "When will you be back?" With effort, she made it sound like a casual question.

"I will try and look in on you each evening."

Don't just leave me here!

"Fine."

What about the wolves?

As he walked past her, heading outside, she battled the urge to grab at the train of his cloak and keep him there.

He paused and looked back at her. "If two nights pass and you have not seen me, you must consider I am dead and make other arrangements. Is that clear?"

She nodded, not knowing what else to say. *What 'other arrangements'?* Darumvale or Edgeway were her only options. "I understand. Call me needy if you like, but I'd prefer it if you stayed alive."

The man's eyes crinkled above his mask as though he was smiling. "I will endeavor to do as you ask. Farewell."

When he was gone, Martha slowly unpacked her things; the task took only a few moments to complete. Lonely and miserable, she dragged her bedroll outside the cave entrance and sat in the late sunshine, watching the shadows lengthen. Pangs of worry gnawed her belly, and not just for her own sorry hide. She stroked Forge's head as it lay on her lap, and looked into the valley below.

The Evil Earl would be at the village by now. How would the villagers fare? She prayed he wouldn't stay long. Martha felt awful, hiding away in comparative safety while her friends had little choice but to face him. But what else could she do?

Darumvale was a small place, and the Earl probably knew everyone who lived there. A stranger would attract many awkward questions. And what if he remembered her from their previous encounter, as Vadim feared he might? What would the Earl do to a woman who'd been keeping company with outlaws?

The truth and her cover story were equally dangerous. If either were revealed, the villagers' fate might be even worse. All she could do was wait and hope.

It was still dark when Forge woke her. His deep rumbling growls sounded blood-curdling in the night.

Martha sat up, heart thundering, her scalp prickling with fear. "What is it?" she whispered, hugging the dog's neck.

Tense as stone, Forge faced the cave entrance. Though he made no attempt to go outside, he continued growling.

Something was definitely out there.

Cautiously, she peered into the dark beyond the cave entrance. Dawn wasn't too far off. Fingers of red and gold already streaked the inky sky. She longed for the comfort of the fire, but it had burned low, its glowing embers casting almost no light.

Wolves? No. Forge would be going off his tree if they were around. These growls were just a gentle warning.

Taking a shuddering breath, Martha kicked off her blanket and got up. Thank God she'd slept fully clothed. Facing an intruder dressed only in her nightwear would've made her feel even more vulnerable. Forge got up too, his growls still rumbling in his throat.

Summoning her feeble courage, she held her breath and tiptoed to the cave entrance and groped for the sturdy stick she'd left propped by the wall. Slowly, she poked her head outside.

Everything looked as it should. The world slumbered on, quiet and still. The various lumps and shadows all looked familiar in the half-night. She strained her ears, listening for anything that didn't belong. Except for Forge's growling, all she heard was the sighing of the wind. She exhaled. But the dog remained rigid at her side.

"You daft old thing, scaring me like that." Martha patted him with a clammy hand. Relief made her feel giddy. "There's nothing out there. Come on. Let's go and make breakfast, hmm?"

To her surprise, Forge didn't follow. He bounded off

several paces and snuffled excitedly at something on the ground. Then he raised his head and whined at her.

"What's that?" Martha picked up her skirts and strode through the dewy grass towards him. "Little Timmy's fallen down a mine shaft?" She stumbled over a sturdy root and swore. "That'd better not be a dead bird, Forge. If you roll in it, you'll be sleeping outside, alright?"

But it wasn't a bird.

"Oh, fuck. No!"

She set off running toward the man lying motionless on the heather. The outlaw who'd brought her from Darumvale.

"Move, Forge!" She pushed the dog aside. "Good boy. Let me see him." The man's eyes were closed. "Can you hear me?" She shook his arm. The man groaned. An unmistakable metallic tang assaulted her nose. *Blood?* Hands shaking, she carefully frisked his body. Two short wooden shafts protruded from his abdomen. *Arrows? My God! This can't be happening.* Hot bile rose up into her mouth, but she swallowed it back. The man needed help. Unfortunately for him, hers was all he had.

"Mister?" Damn. She didn't even know his name.

His eyelids flickered open. "You...must...leave... this place." He struggled for breath. "They may be...tracking me."

"Shh." Martha stroked his hair. "Let's get you sorted out first."

"No!" He wrenched off his facemask, revealing the face it concealed.

Her heart sank even further. She knew then, his wounds must be very serious indeed. "There is...no time." He gripped her hand, but he was so weak she barely felt it.

As the sun peeped over the horizon, Martha could see him properly. Tears blurred her eyes. He was young, barely out of his teens, far too young to be dying on a mountain. Sweat beaded his pale brow. His grimacing lips were tinged with blue. "Leave me," he whispered, his eyes pleading.

"I will." She forced a smile. "Soon." She glanced at the arrows sticking out of his tunic. The leather was dark, saturated with blood. The ends of the arrows were gone. He'd probably broken them off himself. Martha was no doctor, but even she knew the man was beyond all earthly aid. It was a miracle he'd made it this far.

"Are you thirsty?" she asked.

He nodded once then closed his eyes.

She ran to the cave, returning seconds later clutching a bladder of ale in one hand and her cloak in the other. *Please be alive!*

He was. Barely. Martha covered the man-child with her cloak and moved behind him, supporting his head so he could drink from the bladder. Most of the ale trickled over his downy cheeks. But he must have swallowed some for she saw his throat contracting. "Better?"

What a stupid thing to say! He's dying, you fool.

She dabbed his face dry with her handkerchief then carefully laid him back down. She stretched out beside him. Forge lay at the man's other side, whining softly. "Is there any...message you want to leave for anyone?" she asked, clasping his cold hand. Tears ran unchecked down her face.

"My...family...are gone." He drew another rasping breath. "Tell Vadim...I tried to...stop them. I tried to—" He gasped, writhing in pain. Fresh blood welled from the corners of his mouth.

"Hush." Martha put her arms around him and cuddled him against her breast. Resting her cheek on his head, she slowly rocked him like a mother with a restless child. "It's all right," she soothed. "I'll tell him. You did well. Vadim will be proud of you. Rest now. Ssh."

"You are...worthy of him, m'lady. I see...it now..."

He didn't speak again.

Martha held him long after he'd gone, unable to let go, her tears slowly soaking his hair.

Eventually, when her aching arms demanded it, she laid the man down onto the heather. Flakes of drying blood covered her hands and clothes, crumbling into dust whenever she moved. She felt sick. This time, when hot bile rushed into her mouth, she let it out and retched in the grass for several minutes. Forge watched her through sorrowful eyes.

When her stomach was empty, Martha sat up and drew a sleeve across her sour mouth. She stared at the man's body. It was the first time she'd seen a dead person. What an ending to such a young life. After gently closed his staring eyes, she scrambled stiffly to her feet. This wasn't the right time to mourn him, not when he'd died trying to warn her. She owed it to him to escape if she could.

But she couldn't leave him out in the open for the wolves.

After reluctantly reclaiming her bloody cloak, she covered the man's face with a blanket, then raced back and forth across the plateau, gathering as many rocks as she could lift. She stacked them around the dead man in a makeshift, grisly cairn. It wasn't the best grave in the world, but it was the best she could do. At least he was decently covered now.

With Forge at her side, she stood over his grave and said a silent prayer.

I didn't even know your name, but I truly hope you've found peace.

Ten minutes later, she was packed up and on the move. Her options were limited. Darumvale was out of the question, and if she walked toward Edgeway, chances were she'd encounter the Earl or his men on the road. If caves were good enough for outlaws, they were good enough for her. And she knew just where to find some.

Casting many nervous glances into the valley, Martha set off for the mountain she'd visited last winter with Vadim. It was easy enough to spot. Looming in the distance like an anvil, it dwarfed the surrounding hills. It looked a long way off, but they might reach it before dark if they didn't dawdle.

The sun shone bright and warm in a light-blue sky. It was another beautiful spring day, but Martha was too depressed to appreciate it. She couldn't stop crying.

At any moment she expected someone to see her. To hear a cry of, 'there she is'. But it didn't come. Except for the occasional rabbit or startled bird, she encountered no one. Forge seemed aware of her distress and padded quietly at Martha's side, forsaking even the slowest rabbits.

With every heartbeat, she longed for Vadim. With every fiber of her being, she wanted him. Even so, she hoped he wouldn't return home any time soon. Not until the danger had passed. He'd come for her. In the meantime, all she had to do was stay hidden. If he still breathed, he'd find her again.

By the time they reached the cavern of the waterfall, it was almost dark.

Wobbling with exhaustion, Martha threw down her pack and crumpled to her knees before the entrance. Black spots danced before her eyes. Food might have helped, but the thought of eating revolted her. How could she eat when the memory of the man's violent death was so fresh in her mind? His dried blood lay caked beneath her fingernails, and her clothes were stiff with it. More tears slid down her cheeks. She'd been crying off and on all day.

It's just shock. It's natural.

With a sigh, she rubbed her hands over her swollen eyes. She'd never witnessed death so close before. Both her parents were dead, but she'd been a toddler at the time and remembered nothing about it. A car accident was one thing, being shot to death was quite another.

To see someone die like that and be unable to help them was horrific.

Forge whined. He was hungry even if she wasn't.

"Okay." She hauled herself up off the ground. "I'm coming."

She set up camp right where she'd dropped her pack. The cavern entrance was well hidden and afforded her with an unobstructed view of the paths that lead to it. No one would be sneaking up on her tonight. Even the threat of wolves didn't worry her. Forge was a wonderful early warning system, and she had a big stick right where she could get at it. "Let's go see if we can find anything to burn, hmm?"

chapter nineteen

MARTHA HID HERSELF AWAY FOR two days. Although her rations were running low, she was afraid to venture far from the protection of the cavern. At least the weather remained kind. The gentle sun made her isolation slightly more bearable. Time passed and all the hours flowed into a big void of nothing.

She bathed in the chilly waters of the great waterfall. Deafened by the noise of thundering water, she scrubbed her clothes on rocks beside the pool, beating and pounding the bloody garments against the rough granite rocks. But the telltale dark brown stains on her dress and cloak remained, no matter how many times she washed them. The outlaw's blood was as difficult to erase as the memory of his death.

Out, damned spot. She felt like a modern-day Lady Macbeth trapped in a medieval world.

On the third morning, increasingly concerned about her dwindling supplies—to say nothing of her flaking sanity—she decided to risk a trip down the ridge to see what was happening in Darumvale.

She skulked along feeling horribly exposed, grateful she was wearing her dowdiest dress and drab cloak. There was nowhere to hide. No trees to duck behind, and few bushes of any size. But what else could she do?

She couldn't wait forever. What if no one ever came for her? Of course, by 'no one', she meant Vadim. Where was he? An image of the dead outlaw, stuck with arrows, flashed into her mind making her flinch.

No. Vadim wasn't dead. She wouldn't believe it.

Forge enjoyed the change of scenery. Bounding ahead, he sniffed at every new scent with enthusiasm, tail wagging.

Martha envied him. *I want to be a dog. Look at him. Not a care in the world.*

"You're cracking up, girl," she muttered. Isolation wasn't doing her mental health any favors. She needed people—positively hungered for human company, for news. Vadim, as always, was number one on her wish list.

Please, God, let him be okay.

Darumvale was less than an hour away. The village lay quiet in the early morning light, and at first sight, everything looked peaceful. Martha settled down on her stomach, looking down from her secret eyrie, and waited for the village to wake. Gradually, as the sun rose higher, several tiny figures left the Great Hall and walked across the street toward the stables. Who was it? It was impossible to tell from this distance.

Just as she was debating whether to move closer or not, her mind threw out a troubling thought. Why wasn't anyone working in the fields? The sun was up, and there was still a lot of planting to be done.

Suddenly, Darumvale's apparent tranquility looked terribly artificial. As if to confirm her suspicions, a ray of sun struck one of the tiny figures as it emerged from the stables leading a horse. The light bounced off his chest as brightly as any mirror. Her heart thumped hard in her chest. He was wearing armor. And as other figures emerged into the light, she realized he wasn't the only one.

She gasped. Soldiers. *Shit!*

Terrified of being spotted, she shuffled back from the

edge and called Forge to her side. It was unlikely anyone would see them so high up, but she dared not risk it. Not everyone was as short-sighted as she was. Settling back against a grassy bank, she wiped her clammy hands on her skirt. Traveling back along the narrow exposed ridge in full daylight was too dangerous. Her only other option was to wait until dusk. And that lay many hours away.

It proved to be the longest, most nerve-wracking day of her life, spent sweltering in the heat of the sun. By midday, Martha was forced to hide beneath her cloak to escape its hottest rays. Forge was just as miserable—although he'd found himself a small bush and crawled beneath it to escape the worst of the heat.

Fortunately, she'd brought a small bladder of water which she shared with the dog, rationing it carefully, and cursing herself for not bringing more. There wasn't so much as a puddle nearby. As the minutes ticked by, her clothes clung uncomfortably to her body, sweat running between her breasts in a constant, unpleasant trickle. Beneath her scarf, her hair plastered against her head and neck in soggy curls.

This wasn't one of your better ideas, Bigalow.

But at least she was alive. Free. Her situation was better that of her Darumvale friends. How must they be faring? And where the hell was Vadim? Her mood swung from concern to anger and back in the space of a few heartbeats. The lack of information was driving her mad.

Overcoming her fear of discovery, Martha peeped over the edge of the hill again. The horsemen had gone. In their absence, the villagers emerged from their houses. Like timid animals, they scurried about their business then returned home. But not all the soldiers had left. There were four outside the Great Hall: two stationed by the doors, while the other pair patrolled the perimeter.

There was no sign of Sylvie, Seth or Ma. If the Evil Earl ever learned they'd consorted with outlaws... She shivered, praying they'd not met the same fate as Vadim's friend.

Don't be daft. Why would they guard the hall if there's no one left alive inside? Use your brain.

As the hours passed, the evil spectre of the sun gradually sank lower in the sky, and shadows crept along the hill. The longest day was finally almost over. With great relief, she called to Forge then set off back along the ridge, adopting a stooping walk until the village was out of sight.

Her legs tingled with pins and needles as life flowed back into them. Grimacing, she stamped her feet, then took off her scarf, ruffling her sweaty hair in the heavenly breeze. Bliss.

The mother of all headaches pounded away behind her left eye, and an image of Aunt Lulu's well-stocked medicine cabinet floated into her mind to torment her. *Tablets. Lovely tablets.*

On the horizon, only the vivid orange rim of the sun remained, staining the sky with brilliant colors. It was so lovely that, despite herself, Martha smiled. It was like a child's messy painting, shades of blue and violet, red and pink jumbled together and splattered carelessly onto an ever-darkening canvas. She sighed and breathed in the heavy fragrance of flowers, borne up on the cooling wind. The world looked perfect.

Unfortunately, the reality of this land wasn't nearly so pretty.

They came across a little river, and the temptation of its gurgling waters could not be ignored. While Forge bounded about in the shallows, Martha stripped off and wallowed in a patch of deep water beneath the bank. Closing her eyes, she leaned back, sighing as the icy water lapped over her feverish skin.

It was almost dark when they finally started up the hill

to their cave. Even with a full moon for company, being out at night scared her. They walked fast and reached camp in double time.

She looked up at the heavens, and the man in the moon stared back at her from his black, star-studded blanket. How was it the moon and stars looked the same as they did back in the twenty-first century? She still couldn't get her head around that one.

Forge stiffened beside her, rumbling a warning deep in his throat. Martha froze. She felt it too. Something wasn't right.

Gripping the dog's collar, she strained her eyes, looking toward the cavern entrance. It seemed peaceful enough, but she didn't move. A primitive instinct urged her to wait.

Then a shadow detached itself from the external wall of the cavern. She gasped. It was the shape of a man. Her stomach lurched. A man carrying a big, nasty-looking sword.

They'd found her lair.

"Ssh, Forge." Her warning came too late. The man was close enough to hear his growls. The shadow turned in their direction and looked straight at her.

Shit!

A dozen thoughts flitted simultaneously through her mind, while adrenaline flooded her veins and pumped her muscles. She wanted to run. He'd probably catch her anyway. But what else could she do? She certainly couldn't fight him.

She held Forge's collar tighter, the metal buckle biting into her fingers. How far would she get before she learned the pain of an arrow in her back? She'd have to take her chances.

The brutality of the Earl's men was legendary among the people of Darumvale. Surrender wasn't an option. What did his thugs know of mercy?

"C'mon, Forge!" She wheeled around, trying to drag

the dog with her. Unfortunately, he wouldn't cooperate. He stopped growling and began whining instead, his long whip-like tail lashing madly through the air.

"Martha? Can it be you?" a familiar voice called out of the darkness, a voice that chased all of the shadows from her heart.

"Vadim!" She ran to him, stumbling over heather roots in her haste. Her stomach flipped, dancing with happy butterflies. "Oh, thank God!"

"Where in Erde have you been?" Vadim thrust his sword back into its sheath with a horrid metallic squeal then ripped the scarf from his face. "I have spent hours looking for you."

"Where do you think I've been?" Her relief died at the same moment as her smile. "I've been stuck out here for two bloody days and—"

"I meant *now*." He grabbed her upper arms and hauled her to him. "Where have you been until so late? Tell me the truth!"

"Darumvale. Ouch!" What the hell was wrong with him? "Will you let go of me?"

"You went back to the village?" His eyes narrowed, glinting unnaturally in the moonlight.

She didn't like the way he was looking at her at all. Her neck prickled. In a blinding flash of clarity, she suddenly understood the secret workings of his mind. And it wasn't pretty. "You don't trust me at all. Do you?"

He didn't attempt to deny it. A bitter smile curved his lips. "Well done. You see the truth at last." His fingers dug even deeper into her arms. "Please continue. What else do you read in my expression, m'lady?"

Her chest ached as if he'd punched her. "Even now, after all this time..." After all the time they'd spent together. After he'd made her fall in love— She shook her head. What an idiot she was. A stupid, gullible fool. "You think I'm in league with the Evil Earl."

"By your own admission, you traveled to Darumvale and back this day. An impossible task without Lord Edgeway's blessing."

And this was what he thought of her? "Let go of me. Now!" As his grip loosened, Martha pulled free and rubbed her aching arms. If only she could massage away the pain in her heart so easily.

Vadim took a deep breath and stepped back a pace, his hands clenched into fists at his side. "Will you not deny it? I admit I would be most disappointed if you did not at least attempt to convince me of your innocence."

"Deny it?" She widened her eyes. "Of course I do!" she cried, her temper needled by the injustice of his accusation. She had to make him understand. "I didn't—"

"Oh? So how did you manage to return, hmm? Would you have me believe that the Earl simply allow you walk free?"

The softness of his voice didn't fool her. The quieter he was, the greater the oncoming storm.

"What else am I to believe, Martha?" he continued. "Darumvale crawls with soldiers, yet you manage to travel there and back without detection?" He looked down his nose at her, his expression akin to disgust. "Do not take me for a fool, m'lady. You have played me quite long enough."

"*I've* played *you*?" Martha stared up at him in disbelief. This man, her 'friend', didn't trust her at all. He'd shared his darkest secrets with her, fed and cared for her, but all the time...

"You weren't protecting me at all, were you?" she murmured, more to herself than to him. "You were softening me up." As the ugly truth revealed itself, her strength deserted her. "Keep your friends close and your enemies closer. Isn't that what they say, Vadim?" Her legs buckled and she sank down onto the heather, skirts pooled around her.

Vadim remained silent, watching her. His expressionless features gave her nothing.

A mask without a mask. "You only kept me with you to stop me reporting back to the Earl. *That's* why you didn't want me moving to Edgeway, isn't it? Was everything you ever told me a lie?" She laughed bitterly and shook her head. "Oh, Bigalow, you're the biggest fecking eejit that ever drew breath."

Vadim crouched down to stroke Forge, who was still demanding his attention. She battled not to cry as she watched the two of them together. Even the dog had betrayed her. What was it with her and males? For the longest time, Vadim had been her anchor in this strange world. Because of him, she'd learned to carry on.

Now he'd gone and cut the rope. The weight of being truly lost was almost too heavy to bear.

She wanted to look at him, to see his eyes again. This was all a big misunderstanding. Nothing that couldn't be fixed if they talked. But Vadim's hair hung in a long dark veil, shielding him from her.

Tell him the truth. Make him believe you.

When he finally glanced at her, she knew it'd be pointless to try. In that one unguarded moment, she read in his eyes what he attempted to conceal. He hated her. A second later, the expression was gone, but the pain in her heart burned on.

"So, where do we go from here?" It was all she could do to keep her voice steady, but she wouldn't give him the satisfaction of seeing her in pieces. He couldn't have everything. No way.

Vadim dismissed Forge with a quiet word and stood up. "You admit it, then? You are Godric's creature."

Martha stared at his long fingers as they rested casually on the hilt of his sword. A shiver prickled along her spine. "Would you believe me if I said I wasn't?"

"Probably not," he admitted softly. His fingers tightened upon the sword handle. "But you should at least try and convince me."

"Or what?" Her blood chilled. "You'll kill me?" Is that

what he meant?

For the first time, she glimpsed Vadim the killer looking out at her from the cold dark depths of his eyes. Foolishly, she'd believed he was a pussycat of a man, and that none of the killing stuff was real. Now, as fear trickled into her heart, she realized her mistake.

She scrambled to her feet, staggering like a drunk, her mind reeling. "But you found me out on the hill that day!" She flung her arm out, pointing in the general direction. "You've seen my clothes, my phone. How can I be an agent for the Evil Earl? You're the first person I met here."

"So you claim." His mouth twisted into a harsh smile. "Your arrival was most conveniently timed, was it not?"

A hot ball of anger flashed up from her toes and into her chest, melting away her weakness. Let him think what he wanted.

"You've already made up your mind, haven't you? So, what's it to be, Vadim?" She marched over to him, her head held high. "Will you cut me down with your sword? Or, perhaps you'd prefer to stick me full of arrows, like the Earl's men did to your poor friend?" She snorted in revulsion. "For all your manners, you're no better than they are. You make me sick!"

At the mention of his fallen comrade, a chink of emotion cracked the impenetrable mask of Vadim's face. "You were with Guy when he died?" He pronounced the name so it rhymed with 'key'.

"Guy?" So, that was the name of her temporary guardian—or guard. "Of course I was with him. Who do you think buried him—the Earl's men?"

"I found his grave. I wondered if you had built it," Vadim said quietly. "Thank you for that, at least."

"I didn't do it for you. I did it for him. Stuff your thanks! It was the least I could do for someone who bled to death in my arms." She was pleased when she saw him flinch.

Good. I'll make you suffer before I die, you bastard!

"Yes, there was lots of blood, Vadim. I'm still covered in the stuff. Look." She thrust her hand close to his face. "I can't get it out from beneath my nails. See?"

Vadim closed his eyes and turned his head away.

Martha softened. Even now, despite everything, she loved him. "He told me to tell you that he'd tried to stop them," she said gently. "Why would I stay with him if I was meant to betray him, you utter fuckwit? Why would I bother burying him, hmm?"

"To convince me—"

"Oh, for the love of God!" Her simmering temper flashed back to a boil. *If he doesn't kill me soon, I might have to do it myself.* "You're just too fecking damaged to be saved."

She shoved him hard in his chest. He barely moved. The half-smile playing on his lips inflamed her even more. "Go on then. Do it!" She lashed out, slapping his stupid, handsome face. His smile vanished, and his eyes returned to stone slits. *Good!* "Kill me!" Her fingers tingled with the contact. She liked it and raised her hand to hit him again.

But he was ready for her this time, grasping her wrist as she launched her hand. "Witch!"

"If I were a witch, I'd turn you into a toad and stamp on you, mate," she snarled. She was going to die soon anyway. He couldn't do her any worse harm than that.

As Vadim hauled her closer, she struck out with her free hand, only narrowly missing his face. At the same time, she kicked at his shins. His grunt of pain gave her much satisfaction.

"Be still, you hellion!" Vadim roared, securing her flailing hands in one of his and holding them firmly behind her back. He trapped her foot between his legs, preventing from kicking him again. But she kept on struggling, her body writhing against his as he tried to secure her, cursing him with every vile name in her considerable repertoire. She was only dimly aware of Forge barking at them.

“Martha. Stop this!”

“Why should I?” Her hair flew wild about her face. “I’m not...going to make it easy for you to...kill me.”

“Kill you?” Vadim’s eyes narrowed. “I was angry, but I would never do you harm.”

That stopped her. “Wh...huh?” She looked up at him, panting from her exertions. “Why not?”

Rearrange these words, you idiot: Horse, gift, look, never, a, mouth, in, the!

“Does it matter?” He released her hands and stroked a tendril of hair back from her face. As his features relaxed, the ice retreated from his eyes and warmth returned. The Vadim she knew—or thought she knew—had returned.

“Yes. It matters.” He might be thawing, but she certainly wasn’t. She swatted his hand away and tried to take a step backwards. Unfortunately, her foot was still trapped firmly between his legs. She would have fallen were it not for his arm around her back.

He trailed his fingers down her cheek.

Did he have a split personality or something? “Will you please stop mauling me? And take your fecking hair out of my mouth!” She pushed uselessly against the hardness of his chest.

But he drew her nearer, leaning until their foreheads almost touched. His hair fell about them in a dark and private shelter, hiding them from the world, and he didn’t let her go.

Martha flinched beneath the heat of his gaze. Despite everything, after all he’d accused her of, her body responded to his nearness. Her legs wobbled, and heat flooded her veins. Imperceptibly, she swayed towards him.

Hello? Have you forgotten you thought he wanted to kill you only a few moments ago?

Apparently so. And she no longer cared. As if governed by his will, she slid her hands up his chest and linked them about the strong column of his neck. Vadim smiled. The small crooked one that always released killer butterflies into her stomach. She couldn't fight him. Not when she wanted him so badly.

"I really hate you," she murmured against his lips.

"I know," he replied softly. "And so you should."

***

When their lips touched, Vadim forgot everything except the woman in his arms. With a groan of hunger, he gathered her closer, crushing her soft, pliant body against him. Martha did not resist. Tangling her fingers in his hair, she opened her mouth and kissed him back, her tongue sliding irresistibly over his.

How I have missed her.

She moaned within his mouth, and the sound of her pleasure set his blood ablaze. Traitor or not, some things could not be faked. She might hate him, but she wanted him. But not nearly as much as he craved her.

Breathing fast, he cupped one of her soft buttock and held her to the hardness of his body. It would be easy to take her, to make her truly his.

In one smooth movement, he had her down on the ground, pinioned beneath him. Still she made no protest. Her arms only tightened about the back of his neck as she clung to him, demanding his kiss with a rising savagery. The taste of her made his head spin. He wanted to bury himself within her until everything else ceased to exist. What she was, what she had done, no longer mattered.

No woman had ever wielded such power over him.

Martha slipped her hands beneath his shirt and grazed her nails over the hot muscles of his back. He shuddered. The touch of her icy fingers upon his flesh was too good. Taking his lower lip between her teeth, she sucked on it, his body hardening with each pull. Just as he thought he would explode, she moved on, kissing her way along his jaw line.

He exhaled a shuddering breath. But the respite was all too brief. She pressed her lips to his ear, murmuring his name in a manner which was as bold as it was needful. The ache within him fast became unbearable.

He trembled in her arms, as though this was his first time with a woman. Cupping her face in his hands, he looked down into her dilated eyes. The heat of her rapid breaths scorched against his lips.

"What enchantment is this?" He lowered his hand, trailing his knuckles over the exposed swell of her breasts. She shivered and closed her eyes, arching her neck to entice him. Her response pleased him. "You truly are a witch, my love."

Martha's eyelids flickered open. She regarded him languidly, a tiny smile drifting over her lips. "Ssh." She pulled him down to kiss her, and Vadim had no thought of resisting. Burying his fingers in the thick, damp waves of her hair, he surrendered. Her will was his.

Gradually, their frenzied kisses became one deep and endless embrace. Though he was hardly aware of doing so, his hand moved, sliding beneath her skirt, tracing the curve of her calf. He squeezed gently then moved higher, brushing up the side of her knee to her lower thigh. The fever of her skin increased the further he explored, tantalising him, urging him on.

It took all the strength he had not to push ahead with his advance, though it cost him dear. He could barely hear the sound of his own labored breaths for the blood thundering through his head. The throbbing in his trews was becoming unendurable.

Then Martha arched beneath him, parting her thighs to accommodate him, beckoning him nearer. How he wished he could accept. Never had any invitation been so welcome. The softness of her body was as welcoming as a feather bed. It would be easy to assuage the hunger that devoured him from the inside. He longed to possess her whole, to end his suffering. The secrets of her body were there beneath him, waiting to be discovered, to be claimed as his own. Traitor or not, he wanted her.

And what of your honor? Can you set it aside so easily?

With effort, Vadim dragged his mouth away from the sweet oblivion of her kisses. *Easily? No.* Her small mewl of protest did nothing to ease his pain.

But he did not leave her yet. Breathing hard, he withdrew his hand from her hair and, leaning on one elbow, he trailed his fingers across her flushed face. Wordlessly, she looked up at him, a tiny crease forming on her brow. Reality was returning to her again. He watched the passion disperse from her eyes like the clouds after a summer storm.

Vadim watched and listened, committing every moment to memory, storing them with his most precious thoughts, along with the beloved inhabitants of days long ago.

He could not stop himself from touching her, stroking her, prolonging the bitter joy of her nearness. When Martha's hands slipped from beneath his shirt, he knew she was herself again. The expression in her eyes told him clearly what her mouth did not.

Her body tensed beneath him. She wanted him gone.

How long would it take to make her pliant and willing again?

'Twas a dangerous thought. Taking care not to squash her, he rolled away and stood up.

He proffered his hand down to her, but Martha ignored it and scrambled to her feet without his aid. She dusted herself off, adjusting the clothing that had come loose in the fervor of their passion. To his annoyance, she caught him looking at her as his eyes lingered a moment too long on the low neckline of her dress. With a little huff, she pulled her cloak about herself, hiding her luscious body from his sight. He experienced a pang of disappointment tinged with guilt.

With her head held high, Martha met his gaze. Now

her eyes were as cold as the winter snows.

"I didn't go all the way down into the village." Her voice was so quiet that he had to strain to hear her words. "If you must know, I spent the day on the ridge above Darumvale, watching what was going on. I couldn't come back until dusk in case the soldiers spotted me." She ran a hand over her hair in a useless attempt to tame its love-mussed beauty. "That's the truth, Vadim. Take it or leave it. I don't care if you believe me or not."

She turned away and, calling to Forge, walked back toward the cavern. She did not look back.

What a fool he was. He should have waited and let her explain. Instead, he had behaved like a savage. Why?

Because it would be safer for you if she was a traitor. The voice in his heart mocked him. *It is safer to hate than to love, is it not? Ah! She has you shackled now, my friend.*

With a swirl of his cloak, Vadim strode away into the night. The need to escape overwhelmed him. If he stayed, Martha's virtue and his honor would not live to see another sunrise.

Go on, run. His inner voice laughed. *For all your courage, you are nothing but a worthless coward.*

***

Martha watched him leave. After craving his presence for so long, she was now glad to see him go. What she needed was a little time to collect herself.

She tried to light the fire, but her hands trembled so badly she couldn't get a spark. She dropped the flint and it hit the ground with a thud. *Damn him!*

Forge whined, pleading for his supper, so she gave him a share of the remaining dried meat, and a little of the stale bread. "Sorry, lad. That's the best I can do."

Forge didn't mind. He wolfed his food down with quick enthusiasm. Once he was certain nothing else was on offer, he went outside to snuffle in the bushes for rabbits.

Martha wasn't hungry. How could she think of food after what had just happened?

When she eventually managed to light the fire, she sat for a long time, staring into the dancing flames, occasionally raising her fingers to her swollen lips. The memory of Vadim's kiss still lingered. But it meant nothing. Less than nothing. Hadn't she any pride at all? He'd made his feelings perfectly clear, yet she'd clung to him like an animal in heat. She cringed to think of it.

Can't you fall in love with a nice, honest bloke for a change?

She leaned over and threw another piece of wood onto the fire. *Ouch!* She sucked in her breath and pressed a hand to her aching ribcage. It felt bruised and sore. But that was hardly surprising after being pressed against the handles of Vadim's sword and dagger for so long—though she'd barely registered any discomfort at the time.

But it was nothing compared to the pain in her heart. The true nature of Vadim's 'friendship' was her worst injury. She'd trusted him, *loved him.* And all the time he'd been lying to her. He was her jailer. He'd never been her friend. Never.

"You stupid, stupid girl!" She chucked another log onto the fire then went in search of her bedroll.

Wide-eyed and sleepless, she lay for hours, staring at the fire, reliving each hurtful word and every bitter kiss. She was still too angry to cry.

As the light of the new day touched the horizon, sleep finally arrived to claim her.

Her last conscious though was that Vadim hadn't returned.

chapter twenty

AFTER A BRIEF AND TROUBLED sleep, Martha opened her gritty eyes to another beautiful day. There was still no sign of Vadim. He'd probably abandoned her for good this time.

Well, he can suit himself. I'm done with him and his paranoia. She refused to break her heart over another worthless bloke. How many months of her life had she wasted crying about Tony? Well, she wasn't about to do the same thing over Vadim.

Despite the early hour, it was already warm. Today promised to be even hotter than yesterday. Martha snuggled her face into Forge's neck as he lay beside her and closed her eyes, listening to the chorus of joyous birdsong. But the sounds didn't soothe her. If anything, her mood was even blacker than it'd been on the previous night.

Anger simmered in her guts, gnawing at her until she couldn't lie still another moment. Kicking off the blanket, she scrambled out of bed and grabbed her backpack, carelessly stuffing her paltry possessions into it. If Vadim ever decided to return, he wouldn't find her waiting for him like an expectant dog. *Damn him to hell!*

"C'mon, Forge." The dog was still asleep on the bedroll, snoring and twitching. She nudged him with her toe, making him jump. "Get up, you lazy old thing.

We're leaving."

***

As the sun reached its zenith, Vadim arrived back at the cave, a couple of rabbits swinging in his hand.

Martha was nowhere to be seen. Where had she gone now?

But a quick search of the cavern told him this was not another of her exploratory jaunts. Her bedroll and pack were gone. Nothing remained to indicate she had any intention of returning. His heart quickened, whether due to anger or concern he could not tell.

The infuriating little witch!

He had spent much of the previous night deep in thought, examining his uncharacteristic behaviour and wondering at the cause of it. Since Martha had entered his life, Vadim hardly recognised himself anymore. She vexed and inflamed him by turn and seemed to deliberately set out to court his blackest moods. Not only was she stubborn, wilful, and devious, her lack of propriety frequently shocked him. Hardly the kind of woman any man would choose for a wife. She was altogether terrible.

He kicked a small stone with unnecessary force and sent it clattering about the cavern. Something on the floor drew his eye. He crouched down and picked up an old sock. One of his. Turning it over in his hands, he recognised the haphazard darning on the heel. As he traced his finger over the stitches, his heart twisted. Martha's work.

Despite the warning in his head, she had somehow managed to creep beneath his skin and find a place within his stony heart. He smiled and tucked the sock into his jerkin. Not only was she the most beautiful woman he had ever laid eyes on, but she was kind, generous, fearless, and altogether diverting.

Truly, she was perfection in a womanly form. She made him smile when he thought he had forgotten how.

How could he not love her?

He had returned to camp with the express intention of telling her so, directly after begging her forgiveness, of course. His conduct on the previous night had been utterly vile.

Now she had denied him even that. He ground his teeth. When he caught up with her, he would throttle her. Or perhaps he should spank her instead? His lips curved into a grim smile. Both prospects were equally appealing.

***

It was good to be on the move, to be doing something again, instead of sitting back and waiting for life to happen.

Martha marched along at a brisk pace, her arms swinging by her sides. As the warm sunshine caressed her skin, she finally noticed the beauty of the new day. Forge bounded ahead, following the trail they'd taken on the day Guy had died.

Since returning to Darumvale was out of the question, she set her sights on Edgeway. Of course, she'd need money to establish herself there. Perhaps she should take Guy's horse and sell it? *Yes. That might work.* She couldn't leave the poor creature to starve in that overgrown paddock.

For once, she had no fear of the unknown. Anger and betrayal still burned too brightly within her heart. What was left to fear? She'd lost her home world. Except for her own miserable life, what did she have to lose?

Making plans was good. It stopped her mind from dwelling in dark places.

When she reached Edgeway, she'd need to find lodgings and some form of employment. Once she was settled, she'd ask around about this Madoc the Seer fellow—if he even existed. He was probably yet another of Vadim's lies. She wouldn't put anything past that man. And to think, she had— No. It was best not to dwell on it.

Forget about him, Bigalow. The man you loved never existed.

He was an actor playing a role, one designed to suit his own twisted purposes. *Ooh, but he was slick!* He'd known how vulnerable she was, yet he'd deceived her without mercy. Martha scowled and quickened her pace. Two-timing Tony now looked snowy innocent in comparison with such a hardened player as Vadim.

He didn't have a heart. Just a swinging brick attached to a bit of rope.

She should have left him long ago. The sooner she got away the better.

It would take all day to get back down the hill if she dawdled. Martha broke into a jog. She was finished with dawdling. For good.

***

Vadim tracked her as far as the ruins of the old Miller homestead. He crouched in the dust and traced his fingers around the outline of a horseshoe. The freshest tracks did nothing to hearten him. Martha must have taken Guy's horse. He did not need one of Ma's visions to guess her destination.

"Oh, Martha," he murmured. "What have you done?"

Cold needles of fear pricked his spine. If anything happened to her he would never recover from it. All the blame would lie at his feet.

He got up from the dirt and looked along the road in the direction she had taken. He could not let her go. Not now. He would make her listen. There was still some hope. Although she was angry, he knew she bore some gentler feelings for him.

First, he needed a horse. He could have run to Edgeway, but that would only extend Martha's lead. The less time she spent without him, the happier he would be. By all the Spirits, he prayed she would stay safe until he found her again.

***

It was early evening when they reached the lake which bordered of the town of Edgeway, and the sun was already descending in the sky. For the first time that day, Martha felt a nervous fluttering in the pit of her stomach. She ignored it and rode on.

They'd made good time, her riding confidence increasing with every mile. Although it'd been years since she'd done any riding, Guy's horse proved himself a total sweetheart. He obligingly ambled or cantered as required, without any unnecessary skittering.

As they rounded a sharp bend in the road, she reined the horse into a gentle stop and dismounted, absently rubbing at her aching buttocks. It seemed she wasn't going to be alone for much longer.

Edgeway sprawled before them in a messy tangle of narrow streets.

Most of the dwellings were single-storied, not unlike those of Darumvale. But interspersed amongst them were several larger establishments with two, three, and even four floors. These larger buildings leaned precariously, their roofs almost touching 'heads' with their opposing neighbor.

There were people everywhere, milling around like ants as they went about their daily business. After spending weeks in a place with so few inhabitants, the crowds came as a bit of a shock. The last time she'd encountered this many people had been on a shopping trip back home.

What a noise.

After the peace of Darumvale, her ears flinched from the sounds now assaulting them. The constant chatter and laughter combined with the neighing of horses and the rumbling of carts was deafening.

Forge whined and looked up as if to say, *You wanted*

to come here? Fine, we've seen it. Can we go home now?

Martha stroked his big head and smiled. "I know how you feel, sweetie. I wish we were back in Darumvale too." She never thought she'd actually miss the place. *And not only Darumvale.* "Oh, shut up!"

Forge looked up, startled at the sharpness of her voice.

"Not you," she said more gently. "I was talking to myself." Martha gave a heavy sigh. "Anyway, we're here now. We'll just have to make the best of it. Let's see if we can find a place to stay, hmm?"

In the end, she didn't have the heart to sell the horse. Its gentle disposition had won her over. Besides, she'd already named him Eric. With a mental apology to the dead outlaw, she shamelessly looted Guy's leather saddlebags, looking for something she could use to finance her stay in Edgeway. To her relief, she discovered a small hoard of gold and silver jewelery hidden away in a small linen pouch. She selected a brooch from the treasure and traded it for a week's livery at the local stables. The master of the yard gave her a small ceramic disc in exchange for the brooch. A receipt of sorts, she supposed.

Giving Eric a final pat, Martha watched as a gangling stable lad lead him away.

Transaction completed, the Master gave Martha a dismissive grunt before resuming his seat on his tiny stool. With his eyes firmly fixed on the happenings of his yard, the man fumbled beneath his seat with his dirty fingers and picked up what looked like a piece of old chicken bone from the floor. Raising it to his mouth, he began picking at his discolored teeth.

Martha grimaced. "Er...do you happen to know of a place where I might trade goods for money?"

The man looked up, removing the bone from his mouth. "My brother's shop, miss," he said, gesturing with his tooth pick to a narrow building farther along the street. "Emery is a decent man. He will offer thee a fair price for anything you have to sell."

She had little choice but to take him at his word.

With a word of thanks, Martha pocketed the ceramic disc and flung the saddlebags over her shoulder. She took a deep breath and set out on the next part of her mission: To obtain money for her own accommodation.

The swirling crowds paid her no attention at all. Gradually, she stopped feeling conspicuous and began to relax. No one pointed at her, or cried out: *You're not one of us. You must be from another world.* Just like back in the twenty-first century, people here were much too intent on their own affairs.

The smell was almost indescribably bad. Her nose permanently wrinkled as she moved through the crowds. The stench of unwashed bodies combined unpleasantly with the odors of cooking and...feces? She glanced down at the gutter that ran along the street. In the glow of the torch lights, she saw lumps bobbing along in dark liquid. *Oh, God!*

"It's just poo, Bigalow." Stepping carefully over the gutter, she lead Forge through a doorway and into the shop the horse master had indicated.

She emerged a short time later, smiling and extremely satisfied with how the transaction had gone. Emery had given her a small leather pouch of coins in exchange for one of Guy's gold chains—she tried not to imagine where he might have got it from. Even better, the shop owner had told her of a place where a single lady might obtain clean, safe lodgings for the night.

She set off down the narrow street, hoping to find the place before it got much darker. Unlike Darumvale at this hour, Edgeway still teamed with the full spectrum of humanity. Rich and poor mingled freely and, from what Martha could see, frequently lived right next door to one another.

Beggars sat out on the street, begging bowls in hand, many of them missing limbs or disfigured by the ravages of disease. Other more industrious souls played a flute or a fiddle for their charity. Despite the sad circumstances, the merry tunes gave Edgeway almost a party atmosphere.

Emery's directions were good, and Martha soon found herself standing outside a small house on a quiet branch off the main street. "This must be it," she said to Forge, then rapped her knuckles against a plain wooden door.

The door opened and light spilled out onto the street. A plump, wholesome-looking woman stood on the threshold, regarding her visitors through narrowed eyes. "Yes?"

"Mistress Weaver?" Martha smiled uncertainly. "Emery Littleback sent me. He said you might have a room available?"

"Did he indeed?" The woman looked her up and down. "And you are?"

"Martha...Martha Bigalow." She felt herself wilting beneath Mistress Weaver's detailed inspection. Those shrewd grey eyes were taking in every inch of her travel-worn appearance. A little self-consciously, she drew her cloak over her blood-stained dress. As Aunt Lulu was fond of saying, first impressions lasted a lifetime.

"And I suppose I must accommodate the dog too?" Mistress Weaver gave Forge to a long, hard stare.

Undeterred, Forge sat down and thumped his tail, subjecting the landlady to his most appealing look.

Martha almost giggled at such an uncommon display of good behavior. "If that's no trouble. I assure you, he's a very good housedog."

"Come inside, if you will." Mistress Weaver took a step back. "I would speak with you first before making my decision." Her thin lips curved into a faint smile. "This is a decent house, you understand. One cannot be too wary in these dangerous times."

Martha smiled politely. "I couldn't agree more."

She stepped off the darkening street into a bright, snug room. A large, colorful rag-rug lay before the hearth, and four mismatched chairs, each with a plump, bright cushion, sat arranged around the glowing fire. Against the rough, white-washed walls, two wooden settles provided additional seating. The sweet fragrance of spring permeated the air thanks to the small vase of flowers sitting on a small wooden table in the corner.

Martha immediately felt at ease. Although the furnishings were undoubtedly old, everything looked clean and well loved.

After asking her to take a seat, Mistress Weaver left the room. She returned moments later carrying a small tray set with a teapot, two cups, and a plate of home-baked cakes.

Martha's mouth watered. It seemed forever since she'd eaten anything that wasn't either hard, or stale or both.

"Do you care for tea, miss? I know it is shockingly expensive these days, but one cannot be expected to give up every comfort." The older woman's previously severe expression was gone, melted away by the warmth of her smile.

"Proper tea?" Martha widened her eyes. "Really?" How long was it since she'd last tasted tea?

Forge sprawled out on the rug in front of the fire while Martha and her prospective landlady drank their tea. True, it was served black and unsweetened, but she couldn't remember when she'd enjoyed a beverage more. In between slurps, she almost single-handedly demolished the plate of cakes set before her.

Mistress Weaver arched her eyebrows. "By the Sprits! How long is it since you last ate?"

"Something as good as this? Months." She dabbed at the crumbs at the side of her mouth with her finger and grinned. "Sorry. I'm not usually such a glutton." She stifled a contented little burp with the back of her hand. "Excuse me."

"It is nice to have someone who appreciates my baking. In truth," Mistress Weaver leaned forward, almost displacing the large mop cap she wore on her head, "there are few people who linger in town these days. Especially since the arrival of spring."

Martha's heart sank. "Let me guess: the Evil Earl?"

"Indeed." The landlady nodded and her smile cooled by a degree. "Lord Edgeway frequents the town all too often these days, along with his dissolute host of men." She sighed. "If only the winter snows would encase Edgeway castle all year long. We would all be a good deal happier."

Martha almost upset the cup of tea in her hand, but she managed to save it at the last moment. "I-is the castle nearby?" The landlady would have needed to be both blind and deaf not to recognize her distress.

"It lies a league to the north. Calm yourself, my dear." Mistress Weaver patted Martha's hand. "Although the Earl is much about town, he seldom visits this quarter." She pursed her lips in obvious disapproval. "The bordellos and taverns he frequents are at the other end of Edgeway, thank the spirits."

Martha exhaled and leaned back in her chair. A league was roughly three miles away. That was much too close for comfort. But what else could she do? She had to stay somewhere, and the chances of the Earl stumbling across her in a town of this size were minimal, surely? Even if he did, he probably wouldn't recognise her as Vadim's female companion of last autumn.

"So," Mistress Weaver continued, "tell me about yourself. What did you say your name was, my dear?"

"I'm Martha. Martha Bigalow."

"And where is your husband, Mistress Bigalow? How come you to be so alone and..." The good lady glanced at Martha's filthy dress again. "With so few possessions?"

"Please call me Martha." She gave a heartfelt sigh. "I won't lie to you." She was oh-so sick of lies. "I recently separated from the man I called 'husband'." That was true enough at least. "My reasons for doing so are my own." She met the landlady's eyes unwaveringly. "All you need know is that I'm a decent woman who's come to

Edgeway seeking employment. I'm honest, and a hard worker, and I have no love at all for the Earl."

Mistress Weaver nodded but didn't interrupt.

"What you see now is who I am. I have no home or family. Apart from my dog and horse, I'm on my own." She sighed again. It was a very weary sound. "Won't you please give me a chance? I have money. Look." She pulled the leather pouch from her pocket and jangled it. "See? I promise I won't cause you any trouble."

Mrs Weaver tutted impatiently. "Put it away, girl. Money holds no sway over me." But she smiled. "I saw what I needed to see when I first looked into your eyes, out there on the street. Yes, you will do for me, Mistress Bigalow...Martha."

chapter twenty-one

As Vadim reached the borders of Darumvale, he saw curls of thick, black smoke drifting upward, defiling the blue perfection of the sky.

His heart quickened. *No! Not now.*

He ran toward the village, drawing the mask over his face as he went, praying the *others* were not far behind him. As he drew nearer, the terrified screams reminded him of a long-ago day, back when he had lost everything he held dear. Despite the heat of the sun, he shivered.

A small hill at the eastern edge of the village afforded him a good view of the Earl's treachery. At first, no one noticed him, standing against the skyline.

Other matters occupied them.

The villagers stood at the center of the main street, surrounded by soldiers, huddled together like frightened cattle. The Earl, meanwhile, strolled around the perimeter of the human circle. Although Vadim was not close enough to make out Lord Edgeway's words, the calm hum of his voice and its rising inflection at the end told him he was questioning the villagers.

When their response, or lack of one, did not suit him, the Earl waved to one of the waiting archers. Seconds later, a burning arrow arced into the sky. Tinder-dry thatch roofs did not take long to catch light.

Six houses were already burning. Vadim clenched his fists, aching to break them upon the Earl's smirking face. Instead, he drew his bow and strung it, his jaw clenched with rage. He reached back for an arrow. Martha was beyond his aid now. He could not abandon the villagers. He notched the arrow and took aim. The wooden bow gave a few creaks of protest, its complaints as familiar as the voice of an old friend.

She will survive.

For all her strange ways, Martha was clever and resourceful. He let the arrow fly. A scream announced when it struck its mark. Vadim barely noticed. He reached back for the second arrow, and Martha's face swam before him like a beautiful ghost. If he died today, she would never know what she really meant to him. She would go to her own grave believing he despised her. He released the arrow, the action cold and mechanical. Another death cry.

Perhaps it is better this way. If she hated him, she would recover. He would not have her mourn him.

The soldiers saw him at last. Calling to one another, they crept toward his position, weapons drawn, ducking and weaving to avoid his arrows. Vadim was dimly aware of the Earl screaming out orders. He danced around like a madman, his cloak swirling in a purple blur. Were the situation not so dire, the agitation of his enemy would have been amusing.

Vadim fired another arrow, then another. He lost count. How many more did he have?

There was not time to check.

While Vadim distracted their captors, the villagers pushed against the remaining soldiers and broke out of their bar-less cage. With a collective cry of anger, they turned on their enemy.

Vadim smiled to see it.

Using whatever they could find as a weapon—sticks, pitchforks, or hoes—the villagers surged against the Earl's men. The soldiers lashed out with their swords at the advancing crowd. Several bodies fell. Undeterred, the villagers continued to advance, their faces bearing identical expressions of murderous rage. Those without weapons picked up stones, hurling them at the soldiers with deadly force, the aim of the women as accurate as any man.

No more arrows.

Vadim threw down his bow and drew his sword. Taking a deep breath, he raced down the hill to engage his enemy hand to hand.

The long plaintive note of a horn turned his head. His heart soared. *I knew they would come.* A dozen masked men joined the fray. On foot and on horseback, they swarmed into Darumvale, weapons drawn.

The air rang with cries of pain and vengeance. Blades crashed together in a deadly dance, the hideous high-pitched squeal of metal upon metal setting his teeth on edge.

Vadim reached the bottom of the hill. Swinging his sword, he sliced it into his first opponent. The wet sound of human flesh being split open by a sword was the worst sound of all. In one swift move, the soldier's torso gaped from neck to stomach, blood jetting out in a black arc. Vadim swiftly wiped the thick, warm droplets from his eyes and spat onto the dust. But the sweet metallic tang lingered on his tongue. The smell and taste of it sickened him as it always did.

Wide-eyed with shock, the young soldier looked down, watching his guts spill onto the dust in a fast-unravelling coil. Mercifully, he fell down dead seconds later.

Vadim moved on, slipping in the soldier's steaming entrails as he engaged his next opponent, a stocky man-at-arms, clad in gleaming mail from head to thigh. Without hesitation, Vadim raised his arm, plunging the tip of his sword into the man's exposed throat. With a gargling moan of agony, the soldier crumpled to his knees. Vadim withdrew his sword, leaving the man clutching at his ruined neck.

He moved on, mindlessly hacking his way through the enemy line. But even with the villagers' aid, the Earl's men held the advantage not only in numbers, but in skill too. Farmers and trades people were no match for well-armed, highly-trained soldiers—however willing their hearts.

"Vadim!" The cry of warning came a heartbeat too late.

Pain flared so violently, he could not tell where he was wounded. Gasping, he sank to his knees. His sword slid from his hand, hitting the ground with a thud. His life blood pattered into the dust and swirled about the sword's hilt like a muddy river.

It was over.

Dragging his gaze up, Vadim saw his killer standing over him, a silhouette against the sun, sword raised for the final cut.

Vadim heard a roar of rage. Only Seth's intervention prevented his own beheading. In the dim light of his fading vision, he witnessed his old friend stab the soldier savagely through the neck with a pitchfork, freeing his blood in a fast-spurting fountain.

No longer able to support his own weight, Vadim collapsed onto his back, staring up at the fat clouds drifting across the perfect sky.

Martha. His mouth formed her name, but no sound came. Death held no fear for him. It was a blessed release from the pain of living, a time of joyful reunions. *She* was his only regret. *My love.*

"Hold on, son." Seth's gore-spattered face loomed over

him. "You will be fine." But his eyes spoke the opposite of his words. As the sun went out, Vadim felt a firm pressure on his abdomen. One bright flash of agony, and then there was no more pain.

"Stay, m'lord. I will not lose you too."

Vadim tried to smile. *Poor Seth. This battle is already over.*

But blackness took him before he could tell him so.

chapter twenty-two

"I am afraid this is the only bed I have at present." Mistress Weaver hovered in the doorway, twisting her apron in her hands. "But most of my other guests will be leaving on the morrow—travelling east for a wedding, so I understand—so you might choose a larger room then. That is, if you care to stay."

Martha walked about the little room and ducked her head beneath the eaves. The floorboards creaked loudly beneath her boots. Like the rest of the boarding house, the attic room had a cozy feel to it.

Set back against a triangular wall of honey-colored stone was a narrow bed. It looked snug and inviting. A huge patchwork quilt covered the mattress, spilling down the side of the bed and obscuring the polished floorboards beneath a tumble of generous folds. To the left of the bed was a low table, with a pitcher and bowl for washing. An oval-shaped sheet of polished metal lay propped against the stone wall—presumably in lieu of a mirror.

Beneath the solitary window sat a large wooden trunk, topped with even more patchwork—this time in the form of three fat cushions. Mistress Weaver certainly liked her crafting.

"Well? What say you?"

Forge had settled himself on the long rag-rug at the

foot of the bed. His eyes were already closed.

"We'll take it. Thank you." Martha turned to Mistress Weaver with a smile. "It reminds me a little bit of my old room back home." Home. Back in twenty-first century. Would she ever see it again?

On her first night in Edgeway, Martha lay in bed, staring up at the shadows on the roof, long after the rest of the household had retired. As the street sounds gradually died away, a thick silence enveloped the house. It hurt her ears. It was almost a relief when she heard a drunken man, singing his way home in the street outside. She listened harder. Snores drifted up from the rooms below. She exhaled. *I miss his snores.*

She touched the linen neckline of her night shirt and held it to her lips. It was Vadim's old shirt—the indecent one. On impulse, she'd stuffed it into her pack on the day she left Darumvale. It was all she had left of him now. It didn't even smell of him anymore.

She sent a silent prayer of thanks to whichever kindly spirit had accompanied her that day. It was hard to believe she'd been a fugitive in the wilds only a few brief hours ago. Now, she was warm and safe, and nursing a stomach full of good things. Not only that, she had money, transport, and a kindly landlady with definite 'friend' potential.

You have a lot to be thankful for, Bigalow.

Even so, she couldn't help regretting all she'd lost. How were her friends in Darumvale that night? With the Earl and his men as guests, she doubted they were resting as easily as she was. Would she ever see any of them again?

She sighed. Of course, losing Vadim was the deepest cut of all. Despite all that had happened, she'd harbored a secret hope in her heart. A hope that he'd come and find her again. The fact he hadn't, only confirmed what she already knew. He'd never really cared for her at all.

She raised her fingers to scratch at a tickle on her ear. To her surprise, she discovered it was wet. *When did I start crying?* Apparently, quite some time ago. The pillow was damp with tears.

Forge jumped up onto the bed and she flung her arms about him, sobbing silently into his fur. The big dog tolerated her misery with admirable stoicism. He made a few grumbles of concern, occasionally licking at her hand or face, but he didn't pull away.

You just had to go and fall for him, didn't you? The Vadim you love doesn't exist. He's an actor, a fraud, a heartless con artist. What the hell are you crying for?

Because it feels like losing Santa Claus all over again, that's why.

Ridiculous, but all the same it was true—not that she had a penchant for well-upholstered blokes with white beards. As a child, the day she'd finally accepted Santa wasn't real was the day she lost something vital to her happiness. Belief? Faith? Another layer of innocence stripped away? She still had no idea.

Losing Vadim felt the same, only worse. Much worse.

As the weeks passed, Martha gradually adapted to her new situation.

It wasn't easy. At times, she had to force herself out of bed in the morning. But she did what she had to do, going through the motions of normality. A fall from so high up, teetering on the tightrope of misery, would send her plunging into the cold, black abyss of depression. And that was one place she didn't want to go. Not in a world without antidepressants.

Life goes on, and you will too. Somehow.

Edgeway was nothing like Darumvale. The pace of life

was faster, louder, and much more vibrant. People constantly came and went, seldom lingering longer than the time it took to complete their business.

By the end of her first month, Martha could spot an outlander in a crowd from a hundred paces. It was more than the style of their clothes—though it was always a giveaway. The people from the villages appeared timid in comparison with their Big Town cousins. They constantly looked around them, suspicion glinting in their narrowed eyes, as they scurried from place to place like frightened mice.

She'd probably looked the same once upon a time. Not anymore. With a small smile of satisfaction, she smoothed her hands over the skirt of her new blue dress. With the proceeds of Guy's ill-gotten gains, she'd more than rectified the deficits of her pitiful, wardrobe.

Having nice things did much to sweeten the bitter pill of loss.

Thanks to an introduction from Mistress Weaver, Martha was now an employee of 'Abel's Rest', a large inn on the other side of town. Not that she ever mixed with the customers. Her role was in the laundry room, from six until noon every day. Although it was hot, heavy, steamy work, it was exactly what she needed.

The other women who worked in the laundry were friendly, often rowdy companions. In their cheerful company, it was impossible to dwell on the dark thoughts that occupied her solitary hours.

In a weird way, scrubbing the filth from other people's linen, elbows deep in vats of hot water, helped remove the unpleasant stains from her heart. She loved to see the lines of clean garments, flapping in the warm sunshine like prayer flags.

Vadim didn't come.

As the days turned into weeks, she stopped expecting to see him on every street corner. She no longer looked for him or imagined seeing him in a crowd. Gradually, her ears stopped straining to hear his voice. He wasn't coming. Vadim had finally let her go.

This is it. I'm really on my own now.

Martha began making inquiries about Madoc the Seer—though she suspected he was yet another of Vadim's many lies. To her surprise, she discovered that a wise man of that very name actually did exist. By all accounts, he was rather an odd chap who roamed the country all year round. He usually arrived in Edgeway for his annual fleeting visit around harvest time.

It couldn't hurt to see the man, at least. Autumn wasn't that long to wait. Who knew? With a bit of luck, old Madoc might be able to send her home again.

God knows there's nothing left for me here now.

As time passed, she stopped worrying about the Earl. Although she occasionally encountered his soldiers in the street, she saw nothing of the man himself, and her fear of discovery lessened with each day. No one knew her as the one-time 'wife' of a notorious outlaw. In Edgeway, Martha was just another nameless face in a heaving sea of humanity. And that suited her just fine.

She still had a niggling concern about the fate of her Darumvale friends, though. On more than one occasion, she saddled Eric and set off to pay them a visit, only to turn back after several miles. What would she say when she got there? And what if she encountered Vadim? This was enough to send her trotting back to the anonymous sanctuary Edgeway provided. Maybe the past was better off left where it was.

Even so, she began haunting the weekly market in the town square. Although she scanned the face of every stallholder, to her disappointment, she never saw anyone she knew.

The growing anxiety for her friends made Martha bolder. As she got to know the stallholders, she gently quizzed them for information. No one ever had any news, and more than one person shared her concerns. The villagers of Darumvale had always attended the market regularly up until this year. Several people she spoke to promised to make inquiries of their own.

Someone must know something. Why can't someone hurry up and invent a postal service?

Lord Edgeway's anger with Darumvale, however, was a common topic of conversation in Edgeway. The hamlet was a nest for outlaws, or so the gossips claimed. Although Martha despised herself for listening to them, she was too starved for information to have the luxury of morals. What alternative did she have?

Martha moved away from the vegetable stall, clutching her basket, inwardly brooding over the latest dead end in her enquiries.

"Excuse me?" A pleasant male voice recalled her to the present.

"Hmm?" She looked up into the smiling gray eyes of a stranger.

"Forgive my impertinence, m'lady, but I could not help overhearing your conversation just now."

Despite the warmth of the day, Martha drew her shawl closer about her, as though it could protect her from the man's attentions. "My conversation is none of your business, sir." With that, she turned away and plunged into the crowd, hoping he would take the hint and get lost.

He didn't. But although he kept pace with her as she wove a path through the throng, he was careful not to invade her personal space.

"I was raised in Darumvale," he said. "My family still resides there to this day. Though, I confess, I have been unable to visit them for quite some time. The call of duty cannot be ignored."

Hackles rising, Martha came to an abrupt halt. She turned to confront the man, almost hitting him in the stomach with her basket in the process. Every hair on the back of her neck tingled in warning, like a medieval spider-woman. "Let's get this straight." Her eyes narrowed. "*You* are from Darumvale?"

"Have I not just said so, dear lady?" The man's smile widened, his eyes twinkling merrily. He was only slightly taller than she, but he was broad and strong. His hair fell in golden waves about his attractive face.

"How *convenient*!"

"A happy coincidence indeed," the stranger agreed, apparently immune to her sarcasm. "I had not imagined to hear the name of my home being uttered by lips so—"

"Save your flattery, mate," Martha snapped. "Do you really think I'm stupid enough to fall for one of your chat-up lines? Even I'm not that dense. Get lost!"

"You think me a liar? A common swindler?" The man placed one hand on the handle of her basket, detaining her when she would have escaped. He wasn't smiling now.

Inexplicably, Martha shivered.

"Will you not allow me to introduce myself before dismissing me so cruelly?" he continued, not waiting for her to reply. "I am Anselm." He bowed his head. "Son of Seth and Sylvie—"

That got her attention. "You're kidding me?" Her eyes widened and she stopped trying to pull her basket free. This was their son—Vadim's surrogate brother?

"Upon my honor, I speak the truth." The man let go of the basket's handle and took a step back. "Surely they must have mentioned me?"

Suddenly, she felt a little sorry for him. "No," she admitted. "They didn't. But I wasn't with them for very long so..."

"I see." A shadow of regret swept over Anselm's handsome features. "Then, they have still not yet forgiven me." He gave a heavy sigh. "I should have known." Drawing himself to his full height, he gave Martha a stiff little bow. "My apologies for detaining you, m'lady. I meant no disrespect."

"Wait." This time, it was she who prevented him from leaving, clutching at the sleeve of his linen shirt, and releasing it the moment he turned back to face her. "Look, I'm sorry, okay?" She forced an apologetic smile. "I thought you were a pervert or something."

The man looked a little sour. "An honest mistake to make, I am certain."

Martha giggled. She couldn't help it. Now she looked at him, she was sure she glimpsed something of Seth in his features, and his grey eyes held more than a hint of Sylvie. The familiarity gave her comfort. "Sorry. How about we start again?" She stuck out her hand. "I'm Martha. How do you do?"

Anselm's smile returned. Taking her hand, he raised it to his lips and planted a light kiss on the back of it. "I do very well indeed, Martha. It is my greatest pleasure to know you." He released her hand before she had time to become uncomfortable. "Perhaps you would do me the honor of allowing me to walk with you?" He offered her his arm. "I should love to speak of home above all things."

Martha hesitated, but only for a moment. She slipped her hand through Anselm's arm and smiled up at him. "And I'd love to hear you speak of it," she replied. He couldn't imagine how much. Until that moment, she hadn't realized how lonely she'd been.

For the remainder of the afternoon, they wandered aimlessly about the town. Martha couldn't later recall where their path had taken them. The hours passed as swiftly as minutes. Anselm proved to be a most amusing companion, and his stories about Darumvale sent her into fits of laughter. He was a gifted, if brutal, mimic. His impersonations of various villagers were so deadly accurate, she almost wept with laughter on more than one occasion.

Her fears faded away. Anselm was undoubtedly who he said he was. His knowledge of the village was too intimate to be an act. Even so, she was reluctant to reveal too much about herself just yet. For now, she was content to let him do most of the talking. She'd spent so long looking over her shoulder that it was a difficult habit to break. Ma's long-ago words still haunted her. *You will be betrayed by someone close, someone you consider a friend...*

If Anselm noticed the one-sided nature of their conversation, he made no comment. He obviously enjoyed telling his stories as much as she enjoyed hearing them.

Only when the sun hung low in the sky did she realize, with a start of surprise, just how long they had been out walking.

"I have to go," she said, pulling her hand from the crook of Anselm's arm. "My landlady will be wondering where I am."

"Shall I escort you home?"

"There's no need. I don't live far from here." In truth, she was reluctant to reveal her address too quickly, no matter how charming Anselm appeared to be. It suddenly occurred to her that he hadn't mentioned Vadim at all. That struck her as rather odd, considering the two of them had been raised together.

Anselm nodded, almost as if he understood. "Then, promise to meet me tomorrow or I shall not let you go." For good measure, he clutched at his heart and attempted a wounded look.

"Idiot." Her laughter chased away the shadows of suspicion, and she found herself agreeing to meet him the next day.

And so it began. After only a few days, Martha became aware that their burgeoning friendship was fast becoming something very special to her. Barely a day went by when they didn't meet up with Anselm somewhere in town, if only for a few minutes. His light-hearted company was the perfect tonic for her jaded spirits. With Anselm, the pain of the past went away for a while. He felt familiar. Safe. And he never mentioned Vadim once. Not ever. With Anselm, she could forget. In effect, he was a walking, talking Band-Aid for her beaten-up heart.

Their daily meanderings through Edgeway drew frequent disapproving looks from the townspeople. Martha often felt the heavy weight of their disapproving glares following her as she and Anselm passed by. They probably thought it was unseemly for an unrelated man and woman to be out together without a chaperone or something.

Not that she gave a damn what complete strangers thought about her. Her relationship with Anselm was completely appropriate. He brightened her days, and never once put a toe over the line of friendship.

"Why don't you ever talk about your job?" Martha asked. They were sitting in one of Anselm's favourite taverns having lunch, and it was his turn to pay. "I mean, you let me go on and on about my work in the laundry, but you've never once mentioned what it is that you do." It had begun to niggle her a little by now. Why didn't he talk about his job? He was always so open about everything else. Well, apart from Vadim.

"Ah, that." Anselm gave a wry smile. "I wondered when you would ask." He picked up a large pottery jug from the deeply pitted table and refilled their tankards with ale. "Perhaps that is because my employer is...not exactly popular in these parts."

"Oh?" Martha's heart jumped from a walk to a gallop.

Anselm nodded. "You have guessed the rest, I can see it in your eyes." He put down the jug and leaned closer, looking at her with unusual seriousness. "I work in the Earl's stables, Martha." He spoke in a low voice, though there was little danger of being overheard. The tavern echoed with loud talk and laughter, and a couple of drunks were singing lustily from the corner of the room.

"I tend Lord Edgeway's horses, nothing more. In return, he pays me well and provides me with comfortable accommodation." Anselm shrugged his shoulders. "Little wonder you now look at me in that way. My revelation had much the same effect on my parents when I told them. I suppose now you will say, I am sorry, Anselm, but I have just recalled something I have forgotten to do." He sat back in his chair and held up his hands. "So be it. You are free to stay or go as you will, m'lady. I shall not attempt to sway you."

In fact, that was precisely what she'd been about to say. But Anselm looked so miserable that she couldn't bear to prove him right. "Is that what your parents can't forgive you for?" she asked. "Working for the Earl?" Her heart resumed its natural rhythm, once she was assured Anselm wasn't about to sprout horns and start breathing fire.

He nodded. "They took the news very badly indeed."

"Can you blame them?" Martha leaned over the table toward him. "You know the things he's done better than anyone."

"Aye," he agreed quietly. "But why should I not seek to improve my lot in life?" He looked suddenly fierce, gripping her hands as they lay on the table. "Whether it is Godric or...someone else, there will always be an Earl of Edgeway to grind the little people beneath his boot. Noble principles are all very well, but they do not feed us, and they do not keep us safe." He released her hands and flopped back in his chair, a scowl marring his fair brow. "I will not share my parents' fate.

"You have seen how they live, Martha." He gave a snort of disgust. "Has resisting the Earl and harboring outlaws brought them happiness? Are their lives so much better than mine? I think not." He raked one hand through his golden hair. "The more they fight him, the more harshly he is forced to treat them. What else can he do? What example does it set for the rest of the populace when the Chief of Darumvale will not give the Earl his rightful dues? They force him to make an example of them."

Martha said nothing. Clutching her tankard in both hands, she considered Anselm's words. When he put it like that... She gave herself a mental shake. And what about Vadim, the child who'd grown alongside him as a brother? The Earl had massacred his family. There was no excuse for that.

Of course, she couldn't say this to Anselm, not without betraying Vadim's confidence. Even now, she was still protecting him, though there was no good reason why she should. What if Vadim's 'tragedy' was a lie too? No. She'd seen his eyes that day, out on the hill. Suffering like that couldn't be faked. Sadly, that particular truth was gospel.

Anselm smiled, recalling Martha from her thoughts. His face relaxed, tension gone. "You are still here. I admit, m'lady, I am surprised."

"Why?" She shrugged and took a sip of her ale. "Politics have never interested me. Your problems with your family are your concern, Anselm. I'd just like to know they're all right, that's all."

"I can help you there, at least." He glanced about him and beckoned her closer. "What I am about to tell you must go no further. My master only told me this out of kindness, for he knew how I would fret if news of the uprising reached me from another source—"

An uprising? Martha clutched her tankard, her nails digging deep into the leather. Her blood cooled, and a ball of ice formed in her stomach, its bitter chill radiating outwards to her extremities. In the heat of summer, at an inn in Edgeway, winter returned. She shivered.

"Darumvale recently turned upon the Earl and his men," Anselm said. "Fortunately, he regained control before it got too out of hand. I am glad to report that very few lives were lost during the fighting. The majority of the dead were outlaws—including their leader, I am heartily glad to say." Anselm actually laughed, unaware of Martha's horror. "Imagine this: my misguided parents actually took him in as an orphan. Tender-hearted fools. How their precious Vadim has repaid their kindness!" Anselm stopped gloating and frowned. "Martha? Are you unwell?"

Martha stared at him, reeling from the blows he'd unwittingly dealt her. His words were a dagger to her heart, if he only knew it. She felt sick. She wanted to scream. Cry. Run. All of them. None of them.

"You are very pale." Anselm touched her hand but she couldn't feel it.

"I-I'm fine." She managed to respond, but her voice wavered. *Keep pretending!* Her inner drill sergeant yelled at her. *Don't tell him anything.* "It's j-just relief, that's all."

Black flashes blinded her. The voices of the other patrons ebbed and flowed in volume, fading in and out, disorienting her. She took a deep, juddering breath and clutched at the edges of the table. The room seemed to swing like a rope bridge in a high wind. A static noise filled her ears, muffling out the other sounds. The ice in her blood thawed. She was hot. Blisteringly hot. Sweat beaded on her upper lip. She tugged at the neck of her shift.

Act normal, you fool. Breathe. Don't you dare faint!

"I've been s-so worried about Seth and..." It was useless. The charade no longer mattered.

The majority of the dead are outlaws, including their leader. Vadim!

Her head slumped towards the table, landing heavily on her folded arms. The movement dislodged her scarf and sent it fluttering to the floor. Through the static hissing, Martha heard herself groaning.

Now she knew why he hadn't come for her.

He's dead!

"Martha?" She heard Anselm's voice beside her, though she couldn't see him. He slipped his arm about her waist and half lifted her from the wooden bench. "Hold onto me if you can. Good girl."

The next thing she knew, she was outside, perched upon a horse trough. Anselm held her head down between her knees. The sun felt hot against her exposed neck. "Breathe deeply and slowly. In and out.

Excellent, Martha."

She sat up. Too quickly. The world set off whirling on another nauseating carousel ride. "Oh God!" Her head felt too heavy for her neck to support. It swayed dangerously with a will of its own. She would have fallen backward into the water trough if Anselm hadn't held her so securely.

"Have a care, m'lady. Lean your head against me for a moment. Close your eyes."

She obeyed him. All of her strength and will was gone.

Vadim is dead.

For two days, Martha hid away in her room, refusing to speak to anyone. What was there left to say? Even Forge couldn't rouse her from the depths of such grief. She lay motionless upon the bed, staring dry-eyed at the ceiling.

Only her mind was alive, full of its dreadful imaginings.

Mistress Weaver was deeply concerned when she came in to see her and found her so unresponsive. The good lady took the dog away to her own rooms, telling Martha she would call in a healer unless she showed some sign of improvement.

"And that nice young man who brought you home is just as worried as I," she told her later, drawing up a stool to sit beside Martha's bed. "He has called three times already, even though I would not let him see you. He always brings flowers. Oh, and he brought some of those delicate little pastries you are usually so fond of."

One afternoon, she heard Anselm and Mistress Weaver speaking together. It was a sultry sort of day, and the street outside was quiet. They must have left the kitchen door open, for the sounds of their conversation carried quite clearly up the stairs to where Martha lay like a corpse, too stricken with grief to move.

"What can be wrong with her?" She heard Anselm

ask. There was the scrape of a chair being pulled over the kitchen's slate floor. "Is there no fever, or any other symptoms?"

"Nothing at all," the landlady replied. "If you ask me, the girl looks as though she has had a shock."

There was a brief pause. Martha heard the tinkling of crockery being arranged.

"What were you talking about?" Mistress Weaver continued. "At the moment she became so afflicted, I mean."

"Nothing of consequence..."

Nothing of consequence!

"...If anything, my words should have reassured her, dear lady. Martha had been worried about some friends in Darumvale for quite some time. Happily, I had the best of news to impart."

"Indeed?" More clinking of crockery. Mistress Weaver must be making tea. "'Tis a curious malady, indeed." There was the sound of a heavy sigh. "There is nothing else for it. If her condition is still the same on the morrow, I shall bring in a healer."

"A sound plan, m'lady." Anselm agreed. "And I shall pay the bill from my own purse. No, really, I insist. Martha is very dear to me. In time I hope..."

Martha heard the smile in his voice.

"But perhaps it would be better not speak of it. Not until she is herself again."

"Most wise, sir. Ah, she is a very fortunate girl indeed."

I don't think so! Anselm's apparent sweetness now seemed to contain more than a hint of saccharine. And it had a nasty, lingering taste.

Hearing his plans revived Martha better than a bucket of iced water poured over her head.

In the middle of the night, while the rest of the household slept, she set about dashing the hopes of Anselm and her landlady. Staggering a little, she dressed as quickly as she could then stuffed her belongings into her saddlebags. Once this was done, she smuggled Forge out from

Mistress Weaver's room. Together, they crept down the stairs and sneaked from the house, out into the night.

There was only one place she wanted to be. And this time, she wouldn't turn back.

chapter twenty-three

AS THE FIRST PINK RAYS of morning kissed a farewell to the night, Martha slowed her horse to a walk and entered the village. When she reached the centre of the main street, she reined Eric to a halt. Darumvale slumbered on.

"Good boy." She patted the horse's steaming neck and loosened his girth a notch. Forge arrived soon afterwards. Panting and weary, he flopped down in the dust.

All was still. Even the village dogs were silent. Then, almost shyly, the earliest bird began to sing. Soon, the rest of the chorus woke and joined in, filling the air with their sweet song. A cockerel crowed, its raucous cry shattering the fragile peace for another day.

Martha remained motionless on her horse. Dry-eyed, she reacquainted her with the place she'd once called home. It looked the same, but different. There were voids on the street that hadn't been there a couple of months ago. Empty places where a home had once stood, now marked by a cairn of rubble and blackened timbers. Many of the remaining houses were disfigured by tell tale scorch marks, though some were freshly whitewashed, as if to disguise the damage the past had inflicted.

Forge whined. He sat up and looked around, tail wagging. *He's happy to be home, at least.* She knew he wanted to see Bren and Jared again. "Soon," she said.

Where had they buried him, she wondered. Was burial even common practice here? She couldn't remember ever having seen a graveyard. There was still so much she didn't know. Martha bit her lip and took a deep breath, battling to control the rising sense of panic inside. She must remain in control. If she unraveled now, she might well run back to Edgeway again. No—it was time to face everything.

Slipping her feet from the stirrups, she dismounted. Before talking to anyone, there was somewhere she needed to go.

Vadim's house—her home—was gone. Only the shell remained, blackened and gutted by fire.

Oh, God! Letting go of Eric's reins, she walked towards the ruin, her hands covering her mouth as she took in the destruction. Tears slid down her cheeks in a steady stream. The house would have been some comfort. Now she didn't even have that.

There's nothing left of him.

Stumbling and crunching over the broken stone and charred wood, she stepped through the doorway of the house. It was impossible to walk around inside. The roof had collapsed, and a mound of burned thatch and timber roof covered the floor, barring her way. There was nothing to see. Even the cow-horn window panes had melted.

It's all dead.

"Martha? Is it you?"

She turned around slowly. There was Bren, with Forge whining and yipping at her side. But this was a barely recognisable version of Bren. She looked older, much more careworn than Martha remembered. Her once-merry eyes were dull and haunted in the gauntness of her face.

"Bren." Martha didn't know what to say. *What can I*

say? And would Bren even want to hear it? *What must they all think of me?*

"Oh, lass!" Bren opened her arms. "Where have you been so long?"

Martha stumbled from the ruined house and ran into Bren's embrace. They clung to each other, both of them crying.

"They got Jared." Bren sobbed. "They killed my dear, dear man." She repeated the words over and over, as if she couldn't stop.

God, no. Poor Bren.

Bren's grief restored Martha's composure. She cradled her friend's head against her shoulder, stroking her back, while murmuring soft words of nonsense into her grizzled hair. Just as Vadim had once held her.

At length, Bren's sobs slowed, and finally stopped. She raised her head from Martha's damp shoulder and stepped back, swiping her scarf across her swollen eyes.

"Sorry, lass." Bren's lips attempted a smile. "Morning is always my worst time. When I wake up, just for a moment, I feel him laying in bed beside me, and then I remember." Her eyes glistened with another rush of tears. "Will I never stop missing him?"

"No, Bren. You won't." Aunt Lulu had once told her of how she'd lost her own young husband in a terrible farming accident. She'd never married again. "But you might learn to carry the burden of losing him. Eventually. Or, so I'm told." Not that she believed it herself. "But it'll never go away."

"Oh?" Bren smiled properly. "I am so glad to hear that." She took a deep breath. "How are you, lass? I suppose you heard what happened here?"

Martha nodded. "Only recently."

"You may find you have fewer friends here now, Martha. Pay them no heed. Darumvale is still your home."

No it isn't. Not without him.

"I may as well tell you, there are people here who

blame you for everything from the massacre to the lack of rain," Bren continued. "Fools that they are."

Martha wasn't surprised. She hadn't expected a warm reception after being gone so long. "But not you?"

"Silly goose." Bren clasped her hand. "Would I show you the wounds in my heart if I did?"

"Thank you." Martha squeezed her friend's work-roughened hand. Then she voiced the question closest to her heart. "H-how did...Vadim die, Bren?"

"Ah! He was glorious in battle, girl." Bren wiped a stray tear from Martha's cheek with her finger. "You would have been proud. He killed a dozen of the Earl's filth with arrows. Another four died beneath his blade." Bren's smile broadened. "He flew down that hill as if he had wings, not legs, his sword ablaze in the sun. My feeble words do little justice to his valour. I cannot praise him enough. Although he was outnumbered he stayed with us, right until the end."

Martha's heart seemed to swell, until her chest could hardly contain it.

Bren's smile faded and her voice grew softer. "One of Edgeway's men stuck a sword right through him, from back to front. Here." She touched her own stomach, demonstrating how Vadim had met his end. "But the coward responsible died sooner than he. Seth saw to that."

Martha had thought she was prepared to hear this. But she wasn't. Bile flooded her mouth. She bent over, dry retching and sobbing while Bren stroked her back, her rough hands smoothing and snagging against the fine wool of her cloak.

"The minstrels have already put his deeds into song. Mourn him, but be proud of him, lass. He is sure to be seated in the Hall of the Ancestors, with all the heroes who went before him."

At length, Martha straightened up, though her legs still trembled beneath her. She wiped her mouth carelessly on her sleeve. "Wh-where do you l-lay your dead,

Bren?" she asked when she was able to speak again.

Bren frowned. "Walk with me. Dog, come!"

Forge leapt up at Bren's curt summons, wagging his tail. Martha took Eric's reins and led him away from the grass he'd been munching.

The four of them walked down the street and out of the village. They crossed the North road and cut through the hedgerow. In the field beyond was a grassy hill, and at its other side, hidden from the village, was an entrance that burrowed into the hill. A large boulder lay across it passageway, preventing them from going any further.

Martha had seen this hill every day during her time in Darumvale, never realizing its significance.

"Our dead lay within," Bren said. "My own dear…husband amongst them."

Fresh tears blurred Martha's eyes. She let go of Eric and walked slowly to the barrow entrance, tentatively resting her hand on the rough stone. "Oh, Vadim!" She dropped to her knees, weeping, her cheek pressed against the cold stone. "I'm s-sorry…" She couldn't voice her despair.

How can I go on without you? Now you'll never know I love you. Oh, I know you didn't love me back, but I wish I'd said it to you. Just once.

"Martha?" She felt Bren's hand upon her shoulder, squeezing gently. "Vadim is not here, child."

"Huh?" She looked up, frowning with confusion.

Bren sank down on the grass beside her and took her hand. "On the day he…Seth took him away…before he…"

"D-died?" Martha managed to speak again.

Bren nodded.

"Where?" Martha dug her damp handkerchief out from where she kept it, stuffed down the bodice of her dress. "Why did Seth take him away?" She wiped her eyes then blew her nose.

Bren shrugged. "No one knows. He never speaks of it. But perhaps he might if *you* ask him."

Martha scrambled to her feet, determined to do just that, but Bren placed a restraining hand on her arm. "Go gently, child. He is grieving too."

"For Vadim?" It was only right, she supposed. He'd brought him up as his own son.

"Not only for him."

Martha's heart lurched. "Ma's dead too?" Was there no end to the loss?

"No. Sylvie."

It took all the strength Martha had to remain standing.

What a bloody, awful world!

From outside, the Great Hall looked much the same. Although it was singed around the edges, the structure remained sound. It was on the inside Martha noticed the difference.

If she needed an illustration of how it was people—not things—that made a house into a home, this was it.

A damp chill enveloped her the moment she stepped inside. Sylvie always used to have a good fire blazing by now, but the hearth was cold. No friendly red embers twinkled in the dim light. The fire had obviously been out for some time.

Mab—the cow—mooed when she saw Martha and Bren. How long since she was last milked? *Poor thing.*

"Where's Ma?" Martha whispered, reluctant to disturb the awful stillness.

"She took Sylvie's passing very badly," Bren said with a sigh. "Old Mother Galrey took her in. As you can see, this is no fit place to nurse a sick old woman."

Martha nodded. "I'll go and see her later." She looked around, wrinkling her nose. The rushes on the floor smelled sour. In its own way, Sylvie's home was just as much a ruin as Vadim's house. Martha knew what she must do.

Seth's snores started up, resonating from where he slept, screened off from the rest of the hall.

"He will not wake before noon," Bren said. "His fondness for ale has increased of late." She looked about her and shook her head. "I have tried to help where I can, as have the other women, but we have our own homes—"

"Then let me help." Martha attempted a smile. "It's not like I have anything else to do."

Martha spent the remainder of the morning setting the hall to rights. It was hard work, but it helped. She was too busy to think. Or cry.

After milking Mab and the goats, she put them out in the meadow where Eric, her horse, was already grazing. Then she cleaned the grate and relit the fire. The Hall seemed horribly empty without its comforting light, as if its heart had stopped beating. Perhaps it had.

She discarded the soiled floor rushes and replaced them with fresh ones. Then, after attending to the animals' accommodation, replenishing their water and hay, she set about getting something for Seth to eat when he woke up.

His snores had kept her company all morning. It wasn't a radio, but it was company at least. She popped over to Bren's house and returned minutes later with a small pan of pottage, as well as some bread.

A few of the other villagers saw her while she was out and about. Some smiled, a few people were distinctly cool, and one or two blanked her completely.

They can suit themselves. I don't give a shit what they think of me.

When her work in the Great Hall was finished, Martha decided to visit Ma. Maybe Seth would be awake when she returned.

Mother Galrey opened the door of her house and glared at the visitor on her threshold.

"You, eh? They said you had finally decided to honor us by returning, *milady.*"

Martha clenched her fists and battled to restrain herself. Unpleasant words hovered on her lips, just waiting for the green light to launch. Mother Galrey was famously sour at the best of times. Now the old crone was positively revelling in the chance to spit her venom.

"I've come to see Ma," Martha said with great politeness. "Would you kindly ask her if she'll see me?"

Evil old witch. You're loving this, aren't you?

Huddled in her black shawl, despite the heat of the day, the old woman really did resemble a stereotypical witch. She looked down her hooked nose at Martha, a sneer on her toothless mouth.

"Please?" Martha selected civility as her weapon of choice. She'd never win a war of insults with Mother Galrey as her opponent. "Tell her I'm here, would you? I'd be most grateful."

The old woman snorted and slammed the wooden door in Martha's face.

Martha blinked. Anger flashed from her toes to the rest of her body. *You feckin' old besom. I ought to—* She raised her fist, prepared to smash the door into splinters if she had to, when it swung open again.

"Go on inside." Mother Galrey jerked her head, summoning Martha in, albeit grudgingly. "She will see you. Though if I had my way—"

"How very kind." Martha swept past the old woman, stepping into the dark, warm lair of her inner sanctum. She stumbled over a sack that lay discarded on the floor. "And I just love what you've done with the place. It's so very...you."

Deuce, you old cow.

The old woman hissed in reply. Martha ignored her and headed for the bed in the far corner of the room. At first, she thought it was empty, just a heap of rumpled blankets. But as she drew closer, she saw Ma's eyes, shining up in the gloom.

Martha was shocked. She looked so tiny. Ma had always been small, but now there was even less of her. Her skin hung from her bones, and her head seemed much too pronounced, all bony and angled beneath the wisps of white hair. Like a skull covered with tissue paper.

A shiver tingled up her spine, but Martha forced her teeth into a smile. "Hello, Ma. It's good to see you again." She swallowed hard, and pulled up a low stool, close to the bed.

"Will you not tell me how well I look?" Ma's poor withered face broke into a smile, and she chuckled, phlegm bubbling in her throat.

Martha took the knobbled hand that reached out to her from beneath the bedcovers. "You look fine." She gently squeezed Ma's fingers. "I've missed you. And I'm so very sorry about Sylvie." More tears slipped down her face. *Will I never stop crying?* "She was a good friend to me."

"Aye." Ma sighed. "She tried to be, I know she did. Wipe your eyes and help me sit up, girl."

What an odd thing to say. Puzzling over Ma's strange answer, Martha piled pillows against the wall, then propped the old lady against them, handing her a cup of water when she beckoned for it with one claw-like finger.

After taking a sip, Ma called to her roomie. "Agnes."

Agnes?

"Go and check on Seth for me." Old Mother Galrey—*Agnes*—looked up from her darning and scowled.

How could she even see in this light, let alone darn?

"He will be fine," she snarled. "Let him sleep it off. He kept half the village awake last night with his singing and—"

"Agnes." The warning in Ma's voice was unmistakable.

Martha smirked when the old besom leapt up from her chair and hobbled for the door.

"Very well, I shall leave you in her ladyship's care, though no good will—"

"Agnes!"

Without another word, Mother Galrey grabbed her stick. She hobbled from the room like a wounded black spider, and slammed the door behind her.

When she'd gone, Martha went to the window and lifted the curtain. Light, and fresh, sweet air flooded through the small opening, dispelling the smell of sickness and cooked cabbage that permeated the room. She took a deep breath then turned back to face the bed. Ma was looking at her strangely. Almost if she'd never seen her before. Something clicked inside Martha's brain.

"You know, don't you." It wasn't a question.

"About you?" Ma nodded, briefly. "Aye. The night I read your hand. Not everything, mind, but your man told me the rest."

Martha exhaled and sank down onto her stool again. It was a relief to be able to speak freely. "Then you also know he isn't 'my man'." She still couldn't speak of Vadim in the past tense.

Ma shrugged her thin shoulders. "In your heart he is. That is where it matters the most, lass."

There seemed no point in denying it. Ma was too shrewd. As the old woman drew her shawl about her shoulders, Martha leapt up to help her.

"Are you cold? I'll close the curtain—"

"Leave it be. I am weary of being ill and stifled. It does not suit me. Sit down, Martha. There are things you need to hear, and I will not strain my eyes by looking up at you."

Martha obeyed. It was good to hear Ma sounding more like herself.

"Give me your hand."

"No." Martha shook her head and held her hands against her chest. "I don't want to hear anything else about the future—not after the last reading you gave me."

"He's dead. Can the future hold anything worse for you than that?"

Martha flinched at Ma's bluntness. Her eyes stung with tears. But Ma was right. *She might even see a way home.*

Silently, Martha placed her hand in Ma's and waited. Sounds from outside drifted in through the window opening. Children's laughter and adult voices calling to one another as they returned from the fields for the midday meal. The geese were honking and hissing, as usual. A dog's bark set off all the other village dogs. Martha recognised Forge's dulcet tones amongst them. At least he was having fun.

Life goes on. How does that poem go? 'Stop all the clocks. Cut off the telephone—'

More tears leaked from her eyes. She blinked them back.

"That son of mine," Ma muttered, smiling as she gazed at Martha's palm. "I know not whether to hug him or smother him!"

"What do you mean?" What Seth was doing, there on her hand? Whatever it was, Ma looked animated again.

Ma released Martha's hand. Her rheumy blue eyes twinkled. "Do not give up hope, Martha." She cupped Martha's face between her wizened hands. "Speak to Seth. Force the truth from him if you must."

"The truth about what?" Martha still wasn't getting it.

"Vadim." Ma laughed. "He is still alive. I just saw him."

Martha's heart stumbled for a few beats. She felt hot and clammy. "But...he's dead!" Hope wrestled with denial in her heart. But she dared not believe. Not yet. "Isn't he?"

Her ears roared, and the house began spinning, accelerating fast. Martha battled to keep her eyes fixed on Ma, but the old woman appeared to whiz around the room like a frog in a blender. Her peripheral vision narrowed as if she were looking down the wrong end of a pair of binoculars. Then, suddenly, she couldn't see at all.

chapter twenty-four

When Martha opened her eyes, she was on the floor, sprawled out on a mound of sacking that smelled like a tom cat's toilet. Ma was shouting her name, prodding at her with a walking stick.

"Thank the Spirits! Can you get up, lass? I cannot rise to assist you."

"I'm fine." Martha took a deep breath and managed to slither back onto her stool, feeling weak and woozy. At least the world wasn't spinning so much now. She rested her forehead against the prickly mattress.

"How long since you last ate?" Ma demanded, sounding almost herself again.

How long?

The last meal she remembered was back at the inn with Anselm. *When was that?* Time had no meaning since she'd learned Vadim's fate.

"I'm not sure. A while ago, I suppose."

Ma tutted. "And here I thought you were meant to be minding me. Here." She thrust a chunk of bread into Martha's hand. "Eat."

Martha sat up. The bread was past its best, crusty and difficult to chew, but she managed to force a piece down.

"Where were you all this time?" Ma asked. "Edgeway?"

Martha nodded. In between mouthfuls of stale bread,

she told Ma about her job and new home.

"Yes. Very nice. But how did you learn what had happened in Darumvale? Did one of Vadim's friends find you?"

"No." Martha stopped eating. She looked at Ma to gauge her reaction. "Your grandson told me."

Ma paled and sank back against her pillows, hand splayed against her bony chest. "Anselm? You spoke to him...about us? What did you tell him?"

The old lady looked so alarmed, Martha was concerned. Why was she so afraid? "It's all right." She took Ma's cold hand and gave it a squeeze. "I told him I had friends here, that I was worried about them, nothing more." *Are you sure?* Martha wracked her brain, trying to remember if she'd inadvertently let anything of importance slip. She was certain she hadn't.

Ma's eyes narrowed. "How did you meet him?"

"We met at the market. I was there asking whether anyone had heard from Darumvale. He happened to overhear me and...we just got talking." Martha frowned. "Why are you looking at me like that? What's wrong with him?"

"He works for the Earl, Martha."

"I know. He told me he works in his stables—"

"Stables? Hah!" Ma's lips twisted into a bitter line "That is the least of his duties, girl. He is a tracker." She gripped Martha's hand tighter. "He must have followed you there."

"A tracker? Followed me? From here to..." Martha shook her head. "No, you're mistaken. Why would he follow me?"

Ma fell silent and slumped back on her pillows, her expression impossible to decipher.

"Ma?" Martha leaned closer. "Tell me. What's going on?"

The old lady's faded blue eyes clouded. "Sylvie must have told him about you."

"I don't understand." What did any of this matter,

anyway?

Ma slid her hand from Martha's, "Anselm was here, the day she...died." She worried at the blanket with her old knobbled fingers. wringing it between her hands. "He hates Vadim and everything associated with him. The Earl pays him most handsomely to hunt down their common enemy."

Martha felt ill. The bread she'd eaten seemed to be crawling back up her throat. But Ma continued to speak.

"He always was a cruel, cunning sort of lad. As soon as he came of age, he went to see the Earl, seeking employment in his service. He used his information about Vadim to gain His Lordship's favor. Seth disowned him, of course. His own honor demanded it. For Sylvie, though, it was harder. How could she abandon her only child? In spite of his sins, she loved him.

"I know she met with him sometimes, when Seth was called away somewhere, but I pretended not to know. I did not imagine she would tell him anything important. But he must have got something out of her; Anselm could be very persuasive when it suited him." Ma took a deep breath. "On the day she died, while the Earl questioned her about Vadim and his wife, Anselm stood there smiling and watching his mother weep. I was dragged outside then, but the look in her eyes will live with me until I take my final breath. She looked...guilty, broken..." Ma dabbed her eyes on the blanket. "I never saw her alive again."

Martha gaped at her for several long seconds, shocked beyond words. *This is my friend Anselm? Are we even talking about the same person?* Denial swelled in her heart. "No." She shook her head, wanting but failing to dispel the terrible picture Ma had just painted. "You must be mistaken. Anselm was always so good to me. If he thought Vadim was dead, why would he bother with me?" Her cheeks flushed hot at the injustice of Ma's accusation. "What purpose would it serve?"

Ma's lips formed a grim smile. "You did not know him,

m'lady. Not really. As a child, he always wanted anything belonging to Vadim."

"Me?" At this, Martha's eyes widened. "No. He never once tried to hit on me...court me, I mean," she amended when Ma frowned. "We were...*are* just friends. There's never been a hint of anything else." Well, apart from what she'd overheard, that day back at the boarding house when he was speaking to Mistress Weaver. But that didn't count. "Anselm was always so decent, so kind."

"Then, you were fortunate to escape when you did, girl. He was always a patient hunter." The glacial look in Ma's eyes sent shivers goose-bumping all over Martha's skin. "He prefers to see his quarry collapse with exhaustion before moving in for the kill, to watch the eyes of his prey as the end of its life reflects on his descending blade."

Ma took Martha's hand again, gently stroking it. "Are you *so* blind, child?" She leaned closer, her voice little more than a whisper. "Open your eyes and see him properly now. Was there never an occasion during your acquaintance when you suspected him? Not even once?"

Martha's mind transported her back to their first meeting at the market in Edgeway. At the time, his appearance had struck her as too convenient for a coincidence, but when he'd spoken of Darumvale, her suspicion had faded.

"Once...maybe." Had loneliness blinded her to Anselm's true purpose? She'd been so lonely back then, cut off from all that was familiar.

If Anselm was so innocent, why had he never mentioned Vadim until that final day? He hadn't once bitched about him. *You were a fresh audience, just waiting to hear his complaints. He should've leapt at the chance of sympathy.*

"Once or twice," Martha admitted with a shrug. More examples bubbled up in the back of her mind, each one making her squirm.

Hindsight really is a wonderful thing.

The door crashed open, and Old Mother Galrey hobbled back inside. Martha wasn't sorry. She was relieved to press the pause button on this particular discussion.

"Your lad is awake and in a foul mood," Mother Galrey called to Ma. "Someone dared to clean up that sty he calls a home. You, I suppose?" She directed a venomous glare at Martha.

Martha shrugged. "So?"

Mother Galrey cackled, displaying her naked gums. "No wonder his temper burns so hot. If you were planning to visit him, m'lady, I would give it a while yet. Let the ale blunt his rage."

"I didn't know you cared." Martha frowned. "Anyway, why's he angry?"

Ma sighed and patted Martha's hand as it lay on the bed beside her. "He would not let anyone touch the place. Not since the day Sylvie died."

"Oh." Martha felt terrible. "That's why it was so filthy? Oh, feck! Now I've gone and destroyed his shrine." She groaned and covered her face with her hands. "I should have thought."

"Stop fretting, girl." Martha heard the smile in Ma's voice. "It is well past time that someone intervened. Were it not for my feebleness, I would have done so myself."

"Not a bad job either, girl."

A compliment? From the wicked witch of the North? Martha uncovered her face and was disturbed to witness Mother Galrey's smile. It looked...genuine.

Haven't I had enough shocks for one day?

But the biggest shock of all had rekindled the fire in her heart. Flames of hope burned out of control, despite her attempts to put them out. After all, Ma might be mistaken. *Please, God, don't let her spooky powers be wrong this time.*

Martha gave it an hour, then ventured out of Old Mother Galrey's house, the warnings of the older women echoing in her ears. She crossed the street, dodging a horse and cart that were being driven by one of her former neighbours. The man—she couldn't remember his name—turned his head away when he saw her and spat in the street.

I'm crossing you off my Christmas card list, pal.

But she let it go. She had bigger things to worry about.

When she reached the Great Hall, she pressed her ear against the door and listened. Nothing. She pushed the door open a fraction, wincing when it creaked. It was quiet. Taking a deep breath, Martha opened the door a little wider.

"Seth?" Her voice sounded timid.

Why am I trembling? Seth wouldn't harm her. He was a gentle soul.

But she'd misjudged Anselm. Maybe the apple had got his nasty pips from the tree?

Let's just get it over with.

"Seth?" She pushed the door open and walked inside. "It's me, Martha. Are you here?"

"Martha?" Seth's voice drifted through the smoky hall. "It cannot be…she has gone." His speech wobbled, but he didn't sound angry or violent.

"It is me. I came back this morning." Her cautious feet knocked against something solid. She glanced down. A broken pot. Several more lay smashed on the floor nearby. Okay, maybe he was angry. He sounded all right now, though.

"Seth?" Was he crying? It sounded that way. Then, she saw him, sitting by the fire with his head in his hands. A barrel of ale placed at his side kept him company. "Are you all right?" She flinched, annoyed with herself. *Of course, he's not all right. Sylvie's dead, and you destroyed her shrine.*

"She's gone, Martha. My woman is..."

"I know." Martha hovered at the other side of the fire, staring at the Chief. He looked up at her, his eyes red and swollen. His head swayed gently, as if he were on his own private boat. "I'm so sorry Sylvie died..." She'd read somewhere it was important to use the word 'dead' to a bereaved person—not sleeping, gone, or in heaven. "She was a good friend to me. I'll miss her very much."

Seth nodded, gently listing slightly on his bench. "Aye. Thank you, m'lady."

Martha took another deep breath. "There's something else I'm sorry for." She gripped her skirts and prepared to run. *Say it.* "I'm the one who cleaned this place. I didn't know you liked it...the way it was." Seth's eyes narrowed. "I only wanted to help. Please forgive me."

Seth closed his eyes and raked his hands through his long red hair. It looked matted and wild. He exhaled like a bull.

Martha's legs tensed, ready to run.

Suddenly, he smiled. Just a tiny one, but it was something. "Forgive you? For what?" He shrugged. "Your heart meant well. I thought Mother Galrey had done it out of spite." He spoke carefully, as if trying to disguise his drunken state from her.

Her heart contracted with pity for the poor, dear man. No longer afraid, she walked around the fire and sat down on the bench beside him. "Ma told me what happened. I'm more sorry than I can say." She extended her hand to him. Hesitating for only a moment, Seth clasped it with his large, rough paw.

"Aye." He nodded several times, sucking on his lower lip as if he was fighting back tears.

To give him time to regain his composure, Martha directed her gaze to the fire, still holding onto the Chief's hand.

How soon could she ask him about Vadim without

her appearing insensitive?

In the end, she didn't have to.

"You came back to claim your man, then? I wondered when we might see you again."

Martha sighed. *I'm not lying to this man anymore. He deserves the truth.*

"Vadim isn't my husband, Seth. We're just friends—and not even that half the time."

Seth snorted with laughter and let go of her hand, blushing a little. "That is exactly what he said you would say."

"What?" Martha frowned. "You already know? Sweet baby Jesus! Am I the only one in Darumvale who thought this was secret? Who else knows, for fecksake?"

Seth grinned and poured them both some ale. "Just us. Ma and myself." He handed Martha a large mug of the frothing, fragrant brew. "Your secret is safe."

She raised the ale to her lips and chugged half of it down, plucking up her courage to speak. *Ask him. Do it now.*

"Ma read my hand. She says Vadim's still alive." She wiped froth from her lip with the back of her hand. "Is it true?"

Seth studied her for a few moments, as if considering whether to tell her or not. The killer butterflies in her stomach had migrated north, filling her chest and throat with their gentle flutterings.

"Do you want it to be true, Martha?" Seth seemed very sober all of a sudden. His blue eyes were steady now.

What kind of answer is that? "Of course I do."

"Why?"

"What?" Martha scowled.

"Do you care for him? Is that it?"

Why was he interrogating her like this? "Yes. I care. Okay?" *Just tell me.* "Please, Seth, stop arsing around and tell me he's alive, will you?"

Seth smiled. "He lives."

"Oh, thank you, God!" Martha leapt to her feet and did a little jig, spilling the ale in her tankard. "Ye-es!" The killer butterflies buzzed around in her head. She felt light, dizzy with joy. The ale probably enhanced this effect, though.

Seth's jaw dropped as Martha bent her arms and proceeded to waggle her butt from side to side. "Whatever are you doing, girl?"

"A happy dance."

"Ah. Of course." Seth shook his head and started muttering to himself.

"Okay. I'm done." Martha sat back down on the bench. The dancing could wait. Before Seth shut down again, there was something else she needed to know. Desperately so. "Where is he now?"

chapter twenty-five

RED LIGHT AND SHADOWS DANCED over his eyelids. Unfortunately, even with his eyes closed, he could still hear. He yearned for the silence and comfort of the night. The dark was an undemanding companion. It did not speak. Nor did it choke him with unwanted kindness. The night gave him a taste of real peace. The kind only the dead can enjoy.

"How is he today?"

Take your muted concern and be gone!

"He does not improve, Mother."

He could almost feel her tears. *Why does she remain where she is not wanted?*

"'Tis to be expected, child. The wound almost killed him."

Almost. The merest tremble of his sword hand would have spared me this grief.

"The moon has turned two cycles. He has healed. Why does he still not speak?"

He heard her sniffle. Then the pattering footsteps of the mother hastening to comfort her chick.

"Go outside, Orla. Breathe the air. Feel sunlight on your skin. I will watch him—"

"No."

Harken to your mother, girl. Leave me in peace.

"He needs me."

You? I think not.

His mind showed him another face instead. This woman he liked looking at. Chestnut hair blew in a wild tangle around her face, while her cheeks flushed pink with embarrassment. Her lips glistened; the fullness of the lower one seemed slightly swollen, as if she had just been soundly kissed.

I remember her. It was wintertime...in a snow storm. I held her beneath my cloak.

"Look. He is smiling, child."

"Oh, Mother!"

Vadim flinched when he felt a soft hand slide over his, resenting her intrusion.

"Are you awake, m'lord? Will you not sit up and eat? Do you need to...relieve yourself? Or shall I—"

If she attempts that again I shall crawl from this place, on my belly if I must. Insolent maid!

He sat up quickly, startling the two women at his bedside. He glared at them and held his hand out for the walking stick.

"Of course." Orla raced to do his bidding. "Shall I accompany you, m'lord? You are still so weak."

He ignored her and swung his legs slowly from the bed, ignoring the hovering concern of both women. The unaccustomed effort formed sweat beads upon his brow.

"Please, m'lord. Take my arm. Let—"

He silenced her with a glare. Orla's eyes glistened. She stepped back and clung to her mother's arm.

Muscles burning, he finally swayed to his feet and staggered for the door. They did not follow him outside.

***

"Seth, you've got to believe me. I *am not* one of the Evil Earl's minions, no matter what Vadim might have said."

"Yet you admit to a friendship with Anselm? From

where I sit, the evidence against you is damning, m'lady."

Despite Martha's fears, Seth didn't return to the dubious comfort of his ale barrel. Instead, he quizzed her about her whereabouts and doings of the past couple of months until her head spun with his questions, and her patience finally frayed.

"Go and see Ma, then." Finally, Martha stood up, sick of his stalling. "She read my hand. She'll back me up, I know she will." Her need to be with Vadim again made her snappish.

At the mention of Ma, Seth looked down at the ground. "How can I face her, m'lady?" He ran his hand across his dirty, unkempt beard. "I have not seen her since the day Sylvie..."

"Was killed?" Martha's heart softened again. *The poor sweet man.* She went over to him and laid her hand on his shoulder. "Ma will understand. Anyone would after all you've been through. She's your mother. She'll—"

"Sylvie died by her own hand, Martha."

"Say, what?" These words shocked her even more than the news of Sylvie's death. "But I thought the Evil Earl—"

"She took poison. Rather than betray us any further with her words, she ended her own life."

"Holy Mother of God!" Martha sank down onto the bench beside him, her legs suddenly weak. *Sylvie killed herself?* "I can't believe it."

Seth buried his chin into his chest, his shoulders shaking with silent grief. Martha took his hand and leaned her head against his arm in a useless display of comfort. *No wonder he's so messed up.*

"If I could have only seen her. Spoken to her." He said between sobs. "But they kept us apart until it was too late. She died...alone."

Martha felt his arm muscle tense beneath her cheek.

Seth sat up, regarding her with his bloodshot eyes. The wrinkles in his face carried his tears away in tiny, glistening channels.

"Did she believe I would not forgive her?" he asked on a whisper. "Is that why she did it? That thought alone rips me apart."

Say something. Lie if you have to, Bigalow. Make him believe you, or he'll follow Sylvie and kill himself too. But his poison of choice will be ale.

She took a deep breath. "Seth. I didn't know Sylvie long, but I know this much. She loved you with every fiber of her being." Martha dabbed away his tears with her own handkerchief. "Don't you see? It wasn't you she couldn't face, it was herself. Anselm used her love as a weapon. She couldn't *not* love him—her only son. She loved the pair of you, that's the problem."

Martha gave a sigh. "It was an impossible situation for her, I see that now." She held Seth's prickly face between her hands, forcing him to meet her eyes. "But know this," she said fiercely. "The Earl and Anselm killed her just as surely as if they'd shot her."

It was true. Between them, they'd mentally tortured Sylvie to her death. Martha shuddered. What if she ran into Anselm again? She didn't know what she might do. *That little fecker played me from the word go.*

Seth nodded and drew the sleeve of his dirty shirt over his face. "Aye." He sniffed hard and managed a shadow of a smile. "You might be right, lass."

"There's no *might* about it."

"So, what will I do with the rest of my life, hmm?"

Martha shook her head. "I can't tell you that, I'm afraid. What do you want to do—now, at this moment?"

Seth sniffed again, this time at his own armpit. "Have a bath?"

Martha giggled. "That'd be an excellent start." He did smell a bit ripe. She stood up. "I'll go and start boiling the water."

While Seth went to visit Ma, Martha paced and twitched over at Bren's house. This was difficult given the small dimensions of the place. Fortunately, her eldest son, Will, was out at work, having taken over the running of the smithy. Her other two children were out working in the fields.

"Ach! Sit down, Martha." Bren looked up from the dough she was kneading. "You are as bad as the dog." Forge kept pace with Martha, following her across the house and back. "Eat something."

"I'm too stuffed with pottage."

"Then go for a walk. You will not see Vadim any sooner with your mooching."

"Okay. I'll be out on the North road." Martha clicked her fingers at Forge. "You'll let me know as soon as Seth—"

"Yes. Just go!" Bren flapped her floury fingers, dismissing her with a smile.

Summer still bathed the land in a hot golden glow. Everywhere was green and flourishing. Forge gamboled about reacquainting himself with his favorite places, snuffling and rolling in, goodness knew what.

Martha was glad so many of Darumvale's inhabitants had chosen to ignore her. She wanted to think, undisturbed. A couple of people raised their hands in greeting as she marched past the fields where they were working. Lifting her own hand in reply, she walked on.

Eventually, tired from aimlessly marching up and down the road, she settled down in the shade of a huge oak tree.

Somewhere out there, Vadim was alive. Bubbles of excitement floated and burst in her stomach at the prospect of seeing him again.

What kind of reception would he give her when she

next saw him? The last time they'd been together, he'd accused her of being a traitor. But yelling at one another wasn't the only thing they'd done.

Closing her eyes, she leaned back against the tree's rough bark, remembering how he'd held her on that final day. Reliving the kisses they'd shared made her stomach flip. She loved the way he made her feel.

Even though he'd believed she was working for the Earl, there was no denying that he had still wanted her. In what capacity, Martha couldn't say. Maybe he just fancied having a bed-warmer? But if that were true, why hadn't he just taken her? Back then, her resistance had been zero at best.

How severe were his injuries? By all accounts, his attacker's sword had impaled him like a kebab. It must have missed most of his internal organs—God knows how—or he really would be dead right now. Martha hugged herself, shivering as she imagined that strong, vital man cut down. His wounds must have been terrible. Why else would the Earl and Anselm believe he was dead?

She closed her eyes. Her yearning for Vadim was fast becoming a physical ache. Loving him was a kind of painful bliss. A more dreadful and wonderful thing than she'd ever known. Weary though she was, her legs were tense, ready to run to his side at a moment's notice.

If only Seth would give me the fecking directions! How much longer would he be?

She scrambled to her feet and began pacing the road again, her arms still wrapped around her middle.

When Seth finally made an appearance, she didn't notice him at first.

"Martha?" There he was standing beside her, all clean and pink-scrubbed, and smiling. "What are you doing out here, lass?"

"Waiting for you." She blinked and looked around. To her surprise, the sun sat much lower in the sky. She stopped walking. Her legs throbbed with fatigue. "Have you been with Ma all this time?"

"Aye. And Old Mother Galrey was not pleased to be turned from her hearth for so long, I can tell you."

"I'll bet she wasn't." Martha slid her hand through the crook of Seth's arm when he offered it to her. Together, they ambled in the direction of the village. "Come, Forge."

The dog looked up and yawned at Martha's summons. He'd fallen asleep beneath the oak tree. Leaping to his feet, he gave himself a little shake, then padded silently after them.

"So, are you going to tell me where Vadim is, or must I beat the truth out of you?" Martha was too impatient to wait for Seth to broach the question that consumed her heart and mind.

Seth snorted with laughter. "I think I shall like this new honesty between us. Little wonder Vadim finds you so..."

"So?" She had no pride remaining where Vadim was concerned.

"Diverting."

"What?" *Like a road sign?* Not exactly what she was hoping for.

Seth's eyes twinkled. "Amusing."

"Like a clown...I mean, a fool?"

"Ask me no more, lass. Vadim's heart is his to reveal. I cannot know all of his deepest secrets."

"Hmm." Martha scowled. "And I bet you wouldn't tell me anything even if you did."

Seth inclined his head in acknowledgement of this fact.

"Then, where is he?" She scanned his face, searching for answers. "If you still don't trust me just say so. I get the—"

"He is at my hunting lodge."

Martha stopped walking and exhaled. *Finally!* "And where exactly is your lodge? Will you take me there?"

Seth nodded. "In the morning—"

"Oh, can't we go now?" Martha clutched his arm and

gave him her best puppy eyes. "The light will hold for ages yet. Besides, there's a full moon."

"Tomorrow, my lady."

Seth wouldn't be swayed, not now that he'd got his mojo back. Frustrating as this was, it was a good thing really.

They set off walking again, passing the last of the workers as they left the fields for the day. On seeing Martha on such apparently friendly terms with their Chief, one or two people who'd previously ignored her now offered her a smile. She returned the greeting in kind, much too happy to bear grudges. But her thoughts were elsewhere.

Tomorrow.

Her heart felt as if it were suspended on a length of elastic, boing-ing like crazy about her ribcage. At least if they went in the morning, she could spend the rest of the day doing a little self-improvement. Seth smelled better than she did right now, which was a rather sobering thought.

They walked on. The dust kicked up by the person on the path in front of them crunched unpleasantly between Martha's teeth.

Something just occurred to her. "Who's taking care of him? Surely he can't be alone up there?"

"Orla and her mother are looking after him." Seth darted a glance at her, suddenly looking suspiciously red in the face. "Though it seems Orla is the most devoted to his care."

"Oh?" The hairs on the back of Martha's neck all stood up, and heat tingled in her toes. "Is that so?" Pretty Orla with her lovely auburn hair. *She's single, isn't she?*

"Really?" A hissing, spitting green-eyed monster took up residence inside Martha's heart. "How very...kind of her."

Seth's crimson flush spread to his ear-tips. He said nothing more, but a hint of a smile played upon his lips.

I'd say that qualifies as a warning. Fine. If that's how

it's going to be, I'd better get myself weaponed up.

Martha spent the rest of the day preening at Bren's house. The older woman proved to be a great ally to the cause. She sent her offspring to spend the night at the Great Hall while she helped prepare Martha's bath.

Darumvale was no place for the prudish, and Martha was too wired to care. She sat in the tub, scrubbing herself in front of Bren's fire, and all the while bitching about Orla.

Bren listened as she prepared supper, making the occasional sympathetic noise.

"He's a married man, for fecksake." Martha rubbed at her hair, whipping it up into a beehive of fragrant bubbles. "I thought morality mattered here."

"But he is not married, is he, lass? They are both as free as the air."

Perhaps rashly—because she considered Bren her best friend now—Martha had confessed the truth about her marriage. Sort of. But she omitted the part about being from another world. That would keep for some other time. Probably forever.

Martha scowled. "Yes. But unless Vadim told her, Orla doesn't know that."

"And let us, for the moment, suppose he has." Bren picked up a bucket of water that hung warming beside the fire. "As far as anyone here is concerned, you left Vadim when he needed you the most. You went away with his outlaw friend, and you stayed away, long after the Earl had gone." Bren dipped her fingers into the water to check its temperature. "Hold your breath." She poured the water slowly over Martha's head, rinsing the soap from her hair as she talked. "Can you not see how bad it looks, Martha? Caution is one thing, but you abandoned your wounded husband for weeks, and without good reason." Bren sighed. "Can Orla be blamed for wanting to——

"Replace me?" Bren was right. It did look bad.

The older woman shrugged. "I was going to say, offer him solace. But perhaps you are right. Orla may well wish to replace you. And depending on how vulnerable Vadim is feeling, he may well have reconsidered your arrangement, yes." A sudden look of sorrow clouded Bren's hazel eyes.

Martha felt immediately guilty. "I'm sorry, Bren. I shouldn't be talking to you about this." Not now, anyway. Was it fair that poor Jared was dead while Martha's own fake husband still breathed? If Bren felt bitter, who would blame her. *Not very tactful of you, Bigalow.*

But Bren only smiled, and the clouds in her eyes faded. "Talk away, child. It does me good. It stops me dwelling on the things I cannot change. Hold your breath again." She sloshed the remaining water over Martha's head. "Just prepare yourself. Battle alters a man, as you must surely know." With another heavy sigh, she placed the empty bucket on the hearth. "You may never get *your* Vadim back. Not as he was." She handed Martha a sheet then turned away. "I would not have you go there tomorrow so unprepared."

Wrapped herself in a bath sheet, Martha stepped from the tub, water pattering like rain onto the flagstone floor. Then she leaned over the bath and squeezed out her hair.

Had Vadim changed? Thank goodness for Bren. Without her, she might have been completely blown out of the water tomorrow. At least now she was prepared for the worst. If Vadim looked at her with hatred, or if he looked at Orla with affection, she was ready for it. No matter how much it hurt, Martha knew she could act her way out of any situation now.

Please, God. I know. I already owe you big-time, but please don't let Vadim be in love with Orla.

chapter twenty-six

PERHAPS DRINKING MEAD INTO THE small hours wasn't the best way to prepare for what lay ahead. Nursing the mother of all hangovers, Martha trudged up the hillside following Seth and Forge. *What I wouldn't give for a pair of sunglasses!*

Each footstep sent her brain crashing against the inside of her skull. She took another swig from her water-bladder. It was already half-empty, and her mouth still tasted like something from the bottom of a cage.

Good work, Bigalow. How will he ever be able to resist you? I bet Orla's eyes aren't bloodshot.

At least her gown looked good. That was some consolation. She glanced down at her moss-green skirt, swinging elegantly as she walked. It was made from the finest, softest wool— yet another purchase from the proceeds of poor Guy's jewelery stash. To earn the price of the garment herself, she would've had to work for two months at the laundry back in Edgeway.

It was just as well she'd got herself a decent wardrobe. After today, she foresaw that a certain young seamstress wouldn't be accepting any more of her orders.

"We are almost there," Seth called over his shoulder.

Martha hadn't the breath to reply. The sun beat down from a cloudless blue sky. She took off her headscarf and used it to wipe her face while the wind played havoc with her hair. She hoped Seth would give her a few minutes to prepare before they reached the lodge. Facing Vadim was going to be hard enough without looking like a total wreck when she got there.

The hill finally leveled off. Panting a little, Martha looked about her. They were on the edge of a wood. Birds twittered, hidden in the thick green canopy of leaves. It was such a peaceful place. The uppermost branches of the trees swayed and swooshed almost playfully in the breeze.

She followed Seth into the shadows at the edge of the clearing. The cool darkness was a relief after the brutal heat of the sun.

"Shall we sit for a while?" Seth led her to a fallen log. "Catch your breath. The lodge lies a little way along the path." He pointed to a narrow trail, winding through the trees.

Forge was already snuffling there, nose pressed to the earth—reading his doggy mail, as Martha called it.

She dabbed her face and neck with her headscarf then smoothed back her hair before turning to Seth. "How do I look?"

"Hot," he answered with a smile.

And Martha just knew he didn't mean *hot* as in *attractive*. She made room for him to sit beside her on the log.

"I love it here." Seth gazed up at the trees with wistful eyes. "Before Anselm was born, Sylvie and I used to come here often."

"Do you have any other children?" Martha asked, wondering why she'd never thought to ask this question before.

"No." Seth closed his eyes and raised his face to the sun. Shadows of dappled sunlight played across his skin, filtering through the gently swaying trees. "His was a difficult birth, and I almost lost my Sylvie because of it. But good fortune was with me that day." He sighed. "I know I should be grateful for all the happy years we shared, but I am not. The days were much too brief. A thousand years would not be enough to spend with such a woman."

Martha patted his hand, her heart contracting with sympathy. What could she possibly say to that?

While Seth wandered in his memories, Martha reached into her backpack and retrieved a small phial of lavender water. She sprinkled the fragrant perfume liberally over her hair then patted some on her neck and face. It wasn't deodorant, but it would have to do. The fresh, clean scent raised her spirits, quietening the snakes that twisted and writhed in her stomach. Every so often, her heart gave a little flutter of anticipation. The sensation made her feel slightly sick.

As much as she longed to see Vadim, she dreaded it too, fearing his rejection more than anything. Her anxiety reminded her of back when she was a child, and of the night before school commenced after the long summer break.

After a few minutes, Seth roused himself from his waking dream. He turned to look at her. "Are you ready then, m'lady?"

No. Martha stood up. "As I'll ever be."

In single-file, they followed the trail as it wound through the ever-deepening shadows of the trees. Finally, the path broke free of the forest and entered another clearing. There, standing before them was a small log cabin, its timbers bleached by many summers. But it looked sturdy and cosy. Several hens pecked and scratched in the dirt at the foot of the steps.

"Shall I go on ahead?" Seth asked.

Martha nodded. "If you don't mind?" She laced her fingers together, trying to stop her hands from shaking.

Breathe. Just breathe.

Seth strode toward the house and clomped up the wooden steps. After rapping twice on the door, he walked inside.

Interminable moments passed. At last, the door swung

open again. But it wasn't Seth coming out. It was Orla.

The girl's pretty face was twisted in an unpleasant expression. She slammed the door behind her and stomped down the steps. When she saw Martha, Orla's eyes narrowed and she hurried towards her.

A block of ice formed in Martha's stomach.She wasn't going to be intimidated by a child. She set off to meet her rival.

"You finally came back, then?" Orla sneered.

They stood close, confronting one another like fighters at a pre-match press conference.

"As you see." Martha smiled into Orla's glacial blue eyes. The challenge she saw in them was unmistakable. And it was exactly what she needed to reboot herself. Heat tingled up from her toes, warming her blood as it swiftly rose up through her body, banishing her trembling nerves.

"Why did you bother?" Orla planted her hands on her hips, glaring at Martha with unveiled dislike. "Vadim does not want you now, and who can blame him? What kind of wife are you?"

At these words, hope flared in Martha's heart. *So he hasn't told you?* "Keep out of this, Orla. It's none of your business."

"I have been caring for him for the past two months." Orla swung her lovely auburn tresses like a spirited horse. "That makes it my business, *milady*."

"Wrong." Martha smiled coldly. "That makes you his nurse, nothing more. But I'm sure we're both very grateful for your diligence."

It *was* childish, but when she saw the two pink spots of temper flushing Orla's cheeks, she wanted to punch the air and shout, *Yes!*

The girl opened her mouth to speak, but nothing came out. Without another word, she stormed away toward the trees.

Round one to me.

Forge ambled over and Martha bent down to pat him, still grinning to herself. The door swung open again. This time, Orla's mother came down the steps.

Martha straightened up and nodded at the older woman as she approached. "Elsbeth." What would her reception be this time?

To her great surprise, Orla's mother smiled.

"Greetings, m'lady. It gladdens my heart to see you again."

Really?

But Martha returned her smile. "Thank you for taking such good care of Vadim. Orla tells me you've been doing so for quite some time."

"Aye." Elsbeth's smile faded. "And I can imagine her tone too. Forgive her, m'lady. The hearts of the young are quick in their wild imaginings. It is good you have come to break her attachment to my lord Vadim before it grows too strong." Despite the heat of the day, Elsbeth swung a black shawl over her shoulders and tied the ends about her waist. "Not that your man is responsible for encouraging my daughter's tenderness, you understand. Indeed, he has not spoken at all. Not since..."

Martha's heart lurched. *Good God. What's wrong with him?*

"I-I understood he received only the one sword wound?" *Only!*

"That he did, m'lady. No, this is some other affliction." She gave a sigh. "I fear his spirit fled when death came too near." She reached out and squeezed Martha's hand. "Surely it will return to him now that you have come." With a comforting smile, Elsbeth waddled off, following the trail her daughter had so recently taken.

Taking a deep breath, Martha walked towards the lodge. But as she approached the steps, her feet slowed. What should she do? Walk in? Knock?

In the end she didn't have to decide. Seth opened the door and beckoned her inside.

"His eyes are closed," Seth murmured as Martha walked by, "but I believe he heard my words."

Martha nodded. She caught hold the Seth's sleeve as he made to go outside. "D-did you tell him I was here?"

"Aye. I hoped the news might get a reaction but..." He shrugged. "Just do what you can, lass. If you need me, call out. I will be close by." With these words, Seth left.

As the door closed behind him, it robbed the room of light. The gloom was oppressive. *I can't see a sodding thing.* Heart hammering, and hardly daring to breathe, Martha tiptoed toward the tiny window and the faint light filtering through its blanket covering.

She stumbled over what she suspected was a low stool. Stooping to rub her aching shin, she limped to the window and folded the blanket back a fraction. *Better.*

A broad strip of daylight illuminated a path across the floor planks to a narrow bed in the far corner of the cabin.

Martha gasped. *Holy Mother of God!* Her hands flew up to her mouth. *Vadim.*

She hardly recognised him. Boots tip-tapping over the wooden floor, she hurried over to the bed and knelt beside it.

"Vadim?" Her voice was barely a whisper.

He lay on his back, motionless, his face turned towards the wall. In the dim light, the deep hollows of his face were clear, despite his untidy beard.

He did not respond. His eyes stayed closed, sleeping within their sunken sockets.

Martha's lower lip wobbled. The lump in her throat threatened to choke her. All of her previous joy withered at finding him in such a terrible state. His hand lay outside the cover, resting on his stomach. The sight of those long, beautiful fingers, so still and helpless, moved her to tears. She bit her lip, attempting to halt their silent flow.

My poor love. What have they done to you?

With quaking fingers, she touched his hand, half expecting to find it cold. But it was warm. Alive.

She curled her fingers around his. Still no reaction. "Oh, Vadim."

Clinging tightly to his hand, she rested her cheek against his arm and closed her eyes. He smelled just as she remembered: leather, smoke, and his own clean man-scent. She inhaled deeply, reacquainting her lungs with him. Each breath transported her back in time, to a moment within his arms. She could almost hear his voice again—taste his kiss.

"I'm sorry," she whispered. "I should've never left you." His shirt sleeve was already damp with her tears. She turned her head and pressed her nose against him, breathing in his heat and scent as it seeped through the thin linen.

He breathed so low she had to strain to hear it.

Maybe he really *was* dying? *Oh, God, no.*

***

He found her again in his dream. *Martha?* She was the scent of summertime, of lavender and wild mountain air.

Is it her? The woman who always waited for him in his sleep smiled and nodded. The waves of her hair shone like a chestnut fresh from its casing. Her lips moved soundlessly.

Martha.

How had he forgotten her? Consciousness beckoned, but he fought to stay within his dream. The scent of skin-warmed lavender roused him. It was real. His eyelids flickered.

Let me dream a while longer.

He knew that when he opened his eyes, his delusion of joy would fade, becoming the reality of that wretched girl, Orla.

As he recalled Martha's name, the black wall within his mind crumbled. The bad memories were restored along with all of his most precious ones.

Martha.

A dream was all she could ever be. The last time he saw her, he had accused her of falsehood. Then he had almost ruined them both. Of course she would not return to him now.

"Vadim? Can you hear me?"

The ice encasing his heart fractured, splintering into a million tiny shards. Hot blood flowed in, each beat restoring him to life. Still he hesitated. His eyelids remained closed. He needed to be certain she was not Orla. His mind could not be trusted with the truth anymore.

"Please wake up." He heard a sniff. "They say you can't talk."

A gentle hand stroked his hair. Vadim shivered.

She sounds like her.

"Come on." Impatience now. "Open your feck— I mean...your eyes, would you?"

It is her!

Vadim's eyes snapped open and he turned his head to face her. The sudden movement made Martha jump, her blue eyes wide and startled. But she recovered swiftly, and the brilliance of her smile drove the breath from his lungs.

She stroked his hair. "Hey, you."

It really was her, kneeling beside the bed, touching him. Bright tears shimmered in her eyes.

For me?

"Are we good now?" she asked, her voice trembling.

Vadim frowned. "G-g-good?" His mouth felt slow and clumsy as though it belonged to someone else. How long since he had last spoken?

But his lack of coherence apparently delighted Martha. She clapped her hands together and smiled broadly at him. He could not for the life of him imagine why.

"Yes, good," she said.

He liked how her eyes crinkled with the force of her smile.

"I mean, are we friends again? Shall we forget all the bad sh...stuff?"

He smiled back at her for the first time in forever. "Y-yes. We are...good."

To his dismay, she covered her lovely face with her hands and broke into hiccupping sobs.

"I'm s-so s-sorry."

He frowned, straining to make out her words.

"I...I can't h-help it."

He reached out to touch the wild waves of her hair and coiled one long rich lock about his finger. "Shh," he murmured. "Come."

Martha lowered her hands. Her face glistened with tears, lower lip wobbling perilously.

Vadim shuffled up, making room for her on the bed. He patted the mattress, offering her a place to sit more comfortably.

Martha took his hand when he offered it. To his surprise—completely misunderstanding his intentions—she—kicked off her boots and scrambled into bed with him, burrowing her face against his neck.

This unexpected intimacy made his heart to thunder. Smiling, Vadim folded his arm around her and balanced his chin on top of her head.

"Wife." He puffed at her soft hair as it tickled his nose.

Martha giggled and snivelled, still keeping a tight grip on his hand.

He cleared his throat. It was frustrating to be unable to question her as he would like. Was this only a visit, he wondered.

"Stay?"

Fortunately, Martha appeared to understand.

"I'm not going anywhere," she assured him.

"Good." Vadim closed his eyes and was content.

chapter twenty-seven

MARTHA WOKE WITH A START, her memory flooding back. *Vadim!* She couldn't believe it. She'd gone fallen asleep in his arms. The exertion of the early morning walk must be to blame. That, and last night's drinking bender with Bren.

She inhaled deeply. He smelt so good. The familiar combination of leather and man-scent teased her nostrils. She burrowed her face deeper into his linen shirt, savoring the warmth of his body and the sound of his heart thudding reassuringly in his chest. She sighed, and the stress of the last few days ebbed away. *He's alive. Real.*

She felt his hand stroking against her hair. Stifling a yawn with the back of her hand, she looked up at him. His dark eyes glittered, and his lips curved into a smile.

"Hi. Sorry about that." Her voice sounded husky. "Was I asleep long?"

Vadim shook his head and trailed his index finger slowly down her cheek.

Bliss.

"Bren and I had a bit of a drinking session last night. She kept plying me with mead. I never realised it was so strong." She knew she was waffling, but she couldn't help it. The way he was looking at her was as intoxicating as last night's mead. Beneath his intense scrutiny, she felt a familiar heat flushing her cheeks.

"Little...d-drunkard."

She laughed because she couldn't help it. Hearing his voice again filled her with such joy. Her heart swelled with love until her chest felt too small to contain it.

But this was love of a different kind. Although she still wanted him—all of him—her hormones had quietened down to a low roar.

Vadim had always been lean, but now he was positively thin, his muscles wasted. She could feel each one of his ribs beneath her fingers. She wanted to restore him to what he'd been before— to 'fix' him if she could. But it was his mental state that concerned her most. Why hadn't he spoken to anyone before today?

He was still watching her, his eyes clouding with concern.

She turned up her smile dial to full again. "This will have to go," she said brightly, running her fingers over his scraggly beard. "You look like a bad version of Seth."

"Nag. Nag." His familiar crooked grin returned. The one that said 'rosebud' to the killer butterflies in her stomach and commanded them to attack.

Sick or not, I still fancy the pants off him.

But this wasn't the time. First things first.

Ignoring his frown, Martha scrambled from the bed and went to pull the covering from the solitary window. Vadim shielded his eyes as bright light flooded the room.

"Oh, come on, Vadim. What are you now, a bat? I know you like caves, but this is taking it to extremes."

She returned to the bed and held out her hand. "Get up, you...what did you once call me? A slug?"

Vadim chuckled. "Sluggard."

"Whatever." She clasped his hand, pulling until he sat upright. "Elsbeth says your wound has healed, so there's no reason for you to spend the rest of the day idling."

Could he be suffering from post-traumatic stress of some kind? There was no way of knowing what was going on in his mind. She'd read the papers back home in the twenty-first century and watched programs on the subject on TV. Was PTSD even around in medieval times? Although she longed to know about the day he'd almost died, it was too soon to quiz him, and something prevented her from asking him about it.

Get him moving first. The other stuff will keep.

Martha opened the door and saw Seth sitting in the shade of the trees. She felt a stab of guilt. She'd forgotten all about him. *What time is it?* The sun was directly overhead. Lunchtime or thereabouts.

Martha ran down the steps and skipped outside. "Sorry we were so long, Seth. I fell asleep. Come on in, and I'll rustle up some lunch."

Seth opened his eyes and rose stiffly from the fallen tree he'd been sitting on. But he wasn't looking at her. His gaze was on the tall shadow in the doorway of the cabin. Leaning heavily on his walking stick, Vadim slowly tapped his way down the steps.

"Vadim!" Seth strode toward him, arms open. "It heartens me to see you up and about, my friend." The two men hugged and exchanged a couple of back-slaps. "How do you feel?"

Vadim nodded. "B-better."

Seth's jaw dropped. "You found your voice?" He blinked and glanced over to Martha, shaking his head in disbelief. "Truly, the power of a good woman is mightier than any siege engine."

Vadim jerked his head in the direction of the trees. "Walk?" he said to Seth.

"Gladly."

"Is this a boys-only thing?" Martha asked. The look they sent her was answer enough. "Okay. I can take a hint." *Walk must be code for a trip to the big boys' room. Big?* Her cheeks burned at her mind's smutty diversion.

"Okay. You two have fun. I'll go and see what I can find for lunch." Right on cue, her stomach grumbled.

Happiness was a very hungry business.

***

They were away for some time, long enough for Vadim to learn all the sorrow he had missed, adding to the burden of his heart.

When all the bitter words had been spoken, they returned to the hunting lodge in silence, retracing their path through the whispering trees. What more was there to be said?

Seth shortened his stride to keep pace with him. The older man's eyes were red-rimmed and swollen, as were his own. Sylvie—his almost-mother—was dead. Though his own eyes were now dry, his heart still wept tears of blood.

The circumstances surrounding her death were almost inconceivable. Sylvie had betrayed him. Her guilt must be genuine, for Seth would never wantonly defile the memory of his beloved wife. Even so, Vadim bore no anger toward her. He had loved Sylvie as a mother. Resentment was too heavy a load for him to bear, and she had already paid a high price for betraying them.

He prayed the Spirits would grant her peace. He had already forgiven her. How could he not when he had loved her so well? If Martha had not returned he might have felt differently. Despite his sorrow, a warm glow banished the shadows from even the deepest recesses of his heart.

Suddenly, he longed to be hale and whole again—and not only to court Martha. According to Seth, she had forged an acquaintance with Anselm during her time in Edgeway. That could not be mere coincidence.

His neck prickled a chill of warning, and he was not fool enough to ignore it. His treacherous litter-mate may already be hunting for her.

Curse my idleness. How can I protect her when I cannot even stand unassisted?

"M'lord? Listen." Seth held up his hand and stopped walking, his head tilted in the direction of the hunting lodge, just visible through the trees.

From within the cabin came the sound of angry voices. Vadim exhaled. Female voices.

Seth glanced at him. "More trouble."

At least it was not Anselm. Not yet anyway.

He was close enough to be able to discern Martha's voice. Who was she quarreling with? Although he had not voiced the question, Seth answered it.

"As soon as you are recovered, I fear you will need to be harsh with young Orla, my friend."

Of course. The other voice was Orla's. As grateful as he was for all for all the maid had done for him, the weight of her devotion was as a band of steel restricting his soul. If Martha chose to behave in the same manner, however, *her* attentions would be most welcome.

He was still uncertain why she had returned. *Out of pity, perhaps?* That would do to begin with. Where Martha was concerned, he had no pride remaining.

At that moment, Orla flew out of the hunting lodge and stumbled down the steps—almost falling in her haste to be gone. With impressive force and accuracy, Martha pitched a cloak and basket at the girl's departing back. "He's my husband, not yours!" she cried.

Vadim's eyes widened. He exchanged a glance with Seth who appeared equally surprised.

"I think your lady is reclaiming her territory."

Vadim could only agree. Martha's angry words filled him with hope. Perhaps pity was not all she felt? He looked at her and wondered. She stood in the doorway of the cabin, her cheeks flushed and her breast heaving. The soft green gown she wore flattered her shapely figure well.

From her vantage point, she stared down at Orla like an angry she-wolf, watching as the maid scrambled in the dirt gathering her scattered possessions. Even from this distance, Vadim recognised the warning in Martha's eyes. He had felt its weight before.

Foolishly, Orla was not yet daunted by her adversary. "You will be sorry you ever came back," she snarled. "Heed my warning and leave while you still may. Go back to your family."

From the safety of the woods, Vadim leaned on his stick and watched the scene with interest. Unless it came to physical blows, he was reluctant to disturb the fair combatants.

Seth selected a tree to lean against, apparently equally content to watch. "Aye. Their claws are sharp now." He looked pleased. "There is nothing like warring women to make a man feel alive."

Vadim returned his attention to the cabin as Martha stalked down the steps, her attention fixed upon her quarry.

"Vadim *is* my family, you stupid girl. I'm staying. Get used to it."

"Oh?" Orla's laugh was a bitter sound. "Will you still want him when you learn that I have shared his bed?"

"What?"

"What!"

Although some distance apart, Martha and Vadim spoke in unison.

"Ask him, if you dare." Orla stood up, her head held high, flinging back her hair like a glorious red banner. "If the errant wife does not fulfill her duty, a man cannot be blamed for looking elsewhere."

A cold ball of anger formed in Vadim's stomach. This had gone far enough. He made a move from the shadows, ready to confront Orla and her wild claims. But Seth laid a hand upon his arm.

"Words are all they are, m'lord. Jealous lies and poison." The older man smiled. "Wait a little longer. See if Orla's nonsense rewards you with gold."

Vadim scowled. "Hmm?" Anger had him

mumbling again.

"You might learn something of value if we let them be."

Although it was not the honorable thing to do, Vadim conceded. So he remained where he was, watching with Seth from the dappled shadows.

Martha's eyes were shut tight, her hands alternately clenching then flexing at her side. Orla smiled, apparently well pleased with the aim of her poisoned arrow.

To Vadim's surprise, when Martha opened her eyes, she laughed.

"Poor Orla." She shook her head. "You must want him very badly if you're prepared to cheapen your name in this way. But what of Vadim's honor? He values it more than anything."

Almost anything.

"Do you really think he'll be happy to hear how you've blackened him?"

"I speak the truth." But Orla's smile was gone.

"Really?" Martha took a step towards her. "Then you truly are ruined, aren't you? No decent man will ever want you once word of this gets out."

Vadim almost believed Martha was worried about Orla's reputation, such were the gentle concern of her words.

"Your poor mother." She advanced closer to the girl. "I suppose it's only right I tell her about your fling with my husband. Maybe she won't cast you out onto the streets?" Her eyes narrowed, shining with the light of battle. "But if she does, there's a certain Mrs. Wilkes in Edgeway who might provide you with accommodation. But you'll have to work for it, Orla. Mainly on your back, or so I'm told."

Seth spluttered as he attempted to check his burst of laughter.

Orla, meanwhile, grew pale and took a step back. "And what of Vadim? Would you hurt him this way?"

"He'll be fine, you silly girl."

Martha's lips curved into a lazy smile, and the sight

of it aroused him, awakening a fire in his loins. Where had she learned to do that—in bed with a previous lover, perhaps? He ground his teeth and dug his fingers into the tree's rough bark.

"Oh, he'll suffer a few black looks from people, no doubt," Martha continued, "but it'll soon pass." She was face to face with Orla now, but she looked relaxed. "It's different for men, Orla. Didn't you know?"

Orla took several rapid backward steps. "Will you take him back, m'lady, knowing how he has—"

"Bedded you?" Martha shrugged. "Oh, I'll make him suffer for a while. My forgiveness won't come cheaply. A few gold bracelets might advance his cause." She gave another wicked smile.

Vadim shook his head. Why had he ever worried about Martha? She had all the graceful moves of a poisonous snake—beautiful but deadly. He had never admired her more than at this moment.

"What of love?" Orla demanded. "You have not spoken of it once."

"Haven't I? How remiss of me."

Vadim's breath caught in his throat as Martha looked straight at him. Her eyes locked with his and held him there.

"Of course I love him," she said softly. "Why else would I be here?"

His heart threatened to thunder from its cage. He knew her words were meant for him alone. The revelation rocked him to the foundations of his being. Seth chuckled and nudged him in the ribs, but Vadim could not look away from her.

Orla crumbled, defeated by Martha's. "Forgive me for speaking so falsely, m'lady." The girl sank to her knees before her, all her poisonous barbs spent. "I must have been possessed by an evil spirit. Or a demon, perhaps?"

Vadim exhaled an uneven breath as Martha released him from her gaze.

"Demonic possession, eh? Whatever." She extended her hand to help Orla up from the ground. "Up you get."

Orla took the hand Martha offered her. "You never believed he was guilty, did you?" Her tone was that of a repentant child seeking forgiveness from its parent.

"No, I didn't."

Vadim dared not breathe as Martha looked at him again.

"My husband is capable of many things, but such a blatant act of dishonor is beneath him."

"He must love you a great deal, my lady. I am s-sorry for what I said."

At the word 'love', Martha dropped her gaze, her cheeks reddening. For the first time, she looked vulnerable, uncertain. "Whatever. Let's leave it there. Go on home, Orla."

The truth hit Vadim with the force of a trebuchet strike. *She truly does not know I love her?* But then, why would she? Almost from the start of their relationship, he had treated her despicably, blowing hot and cold by turn. His moods had been as changeable as the weather of a spring day. Accusing her of being the Earl's spy had been the final cut.

Orla gathered her things and hurried away leaving Martha alone; the victor on the field of battle. Vadim saw her take a deep breath before she wandered back to the hunting lodge. She did not spare him another glance.

Throughout the meal, Vadim studied her, searching for proof to back up her declaration of love. How would she reveal it? In a look? A touch?

Martha made no mention of her quarrel with Orla, and neither he nor Seth was ungallant enough to introduce the subject. Instead, she regaled them with amusing tales of her adventures in Edgeway, while they ate.

For some reason, she seemed reluctant to meet his eyes, frequently looking at Seth instead of himself.

Avoidance? Most interesting.

Vadim was content to sit in silent contemplation and bask in the warmth of her presence. While Seth and Martha laughed and talked together, his eyes reacquainted themselves with the woman of his heart.

Can she truly feel the same way?

The early symptoms were encouraging. But he would not risk her bolting from him again. Not until he was fit to chase her, at least. Martha certainly liked to run, and thus far, she had led him a very merry dance.

At last she looked at him. "You've hardly eaten anything." Her blue eyes narrowed, and a delightful little crease marred the fairness of her brow. "D'you want something else?"

Vadim shook his head and quickly popped a piece of bread into his mouth. In truth, its texture was as appealing as a piece of horse harness, but he chewed doggedly. He wanted to be himself again, not the shadow man he had become.

"That's better." Martha rewarded him with a smile to melt winter. "Now try some of the cheese. It's good for you, full of protein."

Protein?

She must have read his mind. "It'll help you get strong again."

Seth picked up a piece of cheese and stared at it curiously, as if wondering at its magical properties. But he ate some, Vadim noticed, amused.

"In fact, I really must go shopping and get some decent food for you."

"No!" Vadim did not want her to stray from his sight again. "Stay. Seth?"

Seth beamed his familiar grin. It was good to see. "Lord Vadim has spoken, m'lady. Tell me what you require, and I will bring it."

"Oh, that's kind of you, Seth." Martha squeezed the older man's hand. "I don't really want to leave him now. Okay, he's going to need lots of milk, eggs, fish—if you can get it. If not, chicken will..."

Did she intend to feed an army? Vadim smiled as her list of demands lengthened. Seth would need a mule to carry all of that back up the hill.

When lunch was over, Martha asked Seth to do one more thing before he returned to Darumvale.

"You want me to remove his beard?" Seth visibly shuddered. "Whatever for?" He fingered his own beard as though fearing she might demand that next.

"Because it'll make him feel better." She laughed as she rose from the table. "Don't worry, Seth. Your beard really suits you."

To Vadim's surprise, she came and stood behind him and placed her hands on his shoulders. Her touch seemed to burn his skin through the thin protection of his shirt.

"Just think of it as phase one of Martha's master plan," she said.

Seth cast a worried glance at Vadim. "M'lord?"

He shrugged, indicating he cared not either way.

"Very well." Seth shook his head. "But I fear you will miss it."

Martha found a blade lying forgotten on one of the cabin's dusty shelves. After stropping it vigorously on a leather belt, Seth set to work.

When the task was completed, he called to Martha, who was busily boiling water, filling up an old bath tub she had found outside.

"Well? Does your husband meet your approval, m'lady?"

"Oh, wow!" She hastened to where Vadim sat at the table and gently trailed her fingertips over his clean-shaven cheek. "You're back," she said with wonder.

He smiled. Martha's approval was plain. As he held her gaze, a familiar heat flared between them. Her lips were slightly parted. Unable to help himself, he grazed the pad of his thumb over the fullness of her lower one. Her eyes closed in response, long lashes flickering. The urge to taste her again, to see her mouth glistening with his kiss, overwhelmed him. Surely she would welcome it?

"Ahem." Seth's intrusion was never so unwanted.

The spell was broken, and Martha stepped away.

"If you require nothing more of me, then I will bid you both farewell until the morrow."

It was difficult to gauge whose blushes burned the fiercest. Both very red in the face, Seth and Martha competed to sound easy and natural.

"All right. Be careful going back down the hill, won't you?"

"Of course. Is there anything else you require me to fetch?"

"Erm...you might ask Bren to give you my saddle packs. Oh, and you could bring Forge back with you. He'll be driving her nuts by now."

Vadim chuckled and stood up. "Walk...you...out?"

Seth nodded, beard a-bristling and almost ran from the cabin. Vadim sent Martha a wink and slowly limped after his friend.

***

After they'd gone, Martha sank down onto the bench and exhaled. *Holy feck. What was that? He's supposed to be sick.* She rubbed hands over her hot cheeks and willed her heart to slow down.

It was her own fault. That fight with Orla had fired her up way too much. Maybe that was why she'd gone and told him she loved him. Oh, she'd seen him there, hiding out in the trees with Seth. But it was as if a demon had taken over her mouth, and she'd been so damn angry she hadn't cared.

She took another breath to steady herself. Whatever happened, at least he knew now. The L-word was out there, floating around the cosmos, free at last. The way she'd done it meant Vadim wasn't obliged to say it back or—even worse— to politely decline the contents of her heart.

It's all good, Bigalow. You finally told him—in a round-about and slightly cowardly way. What happens next, or not, is down to him.

By the time Vadim returned, Martha had the bath all ready. The steaming contents filled the cabin with the scent of lavender. The little wooden tub only lacked an occupant.

"Ah. Bathe?" Vadim frowned and prepared to leave the way he'd come.

"Wait. It's not for me, it's for you."

"Me?" He turned back to look at her. "Why?" He smiled crookedly and raised one arm to sniff at himself. "Smell?"

"No." Martha laughed. "It'll relax you." She went over and took his hand. "Call it phase two of Operation Martha." As his fingers curved around hers, her heart missed several beats.

"Yes, wife." Amusement shone from his eyes. "Stay?"

Oh, God. Operation Martha wasn't going to get very far if she couldn't stop blushing. Something told her she wasn't going to be a very good nurse. Perhaps she should have asked Elsbeth to stay? At least she seemed trust-worthy. Unlike Orla. Or herself.

"D'you need help...undressing?" She was determined to help if he needed it, embarrassment be damned.

Vadim chuckled. "Go." He gave her hand a squeeze then gently pushed her towards the door. "I can...manage."

"You're sure?" She frowned, torn between going and staying. "Okay. I'll be out by the steps, but I'll leave the door open a smidge so I can hear you."

Twitching like crazy, she paced around outside, her ears straining for sounds of Vadim in distress. Then she heard a loud splash.

Mother of God!

She bounded up the cabin steps two at a time and pressed her ear to the crack of the open door.

"Are you all right? Did you fall...Vadim?" She felt breathless. "Vadim?"

No answer. *Shit!*

Flinging open the door, she raced into the cabin, sick with dread.

She stopped dead and exhaled. To her relief, she found Vadim sitting in the bath, his skin glistening in the firelight.

He waved the bar of soap in his hand, a lazy smile curving his lips. "Dropped it."

Anger quickly replaced her relief. "Ooh. You fecker! Why didn't you answer me?" She strode over to him, too enraged for modesty. "I thought you'd hit your head or...or..."

"Or?" He arched one dark eyebrow at her.

She couldn't think of anything bad enough.

He calmly handed her the soap then relaxed against the bath's high back, eyes closed. "Phase three?"

She couldn't believe her luck. *He wants me to bathe him?* He didn't need to ask her twice.

Sinking to her knees beside the coffin-shaped bath, Martha dipped her hands in the warm water and lathered up the soap. The scent of warm lavender filled the room with summer. Vadim inhaled and sighed. His eyes stayed closed.

My poor love. He'd lost so much weight. Her heart ached to see him this way.

Her hands shook, finally roaming the places she'd long dreamt of exploring. His ribs felt like a macabre xylophone beneath her fingers. Tears pricked behind her eyes when she remembered how he'd been before she left him, bristling with lean, defined muscles. Only a ghost remained, like the negative of a photograph. A tear escaped and slid down her cheek.

Don't. This is fixable, remember?

She glanced at Vadim. He hadn't moved. Eyes closed, his sooty eyelashes twitched upon his cheeks. Maybe he'd fallen asleep?

Gliding her hands over to the left side of his body, Martha lathered soap over his neck and exposed throat. Despite his recent shave, stubble grazed the pads of her fingers. She moved on, sweeping down to his arms which were balanced on the edge of the bath. She paid particular attention to the exquisite runic band tattoo at the top of his left arm, submerging the ink runes beneath a cloud of fragrant bubbles.

As she worked, Martha chanced a sly downward peek. But she was to be disappointed. *Damn it!* Wisely, perhaps anticipating her lack of restraint, Vadim had arranged a folded linen cloth over his most intimate region.

The soap was getting dry. Almost as dry as her mouth. Martha dipped the slippery block into the water and rotated it between her hands until it frothed. Then, sucking in her lower lip, she turned her attention to his chest and the dark scattering of hair on his pecs, swirling gentle circles around each nipple until they hardened in response.

Vadim's breathing sounded rather fast. *Good.* She was more than a little miffed about the positioning of that linen cloth.

Biting down on her lower lip, Martha attempted to concentrate on her task and not think about jumping him.

Be cool. Pretend you're a nurse.

More soap. The little bar was dwindling fast, such was her attention to detail. She slithered a figure of eight over his heart, but it pounded so hard beneath her hands she stopped.

She darted another glance at him. Nope. His eyes were still closed.

It was quiet. Just the crackles of the fire in the grate and the sounds of their breaths interrupted the silence. Quiet enough to hear the soap bubbles crackling on her hands.

Feeling braver, she moved her hands lower, massaging lazy circles over his lower abdomen, bypassing the old scars, reaching down to the surface of the water.

Vadim hissed, sucking the air between his teeth, his muscles tensing beneath her fingers.

"Oh, I'm sorry." Remorse banished her lustful thoughts. "Did I hurt you?" Her voice sounded so husky that it didn't sound like her voice at all.

"N-no."

Martha felt uncomfortably hot. Touching him like this was easily the most sensual moment of her life to date. She glanced down and gasped. To the right of his belly button was a small raised patch of red, puckered skin. Obviously it was a recently healed injury.

Vadim's eyes flickered open. He sat up and leaned forward, exposing his back so she could see the rest of the wound. "Look."

How could she not obey him?

"Oh, shit!"

Low down on his back, she saw a corresponding wound. But this one was larger than the one on his abdomen, roughly the size and width of a sword blade. It still looked angry and sore.

Martha glided her hand down his back, her fingers glancing lightly over the wound. "D-does it hurt?" She bit her lip again. Hard. How could someone do this to him?

"Not now." Vadim tilted his head and looked at her. His hair hung down his back like a sleek dark pelt, the ends dipping into the water. "Do not...weep."

She hadn't realised she was.

Vadim touched her face with his wet hand. He caught one of her tears and balanced it on his thumb. With a tiny smile, he raised it to his lips and kissed the tear away.

"Better now."

Martha stared. Her tear supply abruptly disconnected. A sudden ravenous hunger consumed her. But not for food. Her stomach clenched. Somehow she managed not to growl at him, though she seriously wanted to. For once, no inner thoughts governed her actions. Her mind was silent, her body free to act as it desired. Her fingers tightened their hold on the side of the bath.

Sick or not, she wanted him. Wasted and weak? Not an issue.

Martha picked up a wash cloth and dabbled it in the bath. Then she raised it, dribbling warm water down his back like a poor man's shower, washing the soap away. Then she leaned over and brushed her lips over the wound. She heard Vadim's swift intake of breath.

Straightening up, she slid her hand up his arm and gently pushed him back against the bath. Now that she had access to the other, smaller injury on his abdomen. It lay dangerously near the water line, and what lay beneath. Martha wasn't afraid. She bent over the bath, her dangling hair floating in the water.

"All...better...now." She applied her personal prescription to his wound, each word punctuated by a kiss. Then she raised her head and looked at him. What she saw pleased her.

Vadim's eyes flared. The tic was back, pulsing away in his firm jaw line. He grasped her arm, water soaking through the fine woolen sleeve of her gown. She smiled and stroked the hair back from his face. It felt like heavy silk beneath her fingers. Leaning closer, she bracing herself against his wet chest with her free hand. His breath played hot and fast over her lips.

When he looked at her like that, she felt like the sexiest woman alive. Martha the bold, the brave, the beautiful. The bad. "Will that be all, my lord?"

Vadim frowned, obviously teetering on the edge of control. His lips moved in soundless speech, as if searching for the right words.

"Hmm?" Martha's index finger danced a lazy spiral through the hair on his chest, *accidentally* encountering a hard nipple. "Is your water growing cold? Shall I fetch you a bath sheet?"

His fingers pressed harder into the soft flesh of her arm, preventing her from going anywhere.

"Then perhaps—"

Cupping her face between his hands, Vadim drew her to him, silencing her with his mouth. She sighed, surrendering to the joy of his kiss, her tongue greeting his. Her arms slid about his neck, while tepid water soaked through the bodice of her gown. She didn't care. She closed her eyes. He tasted just as good as she remembered. In his arms, she found the same happiness as before.

And more besides.

This time, there was no anger to accelerate passion. No deceit. No pretence. This time it was real. Just them.

Eventually they drew apart, panting. Martha giggled then nuzzled up against his ear. Vadim stroked her back.

"You...are...wet." Vadim growled.

How does he... Oh, my dress. Right.

"I don't care." She was too happy, half submerged, sharing the tiny bath with him. She didn't ever want to move.

Vadim seemed equally content to hold her there, his arms folded around her back. "Did you...mean it?" His halting voice was husky, and all too seductive.

Of course, she knew what he was referring to. "What I said to Orla?" She kissed the sensitive skin behind his ear.

"Mmm."

Dare I say it again? She raised her head and looked into his eyes. They looked as black as storm clouds. *I want to say it.*

"Yes, Vadim. I love you." Before he could speak, she placed two fingers over his lips. "Don't say anything now. There's no need. Just get better first, huh? Please?"

"And...then?"

Martha smiled. She couldn't stop smiling. "And then?" She took his lower lip into her mouth and sucked gently on it, making him groan. "Then, we'll see."

***

To Vadim's surprise, she disentangled herself from his arms and began washing his hair, humming softly to herself. The lover turned into a mother. How could she be so calm when he was aching for her so badly?

Afterwards, Martha fetched a bath sheet and assisted him as he stepped from the bath. Then she started to unlace her sodden gown. From his place by the fire, Vadim watched in astonishment, grateful that the sheet draped over his hips concealed his body's reaction to her.

As she wriggled herself free of the soggy garment, all the time, Martha kept her eyes locked on his, baiting him. *Temptress. Let her have her sport while she may. I will not be an invalid forever.*

At last the gown lay in a pool at her feet. She stepped out of it and carried it to where he sat beside the fire.

Vadim caught his breath. The shift she wore beneath her gown was equally wet. Whenever she moved it clung to her, tormenting him with its transparent quality.

"M-Martha?"

"Hmm?" She regarded him with sultry eyes.

He cleared his throat and pointed to his own chest, not wanting to point at hers. Fortunately, she understood. On a previous occasion when he had seen her like this, her embarrassment had been acute. Now, however, she only shrugged and smiled.

"Oh, yes. I know. But I haven't got anything else to wear. Not until Seth brings up the rest of my stuff." She shook out her gown and hung it to dry over a chair.

"Shirt," he said, pointing to a trunk at the other side of the room.

"Oh, thanks. But I'll have a quick bath first. I'm so

hot and sweaty." Her fingers moved to the tie of her shift.

By all that is sacred!

Holding the bath sheet firmly about his middle, Vadim rose from his seat.

"You don't have to go." Her innocent look did not fool him at all.

"Yes...I do." Placing his index finger beneath her chin, he tilted it upwards and brushed her lips with his. "Shameless...witch." Her eyes had darkened, mirroring his own desire. But he knew his body had not the strength to match his need. Not yet.

She slid her arm around his waist and reached up to kiss him again. Then, with a laugh, she sent him outside to sit in the sun.

chapter twenty-eight

As the days passed, Vadim felt strength and vigor return to his body. The hunting lodge became their idyll, a retreat from the outside world and all of its concerns.

At each day's end, Martha dragged their straw mattresses in front of the fire and pushed them together making one large bed for them to share. As Vadim's voice recovered, they spent hours lying there, deep in murmured conversation, watching the fire's hypnotic flames until the night grew old. They kissed frequently, but never overstepped the unspoken barrier they had established early on in his recovery.

Each night, as she slept in his arms, Vadim offered up a silent prayer of thanks to whichever kindly spirit had first sent Martha to him.

In the beginning, back when he found her half frozen on the hillside, Martha had depended upon him to protect her and to care for her. Now their situation was reversed.

He was wholly dependent upon her.

From first light until the sun slid down in the sky, she devoted herself to his care: coaxing, cajoling, and teasing him back to life. He had never eaten so much meat and fish. At first, Martha made him eat eight meals a day, all cooked up on the cabin's small fireplace. Although the portions were small, to his shrunken stomach they seemed like a banquet. But to please her, he cleared his bowl. The warmth of her smile was worth a little discomfort.

Forge proved himself a true friend, discretely disposing of any morsels Vadim dropped to him whenever Martha's back was turned.

The frequency of meals decreased as Vadim's former vigor returned. The same could not be said of the portion size. He consumed fields—or so it seemed— of vegetables, all washed down with quarts of fresh goat's milk.

He made no complaint. He liked her fussing over him.

When she was not stuffing him with food, Martha encouraged him outside. The clement spring weather held, and they spent many hours walking together in the gentle sun, with Forge capering about their heels.

Gradually, Vadim abandoned his walking stick. Martha provided all the support he needed. Even when he was able to walk without assistance, he still draped his arm over her shoulders while they walked. He enjoyed the feel of her arm about his waist, her thumb tucked into his waistband.

They talked as much as they walked, and so he became acquainted with Martha's life in Edgeway. Her resilience filled him with pride, but the particulars of her friendship with Anselm troubled him a good deal. Although she had escaped unharmed, Vadim knew it was far from over. Now, not only had he the Earl to contend with, but his favorite tracking hound too.

Friends visited him at the cabin, outlaws, but loyal men all. Martha always made herself scarce on these occasions, enabling them to abandon their masks and talk freely. There was no news of his treacherous litter-mate, so Vadim despatched several men to hunt him down if they could.

The time for sentimental loyalty was over. Sylvie was dead, and he would not risk losing Martha.

From beneath the shade of the trees, Vadim stared up at her beloved face as he lay with his head cradled on her lap. Martha gently preened his hair with her fingers while she talked. For once, Vadim did not attend to her words. The scattering of freckles on her nose claimed his attention. They had multiplied rapidly of late. Hardly surprising given the continuing spell of fine weather.

But autumn was not far away. The subtle signs of its approach were already visible in the leaves of the trees. Almost imperceptibly, the nights had lengthened, and the sun did not linger in the sky. A new chill in the air carried notice of winter's advance.

Anselm was no fool. He would certainly strike before the snows came. Vadim frowned, and a hot ball of anger burning in his gut. *Treacherous whelp.* Come what may, he would be ready for him.

Forge grumbled and sat up from where he had been sleeping, his chin resting on Vadim's thigh. The sudden tension in his comfortable resting place must have disturbed him.

"Okay. What's wrong?"

Martha's voice finally penetrated his consciousness. "Hmm?"

"You haven't listened to a word I've said for the past hour."

"I have."

"Oh?" She twirled his hair about her finger. "Would you care to put that statement to the test?"

Vadim knew when he was beaten. "'Tis nothing, m'lady. Truly."

"So why are you frowning again? It's the third time today. Don't lie to me. You're no good at it."

"The sun was in my eyes, that is all."

"Vadim!"

More ominous clouds piled in, obscuring the sun. The sky looked almost as threatening as Martha.

He laughed at her sour little face. "Stop fretting.

Let us speak of something else, hmm?" Anything but his thoughts.

"Like what?" Martha scowled and disentangled her fingers from his hair. "The weather? Or the state of the roads, perhaps?"

"Hush, wife." He reached up and placed a finger against her lips. "Do not scold," he said softly. "Not today."

She smiled her frown away. "You must be better," she mumbled from behind his restraining finger. "You've gone all secret squirrel again."

Squirrels are secretive? He bathed in the warmth of her smile, watching as it overflowed into her sparkling blue eyes. Without her, he knew he would be eternally lost. "Are you happy, m'lady?"

She removed his finger from her lips and kissed it. "You know I am."

"What about your home? You must still think of it, though you seldom speak of it anymore."

The light in her eyes dimmed. "What's the point in talking about it? I do worry about Aunt Lulu, though. She must think I'm dead by now." Martha chewed at the corner of her lower lip. "She's old and all alone. How will she cope?"

Vadim sat up. To witness her sorrow was as bad as an actual wound to him. He would do anything to make her smile. Surely there was a way to send her home again? Kneeling beside her, he took her hands in his and raised them to his lips, pressing a kiss upon each in turn.

"Would you return home if you could?"

"Honestly? I don't know." Her sad little smile cut him to the core. "It depends."

"On what?" The tell-tale flush spreading over her cheeks provided him with an answer. "On me?" Vadim smiled. He could not help but be pleased.

"Yes...no. Oh, I don't know. It's a stupid question anyway. It's never going to happen, is it?" She pulled her hands from his. "And you needn't look so smug, m'lord. I only said *it depends.*" In her haste to stand up, her shoe caught in the long folds of her skirt. She stumbled and fell into his waiting arms, knocking him backwards.

As they tumbled into the sweet-smelling grass, Martha landed on top of him, momentarily driving the air from his lungs.

"Oh, feck!" Her remorse was swift and obviously heartfelt. "Are you all right?" She cupped his face between her hands. "I'm so sorry. Did I hurt you?" Before she could scramble off, Vadim secured her in his arms and rolled.

Now Martha lay beneath him, wide-eyed and gasping. Just as he wanted her.

"But, your wound—"

"Is much better now. Thank you." He caught her wrists and raised them slowly over her head until they rested upon the grass and the sweet-smelling meadow flowers. "And as you see, I no longer require a nurse, m'lady."

"Oh?" She pouted up at him.

Yet another of her many moods. Her eyes sparkled bright with mischief. Vadim felt his heart set off at a gallop.

"You no longer require my services then?" she asked.

"I did not say that." Smiling, he hovered over her like a predatory bird waiting for the perfect moment to strike.

"Perhaps I should gather my things and go back to the village," she continued with more feigned innocence. "I certainly won't stay where I'm not wanted."

"I did not say that, either." Quite the reverse, in fact. He dipped his head lower, his eyes flicking from her eyes to her lips, aching with wanting her.

"Oh?" Her eyes widened. "So, what exactly do you require of me, m'lord?"

"Not much." They were so close, her warm breath brushed tantalizingly over his face. "Only everything you are, and everything you will be, my love."

The need to possess her consumed him. She was his now. Whether it was prudent or not no longer mattered.

His life before Martha was a dream, an empty and desolate place. This girl...woman had captured him without ever attempting to do so.

He smiled down at her, watching the rapid rise and fall of her breast. Whether she claimed him or not, she owned him, body and soul. Until death, and whatever lay beyond the mortal veil.

He released her wrists, and Martha reached up to stroke his face.

"You want all of me? But what of my honor, m'lord?" Her soft hands trembled as she touched him, despite the lightness of her words. She brushed her lips against his, teasing him. The lightest touch from her set his blood aflame.

"I value it more than my own life," he murmured. "Just as I value you."

"Really?"

Her uncertainty only made him love her more. She truly had no idea of all she meant to him. But he would educate her, even if it took him a lifetime. "You roused my cold heart long ago." He traced his finger down her soft cheek. "When I ran, my attachment only grew stronger. I no longer want to be free. I love you, Martha."

"You do?" She returned his smile, tears sparkling in her eyes. "Oh, God!"

"I am yours now. Whatever may follow, never doubt it."

"Oh, Vadim!" Laughing and crying, she flung her arms around his neck, showering his face with eager kisses.

He chuckled and swiftly rolled them over again. Martha squealed and held on tightly. The sensation of her ripe body lying on top of his was stimulating, to say the least.

"Oh, Vadim?" He mocked her gently. "Now I have revealed my heart you choose to conceal your own? Cruel woman."

Martha giggled and snuggled her face against his neck. "You already know I love you. I told you ages ago."

"Ah, yes. On the day you fought Orla. I did wonder if you said it out of pity."

"Pity? For you? Hah!" She pushed herself up on his chest and looked down, her eyes glittering like stars. "I should pity myself. I've loved you forever. Not that you ever noticed."

"I was a fool for a long time," he admitted softly. "But no longer." He stroked her wild hair back from her face, while her blue eyes regarded him thoughtfully.

What can she be thinking?

Not for the first time Vadim longed to glimpse the secret workings of her mind. Martha was a constant source of surprise to him. He never knew which way she would leap. She had out-foxed him at every turn thus far in their relationship.

At last, she spoke. Propped up on his chest, she fixed him with a suddenly serious expression. "You say you want everything that I am, but are you sure? I'm not like the women in your world, Vadim. I won't change. I can't. I'm still twenty-first century Martha beneath my disguise."

"Good." He stroked away the frown from between her eyes.

"I'm terrible at darning, and my cooking will never be as good as Sylvie's."

He chuckled. "I know that already. To my cost. Ouch." That comment earned him a jab in the ribs.

"I'm being serious!"

"So was I, my love." He kissed her indignant face then rolled onto his side. Martha slid from his chest and onto the grass beside him. Face to face, he studied her. Something else burdened her mind. He saw it in her darkening eyes.

He took her hands, willing her to believe in him. "Harken to me, Martha. I do not want you to behave like the women of Darumvale, worthy as they are. When we are alone, you may do as you please. Wear your strange

Earth fashions, go off hunting for days if you wish. I will mind the house, for I can cook, darn, and make bread—"

"We don't have a house anymore. It burned down, remember?"

Ah. That *was* a minor set back. "It is of no consequence—"

"It will be when winter comes and we're freezing our butts off in some godforsaken cave—"

Vadim chuckled. "You are missing the point, my love."

"Were you actually trying to make one, my sweet?"

"Vixen." He tweaked the end of her nose, ignoring her squeak of protest. Then he gathered her in his arms and lay back, his chin resting upon on her hair. "Were it not for watchful eyes, I would bid you to be yourself all of the time. But I hold true to my word, I would not alter you, even if I could."

He felt her sigh against his chest.

"But what about...my honor?" She raised herself up slightly to look at him, her eyes clouded with more shadows.

He was puzzled. Had he not already told her what she meant to him? He could not imagine what she meant.

Martha must have read it in his expression. "I mean... my reputation. Y'know, my...virtue?"

Now he understood. "You speak of Tony?" Even thinking about the infernal man made him angry, but he hid it from her as best he could.

Martha nodded, her cheeks flushed pink. "In your world I'm ruined, aren't I?"

"Yes." He could not lie, but he brushed her lips with his and gave a wry smile. "This world is harsh on women. Particularly so, when men are not governed by the same rules."

"Oh?" He felt her body tense. She sat up and looked down at him, her eyes suddenly wary. "I thought you men had that whole honor thing going on?"

Vadim sat up too, shame burning within his heart.

"Not all women are virtuous, my love. Just as not all men are honorable."

As Martha's eyes narrowed, it took all Vadim's courage not to look away. She understood him, and her shock was apparent.

"You mean..." She floundered for the right words, growing pinker by the moment.

He would save her the trouble. "There was a time, back in my youth when I...ran wild."

"Sowing your wild oats, we call it," she muttered, suddenly very interested in examining her finger nails.

He raked his hair back from his face and sighed. For a short time, back in their youth, he and Anselm had forged a partnership of sorts. Vadim still loathed himself for his part in it. The young women they hunted found their combined charms irresistible. Anselm could talk the tightest bud into flowering when he set his mind to it, but Vadim's role was always that of the lure. For a time, he had enjoyed their conquests, but then the situation changed.

Vadim never defiled an innocent, restricting himself to experienced lovers: bored wives, widows, and the like. Anselm, however, developed an appetite for virgin flesh. Their brief fellowship came to an abrupt end when a maiden drowned herself after discovering she was carrying Anselm's child. He fled Darumvale the same day, and sought the protection of the Earl's employment soon afterwards.

When Anselm left, Seth took Vadim aside and made him familiar with the honor code. A man was judged by his actions, and each ill-considered act left a dark smear upon the soul. Because of Seth, Vadim grew to understand the true vulnerability of women lay not in their delicate frames, but in their reputations. What kind of man left a woman to deal with the consequences of his own thoughtlessness?

Honor had been his constant companion and guide

since then, and it had never led him astray.

Martha was certainly uncharacteristically quiet, studying her hands intently.

"Have I shocked you?" he asked.

She finally looked up and met his eyes. "A bit."

He could not gauge her mood. "Did you imagine I was a—"

"Of course not." She glared at him. "Oh, I don't know what I thought."

"Does this change your feelings for me?" He risked touching her, running the pad of his thumb over her glistening lower lip. "Martha?"

Why is she taking so long to answer?

She swatted his hand away. "Did you love any of them...your *women*?"

Jealousy? He could breathe again. "I was fond of—"

"But did you love any of them?"

"No," he admitted with a small smile. "You are the first." Her face relaxed, and her eyes no longer resembled narrow slits of stone. "And the last." That comment earned him the briefest smile. When he touched her face this time she did not retreat. "Now answer me, wife. Have your feelings changed?"

"No." She pressed her cheek into the palm of his hand and sighed. "I was just being silly. Sorry."

"There is no need to apologize. I feel much the same way whenever you mention Tony." He drew her unresisting body closer, gathering her in his arms. "We are both ruined, you and I, my love."

Martha knelt between his thighs and slid her arms about his neck. He could smell the lavender water on her skin.

"Quite beyond repair," she agreed, her words brushing warm over his lips. With a wicked smile she took his lower lip into her mouth and sucked upon it.

Vadim gasped as a pulse of hot desire flashed at his core. He held her face between his hands. "Perhaps together we might find..."

She released his lip and grinned. "Salvation? I doubt it. It's a nice thought though."

Her smile drove the breath from his lungs. In that moment, Vadim learned the meaning of real desire. He ached as if a horse had kicked him somewhere vital. If she kissed him now, he knew his self-mastery would crumble.

He needed her. All of her.

If she finds a way to return home, let her go with your love and blessing. But you must ask her. Then in this world at least, she will always be yours.

"You're scowling again." Martha stroked her fingers over his eyebrows, frowning herself. "Can't you just tell me?"

Vadim was suddenly decided. "I want to be bind myself to you."

"Huh?" The furrow on her brow deepened. "You're scowling because you want to..." Her skin flushed pink. "What, exactly?"

Her confusion was endearing. "I mean," he said, cupping her face between his hands. "I love you, Martha. Will you join with me? Be mine, as I am yours?"

"Yes." She flung her arms about him again, kissing him while she laughed. "Oh, God, yes!"

Her swift response made him the happiest of men.

chapter twenty-nine

MARTHA BLINKED IN DISBELIEF AS Vadim gently set her away from him and began unbuckling the thin belt from about her waist with slow deliberation. She couldn't look away from his dark pirate eyes. Her heart galloped. She wanted to sing with happiness. He smiled as he looped the belt loosely around their clasped right hands.

Hand-fasting? This can't be happening. "We're doing this here?" her voice trembled. "Now?"

"Unless you have any objection?"

She shook her head. "None at all." She watched him weave the end of the belt around the loop. "Is this legal? Don't we need witnesses?" Then again, from what she recalled about hand-fasting, it was only a type of engagement, not legally binding.

Without looking away from her, Vadim whistled, calling to the dog. "Forge. Come here. Your services are required."

Martha giggled as Forge lolloped up, abandoning his search for rabbits at Vadim's summons. He was all pink tongued and laughing as usual.

"Sit there quietly and watch," Vadim said sternly, but he gave the dog's shaggy head a quick rub. "You understand?"

Forge grumbled something that must have been affirmative, for he sat down beside them.

"You're actually serious?" Martha's smile widened. "And I thought I was the crazy one."

Vadim cupped the back of her head and kissed her with a thoroughness that left her breathless and trembling. She sensed something new in that kiss. He wasn't holding back anymore.

"May I proceed, my love?"

Martha nodded.

The first raindrops tumbled from the darkening sky, gradually increasing in number and momentum, hitting the hard, parched earth like hailstones. They didn't move, kneeling before one another, hands bound, their eyes fixed on each other.

"Repeat what I say." Vadim kissed her again, but briefly this time. His slicked back his wet hair with his free hand. Rivulets of water ran over the angles of his beloved face.

"From this day on," he began in a low husky voice, *"I willingly surrender my heart to yours. Together or apart, we are now forever bound. As the sycamore embraces the mistletoe, I will cleave unto you. The storms of life shall only strengthen our bond. I pledge to you my love and my constancy. My life and death are in your care.*

"I will seek your hand on the darkest nights, and your name shall be my talisman against harm. I shall be your shield and your sword, as you are mine. May truth and honor always guide our hearts. This is my vow to you."

As if in a dream, Martha obediently repeated the words, transfixed by the man she was saying them to. She felt like a rabbit in the headlights of an oncoming car, unable to move or look away.

The words of the pledge seemed to sum up all the love she carried in her heart. It was as if it had been written for her. For them.

There were no more words. Vadim wiped her tears

away—although Martha was unaware she was crying—and kissed her.

It was the truest kiss of all.

Wordlessly, he removed the belt from their hands, but he didn't give it back. Instead, he stood, drawing her up with him, and smiled into her eyes so tenderly she could barely inhale.

Though she had no camera, her eyes captured his image, imprinting it on her mind so she could keep him—this moment—forever.

She watched him slick back his hair. It hung down like a luxurious black pelt, the ends of it coiling on the shoulders of his shirt. Martha swallowed. The rain had given the linen an invisible quality as it clung to the beautiful definition of his chest. She placed her hands there, palms down, absorbing the heat of his skin.

The loving gaze of his dark, chocolate eyes felt like a physical caress. His lips curved into a tiny smile, and he rested his forehead against hers.

She closed her eyes, tingles racing up and down her spine. *He's mine. I still don't believe it.* Any moment now she might wake up from this perfect dream.

Duty completed, Forge bounded away for the shelter of the woods, leaving Martha and Vadim alone in the rain.

By common consent, they set off toward the cabin, Vadim's arm about her shoulders while hers curved about his waist. The rain meant nothing. Even though shelter was only a short distance away, they took a long while to get there. Every other step was punctuated by another increasingly hungry kiss.

Martha clung to him, her hands tangled in his hair, whimpering with an unspoken need.

"Soon," he breathed against her lips.

The little cabin felt warm and welcoming, like a dimly lit cocoon. As always, a fire burned in the grate, its blaze settled into a pile of red glowing embers.

Vadim closed the door behind them, muffling the sound of the hammering rain. He slid the bolt into place, and the sound seemed to seal her fate.

Martha sighed and leaned her back against his chest. *I am his. He is mine.*

He swept aside her sodden hair, pressing hot kisses down the side of her neck.

She closed her eyes as Vadim nuzzled against her ear, muttering words of the Old Tongue. It sounded like French, but sexier, the strange, erotic sounds vibrating against her skin.

Was that even possible? "Wh-what are you...saying?" she whispered.

"My love." He moved lower. Translating his words while he tasted the exposed skin of her throat, down to the junction of her neck and shoulder. "My heart's ease." He gently nipped her skin with his teeth. "My destiny."

Martha gasped, and her knees wobbled. She liked him biting her. Almost as much as his words.

Reaching back, she wound one arm about his neck. Eyes closed, breathless with pleasure, she leaned against his strong body, surrendering to his will. She felt weightless, as if she would float away at any moment. Only holding onto him kept her grounded.

Still whispering his ancient words of magic, he turned his attention to the other side of her neck, kissing every sensitive place until her nerve endings buzzed.

Suddenly, Vadim spun her around, and pushed her firmly back against the wooden door.

Her eyes flickered open. *Oh, feck.* He was doing the leaning thing, his hands on either side of her head. So unfair.

With a devilish smile, he lowered his head, kissing along the length of her collar bone. She shivered as tendrils of his wet hair slipped down the bodice of her gown, tickling her.

Holy Mother of God!

She was out of her depth. Drowning in a sea she'd badly misjudged. Her own body felt alien, its movements controlled by his will. She trembled and quaked, even made sounds when he pulled the right string. And he hadn't even touched her intimately yet.

Digging her fingers into his shoulders, she breathed his name over and over again, like an incantation, until she couldn't take any more.

With a feral groan, she tangled her hands in his hair and dragged him to meet her hungry kiss.

Vadim readily answered her demands, kissing her so thoroughly until she was whimpering within his mouth.

Suddenly, she was airborne.

Hands beneath her buttocks, he lifted her, pinning her against the door, his kisses hot and urgent.

Being trapped between a rock and a hard place wasn't always a bad thing.

One handed, she pulled her damp skirts to the top of her legs, the freedom allowing her to curl her legs about his waist. Gripping him with her thighs, she wrenched at Vadim's shirt, desperate to touch his skin.

Without setting her down, he broke the kiss her long enough for Martha to yank the garment over his head and drop it. Before the shirt even hit the ground, his mouth was back on hers, hard and demanding.

She was breathing much too fast. Her heart galloped to keep up.

Arms about his neck, Martha trailed her fingernails over the warmth of his back, gliding her fingertips over the firm contours of his returning muscles.

Vadim hissed and drew back, gasping for breath, dark passion glittering in his eyes

Her core turned molten. No man had ever affected her this way, or made her ache so badly with need. Only him. Her body pounded out a constant tattoo of demands, and for the first time in her life, Martha experienced true feral desire. The kind she'd only read about. A thirst that must be slaked no matter what. She couldn't have stopped now if her life depended on it.

"Vadim, please," she moaned against his lips. It sounded like begging, but she didn't care. "I want you. Now."

His jaw tensed, his breathing as rapid as her own. After one more lingering kiss, Vadim carried her over to their straw mattresses beside the fire, her legs still clamped about his waist. The straw rustled as he set her upon the bed. Then he lay down beside her, sucking gently on her lower lip, grooming his fingers through the damp tangles of her hair.

Kicking off her shoes, Martha tugged at the fastenings at the front of her gown and shift. Her impatience pulled the ties into knots. They were stuck fast.

"Damn it!" She yanked harder at the hateful things. She wanted…needed to be naked with him. Right now.

Vadim chuckled. "Allow me, my love."

To her increasing frustration, he began to carefully pick at the knots she'd made, his head bent low to her heaving chest as he worked.

Yes, bosoms really did heave. Who knew? *What the feck is he doing down there?*

"They are badly snarled—"

"Cut them." She trailed her fingers up his naked back. The feel of his breath on her chest brought her out in more shivering goose bumps.

"Be patient. I think I—"

She ground her teeth. "Cut. Them."

Vadim looked up, his hair slipping around his face in a dark, heavy veil. He gave a slow smile. "Are you certain?"

Martha tutted. Was he deliberately trying to wind her up?

"Very well." The mattress rustled as Vadim searched his pockets—he usually had a blade or three secreted somewhere about his person. He slid a small knife from its sheath. In two swift movements, he cut through the troublesome ties. "You are free, m'lady."

"Finally." As Martha made to shrug her shoulders from the gown, she paused. The knotting incident had allowed her broiling blood to cool a degree. She suddenly felt self-conscious.

If Vadim noticed her hesitation, he made no comment. Instead, he drew her to him, kissing her long and deep, bringing her back to the boil. Soon she was writhing and whimpering in his arms again, all modesty forgotten.

He slipped his hand beneath her skirts, ascending her leg from ankle to thigh in one smooth sweep. The sensation of his calloused fingers moving over her skin was heaven.

Cupping one of her naked buttocks, Vadim gave it a slow squeeze.

His resulting groan vibrated in her mouth, thrilling her. Almost as much as the incredible hardness of his body, positioned between her parted thighs.

Cool air played over her breasts and tightened her nipples. Glancing down, she saw her gown had slipped, taking her shift along with it.

Giving her buttock one final squeeze, Vadim continued his sensual exploration of her body, kissing a fiery trail down her neck.

Martha arched beneath him, indicating where she most needed him to place his hands.

And Vadim obeyed.

She bit down on her lip and closed her eyes as his fingers skimmed her breasts.

He touched her again, growling deep inside his throat. Then she experienced the delicious heat of his mouth as it closed over one of her nipples.

"Oh, feck!"

An electric current flashed from her breast to her lower abdomen. Helpless with pleasure, she thrashed her head from side to side. The fire within her increased, pulsing white heat through her whole being with each suck. She sank her nails into his shoulders, branding him.

Vadim inhaled sharply. He moved to her other breast, cupping it while his tongue slowly circled her nipple.

She couldn't take much more. Her body felt like it was teetering on the edge of a vast precipice. One more wave of bliss would push her over. Her eyes snapped open.

"Vadim. Please!" She barely knew her own voice. It was like a stranger's, husky and raw.

He stopped what he was doing. "Please?" He looked down at her, smiling, but his eyes were wild.

"I need you...now." She'd never felt so hungry and wanton in her life.

He helped her sit up then wrenched the gown and shift down her arms, freeing her from their intolerable restraint. Then she lay back on the bed, raising her hips so Vadim could shimmy the unwanted garments down her thighs.

At last she was naked. Vadim knelt over her, raking her body with greedy eyes. The dark fabric of his trousers was positively straining now. Reaching up, she slipped her fingers between the tight lacing so she could liberate him too.

This amazing man actually wanted her. Loved her. She still found it difficult to believe. She chewed her lip and forced herself to concentrate on not knotting up his lacing too. That would never do.

She darted a glance at him. Vadim watched her intently, his hands clenched into fists at his sides.

When his waistband was finally loose enough, Martha sat up and slid her hand inside his trousers. She caught her breath. *Oh, my life!* He was more than ready.

Vadim groaned as she closed her fingers around him. Eyes closed, black lashes flickering upon his cheek.

Martha smiled. Then she squeezed.

The speed of his reaction shocked her. Suddenly, she was flat on her back, watching him strip. He kicked off his boots and sent them slamming into the wall. Then he tore off his trousers, escaping them in a couple of swift movements.

Her eyes widened. *Oh, yes! He's a very fine thing indeed.*

Without doubt, Vadim was far and away the most beautiful man she'd ever seen. But there was no time to appreciate the view. He returned to her arms, demanding her kiss with a glorious savagery that made her head spin. The feeling of his hot naked body crushed hard against hers almost sent her plummeting over the edge.

Her legs parted of their own volition, inviting him closer. She closed her eyes as his hand slid up her thigh.

Vadim gasped when he touched her, his fingers encountering irrefutable evidence of her readiness for him. He moved higher and slid his fingers against the grateful heat of her most intimate place.

Martha broke the kiss and cried out, her eyes snapping open. She wanted to—needed to—hold on a bit longer. Impossible. Not when his mouth moved to her nipples again, sucking each one in turn while his fingers still caressed her.

A surge of bliss washed over her, dragging her to the brink of oblivion. Breathing fast, she fought to stay where she was, biting her lip so hard she tasted blood. She'd waited so long for him...for this. *Oh, but the way he's stroking me is—*

"Please. Wait." She grabbed his hand, halting its delicious torment. "I need you. Now!"

"Gladly, my love." He smiled his wicked pirate's smile. But his breathing was as erratic as her own.

She raised her hips to greet him as he moved into position against her body. His control was admirable. He entered her slowly, and she was grateful. Despite her readiness, it had been a while—and Vadim wasn't exactly small. Little by little, her body stretched to accommodate him. Neither of them breathed. Eyes locked, they held their breaths until she was finally full of him.

They exhaled together, their lips so very close.

Vadim closed his eyes for a second, unmoving, as if battling for control. To prolong the inevitable. "Martha." Her name was a gentle sigh.

When he looked at her, the tenderness in his eyes made her heart ache. She stroked his tangled hair back from his face and pressed a gentle kiss upon his mouth. "Ssh." *Don't move. Please don't move.*

But being motionless didn't help. Hot ripples of pleasure were already washing over her, building in intensity. She rocked her hips and ran her hands down over his incredibly pert buttocks.

"Now," she gasped.

As Vadim thrust into her, driving himself deep into her body again and again, Martha almost sobbed with the joy of his possession.

When the explosion hit, she clung to him, kissing him, swallowing his cry of release as he swallowed hers. Trembling and gasping, they held on to one another, long after the world had stopped whirling.

Eventually—after an hour or a year, she couldn't tell—reality returned. Still holding him within her body, she became aware of the outside world. The rain continued beating against the cabin, driven by a rising wind. Within his arms, she felt cozy. Safe. Loved.

Vadim's lips curved into a lazy smile as he lay with his head rested upon her breast. Martha stroked his beloved face. *Such beautiful eyes.* So open and warm. Not a trace of their usual watchfulness. He looked...at peace. Vulnerable.

She exhaled. *So this is love?* Everything she'd experienced before this man now felt like a cheap imitation.

And that concludes our sex and love master class. Any questions?

She kissed his head and closed her eyes. They felt so very heavy.

Yes. Where do I sign up for the next one?

THE WORLD SLEPT QUIETLY IN the pre-dawn light. Vadim placed a soft kiss upon Martha's brow.

Will she never wake?

She slept with her head on his shoulder, her wild hair splayed across his chest. Her gentle snores made him smile. As he gazed down at her sleeping face, he still could not believe this was real.

Martha had finally stopped running from him.

She looked innocent in repose, her head tipped back, her mouth slightly parted. Vadim traced a path over her swollen lips. He longed to taste them again. Hot need flared in his groin.

Again? What is wrong with me?

Little wonder she was so weary. He could not now recall the amount of times he had taken her in the night, and she had been most willing to accommodate his demands. He had never desired any woman in this way. Not even back in his wild youth.

They had left the bed only briefly on the previous night. While Martha went outside to find Forge, Vadim got up to throw more wood on the fire before gathering a hasty supper to silence their grumbling stomachs.

Within minutes, Forge was sleeping by the fire, and Vadim was back in Martha's arms, their meal barely touched.

He stroked her hair, smiling at her sleeping face as the words of their vow repeated in his mind. *Together or apart, we are now forever bound.*

The demons in his head were finally silent. Overwhelmed by the love within his heart.

He had forgotten what it was to be happy until the day Martha entered his life. Before that day, living held no joy for him. Its surprises were always bloody, or painful. Frequently both.

The day he found her, down by the river, had changed everything almost overnight.

She erupted into his cold, gray life in a flood of warmth and vibrancy. Vexing and dazzling him by turn. In no time at all, she had turned his world on its head, and set it spinning wildly on its axis. She was disobedient, unpredictable, and infuriatingly irrational.

He pressed a kiss on her sleeping mouth, unable to resist the temptation of doing so.

But Martha had other qualities too. She was amusing and kind, generous and loving. She had managed to snare him without even trying.

Suddenly, he was looking down into her sleepy blue eyes.

Martha smiled up at him. "Hi." Her voice sounded husky.

"Good morning, wife."

"I'm not your wife," she said through a yawn, which she attempted to stifle with the back of her hand. "Not yet, anyway."

Now Vadim smiled. "Oh, but you are, my love." He held her hand away from her mouth, ignoring her warning of, morning breath? "You do remember our vows?"

"How could I forget them?"

She would pay for that sultry little smile very soon. "So, then you see, we are now husband and wife."

"But I thought hand-fasting was like an engagement... a betrothal?"

He stroked the little crease that had formed on her brow. "And so it is. Until that promise is...consummated."

"Consummated?" Her eyes widened. "Oh, feck! And we consummated all night long, didn't we?"

He was not concerned. It was a natural reaction, he supposed. Perhaps he might have taken the trouble to explain the ceremony properly to her beforehand. But she had seemed to know what hand-fasting was, or one version of it, at least.

Maybe it was beneath him. It was certainly not the honorable way. The truth was, he had not wanted to give her any room to wriggle free of the pledge, not once she had agreed to it.

"Do you regret it?" He asked against her lips, already knowing what her answer would be. It was there in her lovely eyes. Such expressive eyes as he had never seen before. "Are you...dissatisfied, perhaps?"

"Oh, God, no." She wound her arms around his neck and pulled him to her, kissing him urgently. Then she drew back with a mock frown. "And just for the record, *husband,* I would have spoken those vows even if you had bothered to explain the small print to me."

Small print?

But he was too happy to ponder the meaning of her latest strange expression. He rolled on top of her and cupped her face in his hands, showering her with ticklish kisses until she was helpless with laughter, squirming deliciously beneath him.

Suddenly, her merriment faded, and her eyes darkened. A sign he recognised of her own increasing passion. But he glimpsed something else too. A flickering shadow of pain.

"Vadim?"

"Tell me." He stroked a strand of hair back from

her face.

"Don't ever let me go again, okay?" Tears sparkled in her eyes. "When I thought you were dead, I—"

"Hush." Vadim kissed her tenderly, his heart aching for her. Since Martha returned, they had not discussed their separation, not properly. Not in the way that mattered. Now, for the first time, he caught a glimpse of the wounds she had kept hidden from him. "Only death will keep me from you, my love. I will always come home to you, I swear."

What must she have thought, all alone in Edgeway for so long? No wonder she had fallen so easily into Anselm's clutches. She had been vulnerable. Easy prey. The thought of his foster brother touching her sent a pulse of white hot anger through his body. Thank the Spirits she had run when she did.

He kissed her until she made the soft mewling sounds in his mouth which so inflamed him, then he thrust hard into the welcome of her body, claiming her as his. She was close. As her eyes rolled back, Martha clung to him, repeating his name like a prayer.

My wife. My love.

He cried out as he spilled into her, filling her with his seed. Then, exhausted, he collapsed beside her, resting his head upon her soft breast. He closed his eyes and listened to the gradual slowing of her heart. Martha held him, preening his hair with her fingers.

It sent him to sleep as sweetly as a lullaby.

***

Martha untangled herself from Vadim's arms and crawled out of bed. She had to. Her bladder was about ready to burst. Forge seemed to have the same idea. He scratched at the door, whining softly to be let out.

"Come back to bed," Vadim said. "It is still

raining outside."

Propped up on one arm with a sheet draped across his hips, it was all she could do to resist his allure. Martha chewed on her bruised lower lip. *He looks so fine, though.* It took all of her will not to obey him, to go over there and pull off that sheet and tangle her hands in his love-mussed hair.

"I don't care," she said firmly and swung her cloak over her nakedness. "I need to pee."

She opened the door a fraction, and Forge darted outside, barging her aside in his haste to escape. Vadim was right. The rain was still belting down from the leaden sky, turning the ground to mud.

She inhaled, filling her lungs with the fresh, cool air as it dispelled the warm, heavy scent of love from the room.

"You could just use the bucket."

"No, I could not!" Martha declared, blushing furiously. "Stop trying to tempt me back to bed, Vadim. I'm going." She opened the door a little wider. *As if I'd let him watch me—*

He chuckled. "Strange creature. I am on intimate terms with every part of your delightful body now."

His voice kept her there, plaiting her legs and holding onto the door while her mind replayed images of just how intimate they'd been. She smiled and looked back at him.

"And you certainly know all of mine," Vadim continued, raking back his hair with a careless hand. "Your lips are nothing if not thorough, my love."

Martha leaned against the door frame with a happy sigh, recalling how freely she'd explored his battle-scarred body. She particularly enjoyed revisiting the newest wound on his abdomen. Her stomach fluttered in memory of it...and of the aftermath.

"So why is it," he continued, "you blush scarlet when I suggest you use the bucket, hmm?"

Her cheeks flashed hot. *Men!*

"It's a girl thing, okay? You wouldn't understand, love." With that, she grabbed her wash bag from a peg by the door and dashed outside into the rain.

Once the most urgent demands of her body were met, Martha wandered to the little stream that ran behind the cabin, intending to have a quick wash. However, the stream wasn't quite so little anymore. In fact, it was all grown up. The heavy rainfall had made it burst its banks. Now water flooded the grass, edging ever closer to the trees.

Martha squidged her toes on the submerged grass, and mud oozed up between her toes. It felt good. Smiling, she closed her eyes and tilted back her head, letting the rain patter onto her upturned face. If only she could introduce Vadim to her aunt her happiness would be complete.

Hey, Aunt Lulu. I've found the most amazing man. Guess what? He loves me. Well, technically, he found me, but who cares. We just got married. Can you believe that?

Only the wind answered. Wherever her aunt was, Martha hoped she'd heard.

The feel of the windswept rain on her face unleashed a mad impulse from deep within her mind. Something she'd long wanted to do, but never dared.

Dare I do it now?

She dropped her wash bag onto a rock and unfastened her cloak. Holding the neck clasp together, she glanced around. Forge was out of sight; he was probably already back at the cabin.

No one else would be about in such awful weather.

C'mon. Be brave. Pretend you're Lady Chatterley.

Taking a deep breath, Martha let go of her cloak. As it

slid down her shoulders, she closed her eyes and raised her arms skyward, gasping and laughing as the cold rain battered her skin. It felt like heaven.

Vadim found her there, showering in the rain. Taking her in his arms, he gave her the solace of his kiss and the bliss of his love. For the first time in her life, Martha knew what contentment was.

chapter thirty-one

AFTER TWO DAYS OF SOLITUDE, the rain finally stopped. Their all-too-brief honeymoon was over. Time restarted, bringing with it brought the intrusion of the outside world.

Once again, the little cabin had visitors tapping at the door. Seth was among the first to wish them joy in their union. Martha was always happy to see the Chief of Darumvale. He'd saved Vadim from death on at least two occasions, and she'd always love him for that. But lately, since the barrier of deceit between them had been removed, she'd begun loving him for himself too.

Other visitors were not so welcome.

Vadim's fellow outlaws began stopping by, bringing with them an air of danger she wanted to forget. But how could she? Vadim was one of them—this masked band of brothers. He was their leader. The Robin Hood of Erde.

She tried not to mind when Vadim and his friends talked together, always in low, urgent murmurs so she couldn't hear their words, but that didn't stop her worrying. Vadim was almost at full strength now. No way was he about to retire from the outlaw life. Not while the Evil Earl still breathed.

One morning, she couldn't take any more. With Forge at her side, she went down to Darumvale to collect more supplies. Not that they really needed them. She just wanted to avoid the whispered conversations for a few blessed hours. Their two latest visitors seemed disinclined to ship out any time soon. It'd been three days already. And it felt like a year.

One of Aunt Lulu's old saying rang in her head. It was true. After a few days, fish and visitors both stank equally bad.

Why couldn't she keep Vadim to herself, just for a little while longer?

Some hours later, Martha returned. The trip to the village hadn't really settled her mind. If anything, she was more worried about Vadim's intentions than ever. Weary and feeling more than a little down, she wound her way through the trees, following the path back to the cabin. As she approached the clearing, she heard the unmistakable clank and squeal of swords. Her heart lurched.

Shit! The Evil Earl's found him.

She set off running, with Forge barking loudly at her side. An overhanging branch yanked off her headscarf, but she kept going. Sick fear fueled her legs. No matter what happened, she needed to get to Vadim. Now.

Still clutching her basket of goodies, Martha burst from the trees and out into the sunlit clearing. Her feet came to a sudden stop. *I don't believe this!*

Forge stopped barking. Tail wagging, he lolloped toward the cabin.

Trembling and furious, she dropped her basket, careless of its contents spilling out onto the grass. She didn't know whether to scream or sob.

Vadim had been sparring with the two outlaws.

As she entered the clearing, the three men all turned in unison to look at her, their swords frozen in a tableau of battle.

Vadim was the first to recover. "What is it?" he demanded, immediately lowering his sword. "Is there trouble?" His eyes scanned the trees for danger.

"No." Not the kind he was imagining, anyhow. "Don't bother," she cried as their two long-stay guests pulled up their scarves to cover their faces. "I'm not interested in looking at either of you."

Her eyes locked on Vadim. "Are you totally insane?" She stalked over to him. "You almost fecking died, remember? What, now you're fighting again?"

"As you plainly see, my love." He sent a rueful smile to other men. "'Tis only a little practise, nothing more."

Her temper flashed. "Don't think I didn't see that look." Unfortunately for him, she was fluent in Man Code. Accompanied by the slight eye roll, he'd clearly given his friends the universal sign for *women*!

She moved back as Vadim tried to take her arm. His eyes narrowed. Good. He was finally getting it.

"What is this about?" he asked. "Why are you so upset?"

She tutted. "You think I'm fussing over nothing, don't you?"

"Yes. I do."

Martha glared at him. The linen shirt he wore clung to his sweat-slicked skin. His hair hung in a damp tangle of rats' tails around his shoulders. Too clearly, she saw how he battled to control his rapid breathing. He looked gray, exhausted.

"This was way more than a little practise, Vadim. Just look at you!"

"And what would you have me do, m'lady?" His patience frayed, as worn out as he was. "Remain an invalid all of my life, hmm?"

"Of course not."

"Then *what*?"

That was a good question. Martha looked away from his flaring eyes and glanced over her shoulder at his outlaw friends. They were picking up the spilled contents of her basket, pretending not to notice their boss getting an earful from his nagging wife.

She sighed. "But you were fighting both of them at the same time. That's a little excessive, don't you think?"

With a growl of irritation, Vadim propelled her toward the cabin, one hand against her lower back. He still held his sword in the other. The very sight of the weapon made her feel sick. A glittering shard of death.

As if he sensed her thoughts, Vadim slid the sword back into the sheath at his belt. They sat together in the sunshine on the steps of the cabin. For a while, neither of them spoke.

Martha concentrated on controlling her temper. Yelling at him wasn't going to do any good. And fighting with him was the last thing she wanted.

Vadim was the first to break the silence. "You do not understand, my love," he said softly. He reached for hands and clasped them in his, his thumbs slowly caressing her skin. "I need to be what I was, and soon. A time of great upheaval is almost upon us, and I must be ready to meet it."

Martha frowned. What was he talking about? "No, I'm going to need a bit more than that, hon. Are we talking about your arch-nemesis again?"

"No. The King, Martha." Vadim's eyes glittered with a strange light. "A new king is coming." He squeezed her hands tighter.

"What happened to the old one?" History wasn't her strongest subject back home, let alone here.

"Nothing. Yet."

Quiet excitement seemed to *thrum* off him in waves. Martha still didn't get why he was so fired up, and it must have shown on her face.

"You remember I told you about the old King? His wife died—"

"—and he was murdered, and someone else stepped

up to claim the throne. Yes, I remember. Go on."

"A challenger has stepped forward. A member of the true house of kings." Vadim's lips curved into a smile. "He is rallying the faithful to arms."

Martha's heart lurched. Now it was starting to make sense. "O-kay. So where did he spring up from after all this time? And what does that have to do with you and"—she jerked her head, indicating his two friends—"your secret squirrel pals?"

Vadim chuckled, and placed his arm about her shoulders, drawing her to him. "Rodmar has been overseas these past years, forming alliances and gathering support for his bid. At last, his forces are at full strength. He is ready to take back what was stolen. They will set sail for Norland at the next full moon."

Martha listened to his heart thudding beneath her ear and the soft vibration of his words echoing through his chest. Suddenly, she wanted to cry.

"You and the squirrels are going to fight for him, aren't you?" Though she phrased it as a question, she already knew the answer.

"We must. Honor demands we keep the pledge our fathers made."

Martha cleared her throat. "And what pledge would that be?"

And what about the pledge you made to me? You promised me forever.

With a sigh, Vadim gently took shoulders and held her away from him. He looked deep into her eyes. "There is something I have not yet told you...about me, about my past."

"Oh?" *I should be used to this by now.* She sighed. "Go on, then. Let's have it."

"My father was...the previous Earl of Edgeway."

"What!" Her voice sounded shrill, even to her ears. She blinked hard attempting and failing to process this new information.

His dad was the Earl, so that makes him...

"Then *you're* the Evil Earl? I mean...you're?" What was he exactly? She couldn't get her head round it.

"I am nothing, my love. Not any longer."

Martha ignored his quiet assurance. "I always suspected you were nobility, but..." She shook her head. "So that's why..." She glanced behind her.

The two outlaws were openly staring in their direction, obviously riveted to every word.

"Then, they must be..." She gesticulated with her hand, moving it wildly from side to side as she struggled to fit the pieces together. *Our fathers.* That's what Vadim had said. "Ex-nobles?" She scrambled to her feet. "Why didn't you ever tell me?"

"What difference does it make?" As Vadim got up from the step, his scowl matched hers. "I told you, I am nothing but the man you see before you. *Husband* is my only title now."

Suddenly she understood. "But that's not enough for you, is it?" she said softly. The fire in his eyes told her all she needed to know. "You want it back. All of it. And so do they." She waved her hand in the direction of the outlaws.

"No—"

"Is that why you're going to fight for this wannabe king—"

"That is not what I said." Vadim's glared down at her, his eyes blazing.

"Isn't it?" Blood thundered in her ears. She was way too furious to back down. "So why are you doing this, huh? What do you stand to gain by—"

"I do it for my honor!" Vadim roared. "To restore the honor of my dead family. Why can you not understand that? It matters to me, Martha. It matters!"

She took a hurried step backward, stunned into silence. Vadim had never raised his voice to her before. Never. Wide eyed and trembling, she stared at him.

His face was white, devoid of color. Rage contorted his

beloved face into that of a stranger. His dark eyes flashed a stark warning.

"My lord?"

One of the outlaws appeared at Martha's side. For once, she didn't resent his presence. It reassured her. Not that she thought Vadim would ever harm her.

Vadim turned away, panting for breath, his hands clutching at his hair. Martha and her masked companion stood motionless for a few long moments, watching him. What the hell was going on here?

Her anger quickly changed to concern. "Vadim?" She placed a cautious hand on his upper arm. The hot muscles tensed beneath her fingers. "Are you okay, hon?" When he didn't respond, she stepped closer and ran her hand gently up and down his arm. She felt him trembling. "Oh, love." She gave a sigh and rested her cheek against his back. "Come on. Let's not make a big deal over—"

"Leave me," he growled.

"Wh-what?"

"I said, *go*!"

Martha's insides liquefied into sludge. *This isn't my Vadim.* Tears stung behind her eyes. What was wrong with him?

One thing was for sure, now wasn't the time to discuss it. Talk about overreacting. A sudden blast of anger burned away her tender feelings. How dare he speak to her like that? If he wanted her gone, fine.

She turned to the outlaw beside her. *I'll be back later,* she mouthed. The man nodded, sympathy shining from his eyes.

Vadim still had his back to her. His body quaked with silent tremors. She wavered, torn between wanting to hit him or hug him. But she dared not do either.

Head held high, she turned away and marched for the trees. *Bloody men!* She didn't look back.

"Do not take it to heart, m'lady." The other outlaw, the older one, fell in step beside her. "Lord Vadim will soon shake off this melancholy. He always does."

"Melancholy?" She shook her head, smiling bitterly. "Is that what you call it when someone rips your head off for no good reason?" As they walked, she glanced at her companion. "Does he often act this way?"

They took the path back through the trees, and the man held back a branch so it didn't catch her face.

"Not often, no. The blackness is an infrequent visitor. It affects most of us at one time or another."

"The blackness?"

"It has many names. Some call it battle fever, the day terror..."

Martha's footsteps slowed.Was he talking about post-traumatic stress? "How long has he had it?"

The man shrugged. "For as long as I have known him."

PTSD? That might explain a few things.

There was a fallen log up ahead. Martha sat down, her mind reeling at this fresh insight into the mind of the man she'd married. The outlaw took a seat beside her.

"Can I ask you something personal?" She glanced at him.

The man inclined his head, indicating she could. His gray eyes regarded her with kindness.

You really misjudged them, you bitch.

"Have you had it; the blackness, I mean?"

"Of course."

Of course, he says. Like it's the most natural thing in the world.

"Battle sickness can fell even the hardiest warrior." He sighed and looked away, studying the swaying branches overhead. "Some seek solace in ale, but its benefits are short-lived and often perilous. I have lost many a good man to the oblivion of the ale barrel."

"Do you ever talk about it, amongst yourselves?"

"No, m'lady." The man chuckled, but it wasn't a happy sound. "The best service we can give our comrades is by pretending not to see."

Surely that was the worst thing they could do? Not that Martha held herself up as any kind of expert on the subject.

Although it probably wouldn't help, she had to say something. "I'm going to ask you a huge favor."

"Anything, m'lady."

"You don't know what it is yet," she said with a smile. There was something about this man she liked. Although his face was always masked, he struck her as older than the other outlaws she'd met. Fatherly, almost. "When Vadim...recovers, will you talk to him? About the battle sickness?"

"M'lady!" His eyes widened as if she'd just asked him to walk naked through the streets of Edgeway. "I cannot."

"Oh, please." She touched his gloved hand as it rested upon the log. "I know it's a big ask, but won't you at least try?"

The man shook his head rapidly from side to side. "I beg you, do not ask this of me—"

"I'm not asking you to have a group hug or to turn metrosexual or anything—"

"Metro...what?"

"Just talk to him. It might help you both."

A heavy silence followed. She'd said too much. She kept forgetting that this was a medieval world. Even in her world, men were often reluctant to discuss what they perceived as their weaknesses. Especially in front of a woman.

"I'm sorry." Martha bowed her head and stared at a line of ants as they marched along in the dust at her feet, each carrying a tiny fragment of leaf. "I shouldn't have asked—"

"Very well." The man gave a heavy sigh. "I will try. Though I will hardly know what to say."

"Really?" She looked up with a smile. "Oh, thank you." Talking wasn't much, but it was something at least. She got up, smoothing the skirt of her gown. "I think I'll keep out of Vadim's way for a bit. Give him chance to calm down."

The man rose to his feet. "That might be for the best. Where will you go?"

"I'll pop back to Darumvale and spend the night with Bren."

"Would you like me to escort you there, m'lady?"

"No thanks. I need you to take care of Vadim for me. Tell him I'm not angry, huh? That I'll see him soon?"

"*That* I will be most happy to do." The man bowed his head and held his hand over his heart.

Martha didn't want to go, but there was no point in trying to talk to Vadim. Not yet. Not while he was still so mad at her. A few hours apart might do them both some good. After all, she was still smarting about his decision to fight for the wannabe king.

There was a sudden rustling sound, and Forge lumbered through the shrubbery towards them, his tail wagging like a skinny whip. At least she'd have some company.

With a final smile of farewell to the outlaw, Martha and Forge set off back down the trail toward Darumvale.

chapter thirty-two

THE WALK BACK DOWN THE hill passed in a blur. Martha's mind was full of Vadim. She hated leaving him, but what else could she do? A few hours alone with his buddies might help him down from the ledge he was on. Or so she hoped.

The blackness. How long would it last?

As she entered the village, a warning bell clanged in Martha's subconscious, focusing her attention back on the present. Her footsteps faltered.

Darumvale looked deserted. Much too quiet for a late afternoon. The place was usually bustling at this time of day. Where was everybody? Where were the workers, returning from the fields? The children? The dogs? The old women sitting outside their homes, gossiping with one another before supper?

Apart from the resident pack of savage geese, there was no sign of life. Only the tumbleweed was lacking. Something was decidedly 'off".

Forge stiffened at Martha's side and grumbled from deep within his throat.

"Shh." As she gripped onto his collar, she felt the dog's hackles rising.

Neither of them moved. They sniffed the air like a pair of wary rabbits, scenting danger but unsure of its direction.

She saw the man too late.

A ray of light from the setting sun bounced off an armored breastplate. A soldier stood outside the Great Hall, leaning against the front wall.

Martha's heart skipped several beats as she met the man's unsmiling stare. He called out in surprise and raised his crossbow, training it on her position.

Oh, shit! She dared not move. Her insides liquefied at the same time as her knees.

Other soldiers appeared, answering the summons of their hard-faced comrade.

Martha tightened her grip on his collar as Forge's growls increased in ferocity. The dog's neck muscles tensed beneath her fingers. She strained to hold him back.

"Don't shoot." She raised her free hand in a gesture of surrender.

The soldier lowered his aim and pointed the crossbow at Forge.

"No!" Without thinking, Martha stepped in front of the dog, shielding him from certain death.

"Go, Forge. Find Vadim," she hissed. "Go to Vadim. For once in your life, listen to me, sweetheart." Tears pricked her eyes as she felt the dog moving against her skirt, still grumbling deep within his throat. "Oh, please, baby. Go back." She loosened her grip on his collar, praying he'd listen. The soldiers were coming closer. She had to let him go. "Go on. Run, damn you!"

With one final disgruntled growl, Forge obeyed. Tears of relief slipped down Martha's face as she heard the sound of his great paws pattering away at speed. The soldier attempted to track the fleeing animal with his crossbow, but Forge was too fast. With a muttered curse, the man lowered his weapon.

In half a dozen fast clumping strides, he closed the distance between him and Martha. "Move! he grunted, shoving her in the back.

Other soldiers arrived, surrounding her in a walking armored cage. No one spoke. The warm, putrid stench of unwashed flesh and clothing enveloped her, making her want to gag. But the naked appraisal of their hungry eyes sickened her more.

I should have read the signs sooner. Why am I so fecking stupid?

Hindsight, she decided, was about as useful as a chocolate fireguard.

The soldiers escorted her into the Great Hall and pushed her inside.

She gasped.

It looked as if the entire population of Darumvale was already there, crammed in a small section of the room. Young and old sat together, shuffling on the reed-covered floor, their every move watched by several more well-armed guards.

Every head turned to look as Martha stumbled through the doors. Someone groaned. It sounded like Bren, but there wasn't time to scan the assembly of terrified faces.

"Sit down." Her captor grinned, displaying an impressive rack of decaying teeth. The stench of his breath made her recoil. "Lord Edgeway will be along soon. Make yourself comfortable." Giving her a final shove, he turned away to talk to his friends.

Martha gladly sank onto the floor, embracing the protection and anonymity of the herd. Now she knew why sheep behaved the way they did.

The villagers remained silent, except for an occasional chorus of coughs. The reeds rustled constantly as uncomfortable limbs sought respite from sitting in one position for too long. More coughing. It sounded like a child this time.

Martha daren't look round. Fear bound her too tightly in place. Her eyes fixed on a solitary floor reed, taking in every detail of its structure, never straying from its study for a second.

Oh, Vadim. Why did I pick a fight with you today of all days?

She missed him already. The floor reed shimmered in and out of focus, blurred by unshed tears. A dull ache throbbed deep within her stomach. She found some relief by folding her arms about herself and rocking imperceptibly to and fro.

Will I ever see him again?

Even if Forge returned to the hunting lodge, and if the outlaws suddenly developed a funky ability enabling them to translate his doggy whines, what could they do? There were only two of them. Three, if Vadim was himself again.

She had to face the truth: There was no hope of rescue, not while Darumvale crawled with the Earl's men.

The floor reed shimmered away in another a glittering haze. Martha held herself tighter and dug her fingers into her ribs. She couldn't cry. She wouldn't.

At the very moment before she crumbled, a gentle hand rested on her shoulder.

"Hush, now."

Bren. Martha reached back and clutched the familiar rough fingers, finding comfort in their touch. The presence of her friend gave her the courage to raise her head and look around.

Most of the soldiers stood clustered about a barrel of Seth's home brew. By the looks of things, they were doing their best to empty it. Their raucous laughter contrasted sharply with the silence of the villagers.

Their merriment came to an abrupt end as the doors of the Great Hall swung open again, and a golden-haired man walked inside, flanked by even more soldiers.

Martha gasped. *Oh, shit!* Her fingers flew up to cover her mouth. *The Evil Earl.*

As the Earl's entourage parted, things got a whole lot worse. Standing amongst the soldiers, talking and smiling, was the ultimate pig himself.

Fecking Anselm.

The Earl swept a look over his captive audience. "I trust my men have kept you entertained?" He cast a brief, glacial glance at the soldiers by the ale barrel. They hurriedly set down their tankards and moved away.

"Excellent," he continued in the same mock-cheerful tone. "I shall not detain you for much longer. Once my men have completed their search, you will be free to return to your homes."

"Aye. What's left of them," someone muttered. But not quietly enough.

"Oh, I'm sorry. Did someone wish to say something?" The Earl raked the villagers with his pale blue gaze. He paced the room, his magnificent purple cloak dragged along the floor, gathering rushes in its wake. "By all means, do speak up."

The Earl's pleasant manner didn't fool anyone. It barely concealed the menace lurking beneath his veneer of civility.

Martha felt sick. Cheeks burning, she bowed her head. Why hadn't she worn her headscarf today? Without it, she was far too conspicuous.

"Oh, never mind." The Earl gave a sigh, delicately tossing his long golden hair over his shoulder. "'Tis probably for the best."

"Martha?"

Shit! And then Martha's day hit the very bottom of the cess pit. She cringed. Anselm had spotted her.

"Can it be you?"

She raised her head, reluctantly meeting the eyes of Vadim's twisted foster brother.

"It is you!" He smiled warmly, as if he were genuinely happy to see her. As if they were old friends meeting unexpectedly. "What happy chance this is. I tried to find you, and suddenly here you are."

The villagers glared at her. Martha sagged beneath the weight of their accusing eyes. Her back tingled, sensing the invisible daggers pointed her way. Despite her innocence, she cringed.

Anselm strode through the crowd toward her, carelessly trampling on anyone unfortunate enough to be under his boots, paying no attention to the villagers' groans of pain.

How the feck do I play this?

Her mind shifted into top gear, racing through her alternatives and the pros and cons of each.

Do I pretend we're still friends? Have I got the stomach for that? No. *He knows I know the whole story by now. What then? Smile? Tell him what I think of him! No. Don't be an idiot. Remember what happened to poor Sylvie.*

Anselm offered her his hand and, because she didn't know what else to do, Martha took it. What she really wanted was to punch the lying little fecker, but the consequences of doing terrified her.

Anselm helped her off the floor. Her legs had gone to sleep, and the pins and needles in her limbs made her stagger.

"Have a care, m'lady." He slid his arm about her waist. "Hold onto me if you will."

Martha recoiled as his warm breath wafted against her cheek. Her flesh crawled, physically itching from his touch. Only Vadim had the right to hold her this way. "No, really. I'm fine." She stamped her feet to restore her circulation. Anger burned hot in her stomach, but she tried to restrain it. Darting him a nasty look, she wriggled free of his restraining arm. *Don't lose your cool.*

She felt the Earl's eyes on them, watching their reunion with rapt attention. He didn't speak.

Did he recognise her? She was about to find out.

Anselm frowned as Martha pulled away from him. "What is it? Have I upset you somehow?"

"Upset me?" Her eyes widened. She couldn't help it. Was he for real? "Whatever makes you think so?"

The Earl saved her from hearing Anselm's reply.

"Is this her? Have you found your friend at last, Anselm? How wonderful."

That's it. I'm probably going to die very soon.

Martha tiptoed her way through the villagers, apologizing as she went, swatting away Anselm's hand as he tried to steady her. "I said, I'm *fine*."

Once free of the crowd, she headed straight for the Earl. *Let's just get this over with.*

The Earl smiled as she approached, with Anselm trailing behind her.

"Hello again, Martha. You never made it to Mrs. Wilkes' after all? You're looking..." He looked her up and down, wrinkling his nose slightly. "Healthy."

Her heart plummeted. *Feck. So he does remember me. Damn it.* She made a small non-committal noise, followed up by a tepid smile.

"Anselm has been most devoted in his hunt for you." Taking her elbow in his gloved hand, the Earl led her to a bench beside the fire. The wall of soldiers scooted as they approached, armor clanking like cooking pans.

The walls of the Great Hall seemed to close in around her until she was breathless. The room went horribly quiet. Even the coughing stopped. Every pair of eyes watched them. Perching on the bench beside the Earl, Martha absently pleated the skirt of her gown with her restless fingers. She was lost. Terrified.

Oh, Vadim.

She glanced at the man with golden hair, sitting there so calmly, all nicely packaged in a disguise of civility. But the glacial depths of his serial-killer eyes revealed the truth. This man was an instrument of pain and death. Strangely, it was his friendliness that unsettled her most of all.

He was older than she remembered. From her previous encounter, and from Vadim's tales, she'd placed the Earl somewhere in his late forties. Now, seeing him close up, Martha mentally added another ten years to her guesstimate. Lines etched his clean-shaven face, and his mane of golden hair showed definite signs of thinning on top.

What had Vadim's sister seen that was worth loving in this man? He was nothing but a well-dressed monster. A murderer. A coward who shot small boys in the back as they ran for their lives. *Sick bastard.*

Anselm took a seat at Martha's other side. Although he didn't speak, she was uncomfortably aware of his eyes burning into the back of her head.

"Tell me," the Earl said at last, twirling the golden tie of his cloak fastening between his fingers as he spoke. "Where is your mate?"

"M...my mate?" Her heart fluttered. Did he know Vadim was alive? Or was he just fishing?

"Lord Hemlock?" The Earl flashed her a brief shark smile, giving her a glimpse of his clean and even teeth. "Vadim? Surely you remember him? Tall fellow. Rather scruffy-looking, from what I recall."

Anger bolstered her flagging spirits, giving her the courage to speak. "Of course I remember him." She fixed the Earl with unwavering eyes. He wouldn't get to Vadim through her. Never.

"And?" The Earl circled his hand, prompting her to go on.

Lie, Bigalow. And make it good. "He's dead."

The icy depths of the Earl's eyes made her skin prickle.

"Come now, my sweet." His voice was gentle. Coaxing. "You can do better than that."

A switch flicked inside her head, and an icy rage took hold of her. She felt calm. Unafraid. The Earl had almost killed Vadim on two occasions. Did he honestly think she'd help him do it a third time?

But he'll torture you. Probably rape you. She ignored her inner mouse. Chances were he'd do those things anyway, whether she cooperated or not. No way was he getting Vadim as well.

The cold rage radiated throughout her body, banishing every tremble. There was still a way out of this mess. Vadim might be lost to her now, but she could still keep him safe.

Death was the ultimate escape route.

Suddenly, she understood why Sylvie had killed herself. Given the same opportunity now, Martha would happily ingest the same poison if doing so meant her beautiful man survived.

Although poison was off the current menu, there were other ways. All she had to do was get the Evil Earl good and angry. *With my mouth? Not a problem.*

She stopped fiddling with her skirt and sat up straighter. "Let's cut the crap, huh? Vadim's dead. You killed him. End of story."

The Earl lashed out with his hand, striking her so hard she almost toppled off the bench. The villagers let out a collective gasp of shock.

Clutching her stinging cheek, Martha regarded the Earl with unveiled loathing.

"Never lie to me." The Earl snarled through clenched teeth. "Where. Is. Vadim?"

Undaunted, Martha gave him a mocking little smile. "In. Heaven."

More shocked gasps rose up from the villagers.

The Earl's face paled. He raised his hand again, slowly this time so she could see the blow coming.

She braced herself, never looking away from his eyes. *Just do it, you bastard!*

"My lord." Anselm intervened. "Perhaps I might speak with her? She might open up better to a friend."

"A friend?" Martha spun on the bench to look at him, adrenaline thundering through her veins. "Is that what you call yourself? Sorry, Anselm, but you certainly don't qualify for that title. You're as bad as he is." She jerked her head to indicate the Earl. "Worse, in fact. At least he is what he is: the Evil Earl."

She heard more rapid intakes of breath.

"What are you, really?" she continued. "That's what I'd like to know. A lying, scheming killer? A twisted psychopath? A man who drove his own mother to her death?" Her bitter smile faded. "Whatever you are, you're no friend of mine."

"Martha, be sensible—"

She scrambled to her feet, pointing her finger in Anselm's face. "You played me from the start, you devious little fecker!" she cried. "You make me sick."

A smooth voice sounded from behind her. "Perhaps I might— "

"No!" Martha turned her head and glared at the Earl. "When I've finished with him, you can do what you want with me." With great satisfaction, she saw the Earl's jaw drop. She'd apparently stunned him into silence.

Good. I have a lot to say before I die.

"Please, Martha." Anselm's blue eyes certainly looked innocent, fearful even. "Stop talking. Let me help you."

"Help me?" Martha almost laughed, too far gone to care. "Like you helped your mother? Where are Seth and Ma, by the way? Have you *helped* them too?"

"Of course not. They are confined to Mother Galrey's hovel."

"Unharmed?"

"Yes. What do you take me for?"

"A mother-killer."

Anselm was a good actor. She almost believed she'd wounded him. Almost.

He stood up too. "This is me, Martha. Remember? We were good friends." He opened his arms as if to display his innocence. Trying to convince her to believe in him again.

Too late, you little weasel.

"I remember all right." She prodded his chest, her finger jabbing out each syllable on his leather hauberk. "You betrayed your own mother—"

"She was sheltering outlaws—"

"Don't give me that crap. This has nothing to do with outlaws. You've despised Vadim ever since your parents took him in, back when he was a child. Don't tell me this is about sheltering anyone. Credit me with a little sense." She planted her hands on her hips, looking at his handsome face with disgust. "This is all about Vadim and your insane jealousy of him." She became aware of just how loud her voice had become. With effort, she turned the volume down. "Let's at least be honest with one another now. It's over, Anselm. Done with. You got what you wanted. Vadim's dead. I loved him, and you took him from me. What more do you want?"

Anselm opened his mouth, then he shut it again. It seemed he had no more to say.

Martha heard the sound of slow applause. She turned her head. The Earl was up on his feet, grinning broadly, whilst the villagers just stared, disbelief etched on their faces.

"Well said, m'lady. Do you know, I think I am beginning to understand what Lord Hemlock saw in you."

Saw? Past tense. That's good.

"His name," she snarled through gritted teeth, "is Vadim."

The Earl ignored her. "I admit, my first instinct was to strangle you—"

"Really? Then you should go with that thought." She didn't want to imagine the alternatives he might have to offer.

The Earl chuckled. "But I think I might actually prefer to keep you alive, my dear. Your candor appeals to me."

Oh, no. This isn't happening. Insult him again.

"That's because I was talking to your boy wonder here." She glanced back at Anselm. "As for you, *sire,* you're nothing but a walking, talking cliché. Do you have a cat back at home in your evil lair, hmm? Do you sit stroking it while you think up your plans for world domination?"

The Earl's smile faltered. He walked slowly towards her. "Or perhaps I might give you to my men as a plaything?"

God, no! Just kill me already. The thought of them sweating and grunting over her was intolerable.

Despite her terror, Martha rolled her eyes, attempting to look bored. "Oh, how very predictable. I thought better of you than that." Her mouth went into overdrive. "Still, the old ones are the best, or so I'm told. But I might not be such a fun ride for your men, though. I seem to have picked up a dreadful dose of cock-rot somewhere along the way." She forced herself to laugh. "Now that's a gift that certainly keeps on giving."

She heard several snickers, some from the soldiers themselves.

Martha bowed her head in their direction. "Why, thank you."

The Earl looked over at Anselm. "Has she always been so..."

"No, sire. I fear the news of Hemlock's death has unhinged her." He sighed. "This aspect of her character is new to me."

"Is it indeed?"

The Earl was wavering. Martha sensed it. Who'd given him the idea Vadim was still alive, anyway? The only people who knew about him were people she trusted. All except for... Orla.

That little bitch! Where is she?

She scanned the crowd of villagers, and her eyes homed in on the girl. As their eyes met, Orla's cheeks flushed scarlet. She looked down at the ground, unable to hold Martha's gaze.

A large gold brooch on Orla's cloak caught Martha's attention. It looked new. She didn't remember seeing her wear it before. The penny finally dropped.

You'd better start praying Lord Evil kills me soon, missy!

The Earl and Anselm stood close together, whispering and muttering furiously to one another.

What was that all about? Martha felt her adrenaline rush fading, taking her courage along with it. Suddenly, she felt weak and wobbly. Her cheekbone throbbed where the Earl had struck her.

Fortunately, there was more than one kind of courage. Dutch, for one. She wandered over to the beer keg and helped herself to a generous tankard of Seth's home brew. No one attempted to stop her. A couple of the soldiers even smiled at her.

It was difficult to swallow the ale. Her throat was constricted with holding back her tears. The thought of never seeing Vadim again hurt worse than a physical blow. With no warning, she'd somehow managed to lose him again.

If only I'd said goodbye. That was the sharpest cut of all. Her courage died as effectively as if someone had pulled out her plug.

If ifs and ands were pots and pans, there'd be no work for tinkers' hands. Aunt Lulu's voice echoed in her mind, another of her nonsense sayings from a time long gone.

There was no pointing in wishing for anything. A quick, painless death was the best she could hope for now.

"Martha?" Anselm was back, standing beside her and looking like a kicked dog.

"Will you come with me?" He gently prized the empty tankard from her fingers.

Martha shrugged and let him take her arm. Her snark tank was flashing empty. Without objection, she allowed him to lead her from the Great Hall. Behind her, she heard the Earl dismissing the villagers, issuing several bloody threats as a parting shot.

As the doors closed behind them, she heard the muffled babble of many voices, but she felt too wretched to wonder what they were saying.

Looking up into the clear inky sky, she saw the first stars twinkling in the dark. They seemed to mock her captivity. Could Vadim see them too? Had he recovered a little by now? Did he know what had happened yet?

Martha shivered. Someone—Anselm presumably—draped a cloak about her shoulders, enveloping her in its heavy folds. The garment still retained his body heat, which repulsed and comforted her at the same time.

Anselm led her to a horse. “Step up onto my hand, Martha.” He linked his fingers, forming a hand stirrup. She silently obeyed him. “Good girl. Up you go.”

He swung himself up behind her and gathered up the reins. Moments later, their thundering cavalcade moved off, cantering into the night.

Martha sat rigid within the circle of Anselm’s arms, riding into the hell of separation. She had only one consolation. Vadim’s love. It was locked up tight inside of her, safe in the shelter of her heart. She closed her eyes and heard his voice again.

I am yours now. Whatever may follow, never doubt it.

And she never would. Not in all the empty days she had remaining.

###

(Coming soon. Summer 2014. Tales of a Traveler Book Two: Wolfsbane.)

a note to the reader

I hope you enjoyed Tales of a Traveler:Hemlock. Please take a moment to leave a review on Amazon.

The next book in the series will be *Tales of a Traveler Book two: Wolfsbane.*

Life in a medieval castle isn't easy, especially as the captive guest of Anselm, Vadim's twisted foster-brother. While twenty-first century Martha attempts to adapt to life in a medieval castle, war comes to Edgeway. As the castle faces siege, Martha's love for Vadim is stretched to its limit, and may prove to be yet another casualty.

acknowledgments

So many people have helped me to get to where I am today. Here are just a few:

To my husband and kids, my home crew, thank you for your constant love, support, and encouragement. I couldn't do what I do without you. Love you.

To all my fabulous family, thank you for believing in me when I finally came out of my writer's closet.

To my friends, Krissie, Andrea, and Caroline, thank you for letting me inflict various dodgy stories on you over the years. You girls were my very first readers. Whatever happens from now on, I'm blaming you!

Thank you to all the people over at Critique Circle who critiqued 'Hemlock' in its various forms. Special thanks to all the friends I made there. In no particular order: Jamie 'petal' Salsbury, Belfast Larry, Yorkshire(Gina G) Chris, Claudia, Cristin, Rox, Shex, 'Highlander' Jill, Shaneen, Brona, Stacey, and Kimberly. You're all amazing writers, and your friendship and support have gotten me through the roughest days.

To Glendon and Tabatha at Streetlight Graphics, thank you for translating the images in my head into such a fabulous book cover and formatting.

And finally, to you, my readers, thank you for giving me a chance. I hope you enjoyed the read.

NJ Layouni lives in Lancashire, England with her husband and two kids. When she's not busy being a wife and mum, she likes scribbling down stories, giving voices to the many characters living inside her head.

Connect with the NJ Layouni:

Facebook:
https://www.facebook.com/pages/NJ-Layouni/405255156236485

Goodreads:
https://www.goodreads.com/author/show/8107337.N_J_Layouni

Twitter:
https://twitter.com/NJLayouni

Website:
http://njlayouni.blogspot.co.uk/

Made in the USA
Middletown, DE
25 February 2015